CW01510400

DEADLY *Dough*

WeNARK GReeN

Nenark Green

Hope you enjoy reading!

WHISPER PRESS

Wenark Green //

WHISPER PRESS
www.wenarkgreen.com
contact@wenarkgreen.com

1st Edition

Paperback ISBN: 978-1-7395943-4-3
eBook ISBN: 978-1-7395943-5-0

from WEN

For May, whose riotous wit and infectious laughter lives on through me, and for all the beloved fur babies who've graced and still grace my days. Love and light.

from ARK

For my beloved cat, Tahlula. Love is truly a four-legged word.

ACKNOWLEDGEMENTS

Endless salutes to all-round good fella and penning partner, Mark. An inimitable curiosity, underrated creative, and endearing eccentric. You are the writing bones to my editing flesh. Keep the Zen, dear friend. Let it flow.

A zillion thanks to some special people.

Freddie, whose bonkers sayings live on in my writing.

My sister, Heather, who'll appreciate the satire, humour, and sarcasm among these witty pages. I hear her titters now. Keep on chuckling!

Bev. For the laughter. The memories. The reminiscing. May our crazy friendship long continue.

Mel. For your warmth, healing, and support, all gladly received. So sorry you had to leave. So grateful you stayed in touch.

Barbara and Nigel. Appreciation and gratitude for welcoming me into a new environment at a time when uncertainty and fear threatened to conquer.

Thanks to my esteemed partner in crime and dearest friend, Wendy. The flesh to my bones and the yin to my yang. Without you, this project would never have been possible. Thanks for all your encouragement, patience, and support. To my parents for your love and support, and to Rosco, for getting me into writing all those years ago.

Readers have a world of choice, and thank you for choosing *Deadly Dough*. We hope you enjoy reading the book as much as we loved writing it. Feedback is vital. To help readers decide their next escape, please give a quick review on Amazon. Many thanks in advance for your valued support. We appreciate you.

DEADLY
Dough

1

In the Tent

P rue Penn loved her Monday masochism. Four hours of slicing, dicing, blending, and beating often whipped up a stink with her scarred nerves, but the victory was worth it.

On this muggy July evening, Prue's zealous hands cranked up the torture. Stretching, knocking, and kneading, all for the love of bread. A flair for food had lured her to the heart of beautiful, rural Treetonshire and the giant marquee in the lush grounds of Biggin Hall, ancestral home of Lord Biggin-Smythe. Equipped with everything for the ultimate baking experience, the hall's estate management team had invited local amateur bakers to claim their chance to enter the tent flaps. Within hours of opening applications, all 16 places had gone.

Lord Biggin-Smythe was a happy man. Mr Hospitality he wasn't, nor was charity his game, but wooing the villagers was paramount to his latest goal. The richest, stingiest man in the county only agreed to the baking class for his own ends, but the idea proved so popular, it urged him to task his team to bolster his image and gain local trust. His proposal to offer a wealth of pastimes and pleasures in the phenomenal grandeur of his historic home was an unrivalled success. From archery to baking through to croquet and golf. All at his expense. All for his own gain. Unless he was profiting, his lordship had no time for the masses. He wanted them in. On his terms.

For centuries, the titled Biggin-Smythe family had wielded power and corruption over stretches of idyllic

1

Treetonshire. Affectionately known as Treet, the county was a rural lover's rapture. Rolling patchwork hills, resplendent meadows, and sparkling brooks made it *the* place to escape to, if you didn't mind a piggish niggard gobbling up pretty villages and everything in between. The notorious Biggin-Smythe estate sprawled and now dominated the county's landscape. But Treetonshire wasn't enough, and greedy hands wouldn't stop grabbing. His ravenous lordship wanted it all.

Prue lived in charming Honest Tor, one of eight villages on the fringe of Treeton, Treet's bustling county town. With its rustic clutch of stone cottages, quaint shops, and cobbled streets, Tor was a prime location. Prue had gone rural following an MS diagnosis, a condition that led to the collapse of her marriage, though she knew her ex wanted an excuse to skulk off into the sunset with his new flame. He'd said some vile things and Prue was glad to see the back of him. Ever since that rotten day, she'd squelched male attention. In time, she'd get a dog, cat, or both, and devote her love and life to four-legged friends, not two-legged toads. At least animals loved you back.

First, Prue focused on health and recovery. At 38, a complete lifestyle and diet change wasn't easy, but her resolve never faltered. When she'd visited Honest Tor to view new homes, she knew this was where she wanted to be, and one cottage stole the show. The delightful, thatched roof, oak stable door, and beamed ceiling enchanted. The nearby Mell Water, burbling beneath Fleece Bank dotted with sure-footed sheep and scores of evergreens, soothed. A cottage offering warmth, sanctuary, and soul. Brambles. The solace Prue needed. Her little piece of peace.

Taking early retirement, Prue took up voluntary work or did a spot of admin for close friend and sounding board, Wendy May. In her free time, favoured hobbies were cooking, baking, and gardening. She also loved reading, or exploring pastoral wonders, so long as her legs could carry her. Every season had its pleasures. Come rain or shine, Prue cherished her happy place. An avid nature lover, she adored humming along with busy bees or basking in the company of wildlife, popping in to say hello. Tending the blaze of flowers and plants in her beloved gardens brought moments of supreme joy.

In warm spells, Prue loved relaxing in her late Grandfather's old deck chair. Catching the sun's smile while topping up her vitamin D, she sensed the Mell Water's healing gurgle working its magic. Even in stormy climes, the river's tempestuous glory fascinated. Gathering pace, rising, clear water turning brown as it rolled and crashed its way to the mighty River Sol. Whatever the weather, the Mell's many moods never failed to beguile.

Living with a chronic condition could be demanding, but MS and all its nasties didn't mar Prue's love of life nor her determination. She was unstoppable. A converted country girl, who respected the pace and beauty of rural living.

Her aristocratic landlord was another matter. Lord Biggin-Smythe looked down on his tenants, his vain, ruthless swagger trumped only by his greed. For generations, control and avarice had surged through his family's tainted blue blood and still reigned.

At 62, with one marriage and four children under his widening belt, Biggin-Smythe's bulging coffers attracted Lucinda Daphne Fanshaw, who was hoping to hook a desirable prospect. Fluttering her lashes and working her womanly wiles, she shot her flirty arrow straight into the eyes and heart of a man thirty years her senior. His lordship fell. Hard. Alas, he was ignorant of his new bride's predatory reputation and one filthy rich husband wouldn't stop her little games. The new lady of the manor's pursuit of any pair of trousers wore out countless pairs of designer shoes. Four years on, she was still at it, but lately, trousers had fallen, and the swirl of a kilt had wooed her. Its wearer, Thomas Trebilcock, Prue's younger stepbrother, now stood at Prue's workbench, casting a critical eye.

'Still chaotic, I see. It's a wonder you get any baking done,' Tom sneered.

'It's a wonder you get *anything* done. Too busy fooling around with another man's wife. Better cut your capers or his lordship'll cut them for you. Won't look so pretty in a kilt, then.'

'Unless you're drunk or drugged, Sister dearest, I'm not in one now.'

'You know what I mean.'

'Don't listen to gossip. It's unhealthy.'

'So's saturated fat, but you still coat your arteries with it. Come on, Tom, I know you and that woman are up to no good. I smell smoke and smoke usually means fire. You'll burn those silly fingers of yours.'

'I'm a chef. Goes with the job.'

'Don't get smart. Unlike your kilt, it doesn't suit you.'

'And sermons don't suit you. I get it. You're six years older. Doesn't mean you're wiser. Don't need or want a lecture on how to live my life. Who I see's my business. Mind your own.'

'Know your trouble?'

'Surprise me.'

'You'll get more than a surprise if his lordship cottons on to your antics. He might already know and is ready to pounce. I'd think twice before riling him. Doubt he'll appreciate some chancer in a skirt seasoning his wife, especially one on the payroll. *It's been done, Tom.*'

'What has?'

'The impotent rich man, fair lady wife, and the handsome drudge. If you want to keep your job as head chef, get a brain. The pig poop ain't working. Now move. My focaccia's burning.'

Prue stooped to pull her bread from the oven, ignoring the sharp shock shooting up her back. She beamed at her creation.

'So, what's my trouble? You didn't say.'

Prue's baking pan clattered onto the bench along with her smile. She stretched her hands, flexing mildly arthritic fingers. 'And won't, Brother, *dearest*. Use your loaf.'

'I'll use yours. Fantastic focaccia. Smells delicious and looks good enough to eat. Pity you're a messy mare, but your bread's damn good.'

'Too good for the likes of you, thank you very much. Go on, get lost. Stop hanging around like a bad smell.'

'Love you too.' Tom blew a kiss and sloped off.

Prue despaired at his swagger. At that know-it-all air he'd gained these past few weeks. She wiped her hands, dusted flour from her beige shorts, then nodded at Wendy May, who'd sidled up to admire Prue's handiwork. Determined to get a "first come first served" place, the friends had applied for the baking class together. Wendy's culinary skills were impressive, but she hadn't quite mastered the art of bread.

As Tom retreated, fiery Sagittarian Wendy stuck her tongue out, tightened a messy topknot fashioned from a mass of dark brown hair and hitched up her jeans.

Assertive and ambitious, forty-year-old Wendy was content to be single. A martyr to her legal career, the editor and writer concluded long ago that the trappings of matrimony and children weren't her destiny. Three times she'd readied to walk the *Wedding March*. Three times she'd marched the other way. During each of her engagements, something didn't feel right, and Wendy decided that squandering empty words on frivolous vows was a foolish venture. She didn't have to marry to enjoy male company. Besides, divorce could be a messy affair. She'd seen the ravages first-hand.

'Ignore him, Prue. You're a star, and your bread's divine. Alas, mine's a tragedy. Overbaked and hard as a bleeding rock. I must learn to tame the dough, then bridle the bake. 'Tis official. I find proofing words easier than proofing dough. Or should that be proving? Whatever word takes your fancy, all's not lost for me, friend.'

'How?'

'Because I'll donate my disaster to you. Will come in handy to knock some sense into that brother of yours. If that brick doesn't do the trick, I'll eat hay with a mule.' Wendy's charred ciabatta landed with a dull thud on Prue's workbench.

'You're a darling, Wendy, and so funny. Sorry about your bread. You have baked it to death.'

'*Dead bread.* No chance of revival then?'

'Nope. Don't think Arnaldo Cavallari would be impressed.'

'Who's he when he's out?'

'The Italian baker who invented ciabatta in nineteen eighty-two.'

'As late as that? Interesting.'

'Wanted something to compete with the French baguette, which was so popular at that time. At least your effort lives up to its name. Ciabatta means slipper in Italian, and that thing looks like a well-worn one, even charred as it is.'

'Looks more like a kipper to me. Smoked and flat, without the whiff. What a shocker. Are you all right?' Prue's flinching and squirming hadn't escaped Wendy's eagle eye.

'Yes, and no. My bread's a success, but Tom's being a twit and this new cool vest's crippling me. Nifty when it's hot but digs when I'm triggered and symptoms start. It's coming off.' Prue unzipped the costly vest, draped it on a chair, then slipped off canvas deck shoes and stretched her toes.

'Where's the pain? Can I do anything?'

'Twinges in the back and feet. Shocks in my legs, too, but I'll be fine.' Prue sat down. 'Lifestyle changes can take months, even years, to kick in. Nerve damage, Wendy. Scary stuff. No guarantees, mind, but I'm doing all I can to slow the progression.'

'And doing a sterling job. Forgot to say I'm loving your new hairdo. Cropped chestnut chic. Definitely a winner.'

'Chic? With a scruffy apron and sweaty T-shirt! Do the dirty white decks add a touch of glam, too?'

'You're baking bread in a hot tent, Prue, not strutting your stuff on a catwalk. I ask you. What's the point of open tent flaps in a tropical summer? Look at the state of me. Rocking it big in faded denims, grimy, old top, and knackered flip-flops. Won't be walking the glitzy red carpet anytime soon. I'm a frazzled mess. Hardly matches my shrewd, nobody's fool kudos. My hair's a sight. Wore a cap to hide it, but my head boiled, and I flung the thing to hell. Think it landed in a bag of flour. Or did I bake it? Yikes! Maybe that's the ciabatta.'

Prue got up and dumped her baking pan into the sink full of grubby dishes, giggling at Wendy's antics.

'Well, blinker my eyes. 'Tis the fulsome front,' Wendy whooped.

'What?'

'Your vest isn't the only thing you've whipped off, Madame Penn. I'm here to battle dough, not two frisky ferrets in a windsock.'

Prue's shrieking drew looks around the marquee. 'You're outrageous. I assume you mean no bra. Didn't bother. MS, heat, and undies don't always agree.'

'Where there's no hold, jiggling's a certainty. Loose and lethal. You should've warned me I was in dangerous territory.'

'One digging vest's enough. Can't cope with double trouble.'

'And I can? Scandalous.'

'That's the way it is.'

'Still love you, friend. Sorry to mention your unmentionables.'

'Wouldn't have you any other way. I appreciate your offer to help with that brainless brother of mine, but it'll take more than a stone loaf to bring Thomas to his senses. It's the thrill of it all. He gets a kick out of handling expensive goods and doing the dirty on his boss, but Lady Chatterley, this is not. Can't see a happy ending to Tom's story. More like a tragedy. Illicit thrills often end in woe, but that numbskull won't listen.'

'He's an apostrophe. Or can be.'

'How so?'

'Niggly and difficult. That's how many see the impish little punctuation mark. Poor thing gets a bad press.'

'How quirky. D'you have a mark for everyone?'

'Nope. And don't ask me why some people get marked and some don't. Blame the editor and writer in me.'

'Do I have one?'

'You do. An elegant em-dash. It speaks volumes in one simple line.'

'Thanks. That's a lovely thing to say about me. Niggly and difficult sounds right for Tom. Always was pig-headed.'

'He's tampering with trouble, dumping on the master's doorstep. Where's his head?'

'Up his rump. Did you hear everything we said before?'

'Guilty.'

Prue lowered her voice. 'That means others would've heard. It's bad enough locals earwigging, but people from other villages isn't a smart move. Or elegant. Me and my big mouth. Tom'll be the talk of the place.'

'Wouldn't be Honest Tor without its steamy gossip train. Don't worry. When folk trash Tom, they're leaving someone else alone. Gas about him for a while, get bored, then pick at another. He'll be yesterday's news and some other poor sap'll be the talk of Tattle Tor. Serial yappers are programmed to snoop, blab, and spout lies. Make it an art. Ugly, isn't it? Practicing law for years only cemented my belief. People love scandal. The juicier the better.'

'I can't remember the why and when, but it's no wonder you gave it all up.'

'Had to. Practiced law for thirteen years. That's thirteen years too long. The why? An intense distrust of the legal system and limited judicial reviews made it so. There I was, a legal eagle with a social conscience, and it got me thinking. I'm all for justice and fair play but saw little of that. The when? Six years ago, I turned to editing legal documents, thinking I'd kill the frustration with only the wordy side of correction. Wrong. I'd lost my passion for law and order. Took a twelve-month editing and proofreading course, passed with distinction, then went freelance. As you know, I'll nitpick anything and everything. Even legal stuff, but not if I can help it. Do copywriting too. Found myself a talented assistant. Turns out she's not only an ace cook and baker, but a damned good friend. If I'm a darling, you must be a darling's darling.'

'Don't. You'll make me cry. I admire your no-nonsense confidence and compassion. And your way with words.'

'Love them. Swallowing dictionaries, encyclopaedias, and the odd thesaurus is far healthier than guzzling legal tomes. More nutritious than fighting the corruption of this prejudiced world and those playing the system. The privileged elite, who know how to twist the rules. Money means buying. Anything and everything, from luxuries to people. Milord Biggin-Smythe's a member of that odious breed. Probably pays government salaries, kits out the cops, and frequents judges and barristers' balls.'

'It's odd. Tom works for the man but can't stand him. In little brother's crazy mind, he's getting one up on the boss, but could lose a lot more than his job. He's a clown. She's no better. When naughty's in, brains are out. Is that me being a grouch, or do you agree?'

'Always.'

2

Down Among the Drums

I t wasn't the fat-faced corpse that baffled Jon Windup on his morning routine down in the cellar of the Noose & Gibbet. It was five rolled-up banknotes jutting skywards from mottled lips, and a fistful of silver coins slung on the concrete floor.

Propped up against a stack of beer barrels, the stiff looked fishy. Pale. Mouth agape. Cold, wide staring eyes. Bloated cheeks convinced Jon that something lurked inside the dead man's mouth, but without prising it open, he was clueless. *A bizarre crime in a historic hilltop inn in tranquil Honest Tor?* Seemed someone had gone to a lot of trouble to make a point.

Jon knew not to touch. Fingerprints at a crime scene wouldn't sit well on his CV and landing a job in the environmental science field was hard enough without further snags. But there was no harm in snooping, and snoop Jon did. He found more dough, this time the edible kind. A broken baguette splashed with tiny red dots, one half resting at the foot of the concrete steps, the other wedged in the man's right hand.

Jon counted the coins. Twenty-five shiny 5p pieces. He couldn't decide what was crustier. The broken loaf or lifeless corpse? The corpse was definitely richer. *Like he needed the money!* Who'd kill a man, stuff cash in his face, and fling a stack of silver on the floor? Odder still, why?

'The police'll love this freak show.'

Jon's verbal musings, a seasoned quirk that got him when still in short pants, helped him join the dots in his ever-probing mind. His love of crime books and films, hunger for knowledge, and an insatiable zest to channel Sherlock Holmes got him while still in nappies. Or was he born with it?

Either way, Jon's ambition often got the better of him. He knew calling the police was the wise thing to do, but his big nose had taken charge and that was that. He checked his watch, then took off, lanky legs sprinting upstairs into the Noose's deserted kitchen. The pub was closed for business and neither head chef, Tom, nor his little helpers, had turned in yet. Jon snatched a pair of food prep gloves, tugged them on monster hands, then dashed back to the cellar.

He squatted next to the corpse, felt for a pulse, and shook his head. 'It's good, but it's not right. He's dead, you plank.'

Long fingers moved to the dead man's forehead and face, careful to avoid the rolled-up notes. Jon couldn't make out if the flesh was cold, but a little more probing determined the stiff *was* stiff. In rigor mortis. 'Must've snuffed it hours ago when everyone went home,' he muttered.

From his jeans pocket, Jon pulled his loyal drat pack. A small zipper pouch crammed with whatnots and thingummies, the unrivalled ally of an inquisitive mind. He hoped today's jumble of tweezers, a bunch of hairpins, nail file, cotton wool, and plasters would prove useful. He fished for his notebook and the battered tape measure he'd pocketed before leaving home, mumbling as he meddled.

'When sleuthing, logging and accuracy are key. Pencil! Here, you scamp.'

Jon jotted and sketched while scanning the scene, ill-fitting prep gloves resulting in scrawl the Rosetta Stone couldn't decipher. He was 34, for pity's sake. Would his hands ever stop growing?

A patchy red trail ran from the bottom of the cellar's concrete steps to the barrels. Jon suspected the killer had dragged the dead man across the floor. He probed the stiff's mouth and chest. Traces of goo. Blood, vomit, or both? Looked sticky, whatever it was. *Had that helped secure the banknotes?*

The gloomy cellar's stale stink and odious company were closing in. Jon drained two cups of espresso and decided he'd seen enough. Time to get out of there. This was a job for the experts, and he must make that call, but not before his shift was done.

Jon pulled out his mobile phone. He must have pictures. A couple of videos wouldn't hurt either. The police wouldn't like it. Could even snap on the cuffs and arrest him, but what was a bloodhound brain supposed to do? Wasn't his fault he'd stumbled upon a crime scene. What harm was a little souvenir? Scientists craved evidence, and nothing would stop Jon sniffing, snapping, or shooting. Besides, no one was about, and old fish face could hardly snitch.

3

An Impossible Crime

T he Noose & Gibbet was a crime scene. Cordoned off, only police and forensics allowed inside. Around the village, word spread. Outside, a small crowd of locals jostled and jabbered at 100 miles an hour. Nothing ever happened in little Honest Tor, and this *was* a happening. Marked cars came and went. Authorities milled around. Contamination suits and evidence bags provoked excited whoops and whispers.

Down in the cellar behind the beer barrels, Jon Windup, who hadn't got out of there, caught an exchange between two men.

A loud boom that could cut granite shook the room. 'Albie, my good man. You came, you saw, but have you conquered? What's the verdict?'

'He's dead.'

'Very funny, but I don't have time for gags.'

'Patience, Jim. You've been in this game long enough to know after a quick probe, the cause of death isn't concrete. Won't be certain until I get him on the slab and have a good poke around. Vague's all you'll get.'

Detective Chief Inspector Slate grumbled. 'Rules and regulations be damned. All that does is slow down the operation and give me bellyache. Still don't understand why we go through all this ritual.'

'Still don't understand? After how many years of service? I'm a pathologist doing my job, Jim. You're a senior detective. Do yours!'

'Right. Give me the vague verdict,' Slate growled.

'Not suicide. Likely fell down the stairs—maybe pushed—dragged across the floor, then propped up. Suspect he choked on his own vomit, after other—'

'Other what?'

'You're testy this morning. Not had your bacon roll yet? Like I said, must get him down to the morgue. Doesn't look like robbery. His wallet, watch, and other valuables are intact. A scuffle, or something more sinister? Whatever, it looks like an impossible crime. We both know this chap, Jim. He was hardly a beggar, but look here. Rolled-up notes. Small coins. What's that all about? Strange old business. Let forensics thrash it out.'

'Are you done? Need to get a closer look before … what the devil's that noise?'

'Sounds like a duck.'

'In a pub cellar? Don't be stupid. There it goes again. From behind those barrels. Who's that? Come out, whoever you are.'

Jon inched out sideways to brave the boom and got smothered by baggy brown eyes and a crushing scowl. Fuzzy eyebrows did a funny little jig, then met in a passionate clinch as a warrant card flashed in Jon's face.

'I'm Detective Chief Inspector Slate, Treeton CID. Who are you?'

'Jon.'

'Jon who?'

'Windup.'

'Tell me, Jon Windup, why are you loitering down here?'

Jon's neck toasted and sweat gathered on his brow. 'I'm not loitering.'

'So, what *are* you doing? Who let you in?'

Jon shuffled on the spot, removed his glasses, and rubbed his eyes. He breathed on the lenses, then popped the specs back on.

'In your own time, Mr Windup.'

'I let myself in. I'm a barman. Managing the cellar's one of my jobs, and if I'm doing a morning shift, I have to check all's good down here.'

'Convenient.'

'What is?'

'You being here.'

'Convenient how? Not the best place to be when a stiff says hello, especially when he ain't your best buddy. That fat fishy face wasn't the first thing I expected to see this morning. Horrible.' Jon curled his lip.

'What time did you arrive?'

'About seven, I think.'

'What time did you find the body?'

'Not sure.'

'What time did you call the police?'

'Don't know the exact time. Just know I did.'

'Time isn't your thing, is it, Mr Windup?'

'Depends what you mean. Time's a manmade concept and nature couldn't care about human invention. Did you know—'

'I know that you're wasting *my* time.'

Social anxiety either muted Jon or made him gibber like an idiot. Trust it to choose the gabbler this morning. To turn the introvert extrovert. 'I called the police. Not sure where my watch hands were pointing.'

'But I'm sure you were told to leave the premises and not touch anything. Except you didn't, did you? A couple of hours later and you're still lurking down here.'

'Doesn't mean I touched. You won't find any fingerprints down here.'

'A lack of fingerprints doesn't mean you're innocent, Mr Windup. Never heard of gloves? Surely you heard officers coming in and out. Heard Mr Drew doing what Mr Drew does.'

The chilly cellar was now a sauna, and Jon wanted out. He grasped for words. Hoped Slate wouldn't ask him to turn out his pockets. *Think, man. Think.* He didn't know forensic pathologist and police doctor Albie Drew, but knew of him and his warm, but no-nonsense reputation.

Jon shot out his hand and smiled. 'Mr Drew, that must be you? Jon Windup, how do you do?'

'I do well, thanks, and it's a pleasure. Do you always speak in rhyme?'

'Only on Tuesdays.'

Albie chuckled and made to reply, but Slate cut him off.

'Never mind all that nonsense. Pleasantries don't help my enquiries. I want to know why you're here.'

Jon could've kicked himself. The heat was rising. Why hadn't he left earlier? His big nose, that's why. The craving to establish facts and doings and dissect every iota. He swallowed the pesky lump in his throat. 'I called the police, then came back down to the cellar because I left my jacket. Cellar work's hot and thirsty, you know.'

'But you didn't do any cellar work. There was the small matter of a dead body greeting you. That horrible, fat fishy face, remember?'

'Took off my jacket while heading down the steps. Did that *before* finding the body.'

'You're not making sense, Mr Windup. Remind me what time you phoned the police?'

'Don't know.'

'So, you did your civil duty, then thought you'd hang around? To snoop.'

'No! After I got my jacket, I felt dizzy, and didn't want to tackle the steps until I'd had some gloop.'

'Gloop?'

Jon held up a small bottle of pink liquid. 'Antacid. I take it for my sweet GORD. That's gastroesophageal reflux disease. Call it gloop because it's well … gloopy. This is aniseed flavour. The white stuff's peppermint.'

'Intriguing. Do let me know when it comes in chocolate flavour, won't you? No doubt that'll be the brown stuff. Now, where were we? I know. Why were you hiding behind the barrels?'

'Wasn't hiding. Ducked behind for privacy. Didn't want old popeye putting me off. Nothing worse than a deadpan audience.'

'And?'

'Guess the police came. Then, Mr Drew, but I wasn't interested in comings and goings. Not with acid reflux burning like hell. Hoped the pain would go away and hung around until it did. Sorry for being here, but I've done nothing wrong.'

'I'll be the judge of that. I may not know the workings of a pub cellar, but I know the difference between cider and ale. Is that the miraculous gloop in your hands?'

'Yes, but I wouldn't call it miraculous. Doesn't always—' Jon's mouth broke into a wide grin, then he roared with laughter.

'And what's so amusing?'

'He is.' Jon pointed to a fluffy ginger cat giving his white bib and socks a wash and brush-up inches from Slate's feet. 'That's the pub cat, come to say hello.'

Slate jabbed his forefinger towards the wary animal, baggy eyes wobbling as he bawled. 'Albie. Corner that cat. It could harbour DNA. Won't have it tampering with my crime scene, contaminating evidence.'

Albie tiptoed past Slate, but the cat was quicker. He shot off and scuttled behind the barrels.

'He's lightning fast, inspector. You'll need a better strategy,' Jon advised.

'So I see.'

'Can I go now?'

'Better had before the burn comes back. And shut that cellar door. I want that cat!'

'Anything else?'

'Don't loiter upstairs.'

Jon nodded to Slate and Drew, then took off on never-ending legs. Halfway up the stairs, Slate's boom stopped him.

'One more thing, Mr Windup. The coffee cups. What time did you have coffee?'

'Can't remember.'

'Get out!'

Even in his school sprinting days, Jon had never moved faster. Damn social awkwardness. Making him babble like an idiot and causing a mild panic attack. At least he'd had the sense to remove the prep gloves and keep his drat pack and gadgets intact. Mr Quince was a gentleman and star to offer a reprieve. Shut the cellar door? Never. Closed doors and cats were mortal enemies.

4

Slated!

O nce outside, Jon stashed his booty in a rocky safe
place, then headed to the far edge of the cordon. He
was in deep thought when Slate collared him again, with
a plainclothes detective in tow. A younger man, shorter
than Slate, wearing a crooked grin, immaculate brown
hair, and a gallon of cologne. When it came to ages, Jon
was hopeless. Age blind, he said. This bloke could be late
twenties or thirties, but Jon knew one thing. The stride,
the suit, the intense whiff convinced him that here was a
cop too sure of himself, but unsure how to be humble.

Jon's gaze shifted to Slate. Of average height and
build, wearing a washed-out brown suit, dirty white shirt,
and faded tie, he didn't look like a senior detective. More
like a litter picker Jon had seen around Treeton. A proper
grump, altogether too testy with his lot, who wore a
permanent frown and stabbed at discarded rubbish with a
rotatable claw.

Hard to guess Slate's age. Rumpled skin, and his
rank—surely it must take years to reach chief inspector—
the detective could be mid to late fifties, even sixties, but
the hair told a different story. Thick and dark, with no hint
of receding or thinning. No obvious grey either. What was
plain was the man's pride at his magnificent mop. The
way he stroked it back from his baggy face, with a warm,
gentle touch and the vain smirk that followed. *Could be a
wig. Or a hair transplant. Or—*

'Mr Windup, we meet again. DCI Slate, remember, and this is Detective Sergeant Uttley. Show the man your warrant card, sergeant.'

Full of inflated importance, Uttley flashed his ID, stabbing Jon with startling blue eyes. 'A few minutes of your time,' he said, waving a notebook mid-air.

'What for?' Jon's toasty neck was back, and it had nothing to do with the scorching sun. Uttley's cocky face and manner unnerved him.

'Just a couple of questions. What time did you phone the police?'

'I've already told you. I don't know. Can't remember.'

'But we know. Emergency services logged your call just before eight, almost an hour after you got to work. Explain.' Uttley couldn't have looked smugger.

'Explain what?'

'The reason you took so long to call the police, Mr Windup. Did your dawdling have anything to do with aniseed gloop?' It was Slate's turn for smugness.

'No, but I didn't find the body straightaway. Had other things to do before going into the cellar. Think I said it was *about* seven, not on the dot. I went into the kitchen to look for Tom. As head chef, he's usually the first in and often the last out, but there was no sign.'

'Why were you looking for Tom?'

'Needed coffee for the machine in the bar. We always make fresh coffee for breakfast. The ground stuff's kept in a locked kitchen cupboard. Expensive beans. Because Tom wasn't there, I had to find the keys, get the coffee out, lug it into the bar, and set everything up for brewing and serving. Coffee lovers know the most important cup's that first one in the morning. It's no different in the Noose, providing we're dishing up breakfast, of course.'

'Then you went down to the cellar?'

'No. Did a few other bits. Getting the place ready for business stuff.'

'How long did it take to sort the coffee and do your *other bits*?'

'Don't know. Half an hour or so. Finding the key for the coffee cupboard set me back. Like I said, Tom usually gets here first and opens everything up.'

'I see. You didn't call the police until just before eight. That leaves half an hour.'

'Like I said, don't know exactly.'

'Yes. Like you said. And keep saying. Where were you last night?'

'Never fails to crack me up why police ask that question.'

'We could always take a trip to the station and continue the chat there, Mr Windup. A formal setting might help you take this serious crime seriously.'

'Not so fast. It's not every morning I turn up for work and find a stiff in the cellar. I'm still in shock and that's not a crime.'

'Of course not. I'll leave things for now, but want a full statement soon. Don't leave the village.'

'*What?* But I don't live here. I live in Treeton.'

'You can go home, but make sure you're available when I'm ready to see you again.'

'When will that be?'

'Soon.'

'How soon?' Jon fought the temptation to yell.

'Police are never off duty. You live in Treeton. When you have a spare hour, pop into the station and have a cup of tea. We'll take your statement while you're sipping. Failing that, I'll get you another time. Come along, sergeant.' Slate turned to leave, then turned back.

'One more thing, Mr Windup. Why didn't you close that cellar door when I asked?'

'Did you? Didn't hear, inspector. Blame that on my gammy ear.'

'And the duck?'

'That's a message tone on my phone. I got a message reminding me of a dental appointment.'

'Or whatever else you rustle up. We're off, sergeant.' Slate scurried away.

'By the way, my governor's a *chief* inspector. Don't forget that.' Uttley snapped his notebook shut in Jon's face, slipped it in his pocket, and dashed after Slate.

Jon headed the other way, murmuring under his breath and dodging the swarm of feverish villagers dying for an update.

'Who've you been poisoning with your pints, Jon?' a voice called.

Ignoring the quip, Jon caught up with a familiar face further down the road. Close friend and confidante, Wendy May, had been his saviour when he was scouring the net for an editor during his environmental science studies. He hoped for a sharp eye, and a sharper mind, to cut his wordy—or windy, she said—dissertations, and got more than he bargained for. Poles apart, but Zen connected, the pair had become besties, Jon even offering Wendy a roof in Treeton, while her cottage in Bogus Hole underwent extensive renovation. For this bantering pair, the push and pull of diversity worked.

In a riot of lime green, purple, and white, sporting the essential hat of the day, Wendy waved and rushed to greet Jon. 'Just the man. There I am in Beans and Leaves, deep in coffee paradise, when Ross Pengelly charges in saying someone's snuffed it in the Noose. He's all mouth, so I ignored him. You had an early start this morning, my windy friend. What's the scoop?'

'In the words of a popular murder mystery board game. Lord Biggin-Smythe. In the cellar. With a baguette.'

5

Double Dough

'**M**ilord? A killer? If you mean the game I think you mean, *that* game names the doer, not the done. Which game?'

'I said in the words of. Not verbatim. The old boy's the done, not the doer. A fish-faced goner!'

'Got it. Milord's dead.'

'As the proverbial doornail. Miserable old nark. I know he didn't like me, but he could've invited me to his leaving do. I love a good send off.'

'This must be a wind up.'

'That's my name, Wendy, not my intention.'

'Not the same thing. Your name's wind, like the movement of air. Not wind, like turn. One's a noun, with a short, sharp *i*, the other a verb with a long one. Heteronyms, Jon. A cranky old quirk of the English language. Same spelling. Different sound, meaning, and pronunciation. And beware those vowel movements.'

'Does the editor ever sleep?'

'Don't be silly. After years of nitpicking, pedantry's a lifestyle, as well as a job. Words. Syntax. Punctuation. I love it all. Dictionaries, libraries, and books-books-books. I swallowed good grammar with baby food and sicked up all the bad.' Wendy's monologue moved at a fresh pace, expressive hands and face matching her enthusiasm.

'You don't say, and yes, my name *is* pronounced wind, like movement of air, but people often get it wrong. Won't get wound up over it.'

'Clever.'

'See you're kitted out in full technicolour. Can't miss you, or that cap.'

'You know I have a wicked love affair with hats, Jon. What you don't know is how it all started, but hat's another story. Tell me do about your date with the dear departed rich boy.'

'Not here.' Jon made to move down Bluebell Lane, known locally as heart attack hill for its challenging incline.

'Why all the mystery? Out with it and stop faffing. The suspense is killing me.'

'Well, get on my good ear. You know the right one's broken.'

Wendy shuffled around. 'You and your iffy lug. Happy now?'

'Better.' Mindful of the hive of police activity and villagers still nosing around the pub, Jon kept his voice low. 'Like I told you. Lord Biggin-Smythe, cold in the cellar. Alive or dead, he needs no introduction, even propped against a stack of drums with a bloated fishy face. He'll be celebrating with Satan, with a mouthful of cash and a little bit of bread, but no cheese.'

'That's dark, Jon. Explain.'

'Possibly fell down the stairs, or got pushed, then whacked with a baguette, of all things. But here's the first rub. Whoever did it was creative. Shoved five rolled-up banknotes in his mouth. Like slick cigars. I know the old boy loved a big Havana. Some joker knew that, too. He had something else stuffed in his mouth. Don't know what. Could be more money. His cheeks were all puffy. Looked like the fat fluid sacs of a bubble eye goldfish.'

'I'll take your word for it. What else?'

'A patchy blood trail. Not gory. The killer could've dragged the old boy across the floor, then propped him against the kegs. His hair didn't make the journey. It was on the ground, loafing around as hair does. Must've fancied a snooze,' Jon sniggered.

'*Mr Windup*. You're talking about a man's life. Or death. Same thing.'

'No. I'm talking about a man's wig. Anyway, why should I be kind to Mr la-di-da? My natural caring streak doesn't run to unscrupulous unthinkables like him. I work for him, remember, and he's a ruthless, filthy rich rotter, who doesn't give zip for his staff, or anyone else.'

'Was.'

'Was what?'

'A ruthless, filthy rich rotter. He's dead. Expired. Amen.'

'And good riddance. Doubt I'll need a bereavement counsellor.'

'Nor me. By the way, unthinkables is super-duper, by golly. Not sure if the OED will accept it though. Oxford boffs are a fussy breed.'

'Glad the editor approves, and if Oxford won't bite, I'll try Cambridge. It's one for my new dictionary, regardless.'

'What's all this?'

'Windy's Wacky Words.'

'Let me guess. Nutty words and phrases only for geeks like you. Your own nonsense language.'

'My lexicon for life. But now it's back to death. Did you know the old boy was quids in? Won't be long before the vultures circle.'

'Think I figured he was worth a pile. Arrogance gave it away, or the fact he's snaffled half the bleeding county. Is "quids in" your attempt to roll out a crude slice of dark wit because of the cash in his mouth? Does the quipster ever sleep?'

'Not if my circadian rhythm's playing up.'

'Let's leave his fortune and get back to the crime scene. You mentioned the first rub. What's the second?'

'The bread. I know Eddie's trying out a new supplier and buys in frozen loaves. Those home bake types, but I don't know if the bread came from the Noose's freezers. I'm Jon Windup, not Dan Fahrenheit.'

'What sort of bread?'

'A golden baguette. Likely baked in the pub kitchen. Unless the killer was peckish and brought it along to make a sandwich. There's your motive. The old boy tried to swipe the thug's supper and got walloped instead.'

'So our murderer has a sense of humour. Why a baguette? Must've used it as a joke. Unless there's another logical reason. Why do you think someone clonked milord over the head?'

'Just a feeling. Spots of blood here and there. Think the bread had something to do with the murder, but I doubt it killed him. It was snapped in two. One half at the bottom of the cellar steps, the other half stuck in the old boy's fist. Maybe the killer had it all planned out, then it all went wrong. Whatever happened, bet people think the killer's done Treet a big favour. Won't be many who'll miss that old codger.'

'Many? Any's closer to the truth. I know Prue won't. Let's talk dirty cash.'

'Hold on. Don't you want another rub?'

'Not now, Jon. I've just had me cake.'

'You know what I mean.'

'Out with it, then. Don't stand there with your finger up your beak.'

'More props.'

'Props?'

'Twenty-five coins on the floor. Five pence pieces, all bright and shiny. Don't know what to make of it. Did some scouting around, but the gloves I had on didn't fit and it was all a bit fingers and thumbs. Not everyone has monster hands.'

'Or Yeti feet. Notes *and* coins. Gets weirder and weirder. Sounds like you got something, though, despite the fingers and thumbs.'

'Of course. Had my faithful friend with me.' Jon wiggled his drat pack in mid-air. 'Had to hide my stash, then retrieve it later.'

'I love it. Your twee pocket pouch jammed with every little gizmo for every big fix. *Who'd do that?* Stuff a zipper bag with an odd bunch of whatsits, then give it a name? You're a fruitcake, Jon Windup.'

'Only part-time. Rest of the time, I'm just cake. Anyway, back to poking around. Couldn't do too much. Was getting all hot and bothered and knew I had to call the cops.'

'A sweaty yeti. Ugh. Nothing worse.'

'Took a pile of pics. And a couple of vids.'

'Let's have a gander.'

Jon tapped the screen of his phone and scrolled.

Wendy's eyes opened wide, then squinted. She tipped her head from left to right for a better angle and effected an affected voice. 'Frightfully sharp suit, milord. Jolly decent tweed.'

'See the puffy cheeks? That's the bubble eye goldfish look I was on about. Megantic fluid sacs. You need to see a picture of one to fully appreciate it.'

'Can't wait. Wonder who wanted him dead? Imagine the shyster had a ton of enemies. Most of the village, I bet. For years, he's been bleeding the people of Treetonshire. Now someone's finally bled him.'

'*Shyster*. Isn't that a term for crooked lawyers? You should know all about that.'

'Are you itching to be milord's drinking buddy, Windup? You're going the right way about it.'

'Rather stick pins in me eyes.'

'Just as well. Alive or dead, Seymour Richard George Royce Biggin-Smythe wouldn't associate with riff-raff.'

'Blimey. I'm surprised he fit in the cellar with a name that long. Are those his full credentials?'

'All that.'

'What *is* the point?'

'Tradition, I suppose. Foot-long names are required. Especially for boys.'

'And the delights of hunting, shooting, and fabulous fornication. The elite sure know how to party. I remember you told me his name when you interviewed him for that fancy mag. Wasn't that long ago, but my short-term memory's shot. I only remember Seymour.'

'Alas, poor Seymour didn't see more. Certainly not the deadly dough. Did you phone the police?'

'Indeedy and got on their wrong side.'

'How?'

'Snooped a lot, but didn't get out before the coppers came. Hid behind the barrels and DCI Slate collared me. Had to answer some tricky questions and thought that was it, but he wants a full statement. That theory of what possibly happened came from Albie Drew. I swiped it.'

'Good old, Albie. Know him from my legal days. He's been cutting up corpses for years. You'll get on well with him. His humour's as dark as yours. He's sweet on Prue, but she won't return the sweetness.'

'Because of her ex?'

'Yes. Mr Daniel Foster said he couldn't cope with an invalid, wouldn't be a wheelchair pusher, then packed his bags and left with some other poor sap in tow. Prue went rural. Divorce followed. She went back to her maiden name, and that was that. No surprise she's off relationships.'

'Foster sounds like a nasty pasty.'

'Worse than a semi-colon. Even that has one use.'

'Is Prue a Penn and Tom a Trebilcock because they're stepsister and brother?'

'Yes, but Prue's always treated Tom like blood kin. Probably knows him better than he knows himself.'

'Is he the same with her?'

'Was, but things change. Don't know the full ins and outs. Ask Prue. Anything else to report, Sherlock?'

'Plenty, but later, although I must tell you this. Mr Quince came into the cellar and Slate wanted Albie to nab him. Something about DNA and contaminating evidence. Quincy scarpered behind the kegs. Slate wasn't best pleased. He told me to get out and close the cellar door.'

'So you got out and didn't close it?'

'That cat saved me from a nasty panic attack. No way would I impound him. Shame I couldn't hang around to find out a bit more, but I think Slate and Drew had done with talking. Nothing else to report on that score.'

'A childish prank, with a drum of theatre. Are you sure it wasn't you, Jon?'

'Is that supposed to be funny?'

'For those with a sense of humour. Not in the best possible taste, I admit, but don't be so touchy. Blame your love of the dramatic. It's that quirky theatrical spirit of yours that opens all doors to my biting wit.'

'I hear you. Will there be a post-mortem?'

'Violent, unnatural death. Cause unknown. Coroner must investigate. A certain inquest.'

'Thought so.'

'Well done, you. Anything else?'

'Met Slate's sidekick. DS Max Uttley. He's one to watch. A proper, cocky ladies' man. Looks nothing like a copper. Come to think of it, neither does Slate.'

'*M Uttley*.' The name rolled off Wendy's tongue in an exaggerated giggle. 'His parents must've had a dastardly sense of humour. Could have some fun with that.'

'Yeah, it's a bit of a woof name!' Jon expelled a wheezy snigger.

Do you know Slate's name?'

'Jim. Probably a James.'

'Anything else to tell me?'

'No. What's in the bag?'

'Provisions. Though Pengelly's story sounded far-fetched, thought I'd grab lunch just in case. Knew you wouldn't get your free grub in the Noose if he was telling the truth and, without sustenance, I'd never hear the last of your whining. Can't let you starve, my windy friend.'

'Get proper irritable when I'm hungry.'

'And doubly so after interrogation. A whiff of anxiety and you morph into a sad, gibbering wreck. Methinks panic still lingers. Come on. I'll treat you to a—'

'Yoohoo!'

'Not now,' Jon groaned, spying village muckraker Annie Clegg furiously pedalling towards them on her clapped-out old bike.

6

Every Village Has One

'She's late. Wonder what kept her?' Wendy's words were slow. Deliberate. 'The carper of contrary triumphant again.'

'Every time there's an incident, she turns up.'

'Always. Wouldn't be a show without the village scold. Village communities breed big mouths, but the unwritten rule expects locals to rub along with each other. I'm not the rubbing type. Especially where Annie Clegg's concerned. She can't, won't, and don't blend into the background. Should've stayed on the hilltop. Up on the hump. Free from the grump.'

Annie stopped beside Jon, scrawny white legs akimbo. She blew cold air onto her crumpled, red face, bony frame heaving and sighing as mean, bulging eyes sneered and accused.

The woman was an oddity. Once a pretty girl, or so said the rumour, over the years, she'd let herself go. Now, at 71, wild grey hair doubled for a rat's nest, and a big wart on the end of her wonky nose made it wonkier. Her eyes popped and the ability to stretch her face into the weirdest shapes convinced Jon and Wendy it was made of rubber. Jon joked that Annie had a doctorate in mugology. So many lines, it looked as if she'd fallen headfirst onto a train track.

But of all Annie's peculiarities, an overzealous overbite was her greatest liability. Soaking her crinkled, hairy chin in bubbling spit as that cackling mouth tirelessly yakked.

Always hurried, or angry, or both, Annie whizzed around Tor on a bike so old, she must've ridden it in another life. Perhaps in the 19ᵗʰ century when bicycle face came about. Allegedly brought on by cycling strain, Annie certainly had the symptoms of the spurious disease. A pale, flushed, fatigued visage. Pinched lips. Dark circles under the eyes. Of course, it was bogus. A scare tactic and ploy by male doctors to discourage women from cycling. Any condition would do.

It wasn't long before the cackle started, addressing Jon as if her drama bothered him.

'This heat's a killer. I'm going to pass out. Talking of killings, I hear that old boot Biggin-Smythe copped it in the pub cellar. Someone did for him, and you found his body, Mr Windup. Fancy that.' Annie wiped her chin with the back of her hand, rubbed it on a faded blue blouse, then stuck a battered old white bucket hat on her head.

'Speak up, Annie. They can't hear you in Scotland,' Jon said.

'Go on with you. Can't help how I talk. Funny you should mention Scotland. That's where that chef Tom thingy's from. He must've done it. Carrying on with the old lord's missus, you know. She's a one. Likes a man in a kilt, they say.'

'Who says?' Wendy's direct, controlled tone cut Annie to the quick.

'You should know, Wendy May. The locals, and that friend of yours, Prue Penn. Don't tell me you didn't hear her in the tent last night. Having a go at thingy over his frolics with the posh piece. No smoke without fire, she said. I agree. The old boot caught them at it and now he's dead. Has to be the kilt. Who else?'

Jon and Wendy said nothing. Unless they wanted privileged news trashed from here to Nantucket, best keep quiet. Discretion and Annie Clegg didn't share the same pod.

'So, Mr Windup, did you find him? You didn't say.'

'Belt up, Annie. We'll let you know when we want a foghorn on call. I suspect you'll have an infinite wait. The matter's in the police's hands.'

'Since when was your name Mr Windup?'

'Since you wheeled up and the real one lost the will to live. Unless you didn't know, this is a private conversation. Think you said you were going to pass out? Right now would be a good time. Failing that, on your bike and push off.'

'Haven't you got funny eyes?'

'Not as funny as your malocclusion.'

'What's that?'

'Call yourself a schoolteacher. Sorry. Former schoolteacher. Your overbite.'

'One's blue and one's green. You're not normal.'

'That's the rumour. What some call an acquired taste. Much like you, except I'm nothing like you at all. Tell me. Has your top set of teeth always stuck out that far? Ever considered braces?'

'Freaky.'

'You said it.'

'Were you born that way? With different coloured eyes?'

'Thought I told you to shove off.'

Annie didn't budge. She'd clocked Prue Penn and her malicious muckrake itched for scandal. 'Five minutes.'

Wendy was having none of it. 'How about now, if you know what's good for you?'

Annie Clegg knew of Wendy's kickboxing days and didn't fancy being on the end of a mighty right hook. Either that, or Wendy would wrap her up in words. Either way, she'd get bounced. Muck would have to wait. Grudging, Annie took off on her cranky old bike, fleet feet zigzagging down the road and pity help anyone who got in her way.

'Thank goodness that mad cow's gone. Yak-yak-yak. Surprised she hasn't worn her tongue out.' Prue sat on a wooden seat, one of many scattered around Honest Tor dedicated to some dear departed soul. She was glad she'd worn shorts, sleeveless tee, and trainers. The fickle cool vest had come out to play, too.

'Every village has one, Prue. Annie Clegg takes pleasure from other people's misery. It entertains her. She's never evolved as a human being. Something's turned her into a bitter old shrew. What, I don't know exactly, but have my suspicions. No matter, that isn't a licence for spite. No excuse for spreading malignant gossip. How she became a primary schoolteacher's a mystery, but she did, and for years. A shrill, snaggle-toothed she-devil. Eek! The kids probably found it hilarious when her overbite did its thing. You know what kids are like. Would've been scary funny. The bite that is not a soaking from the spit stream. Hope you've fettered your ferrets today, Madame Penn.'

'Behave, Wendy,' Prue giggled, 'you'll make my belly ache. Annie's twin sister lives in Bogus Hole, doesn't she?'

'She does, and Kitty Clegg's nothing like her. Fraternal twins, but poles apart. Annie came first. Married once to henpecked Stanley Watt. No children. Widowed when Stan choked on a fishbone while dining out. Story goes, no one could do the Heimlich Manoeuvre, and he staggered outside, clutching his throat and flapping about. Paramedics found the poor old soul flat out on the tarmac. Eyes wide open. Mouth agape.'

'He didn't eat the whole fish then?' Jon thought it was time he put in an appearance.

'Wrong soul, Jon. Homophones. Another one of those cranky old quirks of the English language. Pronounced the same, but different in meaning, origin, or spelling. I suspect that wily grin on your face warns me I've fallen for a dark-humoured Windup wind-up.'

''Fraid so. What type of fish did the dastardly deed?'

'Mackerel. A fish packed with teeny pin bones, and filleting's tricky. I bet Stan's goggle eyes and open mouth made him look like the thing he'd just scoffed. Don't know if medics ever dislodged the bone or left it inside his dead body.'

'Revenge of the Mack. Coming soon, to a cinema near you. Sounds like a B-Movie from the fifties. Or that song from the nineties, Return of the Mack,' Jon said.

'How come Annie's a Clegg and not a Watt?' Prue asked.

'Went back to her maiden name after Stan died. Vowed she'd never forgive him for eating mackerel that day. Served him right, she said. Maybe that's why she's such a mean old misery. Embittered. She and Kitty don't speak much. Kitty has no time for her,' Wendy said.

'Does anyone?' Prue said. 'What's her punctuation mark?'

'Has to be the exclamation. Long and thin, with a wart on the end. Better still, inverted. Turned upside down, it looks like a skull on a stick. The editor in me squirms at the overuse of any mark, but I'd gladly keep lining up the exclamation to typify Annie. Any way up.'

'I second that. Anyway, what's doing? Heard you found his lordship's body, Jon. Dead as, and drunk. Is that right?'

'That's half Annie Clegg and half Ross Pengelly, Prue. Dead, yes. Don't know about booze drunk. From what I made out, he *was* drunk on money, but I was careful not to contaminate the scene. Didn't smell drink but did smell something.'

'What?'

'Murder.' Jon gave a rundown of that morning's findings, broken bread and all.

'A baguette? Funny that. I'm into bread at the moment.'

'Me too, except my baked offerings aren't pretty,' Wendy snorted.

Jon's revelation about the money made Prue chuckle. 'Double dough. Or is it double bread? I've often wondered why dough and bread mean money. Strange.'

'Like our sense of humour. You wouldn't think a man was lying flat out over the road,' Wendy said.

'He isn't flat out. He's propped up. And technically, it's triple dough. Bread, notes, *and* coins. Double's fine, though. Don't mind mashing up the cash.'

Wendy laughed. 'Last word Windup strikes again, but good call. Triple's too much. Let's mash 'em. What's your take, Prue?'

'Nobody liked the mean old goat. He'd never win landlord of the year. You remember how many times he tried to hike my rent, and how long I waited to get my boiler fixed last winter. It's a fact. Money goes to money.'

'I told you to move out or hold your rent. Wouldn't put up with that,' Wendy said.

'But I love Brambles and didn't want to risk a notice to leave. I'll buy a place when I'm better fixed healthwise. Anyway, stingy landlords are everywhere. They take ages to cough up for repairs and when they replace anything, it's always junk.'

Jon agreed. 'El cheapo poop. The old boy was a typical toff. Best double Jersey cream for him. Skimmier than skimmed milk for the peasants.'

'Skimmier? Is that another wacky word for your new lexicon?'

'Yes. It's coming on.'

'If you didn't like him, why did you work for him, Jon?' Prue was curious.

'Didn't like him's an understatement. I loathed the man but was doing Eddie Rutter a favour. He's a mate and was stuck for a pint puller. I've temped as a barman in all the local villages, so, when he asked if I'd do a few shifts, I agreed. Not how I want to spend the rest of my life, but finding a job in my field ain't easy. Bet Newton didn't have such trouble. Anyway, for Eddie's sake, I put up with the bull but didn't have to like it.'

'And now someone's shut him up, you won't have to put up,' Wendy said.

'Is that why people call him BS? Was he full of dung, then? Pooh.' Prue wrinkled her nose.

'Chock full. Lord Muck. Any sign of Tom? He hadn't shown when the police arrived. No doubt they'll want to talk to him. They'll question everyone who works in the pub and probably know about Tom's close connection with the old boy's missus. You know how locals gossip. The biggest mouthpiece's already at it. Could be tricky.'

'Haven't seen him, Jon. He took the bakery class, then did off. Probably to join his lady love.'

Wendy dragged her hands down her face. 'He better watch out when Annie's about. That woman gets worse. If it moves, she criticises it. If it talks back, she shouts. That's the downside of close communities. People sponge everything up. Tor's a nest for scandal and Annie's no feathered friend. She overheard you in the tent last night and is twisting your words to her advantage. Perhaps got the idea into her head when I joked about using my stone loaf to knock some sense into Tom.'

'You don't think he did it, do you? I know he's been an idiot, but he wouldn't kill someone. Even a rotten old moneybags.'

Prue had gone a funny colour. She'd warned Tom many times about his folly, knowing nothing would come of it, but he'd ignored her and made a cuckold of Lord Biggin-Smythe. Now the aristo lay dead, and Tom was chief suspect.

7

The Noose & Gibbet

S afe from Annie's venom, Jon, Wendy, and Prue hiked back up heart attack hill, then stood at the corner of the Noose & Gibbet behind the police cordon to watch the goings-on. For decades, the popular inn had soaked up an odd bunch of characters, its hilltop site, jaded facade, and worn, pendent sign lending an aura of adventurous, bygone days.

'Time for a bite. What delights you got, Wendy?'

'I adore Adam's wacky fillings, but veggie lasagne drizzled in chocolate lemon pesto, nor guacamole and chilli jam haven't made the bag today. There's egg mayo, cheese and pickle, or falafel and charred pepper wrap. Help yourself. Juice and crisps too. Just a drink for me. I'll eat later. Guess you had a lovely breakfast, Prue?'

'Yes. Smoothie bowl and a big bowl of berries. Yum.' Prue rested on her trekking poles. 'Love old stone buildings. So full of character. Never really thought about it, but wonder how old this place is.'

'Ask the expert,' Jon said in between bites of falafel wrap and pickled onion crisps. 'Wendy knows more about the past than Herodotus, the father of history himself. What she doesn't know about Treetonshire county isn't worth knowing. Take the stage, darling.'

'Why, thank you, my windy friend, but I've told you a zillion times, don't exaggerate. History's infinite. Always something new to learn. 'Tis true, I hold a fascination for local archives and have written dozens of historical pieces. The Noose and Gibbet can tell many tales. Only last week, I researched a tiny scrap of its past. Funny how days later, we're standing here among strange happenings. I don't believe in coincidence.'

'Want to know the great thing about Wendy's memory, Prue? It remembers. Unlike my fickle pickle, Wendy's gherkin's a whizz at saving what she reads and writes. May not be exact, but near enough,' Jon said.

'Revision and public speaking help,' Wendy said.

'Tell us a few things,' Prue enthused.

'I'll do my best. The pub's centuries old. Started its life as The Swan, a fashionable coaching inn, refreshing and housing hundreds of thirsty travellers and their horses on long journeys. It soon became a haven for robbers, poachers, and highwaymen, indeed, any scoundrel who dared to ply their trade or plot their next fiendish crime in dark corners.'

'The way you tell it makes me want to be there, Wendy. All mysterious and exciting. Go on,' Prue bubbled.

'Taking pride of place in the darkest corner was a hallowed stone throne called Buccaneer's Booty, reserved for dashing dandy Patcheye Peg, Treet's most notorious pirate and seadog. Peg started his swashbuckling life as quartermaster and first mate to the captain of The Salty Squid, then ended up captain himself. His reputation stretched far and wide. Not only was he the cream of corruption, he was also the most feared *and* most admired rascal in Treetonshire. The illustrious plunderer was a frequent visitor to the inn. Parking his bones and summoning his best wench, Sal, to serve ale in his special silver tankard. He'd down a few, then glug a brimful of bumbo.'

'What bo?' Jon said.

'Bumbo. A heady brew of rum, water, and spices. The favoured grog of all revered sea robbers, it's said. Salacious Sal, of ample bosom and generous hip, was the only mortal who could handle Peg. She kept him in check with her teasing and a playful ritual.'

'What did she do?' Prue was agog.

'She'd steal Peg's drink, give a naughty wink, then tickle him under the chin. She was an alluring temptress who did what she did to let the pirate know she was offering her favours. Raunchy rascal Peg needed no further come on. Whatever the pleasure, his boots were never full. So the story goes.'

Prue took a sip of water. 'Wonder if Lady Lu descends from Sal the Gal?'

'Floozies both,' Wendy said. 'Cut from the same cloth.'

'I'm loving this. Carry on.'

'When The Swan's reputation as a rogue's den spread, the authorities stepped in. They adopted the inn's hilly location and erected primitive gallows to hang executed or tortured criminals. Known as gibbeting, the grisly practice served as a warning to crooks who plied their trade. Adding chains and a gibbet cage made the custom more gruesome. Many outlaws hung and rotted there, the swan flew, and the inn's name changed to the Noose and Gibbet. Ta-da!'

'What about Pegleg? Did he have a bumbo ending?' Jon roared.

'A fitting question, asked in your inimitable windy fashion,' Wendy giggled. 'Patcheye Peg held celebrity status in the county, especially with the ladies. He was a rake, but people respected him for his intrepid exploits, daring ways, and kind heart. He was like Robin Hood. Helping the poor. Scorning the rich. The law wasn't so tolerant and wanted his neck, but it was a savage called Nasty Ned who ended Peg's piracy days.'

'How?' Jon and Prue asked in unison.

'Ned collared Peg for dabbling with his wife, Sal. He stole his cutlass, slit Peg's throat, then strung him up in the gibbet cage. Depending which way the wind blew, jangling chains and a clanking cage were a grim reminder the pickled pirate rotted there, swinging for all to see. It's down in the archives.'

'So, poor Peg pegged it. What a way to go,' Jon said.

'But the story doesn't end there. The law nicked Ned and hanged him as a wrong'un, though spared him the evils of gibbeting. It's said devastated mourners cut the famed dandy down and buried him next door in Saint Mark's cemetery under a gnarled yew tree. People turned out in droves to bid farewell and tears flowed as freely as the bumbo that kept him soused. Or something like that.'

'I bet Peg was a real ladies' man,' Prue bubbled.

'I want to visit the graveyard. See if I can find Peg's headstone. Imagine it'll be wonky and battered, but I'd love to see it. I'll nab the rector. Ask to have a peek at the church and parish archives. Heaps more to research, friends, but today's lesson's over.'

'That's a shame. Not even a morsel?' Prue urged.

'Only recent stuff about the inn, if you're interested.'

'Yes, please.'

'As expected, the clientele, decor, and ambience have changed, but not the name. Buccaneer's Booty crumbled, but we know of one infamous rig that hangs around. At the foot of the beer garden stands a replica of the grisly gibbet. Some parts are original. Some not. Still swinging and swaying. Still groaning when the wind blows a certain way. For years, that gory relic's attracted ghoulish lovers of dark tourism. People flock to lap up its macabre history. Aren't humans a weird lot?'

'Fact,' Prue said. 'Do you think his lordship's plans to make big changes have anything to do with his death, Jon?'

'Maybe. I know his zealous scheme to tear down that grumbling, clanging eyesore, rename the Noose, and convert it into a gastropub incensed the locals.'

'That's why a petition went up, accusing Biggin-Smythe of vandalising the village and killing a piece of celebrated history. A petition started by Annie Clegg, of all people. Milord didn't care. He dismissed pleas and surged ahead, saying his heritage was all that mattered. He wanted an end to archaic devilment. Thoughts, Jon? Or do you have to go away and think about it?'

'Not this time, darling. Sounds like someone had their own devilment, wouldn't let matters hang, and ended the old boy instead.'

8

It's All About the Bags

Colin and Joanna Sower, glum undertakers, who worked with police on "delicate" matters, clung to their trusty trolley, waiting impatiently to bag a body.

Wendy knew of the Sowers' testy reputation. 'Sower by name, sour by nature. There's not a pair better suited to their vocation than those two miseries. And here comes milord. All bagged up and ready for the off.'

'Don't think much of his new tweed,' farmer Jack "Figgy" Figgis growled. 'Go on. Get to hell and take the rest of your stuck-up lot with you.'

As the Sowers loaded their cargo into the back of a van, the crowd tussled to get a better view. Amid a shower of hoots and mutterings of get lost, the grimsters took off to the morgue.

'The cadavan,' Jon said, 'A new class of caravan to carry stiffs. Did you get that, Wendy? Cad-a-van. For cad-a-vers. The next entry for Windy's Wacky Words.'

'Love it, Jon,' Wendy chuckled. 'And there he goes. Stingier than Scrooge, but he'll be the richest man in the graveyard.'

'Think they'll bury him next door, Wendy?'

'Doubt it, Prue. There must be a family crypt for the tribe. Suspicious death means the funeral must wait. Could be weeks before the inquest's over. Of course, if he's happy to, the coroner can sanction a funeral. It's all at his discretion. There may be a memorial service. Meanwhile, until Albie Drew lugs him on the slab and puts his gruesome cutters through a vigorous workout, milord and the chiller will keep each other company. No creeping into the crypt just yet. Imagine the family's clout will demand an early post-mortem to determine the cause of death.'

'See old baggy-eyed Slate's still mooching around,' Jon said.

'Is that him in the brown suit?' Wendy said.

'Yes. And there's Uttley, not a hair out of place. I'm sure you'll meet them both soon. Slate looks like he hasn't slept since time immemorial.'

'Pressures of the job. Cuts, staff shortages, and long, long hours.'

Annie Clegg, who'd gawked at the crime scene most of the morning and couldn't get enough, cranked up her tongue.

'Yes, that old boot'll rot away while his gold-digging wife spends all his money and frolics with the kilted killer. I'm telling you. That Tom thingy's behind all this. The old lord knew his missus was up to no good and ended up a goner. Stupid fool. What did he expect, marrying a girl half his age? He was always heading for a sticky end and now he's stuck in a bin bag.'

'So, jabberjaws beat the hill and is now living up to one of her nicknames,' Prue whined.

'She did and is. Revved up on slobber power from that overactive overbite.'

'Someone should bag her up and dump her in a dung heap,' Jon growled. 'There's a big, massive pile on Snell's pig farm in Old Farrow. What's she doing now?'

'As well as carping, she's cooling herself down with cold tea. Always has a flask. Loves the stuff,' Wendy said. 'Betsy Figgis tells the hilarious story of seeing Annie nagging a photo of Stanley. Delivering eggs and honey one day, Betsy looked through Annie's kitchen window, and caught her saying something like, make me a cup of tea, Stan. Don't care if you're dead. The scold's never forgiven poor old Stanley for choking on mackerel and leaving her high and dry. Still nettled that her dedicated tea boy would rather brew up for the angels. If that woman's right, I know where there's a houseful.'

'Where's her bike?'

'Over yonder, propped against those bushes. She rarely leaves that old bike of hers alone, even though she struggles to pedal up Bluebell Lane. It may be short, but it's steep. You'll appreciate that, Prue.'

'I do, and I'm wary when going downhill. Any hill. Ever since I was told, well, you know, these moody legs of mine can suddenly wobble. If they do, it's keep on rolling, Prue. Thank goodness for sticks and poles.'

'Yes, thanks to them. But no thanks to Annie. If there's muck, she'll be there.'

'Thought we'd be safe for a while up here.'

'Behave. She's here for the duration. Brought her knitting. If it was raining poop with a face wind, she'd be out raking it in. Hear she's bought herself a big wooden spoon to stir things up when rakey's on a breaky.'

'Indeedy,' Jon chipped in. 'She'll cause mischief any which way. Watch out, Atom Annie's about. Gets where germs can't.'

'Well, Prue Penn! Where's the kilted killer?' Annie wouldn't leave it alone.

Prue turned on Annie, waving a trekking pole in mid-air. 'For someone who had no time for his lordship, you're making a lot of noise. You should be glad he's gone.'

'So, that's your game. Little brother kills the rich old boot, and you excuse him by saying he's done everyone a favour.'

'I'm warning you, Clegg. Get lost, or I'll push that old scrapheap bike of yours down the hill. With you on it.'

'You touch me, or Jemima, and it won't just be your murdering brother the law's after. Bet you were a problem child. Him too. Violence must run in the family, and you have the nerve to call me a troublemaker.'

Wendy wanted no more truck with Annie Clegg. Not today. 'Hold your tongue, woman. You dribble like a baby. If you must skulk around here, wear a bib. And use that mop you call hair to clean these pretty cobbles. They don't want your slop and neither do we.'

Malice would never make Wendy's list of darlings, but she knew Annie voiced what many thought. The Tom and Lady Lu rumour was rife, holding with Wendy's observation that people loved scandal. Her head and heart were with Prue. Untold stress could lead to a tragic relapse, and Wendy's focus was on keeping her dear friend in good spirits. But for how long, when poor Prue was at breaking point?

'Let's move away. There's space near the end of the cordon,' Wendy said.

The trio moved off, nestling beside Eddie Rutter and commis chef Will Dalton.

'Has Tom turned up yet, Eddie?'

'Haven't seen him all morning, Will. Sure it's not his day off?'

Eddie looked muddled, then smiled awkwardly at Prue. Tom's absence and Annie's cackling were doing nothing to quell suspicion. It didn't look good for the head chef.

'He's definitely on today. Should've been in early to start breakfast. Guessing he hasn't phoned in sick?' Will asked.

'Nope.'

The no-show had both men puzzled. Jon too. It wasn't like Tom to miss a day's work. He overlooked the long hours and poor pay that came with the job. Even on days off, he'd don his metaphorical chef's toque and run his bakery classes, ironically on land owned by Biggin-Smythe. For Tom, gastronomy was a labour of love.

The screech of a sleek red sports car halted all conversation, goggling eyes fuelling the vanity of the bronzed, made-up driver. She stepped onto the pavement, clutching a jewelled handbag to her chest and drawing gasps from the curious crowd.

9

The Usual Suspects

H onest Tor rarely saw outrageous lustrous heels shimmering in the sunlight, or a knee-length white dress clinging like a second skin. The woman's oversized sunglasses, bigger than her hair, masked any emotion. She flicked back lashings of golden waves, yanked on a shocking pink sunhat, and took in the scene before her.

Wendy blew out her cheeks. 'Good God! The ego has landed.'

'Is that …?' Jon spluttered.

'The one and only merry widow. No one makes an entrance quite like Lady Biggin-Smythe.'

'You're not kidding,' Eddie sneered. 'Who stitched her into that dress? And what about those dumb heels and stacks of bling? *What's she on?*'

'Stilts,' Jon quipped.

'Seems no one's taught milady the upper-class dress code,' Wendy said, 'or she just ignores it. I'm no expert, but I suspect wearing duds way too tight or way too short isn't proper. Doesn't fit the etiquette of good breeding. Can't imagine skyscraper heels fit protocol either. Or a bling binge, even if that means real diamonds of every colour. I'm no hotshot fashion designer, but that gaudy hat does nothing for her outfit. What would?'

'What's she doing here?' Prue craned her neck for a better view.

'On principal, milady avoids the village and all its *common trappings*. That's my understanding. Lucinda only cares about Lucinda. So, why the sudden arrival? A genuine visit? Or does she have something to hide and is aiming to quell suspicion? Does she or doesn't she know about milord's demise? Here she comes.'

A uniformed officer stopped Lady Biggin-Smythe from advancing further. 'Excuse me, madam? Are you a relative of the deceased?'

'Deceased? Who's dead? What's going on here? I'm Lady Biggin-Smythe, as if you didn't know, and I have business with my husband. Get out of my way.' The voice was shrill. Excitable. And loud enough to let everyone in on the exchange.

The policeman's vacant look said he didn't know and cared less about this stuck-up woman or her dead husband. He called DCI Slate. 'Sir, you'd better come over here.'

'What is it?'

'This woman's asking questions. She's—'

'Lucinda Biggin-Smythe, I presume?' To the seasoned inspector, Lucinda's look and manner were enough to confirm her identity.

'*Lady* Biggin-Smythe to you. Only my friends call me Lucinda. Who are you?'

Slate shot the constable a sharp "shut your trap" glance before showing his warrant card. 'Detective Chief Inspector Slate, Treeton CID. Please, come with me.'

'Why?'

'Follow me and you'll see why, your ladyship. You can stay put, constable.'

Slate ushered Lucinda towards an unmarked police car and gestured her inside, masking the crowd's view.

'She's fooling no one. Knows hubby's dead and is over the moon. Only married him for his money, she did. No doubt she'll inherit his fortune, then carry on messing around with any man she likes. There's a name for women like her. Yes, a name! One good thing's come out of it. At least we don't have to see that misery guts lord anymore.

Surprised it took someone this long to bump off the silly old fool. Down with the toffs.'

No one was listening to Annie, except one man who'd revved up in a car slicker than Lucinda's. His blatant disregard for narrow roads and milling pedestrians incensed the villagers, but he didn't care. His swagger had no bounds. He stepped out of the car and strode across to Annie, arms swinging military style.

'Despicable old crone. Whoever you are, shut your foul mouth. Regardless of how I feel about my stepmother, I won't hear you disrespect my father.'

The man's thundering held Annie's wagging tongue. It was bad enough Wendy May telling her to scoot, but Lord Biggin-Smythe's eldest son at her throat was another matter. Dressed down twice in one day, Annie couldn't get away fast enough. She mounted her bike and took off, forcing locals to dart and dive as she hollered and weaved through the crowd. Richard Biggin-Smythe went back to his car and jabbed at his phone.

'That's her told,' Prue said. 'Wonder if she'll walk Jemima back downhill.'

'Freewheel, probably. Seen her do that before. *Jemima*. Who knew Annie had a pet name for that beat-up old bike? That, my lovelies, has made my day.' Wendy punched the air.

'She'll make mine when she coasts into a dirty ditch,' Jon sniggered. 'Doubt anyone'd drag her out. Leave her to rot, I say. Don't bank on her being away from here too long. She won't want to miss the Biggin-Smythe show.'

'Ah, yes. The usual suspects.'

'What do you mean, Wendy?'

'It's not unusual for the usual suspects to be family. Of course, all of milord's kids aren't here. Only Richard, the angry man. Dickie, to his intimate friends, eldest, and by far, the most obnoxious of the tribe. It's common knowledge he and Lucinda don't get on. Tension ever since milord remarried and when the will changed without a prenup, yikes. The kids, especially Dickie, resented the prospect of sharing their inheritance with "that woman." They say she only married daddy dearest for money and status and believe Lucinda bided her time to grab a share of the will. How convenient that time's sooner than expected. From what I understand, the kids also know about her romps with a string of men.'

'Including my brainless brother, who still hasn't shown his face. How come you're so well informed, Wendy?'

'One day, I chanced upon Antonia Biggin-Smythe, daughter and third child of the dear departed. Remember when I went to the big house to interview milord for that swanky mag? The editor wanted a scoop, and I landed the job, but milord had a pressing engagement and cut short my audience with him. I got turfed out, but damned if I was leaving without a nosy around the grounds.'

'What are you like?' Prue laughed.

'Shy kids get no treats. Anyway, mid-snoop, I met Antonia, who was happy to spill a few family secrets. Now milord's gone, the magazine's undecided about my article and could rescind our contract. Drat the man. He could've waited to hit the slab. Doubt a story about Seymour Bones'll cut it.'

'It will if you have anything to do with it,' Prue giggled. 'You have a way of making things happen, and the nerve. I've never met Antonia. You've seen her in Tor a few times, haven't you?'

''Tis true. Think she has a secret beau, but that's a tale for another day. *Mind your manners. Here's Dickie.*'

Richard Biggin-Smythe and his stepmother had little in common, but arrogance and a taste for snazzy, loud garb were obligatory. He looked solemn, but not like a man recently bereaved. His approach was casual, the glower exaggerating cold, narrow eyes and a hook for a nose too big for his snotty face. Dickie's shapeless, wide mouth and long, long neck made it look as if he'd swallowed an ironing board.

'That's his resting face,' Wendy said. 'If he cracks a smile, it's wind.'

'A staff member called about the ghastly goings-on here. Is it true someone found Daddy early this morning?' Dickie's mean eyes darted from left to right. He licked his fingers and patted his head, trying to tame rogue strands of hair, but failed to stop them from sticking up.

'Yes, someone found him,' Eddie said.

'Who?'

Jon saw no reason to keep quiet. 'Me.'

'And what were you doing poking around in the cellar at that hour?' Dickie's nostrils flared. His neck stretched a little further.

'Wasn't *poking around*. I was doing my job, thank you very much. Checking barrels and crates. Tidying up. Like I said, doing my job. Cellar hygiene is vital, don't you know? No, of course you don't. It's crucial to keep the place clean. Stagnant wastewater sloshing around makes an ideal breeding ground for bacteria. People don't want that in their beer. The walls and ceiling need regular cleaning, too. Don't want mould or yeasts lurking with intent. Spores aren't pretty. They—'

'Enough, you silly little man. I didn't ask for a science lesson.'

'No, but you asked what I was doing in the cellar so early and I'm telling you what. You wouldn't understand. To get it, you'd have to work in the trade and that's something *you'll* never do. By the way, last time I looked, I wasn't little. Taller than you by a good four inches, even with that sticky-up hair. The silly side's debatable.'

The others snickered, the loudest being Wendy, who wanted to bounce this pompous buffoon. Jon hated confrontation, and she knew it would've taken phenomenal courage for him to speak out so. Either that, or he couldn't bear not having the last word.

'Sorry about your daddy, sir. You have my condolences.' Eddie choked on the lie.

'I should think so. We had our differences, but his death has hit hard. When I say differences, I mean different hobbies and pursuits, but, oh, Daddy was jolly decent at nurturing and encouraging his sons. We spent many happy hours together and I'll miss him dreadfully. It's all a frightful mess.'

'Excuse me, sir?'

'What do you want?'

'I'm Detective Sergeant Uttley from Treeton CID. The chief wants a word with you. Follow me.'

Uttley held up the cordon tape and led Richard to the unmarked police car. Lucinda stumbled out, looking whiter than her dress. She dabbed sobbing eyes, ignored Dickie, then popped her shades on. Uttley watched her totter to her car, feet click-clacking across the cobbles.

'See that. It's all a show. Sackcloth and ashes, crocodile tears and all. She's not sad. I bet she'll be off soon to see that handsome Scot. Hey, Prue Penn, where's the villain? You know more than you're letting on.' Wearing a battered old straw hat and clutching crooked sunglasses, Annie was back. She'd parked Jemima near the telephone box and snuck in among the crowd.

'Claptrap Clegg's at it again. She's worse than a bad smell,' Prue said.

Wendy knew Prue was feeling the heat, and it wasn't just the savage sun. Once an arbitrator, always an arbitrator. Time to step in and silence the yak. 'When I told you to clear off earlier, I meant for the whole day. For life, suits me. You have a choice. Keep a civil tongue in your head or go. No one wants to hear your piffle.'

Jon, Eddie, and Will exchanged glances. A dribbling klaxon she may be, but this time, Annie may not have strayed too far from the truth, even putting her own spin on events. Occasionally, when the three men sat at the bar with Tom after closing, Tom had let them in on a few observations. Notes he'd made about Lord and Lady Biggin-Smythe, their marriage, and children. The picture painted wasn't the clover most would assume.

'Four kids, that's right, Jon? Three boys, one girl, all with names that last forever?'

Wendy stepped in to answer. 'Right about the number of kids, Eddie, but not all have extended names. The sons, yes, not the daughter. Biggin-Smythe protocol says sons must have four Christian names, daughters two, or one if born with a "ber" in the month. Mad, I know. Centuries of breeding. Family custom determines son's names. The firstborn takes daddy's second name, second takes the third, third the fourth, and so on. Milord was Seymour Richard George Royce. His three sons are Richard, George, and Royce. Plus a string of other forenames I know not and care not.'

'And that, folks, is the biggest heap of twaddle I've ever heard. Except for the bit about not caring.' Eddie screwed his face up to the sun.

'Not far off the mark, Eddie. Save for wealth, education, and a gorge of pomp and circumstance, there's no fundamental distinction between the classes. We come into the world the same way and leave the same way. Death doesn't discriminate.'

Jon was curious. 'The old boy had four names. What if there'd been another son? What would he be called?'

'Useless.' Wendy's well-timed delivery caused a spark of laughter.

'Ask a stupid question,' Jon said.

'I don't know, is the honest answer, Jon. Haven't delved that far into the family history.'

'What about daughters?'

'Daughters, Prue? Mercy me, what are daughters? Girls' names aren't important. Etiquette doesn't warrant such trivia. They get what they're given, although an established name for debutantes and finishing school is preferable. After all, we're talking nobility, with a colossal mansion, coat of arms, and family tweeds. Milord was so up himself, he petitioned to rename the county Bigginshire, but nothing came of it.'

'He went further than that,' Jon said. 'Wanted Great Britain changed to Great Biggin and was going great lengths to do it. Nothing ever came of that either, but I remember the old boy yapping about it in the Noose. Boasting about his status and how his rules were law. He said changing the country's name would "benefit the common people." Who knew a month later he'd be chilling with the commoners down at the morgue? Some status. The man was a stinker.'

'I remember that, Jon, but how come you know so much, Wendy? I worked for BS and know zilch.'

'Tell you another time, Eddie, but right now, please excuse me. Just spotted a chance too good to miss.'

10

Heirs and Graces

Hawk-eyed Wendy had spied Slate, Uttley, and Dickie deep in conversation on one of Figgy's Fields. Ankle-deep in cowpats and daisies, DCI Slate had the chair. Wendy silenced her phone, turned her ears up, then took position behind a stone wall. She couldn't see, but she could hear, and that was enough.

'Did your father have any enemies?' Slate's customary boom was temporarily subdued.

'Any? Try many. Daddy didn't get where he was by being a pleasant fellow. He's way up the rich list. Not just in the county, the country too. A ruthless businessman who'd tread on anyone's toes if there was profit in it. He amassed a fabulous fortune over the years, but he was a good man. A philanthropist, who gave thousands away. Not many can say that.'

'No, sir, not many, but his lordship could afford to be charitable. Being in a privileged position, I mean. But that isn't important. What is important is gathering evidence. Can you think of anyone who'd want to harm him? I know you said he had many enemies, but not everyone is capable of murder. Any idea who would be?'

'If I had time to think about it, I'm sure names would come, but I don't have time. There was one ghastly fellow from years back. Daddy toyed with the idea of a partnership with him, but changed his mind and pulled out at the last minute. Don't know why. I recall a few unpleasantries.'

'Unpleasantries? That has overtones.'

'*Rather*. Big threats after Daddy said no. Apparently, this fellow's noted in the county for his vile temper and beastly nature. At the time, the family dismissed it as hot air. He vanished yonks ago and we haven't seen him since. I simply can't remember. Any deal would've involved big money. Refinancing and such.'

'Your father would refinance?'

'Absolutely not! Daddy a debtor? How positively frightful. The Biggin-Smythes don't do credit. That's a practice for peasants, don't you know?'

'What was the name of this *ghastly fellow*?'

'Golly. What was it? King, I think. Can't recall his full name. Ask my stepmother. She'll know. After all, he is a man.'

From the silence, Wendy knew both detectives had caught Dickie's slur.

'What about your real mother, sir?' Uttley said.

'What about her?'

'Will she know anything about this man, King?'

'I doubt it. After the divorce, Mummy moved away. She had a beastly time with Daddy. Actually, they had a beastly time with each other.'

'Not suited?'

'*Rather.*'

'Are you still in touch with your mother?' Slate picked up the pace again.

'What has that to do with anything?'

'We must pursue all lines of enquiry, sir.'

'I have no reason to avoid Mummy. She's a marvellous brick and we have a jolly good relationship. Now, will there be anything else? I'm awfully busy. Estate matters, you know. A frightful bore, but necessary. Also have a rugger match to watch. See Treetonshire give Essex a damn good thrashing. I have a portrait sitting, too. An age-old tradition. Looking dull for the artist simply isn't done.'

"That'll do for now, sir, but this investigation's at an early stage. We may need to speak again. If anything comes to mind, please call me or come to the station. My business card."

Wendy heard a grunt and assumed Dickie had taken Slate's card and flounced off.

'Didn't like that tie he was wearing,' said Uttley. 'Bit big and bright. If nothing else, we should do him for speeding. Look at him go. In wellies too. For a man who's just lost his dad, there wasn't much emotion.'

'Isn't that the way the upper-class should behave, Uttley? Don't show your feelings. Stiff upper-lip and all that nonsense. Seems the wealthy have their own code for life's happenings, including death. Even foul play. But, and this is a hunch, I think the heir apparent, and his stepmother are hiding something.'

'Like what?'

'That's for us to find out.'

'What about that chef? And the pub manager? King, if that's his name, and the joker who found the body? Then there's that big-mouthed old crow on the bike with the funny hair and teeth. That's a long list. You can't suspect them all.'

'I'm a chief inspector, Uttley. Until the three necessaries between suspicion and conviction are absolute, I suspect everyone. Motive. Opportunity. Evidence. That's why we're here. Her ladyship's still around. I want to know about this King chap. I want answers.'

'Where is she?'

'In her car. Off you trot. Tell her I have a few more questions.'

Wendy bit her lip. She was proud of her sharp memory, but doubted her head could hold anymore. Wilting under the rising sun, she didn't know whether to stay or go. Click-clacking across the concrete stopped her indecision, but it wasn't long before Wendy regretted hanging around. The merry widow's squeak grated. Like long fingernails dragging down glass.

'I'm not coming into that field.'

'You have no boots in your boot?'

'No.'

'Stay on the cobbles, then. Thank you for your time. Just a couple of questions.'

'Who inherits the Biggin-Smythe estate?'

'Is that question relevant?'

'Indeed, it is. I'm investigating a serious crime and I'd like an answer.'

'I do.'

'Just you?'

'No. Seymour told me his children would benefit, but, as his widow, I would get the lion's share.'

'When did he tell you that?'

'Before we married, and many times after.'

'You know a man named King. I don't have his first name. Your stepson told me to ask you about this man. A ghastly fellow, I'm told.'

'Ask me what?'

'I understand he got mixed up in a business deal with your late husband, which came to nothing. A partnership his lordship decided not to entertain and there were *a few unpleasantries*. King became violent, noted for his temper he was, but the family dismissed his threats as hot air. This all happened ages ago. King vanished and no one's seen him since. Much like Tim Tresslehock, that runaway head chef from the local pub.' Slate chanced his arm.

'You mean Tom Trebilcock.'

'That's him. Know him well, then?'

'Only that he's the head chef. The pub forms part of the Biggin-Smythe estate, remember?'

'Of course. I'd like King's full name, thank you. '

'I don't know his full name. Why would I?'

'Richard was sure you'd know. What can you tell me about the deal King had with your late husband?'

'Nothing. I only know of him. I wasn't privy to everything Seymour did. He had his own pastimes and pursuits. Could take himself off for hours doing whatever he did, and that suited me just fine. Suited him too. As for my stepson, we don't dance the same tango. Now, if you'll excuse me.'

11

The Unusual Suspects

B ack at the Noose & Gibbet, head fit to burst, Wendy joined Jon and Prue. The crowd had dwindled, but animated whispers still kissed the air. Plainclothes police had left, leaving a couple of uniforms standing guard.

Eddie was still around. Will Dalton had said so long when talk turned to Wendy's encounter with Antonia.

'Well, eagle-eye. Something tells me you have news.'

'Talk you through it later, Jon. Anything doing here?'

'Just about to find out. Hey, Ed, what's happening? When will they let us back in?'

'Don't know. Could be a few hours, could be a few days. You know what coppers are like, especially out here in the sticks.'

'A day off then.' Jon was hopeful.

'Looks that way.'

'That's the ticket. Who's in charge now the old boy's snuffed it?'

'He ran the pub through his principal company, BS Estates. It'll pass to his widow and sons, probably. Until one of them takes over, guess I'm in charge.'

'No change there. The old boy was a typical backseat boss. Loved delegating the day-to-day running to the underlings. Only showed his face when he wanted to poke his nose in or ram his agenda down the plebs' throats.'

'Saw you talking to the police, Eddie. Any clue to suspects?' Prue said.

'Biggin-Smythe had many enemies. Even though he was desperate to get locals on side, many in Tor hated him. Probably the case in other villages, too.'

'Putting on fancy games and pleasures at the big house. He had his spin doctors out in force to coax people in,' Jon scoffed. 'Spouting a heap of lies as spin usually does. One big smokescreen for whatever trickery he was up to. Anything to divert the truth. He had the money. And the influence. Scruples and ethics fly out the window when money's involved. Screw the world over as long as it's profitable. Greed and corruption. Says a lot about our species. It's disgusting.'

'Anyway, now he's gone, the police'll have a few suspects on their radar, including Tom. Sorry, Prue. He'll be near the top. Even at the top.' Eddie shook his head.

Prue wore a troubled look. She'd warned Tom of his frolics, but he was headstrong and hadn't heeded advice. There was no point in digging at Eddie. 'You still haven't heard from Tom?'

'No sign. Not answering his phone. Tom and the boss weren't exactly matey. As you know, against the village's wishes, BS wanted to change the Noose. Tom was with the locals.'

'Heard heated words between the old boy and Tom a few nights ago,' Jon said.

'From what I gather, Tom was told to toe the line or go.' Eddie shrugged and looked blank. 'Tom had a fierce temper, but doubt he'd kill someone, even a miser like BS. Anyway, I'd gone home when it all happened.'

'What time was that?' Wendy asked.

'From what the police said when they questioned me, between closing and two in the morning, I think.'

'No. What time did you go home?'

'Around nine. It was quiet, so I left Jon on his own to cash up and lock up.'

'I left before midnight. Didn't see or hear a thing. Took the scenic route home and didn't get home 'til late,' Jon said.

'Must've been late. Didn't hear you come in.' Wendy said.

'Yeah, you were like the old boy. Dead to the world.'

'*Mr Windup*. Your darkness has no bounds.'

'That's me. Anyhow, I was in work late, up first thing for cellar duty. Saw nobody between leaving and coming in this morning. No alibi for me. Guess I'm in the frame, then.'

A bicycle wheeled up. Not rickety old Jemima, but the bike with no name ridden by village postman, Ross Pengelly. He'd come for a nose on the last leg of his round and was doing his usual routine. Parked the post van, stripped to luminous Lycra, then biked from home to Tor and up heart attack hill, postbag and all. Did it, whatever the weather, and nobody did it better, according to proud Pengelly. Wendy couldn't bear the man, nor his glaring orange tan, waxed body, and conceit. His bigoted, sexist attitude to women didn't help either.

Ross propped his powerful mountain bike against a wall and pushed through the small gathering. 'What's doing, folks? Have they brought the stiff out yet?'

'A while back,' Jon said. 'The Sowers flung it into the back of the cadavan and took off to the morgue. No first-class ticket for the old boy today. Only ticket for him'll suit his big toe. Not that he needs any ID. Guess he'll have a fitting later today. No tweed, just card.'

'Gross,' Prue shuddered.

'It's all dead exciting.' Jon was enjoying himself.

'Okay, Windy, time out.' Wendy's tone brooked no argument.

'Sorry.'

'Don't be,' Ross snarled, 'and ignore her. She's old and confused. Time out, why? No one's sorry to see him go. Every Christmas, I wished three ghosts would visit, but they never did. So much for that stupid story that's on every year. Biggin-Smythe didn't change. Won't get a chance now, but suits me. He was a stingy old git and can rot in hell for all I care.'

'That *stupid story* is A Christmas Carol, Mr Pengelly, and it was four ghosts. Three spirits of past, present, and yet to come, and Marley's ghost. Jacob Marley, Scrooge's penny-pinching partner. Everyone knows.'

'*I don't*. Not a fan of such rubbish. That Shakespeare dude wrote some junk. Three ghosts. As if.'

'Alas, poor Pengelly, he's not read well. Think you'll find it was that Dickens dude, and it was four ghosts, but we won't split spirits.'

'Well, I say three. Annoying ex-coppers, and a woman at that.'

Ross Pengelly's attempt to flap the unflappable fell flat. 'Annoying ex-lawyer, if you please, and what's your problem with women? Does the female form scare you? Why so hostile?'

'I'm not. Biggin-Smythe was my landlord, too. He loved to take money but gave nothing back. Hated putting his hand in his pocket unless it was for the family name and to make his life better. How much better did he want it?'

'What has that to do with anything?'

'I'm telling you, that's all.'

Unlike Jon, Wendy didn't crave the last word. If she had a mind, she could wrap Ross Pengelly in knots. Buy him at one end, sell him at the other, but had neither the time nor inclination to do either. Why invite stress into her life? If a peacock must strut, let it strut.

'What you've said sounds familiar, Ross,' Prue said. She wasn't Pengelly's biggest fan, but thought it best to pour oil on troubled waters.

'Yeah. Leaky roof. Mouldy ceiling. Broken boiler. Rubbish cooker. You name it, he wouldn't fix it. And guess my reward for complaining?'

'Don't tell me you've had notice?' Prue said.

'I'm telling you.'

'That's awful. What will you do?'

'Nothing. They can drag me out kicking and screaming. Who knows, now the old git's dead, I might get to stay.'

'Don't get your hopes up,' Eddie warned. 'I've heard Dickie's just as ruthless. As for the widow, she's in a league of her own. Not sure about the other two sons. They don't make the headlines. I've had notice too, but don't want to talk about it. Got anything for me in your postbag?'

'Funny you should ask, because I do.'

'Good show. I've been waiting for this.' Eddie grabbed the big envelope and hugged it to his chest.

'Anything interesting, Ed?'

'Just stuff, Jon. Much more to do, Ross?'

'A couple of drop-offs, then the afternoon's mine.'

'Well, don't hang around here making the place look untidy,' Wendy muttered to the air.

'If time's on my side, think I'll enjoy a spot of village life,' Jon mused.

'How about munchies, Jon? I see you're craving caffeine and sugar.'

'You see too much, darling, but you're not wrong. Beans and Leaves?'

'Deal, and you're paying.'

Jon opened his mouth to reply, then stopped. A smile danced across his lips.

'What is it?' Wendy said.

'*It* is Mr Quince. Hope he's not contaminating the crime scene again.'

Heads turned to see the big ginger cat skulking around the pub's entrance. He bolted when a uniformed officer shooed him away. Much to the onlookers' amusement, the copper gave chase.

'Good old Quincy. Can always count on him to cause a stir,' Jon laughed.

'I remember when he arrived,' Eddie said. 'Just wandered in, jumped on a bar stool and went to sleep. I still don't know where he came from, but who cares? He's been my friend ever since. Spends a lot of time in the pub. More regular than the regulars.'

'Wouldn't surprise me if he did it.' Jon said.

'Did what?' Prue asked.

'Killed the old boy. Biggin-Smythe wasn't an animal lover, and there was no love lost between the two. The other day, he clocked Mr Quince, called him vermin, then had a go at me. Said he'd call environmental health. Bet Quincy waited until the pub was empty, jumped on the old meanie, and made him fall down the stairs. He had the purrfect motive.'

'Absolutely. Don't know how the rest fits in, but Quincy's one of the unusual suspects,' Wendy said.

'That sergeant told me they might want to analyse his fur for DNA. I said he's a typical curious cat and often sneaks into the cellar. Could've been there when Biggin-Smythe got killed, apparently.'

'Interesting, but they'll have to catch him first, Ed,' said Jon, remembering Slate's insistence on him closing the cellar door.

'Good luck to them. Anyway, must dash, folks. I'll let you know when the police are done, Jon. Doubt they'll finish today.' Eddie was gone before Jon replied.

'Should let me catch that stupid cat. He won't get away from me.'

'Don't you have a post round to finish?' Wendy snarled.

'Mind your own, bossy boots. Ex-coppers. All the same.'

'Ex-lawyer, and only ex because I no longer practice. From ghosts to classic authors to occupations. Seems you can't get anything right today, Mr Pengelly. Better get on your bike and hit the cobbles or you could end up jobless *and* homeless. At least you won't get bicycle face. That's a woman thing.'

Ross curled his lip. 'I'm going. Anything to get away from you. Keep me *posted*, friends.' Laughing at his own feeble joke, he mounted his bike, taking off in a blaze of vanity.

'I have an intense loathing for that man,' Wendy spat. 'Puts me in a right snark.'

'Bicycle face! Classic,' Jon snorted.

'Overbearing, overfamiliar, overkill. A is for arrogance. He has that in spades.'

'A's also for ass.'

'Non, Jon. Unlike Monsieur Pengelly, le derriere has a use. If you meant the four-legged type, don't insult the animal.' Wendy returned Jon's wide grin.

'Do you have a mark for him, Wendy?'

'Many, Prue, but two stand out. First, the exclamation mark. When used on its own, it serves as a warning. Ross Pengelly should wear one. Permanently. Second, the comma. There are four types. He's the listing comma, which can appear where it shouldn't. If that's the case, get rid of it. Where that man's concerned, getting rid's a brilliant idea.'

'Blimey. Didn't realise you felt that way,' Prue said.

'Always.'

'Anyway, much as I'm loving the banter, I have chores back home. I'll catch up with you for coffee in an hour or so, and here's a thought to mull over. Have you pair ever considered teaming up as a double act? See you.'

Prue's lopsided gait took her to the end of the lane where a taxi awaited. Wendy made a mental note to check on her over coffee. 'So, my windy friend. From your perspective, who's in the frame?'

'Well, not me.'

'Drama, drama. I wasn't implying.'

'Good.'

'Anything you must go away and think about?'

'Solving crimes needs energy, darling. Time for that caffeine and cake, and yes, I'm paying.'

12

The Odd Couple

Save for tall, aproned Adam Brown, joint owner, barista, and all-round good fella, Beans & Leaves was empty. Unusual for the trendy cafe, where coffee and tea appreciation reached giddy heights, but this was an unusual day.

Coffee freaks both, caffeine had polar effects on Jon and Wendy. Jon preferred a strong brew, but his delicate gut surrendered at three mugs per day. More than that, and he bounced. Off the walls, ceiling, and everywhere in between. Then came the headache. Then another, if caffeine withdrawal had its way. Not so for Wendy, who took her coffee weak or strong and was immune to overfill. Jon quipped she was caffeine-proof, marvelling at her ability not to fly after downing a few big cups of number ten.

The couple each chose a two-shot oat milk latte and a slice of sticky sin—Adam's bestselling, loaded ginger cake—then bagged a corner table to deliberate.

Wendy removed her cap and, for the nth time, admired the tasteful decor while absorbing the heady hit of aromas of the world. Coffee shops hurled her back to crazy legal days. To times of crime and courtrooms and counsel. Suited, booted, and armed with briefcase and knowledge, Wendy's resolve to see justice done often left a sour taste. To her and the clients she supported. Too many wrongs. Too few rights.

A gregarious, warm extrovert, no-nonsense Wendy had zero tolerance for those who pushed her limits.

Viewing cynicism as both her friend and enemy, she had an opinion, but wasn't self-opinionated, invariably voicing her view at the right moment when a debate got stuck in a groove. That wasn't always the case. Her sharp wit and sarcasm were often blunt, but an iron will could and often weakened. Wendy kept her soft spots well hidden, but kindred souls knew where to find them.

Introverted dawdler Jon Windup knew. Unless he was a genuine friend, you'd never comprehend his razor-sharp mind, quick wit, or sweeping intellect. Harebrained and often lacking common sense, Jon's clumsy exterior contradicted what bubbled within. A thinker. A defender of the underdog. A compassionate, sensitive man, who'd dabbled in a long romance, had his heart broken, and dabbled no more.

Jon's silly and oft dark sense of humour was a gift, Wendy said. Full of daft jokes, his sense of timing and deadpan face and voice left her helpless. For all his qualities, complex Jon saw himself as an underachiever. The Aries failure. The fire sign, whose flames had never quite sizzled.

While his hectic mind trawled the morning's madness, Jon's exceedingly sweet tooth munched gooey ginger cake. Convinced there was a reason for this morning's grim experience, there was much to digest. So many suspects. So little time.

Away from Atom Annie's spite or Slate's suspicious finger, the still, yet soulful cafe was a chance to recount and rethink. Never had such a feverish wanting to get to the truth provoked the keen minds of yin and yang. In both heads, curiosity courted intrigue. Following different paths but seeking the same answer. *When? Why? Who?*

'Could I be cheeky and ask you to watch the place for half an hour? Have an errand to run and don't want to kick you out. Any problems, shoot me a message.'

'No bother, Adam,' Wendy said.

For her trouble, Adam handed Wendy his number on a scrap of paper. Jon got another slice of heaven.

'See you soon,' Wendy called.

'Cheers!' Jon smiled, rubbing his hands together. 'That's a stroke of luck. More cake and this place to ourselves for a while. The acoustics in here mean even whispering's audible, but now we can speak freely, though not too loud. Walls have ears.'

'Drama and you are so together, Jon. Your middle name should be theatre.'

'Hit me with some of your own scenes. What did you get when you did off earlier?'

Wendy retrieved the detectives' Q&A stored in her memory. 'That's pretty much the gist. Anything I've missed'll come to mind. Now it's your turn. Go on. Kill me with action.'

From the day the midwife smacked his bare bottom, Jon Windup had an insatiable thirst for knowledge. He was no exception to the sceptical nature of scientists. Always questioning. Needing to prove or disprove a theory and going to extreme lengths to do so.

He took a sip of coffee, licked his lips, then attacked a slab of double chocolate sponge, sandwiched with cream and strawberries, and frosted in icing sugar. The bite disappeared in seconds. 'We're right in the thick of it. Foul play, no froth. My brain's buzzing with possibilities. I can't leave this alone. Not now. A novice bloodhound I may be, but once a sniffer, always a sniffer. What do you say? Do we stand together to find the truth?' He forked in another mouthful of chocolate bliss.

'Unlike you, I don't need to go away and think about it. I'm game. You're way nosier, but the role of nebby secret agent tickles me. My legal background helps. And a thirst for research. With your appetite for formulae and rebellion and my fondness for method and level-headed calm, we're solid. You're chaotic. I'm organised. You crawl around a problem. I zoom straight down the middle. Despite stark conflict, we fuse. It's a logical recipe. A mind romance.'

Wendy's cake begged her to take a bite. She obliged and worked the ginger softness into a wad. The sticky treat had a devilish way of clinging to tongue and teeth and soon her mouth was all caked up. Wendy craved liquid to shift the goo. Gulping coffee, she held Jon with her blue eye. 'You know in films and TV shows how cops or detectives have a nickname? We should have one.'

'Good idea. Any suggestions?'

'What about JW Sleuths?'

No sooner had the words left Wendy's mouth, the pair looked at each other and shook their heads.

'Windy and Wendy has a ring to it,' Jon said.

'Bit bland. Besides, don't want to use my name. Think again.'

The pair sat motionless, every breath in tune with the tick-tock from the huge wall clock. Like Big Ben, in a memorable scene from a much-loved childhood film, the giant face and hands drew Wendy in. She shifted in her seat. 'Well, I'll go to Neverland. The perfect handle's sitting here in my lap.'

'So, what's the perfect handle?'

'Windy and Darling, TA.'

'TA?'

'Team Awesome.'

'Not sure.'

'About what, Jon?'

'I'll have to go away and think about it.'

'Someone once said procrastination's the art of keeping up with yesterday. What's to think about? Windup becomes Windy. Darling from Peter Pan. Simple and effective. We use the names every day. And it's our quiz handle. A brand. *A legend*. And the TA adds that je ne sais quoi.'

'Still have to think about it.'

'You and your dithering. Just as well you have redeeming qualities.'

'Thanks. Still—'

'You're always the cow's tail, Mr Windup. An infuriating faffer. No sense of urgency and everything last minute. If you must go away and think about it, please, don't take all day. Now, can we run over a few things you don't *have to go away and think about*?'

'Think the ditherer can stretch to that, but first, can I swipe *faffer* to add to Windy's Wacky Words?'

'Don't push it.'

'As if.'

Although it often worked, Jon Windup had to have the last word. The do or die quirk, inherited from his father, was often an irritating fancy. So was his sense of no urgency and habitual lateness. There was Greenwich Mean Time, British Summertime, and Jon Windup time. Arguably, flaky timekeeping was a branch of Jon's remarkable talent for fussing. Thank the stars he hadn't picked up his dad's "I'm always right" peeve. If that crept into his repertoire, Wendy would disown him.

'By the way, you may be interested to know that the beer cellar's known as the engine room. That's where all the scientific stuff goes on with the pipes and temperature and cellar gas. Think. Secondary fermentation takes place in the cellar. Best part of the job for me.'

'Fascinating. You're obsessed with gas, Jon. And random. Windy right enough. Never was there a more fitting name. Let's get back to business.'

'If Annie has anything to do with it, Tom's guilty, no question. His absence today adds weight to her rancid ramblings, but there could be a good explanation for him going AWOL.'

'Such as?'

'The usual. Illness. He can't be bothered and is pulling a sickie. Thinks because he's head chef, he doesn't have to report his absence. I don't know, but it doesn't look good.'

'From what I've learned of Tom, he isn't Mr Sick. He loves his work. It's not like him to be absent without saying so. He could be ill, but it'd have to be serious to warrant not phoning in. Or he could be dead. Two killings, not one. Wouldn't say that to Prue, of course. She has enough worry. Alive or dead, where is he? The whole thing's a mystery.'

'Unless he's dead, I'm not buying. He must be able to get to a phone.'

'Just because he can get to a phone doesn't mean he can use it. Or wants to.'

'True. I'll take back what I said. So, what about reasons for bumping off the old boy? I know many people despised him, but they've done that for years. Why now?'

'Going back to Tom, the obvious reason. The husband, the wife, and the rough bit of fluff. The typical love triangle. Milord caught them at it. There was a scuffle, and the rich man lost. Sounds simple.'

'Caught them at it? Across the barrels?'

'Don't be a nit. Could have been anywhere in the pub, or outside. Milord may have suspected all along and planned to take revenge when he had his chance.'

'Okay, but surely it must be more sinister than that. Money suggests premeditation. Stuffing money into your victim's mouth isn't a spur-of-the-moment thing, regardless of how it's stuffed. And what about the coins? If Tom killed in self-defence, or not, why fill the old boy's face with cash? And where did it come from?'

'Could've been in cahoots with milady. Tom has the brawn, she has the money, and the brains. The brains to bump off the old man, anyway. Another thing. What about CCTV?'

'Only covers public areas in the bar, restaurant, and beer garden. A savvy killer would've disconnected it. Sensor lights too. Okay, let's rewind. We've said loads of people loathed the old boy, so it figures loads of people could've killed him. The crux here's the money. Find the logic behind the dough to solve the puzzle. There are loads who would want to, but probably wouldn't or couldn't. One or more of the family seems logical, or one of the estate management team. There's that ghastly fellow Dickie mentioned, but he didn't elaborate. Could be a lead to follow, but where to start? All my thoughts are just theories. Apart from the money. That must be crucial to this whole dirty business.'

13

Windy & Darling, TA

L ost in a maze of mayhem and mischief, Jon and Wendy hadn't spotted Prue heading to their table. Adam followed, saluted his thanks, and offered more goodies on the house. Wendy chose another latte, but no cake. Jon favoured espresso and a caramel slice.

'The day Jon refuses a sweet treat, I'll show my butt in Figgy's Farm Shop Window,' Wendy quipped.

'Freebie, Prue?' Adam said.

'Didn't want to assume. Haven't paid for anything yet.' Prue plonked beside Wendy.

'Think I can spare a coffee. You spend enough money in here.'

'In that case, Americano and soy milk, please. I've brought carrot cake.'

'No worries.' Adam knew Prue's diet and lifestyle helped her condition and didn't mind if she ate her own dessert.

The three friends made small talk as Adam worked coffee magic, then dished them around. 'It's deathly in here. Fancy a singalong? Anyone know the words to Don't Fear the Reaper?'

'Ouch, Adam. You're worse than Jon. What do you think of the Biggin-Smythe goings-on?' Wendy dipped her spoon into Adam's stylish latte art heart and broke it in two.

Adam pulled up a chair. 'He had it coming. When he started bulk buying, I was determined not to let his greedy hands suck me up. A couple of cottages here, a shop or two there and before you know, the slimy weasel owns half the county.'

'What did he want?' Wendy's jabbing spoon demolished the heart.

'Everything.'

'The greedy git,' Jon snarled.

'Me and Kate have a Beans and Leaves in six villages and a Half-Baked sandwich bar in two. We've sweated to get where we are and still sweat. When Biggin-Smythe's silver tongue tried to seduce us, we refused his offer. It's a sin for one family to own so much. Buying up small businesses to expand the empire and boost its millions. In the end, the offers got silly. Hundreds of thousands to snatch up what we've worked for, just to brag about his latest gain. He even said he'd buy up and lease back to us.'

'What did you say?'

'To be honest, I spent a bit of time thinking about it, but his lordship couldn't sway my lovely Kate. She stayed inflexible and had the final say. Said leaseback sounded like fleece back and told him what he could do with his generosity. She wasn't charming. She wasn't proper. *She was bleeding marvellous.*'

'Bet you were proud of her, Adam. Wish I'd been there to see the old boy's face.'

'Mighty proud, Jon. No wonder he copped it. Pampered old prat. No doubt the heirs'll be picking up where he left off. Who knows? Maybe that dolled-up airhead of a wife will insult us with more crazy offers. Sorry, Prue, no offence to Tom, but crikey, what's he thinking?'

'None taken, and I agree, but that doesn't help Tom's cause when everyone's pointing the finger at him for murder. He's keeping a low profile. Why, I don't know. No one's seen him and the fact he didn't show up for work this morning doesn't look good.'

'Have you tried contacting him?'

Prue looked uncomfortable. 'Yes, but nothing. He's probably still miffed with me for having a dig at him at the bakery class. Wish I'd zipped it. Should know better when Clegg's around. She'd start world war three with that malicious tongue.'

Adam sucked in his breath. 'This sorry saga's keeping my customers away. People are too busy sticking their snouts into the Noose and rabbiting for England—'

'While Clegg's whizzing around on that old bike like a foghorn on wheels. She calls it Jemima.' Wendy's sardonic, infectious laughter filled the room.

'Calls what Jemima?' Adam said.

'Her bike.'

'And I call it a battered old wreck. Someday, it'll turn into a broomstick and her face'll go all green like that wicked old witch in Oz. Take it the singalong's out then?'

'Go grind your beans, Adam.' Wendy made a face.

'Sounds painful, but message received.'

'What's on your mind?' Wendy asked Prue.

'I've tried Tom so many times. His mobile's switched off and his landline's going to voicemail. Left heaps of messages.'

It wasn't often Wendy struggled for something to say, but words wouldn't come. Jon had the same problem, except his answer was to fill his face with another chomp of caramel and a slurp of espresso.

'Clegg's making waves. She doesn't need a megaphone. Wish something would knock that nasty old hag off that bike of hers. Now the MS gremlins are acting up and I wish they'd go away.' Prue knew she was powerless to stop the village scold, who furiously pedalled over concrete and cobbles, dribbling tidings of hanky-panky and foul play.

Wendy found her voice. 'I'm sorry, Prue. Have you tried Tom's house?'

'Yes. Blinds and curtains drawn, but his car's gone and here's a thing. He always closes the gates before going anywhere, but they were gaping wide, as if trying to tell me something. On that note, I'm off. Fatigue and stress have it in for me today. Must rest.'

Wendy squeezed Prue's hand. 'I feel responsible. Me and my meddling. Remember, we're here for you. Don't be alone.'

'You're such a darling, Wendy. A precious heart.'

'Thanks, Prue, but don't go putting it about. Wouldn't want to ruin my biting reputation.'

'Thank you for your support, Jon. See you both soon.' Prue got up to leave.

'Bye,' Jon and Wendy called in unison.

Prue took a few steps, then turned around. 'Keep on meddling, please. I love you for it, and Tom will too.' She disappeared through the door.

'What do you make of that, Darling? Windy or what?'

'Does that mean you've stopped thinking and agree on the handle?'

'I never stop thinking, but we'll crack open a bottle when we get home.'

'To Windy and Darling, TA?'

'Yes. And deadly dough.'

14

Fizz, Facts, and Fakes

'Y ou did what?' Wendy's mouth fell open. 'You kept that quiet. Just when I thought it was safe to trust you!'

Jon's two-bedroomed flat, nestled in a quiet cul-de-sac in Treeton, had never heard such a shocker. While toasting the Windy & Darling sleuthing partnership with a superb bottle of bubbly to fit the occasion, Jon had dropped it into the conversation. The day had been long, tiring, full of shocks, disputes, and surprises. Dinner was later than usual. Amid mouthfuls of smashed avocado salad, warm ciabatta dipped in herby EVOO, and sips of fizz, Jon and Wendy were discussing their next move.

'Doubt I'll ever grasp all your whims, Windy. Dramatic announcements. Boohoo tantrums. An insatiable curiosity. But what you've told me's a curiosity too far.'

'Darling, you should know the scientist in me wins every time. Besides, I couldn't resist. Yes, the gloves I was wearing were too small, but my tweezers were twitching, and that was it. What's a nosy egghead to do?'

Wendy shook her head. 'That sniffer of yours'll get you into trouble. Tampering with a crime scene's a punishable offence. Intention, or lack of, knowledge, and meddling by accident, are all points for mitigation, but you shouldn't take risks in the first—'

'Yes, yes, I get it. You don't want to know what I found, then?'

'*What?* You dangle a juicy carrot and expect me not to bite? Suspense is pungent and kicking. Hot off the Scoville Scale, like this chilli dressing.'

'Your asbestos tongue and iron guts can cope with fire. Don't mind a little flame, but too much and I'm gone.'

'I know. Poor you. When the heat's on, it's gloop central. Let's eat up and get comfy, then you can give me the lowdown on your rascality.'

'And there's me thinking I had all the wacky words. That comes from rascal. Right?'

'To coin a Jon or Windyism, indeedy. Means mischief or a stream of other synonyms. Take your pick.'

After dinner, Jon stacked the dishes, and the couple moved from the dining kitchen to the lounge. A modest affair, with magnolia walls, two-piece grey settee, and a dark pine coffee table. The decor was simple, but practical. A typical rental, with the obligatory bargain carpets, furnishings, and fixtures. Jon longed to live in the country, in a charming cottage like Wendy, but, until he secured a regular job, Treeton's outskirts would have to do.

Jon topped up the fizz, then slapped a £50 note on the table.

'Thanks, mate, but that won't pay for your meal and drink. Another tenner and we'll call it quits.'

'Shut up and listen.'

'Have you just shushed the duty chef? This better be good.'

'Forget good. This is a right old revelation. I'm no expert, but I'm convinced this is a fake.'

'How can you tell?'

'A few signs, but two crucial giveaways. At a glance, this looks like a new fifty-pound polymer note. All new notes have holographic images on the front. Looking at the bottom left when tilted, the words should change between the value—in this case fifty—and pounds.

Look.' Jon tipped the note and grinned at Wendy's fervent shriek. 'Exactly. Easy to spot that one. *Fifty* doesn't change to *pounds.*'

'And the other giveaway?'

Jon pointed to the centre. 'All new notes should have a translucent window. Gold and green on the front, silver on the back.' He flipped the note over, then flipped it back. 'On the front, there should be an image change, like with the holographic image. When it's straight, you can see both the number fifty and the pound sign, but skewed, you should only see one or the other.' Jon handed the note to Wendy.

She held it up to the light, tipping it back and forth. 'It doesn't change. I see fifty and the pound sign.'

'There are other ways you can check the authenticity of a banknote, but I'm sure you get the picture.'

'You're such a clever clogs, Windy.'

'Not really. That info's easily available. For about fifteen quid, I could pick up a UV detector. I'm tempted, but a visual inspection's sufficient.'

'If it's that easy to spot a fake, then the police will know without forensic analysis. They'd have to be blind to miss telltale signs. Wasn't the point of these new polymer notes a way to make counterfeiting difficult?'

'Indeedy. The composition of the plastic's secret, so forgers must produce their own material, then copy a bunch of security features and get the serial numbers right. A fraudster could produce a substitute material that'd probably look right to the naked eye, but wouldn't feel right. Of course, the security features would give it away, unless that crook knows top level staff in the Bank of England.'

'I'm not convinced. Something doesn't add up. If you're saying these fake notes are easy to spot—'

'Years ago, when I worked in retail, I was told forgers would produce high denomination banknotes—say fifties—then buy goods for a fiver and grab the change. That way, they'd ditch the fake fifty and get themselves a genuine forty-five. They train cashiers to spot duffs, but vigilance goes when staff's rushed or haven't had a break for hours. Also, there are those too lazy to check. If you know what you're doing, it isn't impossible to print your own money.'

'All the same, it sounds amateur, producing fake banknotes that are easily identified.'

'Come on, Darling. You've had enough truck with criminals. You know what they're like. Forever hoping someone's stupid enough to be taken in. Greed and the love of money clouds judgment. That aside, think we can safely say whoever killed the old boy either has a fake money operation on the go, or knows someone who has.'

'Or the killer wants the police to think they're mixed up with bogus money. Again, something doesn't feel right. It's just too obvious.'

'It's quite a fitting statement, though. Stuffing money cigars into a rich man's mouth, perhaps a wad of cash, too. The bubble eye goldfish springs to mind. Who knows, maybe one of the old boy's kids wanted to make a point. My daddy, the rich aristocrat who only cares about his fortune, and couldn't give zip for his children. Maybe they were all in on it.'

'All his kids? Trust you to ham it up.'

'I don't think he was renowned for his warmth or parenting skills. Bet he sent them to boarding school. The strictest school, full of bullies. If my dad was a tyrant, I'd be resentful too. Could have been any one of the tribe. They all pee in the same pot.'

Jon's blank face creased Wendy up. 'Imagine Biggin Hall has more than one pot to pee in. Dozens, surely, but I get your angle. Do I get the slant, though?'

'Just a thought.'

'Then let's run with it. So, one or more of the kids resented milord caring more for cash than he did for them. Dickie's a maybe. He's a prize jerk.'

'First prize.'

'Don't know much about the other two sons, although Antonia gets along with them, especially Royce. Doubt she'd be involved in any skulduggery. Who knows? Anything's possible but doesn't explain why Tom's missing. Unless it's what everyone's thinking and he's a killer. Or dead. Poor Prue. It's the last thing she needs in her condition. You know how stress affects MS, and she's been under the cosh lately.'

'Bottom line, whoever did it wanted to make a point. The old boy craved money and someone, or some people, didn't like it. Tom's prime suspect, but one or more of his sons could've done it.'

'Dickie's top man.'

'Don't rule Antonia out. Then there's Lady Lu, or that ghastly fellow who no one's seen since his run-in with the old boy. Don't forget Mr Quince and even atom Annie. She started up the petition to save the village, remember? Couldn't stand the old boot. Down with the toffs, she said.'

'Now you're being ridiculous. Yes, Annie Clegg's toxic, but if she's a killer, I'll show my butt in—'

'Yes, I know. Figgy's Farm Shop Window. Jack'll be asking for rent soon. More fizz?'

Jon drained the wine into two glasses, scooped up the fake note, and put it back with his stash.

Wendy binned the empty wine bottle into the glass recycling box, nestling it between four spent bottles of ginger kombucha. She frightened the life out of Jon with an excited squeal.

'*Mr Quince.* You said it, Windy. But it wasn't Quincy who made milord fall down the stairs. It was the killer. Pushed down with a baguette, then whacked for good measure. And yes, like you first thought. To prove a point. But why a baguette? Initially, I assumed it was a joke. Now I'm confident there must be a reason. A simple connection, but what? Hold it there while I take this call. Prue? Slow down. What's wrong? Tom! Where is he?'

15

Cooking Up a Cover

Despite living with a chronic autoimmune condition, Prue Penn's optimism had opened many doors since her MS diagnosis. A new diet and lifestyle provoked changes she never thought possible, bringing focus and new purpose to her life. Pushing boundaries could trigger flare-ups, but total relapses had lapsed and for that, she was grateful.

'How is she?' Jon polished off a breakfast bowl of bran and fruit and drained his strong morning coffee.

Wendy munched on a banana, flung the skin into the food wastebin, missed, and threw it again. 'She's had a terrible night. At least we now know Tom isn't dead, but seems his flit and Annie Clegg's malice aren't enough.'

'What do you mean?'

'Tom's phone call sparked nasties galore. The worst in a long while, Prue says. Lasted all night and still niggling this morning. She's hardly slept, but you know what Prue's like. She just carries on.'

'Perhaps too wilful.'

'Can be. She was adapting, and well, but Tom's disappearance has pushed her back. Everything's raw, like an open wound she's scared to touch. I'm concerned if she keeps nudging that symptom ball, it'll roll, but she won't stop prodding. Wish she'd let me see her last night. Could've offered support, but she said she'd be terrible company. I can cope with that. Do it every day living with you.' Wendy's grin assured Jon that no matter the dire situation, humour was never far away.

'Let's finish here and I'll drop you at Prue's place. Gives me a chance to check progress at the Noose. The cordon may still be there, but hope not. It's been twenty-four hours. What do you think?'

'As I recall, police procedure requires reopening of a crime scene as soon as possible, especially where livelihoods are involved. Keeping drinkers from the local watering hole won't make the cops popular. Not that they are anyway, but a necessary evil under the circumstances. Finished faffing, have you? I'm ready to go.'

'All done.'

Jon dropped Wendy at Brambles, then headed to the Noose. Prue welcomed her friend with a hug and let Wendy carry coffee and cups to the table. For once, that fierce, independent streak had no fight. Prue tried to speak, but words didn't come easy. Jumbled and confused, they tumbled over one another, struggling for an audience.

Wendy took Prue's hand. 'Slow down. Relax and tell me from the beginning.'

Prue's anxiety was sky high. This ordeal had her beat. She'd said little of substance. Lots of crying, sniffles, and shrieks of pain, when spasms and shocks worried her body, but nothing concrete about Tom's call. Except the fact he was alive and kicking.

Knowing it was pointless to rush anyone when panicked, Wendy's guiding hand let Prue dump all the madness her way. Vast legal experience had taught Wendy robust patience was key. 'I'm here for you. Easy does it.'

'Thank you for being my friend. Everyone needs a Wendy in their life.'

'Such kind words. *Thank you*. When you're ready, I'm listening.' Wendy sipped coffee and waited.

'Okay. Stop me if I start blabbing. Or blubbering. Must get this out without cracking up.'

'Take your time.'

'I was watching a film when my phone rang. Usually, I ignore calls from unknown or withheld numbers, but had a strange feeling it could be Tom.'

'Go on.'

'It's been hard to stay calm when I've been worried about him, and he hasn't answered my calls or called me. Even harder when people want his blood. I didn't know whether he was dead or alive. Even though we'd had words, and he knew how I felt about his capers, he's my brother and I care about him. I wanted to lash out, but had to hold back. Stress was high and got me all over. Don't know how I got through the night. Still suffering, but the burn and spasms aren't as bad. More tired than anything.'

'I should've been here. Should've insisted.'

'I didn't want to spoil your celebration and would've been lousy company. Congrats, by the way. Love the name. Windy and Darling was there all the time and Wendy Darling's here now. That's what matters.'

'Thanks. You know Wendy was J M Barrie's invention for Peter Pan. Reckon I'm a good fwendy, even a darling like you say, and Jon Windup's definitely the boy who never grew up. Being polar opposites makes a potent mix. But enough of that, tell me about Tom.'

'At first, he didn't say much, except that he's okay.'

'Did he say where he is? Why he didn't show up for work?'

Prue's shaking hands grasped a glass. She gulped water. 'Awful dry mouth.'

'Where is he, Prue?'

'Wouldn't say. Just told me not to worry. I exploded. Told him I'm strung out worrying and his disappearing act makes him look more suspicious. He asked me if I thought he was guilty. I said no, but staying away isn't helping. He said he understood, then told me not to worry again. He knows things look bad.'

'Did he say why he'd gone to ground? Give any clues at all?'

'Nothing concrete. He goes missing during a murder investigation and most of the village assumes he's the killer. Phones me out of the blue, won't tell me where he is, and gives glib answers to my questions. I wouldn't accept his casual manner. Was determined to get something out of his call. He asked me to say he stayed at my house that night. Be his alibi.'

'How can you? If he'd turned up for work, no ache, but he didn't and still hasn't. No one'll believe that story. He's vanished, won't say where, and asks you to cook up some crazy cover. You couldn't make this up. Anything else? Did you ask why he wanted you to be his alibi?'

'Not directly, but I did ask why I should tell lies and what he was up to.'

'And?'

'He clammed up. I wouldn't let it go and dug some more.'

Wendy had a feeling something stronger than espresso was brewing. 'Did the digging pay off? Any treasure?'

'Said they're doing a great job covering their tracks, but he was onto them and just needed time. Whatever that means.'

16

A Brush with the Law

J on parked at the Noose and Gibbet and looked around. Free from the cordon, the pub looked ready for business. No blue and white barrier tape screaming police do not cross, police presence now down to one marked car. The only other vehicle was Eddie's.

He pushed the main door and walked into silence. Instead of the familiar sound of voices, piped music, and clattering cutlery, a soulless aura greeted him. Even this early, there'd be movement. A couple of regulars sipping coffee. A member of staff hovering behind the bar or in the kitchen beyond.

'Hello?' Jon called out.

'Hey!' Eddie's muffled voice came from a room behind the bar, then he appeared.

'This place looks deader than a fungal toenail.'

'Wouldn't know, never had one, but sounds gross. We're not open yet. I only came in to make sure orders and deliveries are up to date. Had to call the supplier and tell them to postpone this afternoon's craft delivery.'

'Why?'

'Cops are still here.'

'But the cordon's gone. Thought they'd be done by now. I'm here to see when I'm next in.'

'You should've phoned, Jon. Saved yourself a trip.'

'Was in the area. What's the deal with the police?'

'Guarding the cellar. Forensics still poking and prodding.'

'For how much longer? Wouldn't want to be in their shoes when the local drinking mob turns up and beer isn't flowing. There'll be a riot,' Jon chuckled.

'Would hardly call old Lenny and Frank mobsters, but I know what you mean. If those two can't have a pint and a civilised game of dominoes, there'll be trouble. Got my crash helmet on standby,' Eddie guffawed.

'Mine too. And my armour.'

'The police know they can't keep a crime scene sealed off too long, especially when a game of dominoes is at stake. Joking aside, forensics want every shred of evidence. With luck, they'll be gone tonight, and we can reopen tomorrow morning.' Eddie leaned forward and spoke in a hushed tone. 'The detectives were in earlier, quizzing me again.'

'What did they say?'

'Apparently, the murder happened between midnight and two, so they wanted a reminder of who was here. Told them I was at home with Gina watching a film. Gave them a copy of the rota and said apart from our missing comrade, no absences today. You closed the bar last night, so I assume they'll want a chat with you.'

'Great. I was on my own in the bar and the lights were on in the kitchen, so I assumed someone was in. Either way, the place was dead at closing time. There goes my alibi.'

'Don't worry. Unless you have a money printer and piggy bank at home, it's safe to say you're in the clear. By the way, why are you in the area?'

Jon wondered if Eddie's shifty look and quick change of subject had anything to do with the crime. What was in that big envelope Pengelly delivered yesterday? The one Ed clutched to his chest that sent him all cagey.

'Anyone in there? What you doing in Tor?'

'Sorry, Ed, miles away. Dropped Wendy off at Prue Penn's.'

'Don't suppose Prue's heard from Tom? I've heard nothing. At this rate, looks like it'll be Willy No Mates on his own in the kitchen tomorrow. I'll ring the agency to get a relief chef. Piles of other rubbish to sort, too. The stresses of running a pub.'

'You're a good manager, Eddie. You'll have things under control in no time.' It was Jon's turn to look shifty and avoid the Tom question. He knew Prue wanted to keep the call quiet.

'Hope so. Assuming we open tomorrow, can you do a lunch shift? Start at eleven, finish three?'

'Yeah, no worries.'

'I'll call if there's a problem, but if you don't hear, we're on.'

'No probs. Think I'll use the gents before heading off.'

'Okay. I'll crack on with my calls. See you tomorrow.' Eddie hurried back to the office.

Jon headed to the gents and was about to step in when heavy footsteps stopped him. He turned around and looked straight into the face of a surly police officer.

'Where's the manager?'

Jon didn't care for the policeman's abrupt manner. 'In the office. He won't be—'

The uniform took off through the door leading to the office, kitchen, and cellar. Jon followed on tiptoe. Normally, the area was off limits to the public, but Jon was staff, and allowed. He crept past the closed office door. Heard Eddie talking. The door to the cellar was at the end of an L-shaped corridor. Jon couldn't see it, but guessed another uniformed officer guarded the entrance and the surly one was his relief. Jon hid inside a cleaning cupboard with the door ajar so he could listen in. He hoped his gammy ear wouldn't play up.

'All right, Gus. How's tricks?' Jon spotted the rude voice.

'Not all right, I can tell you. Rather clean the super's boots than work this shift.' The reply was that of a grumpy officer fed up with sentry duty.

'That'll be the day when you clean Superintendent Scott's boots. Take it nothing's happening?'

'Got it in one. Forensics haven't finished here and there's another job in Treeton, so we'll be on statue duty for another few hours at least.'

'Statue duty. Ha. Makes me laugh when I hear that, but not happy laughing. Interesting crime, don't you think?'

'Interesting, how? All I know is some posh old coffin dodger snuffs it and I'm told to guard the scene.'

'They found him in the cellar with a wedge of cash in his mouth, so I've heard. Not just notes sticking out of his mouth, but a wad inside and a load of coins. Some on the floor. The rest shoved down his throat.'

Jon slapped his hand over his mouth to stifle his cheer. He'd seen the rolled-up notes, but the wad and coins revelation floored him. His theory about old fishy face was right. There *was* more cash in his mouth. But coins shoved down his throat? What was that all about?

'Sounds like someone hates the rich and came up with some crazy plot. Anyway, Rob, how do you know?'

'CID.'

'Get away. Some detectives don't look at us minions, never mind talk to us.'

'DS Uttley does. Can't keep his mouth shut, that one. It's a miracle he ever got into CID, never mind made it to sergeant.'

'When did he tell you this? What else did he say?'

'When me and Carter were having a drink, Uttley was mouthing off about the crime scene. About finding the body. Face full of cash, blah blah. He said the old guy fell down the steps, pushed probably, then choked on his own sick after the killer shoved coins down his throat. Probably half dead anyway before the coins. When the old guy snuffed it, the killer stuck rolled-up notes in his mouth. Oh, and somewhere along the line, he got thumped by a lump of bread. Don't ask me why.'

'Uttley's having a laugh, surely.'

'Probably, but he sounded serious, or as serious as you can be after a few pints. Anyway, the stiff's missus is having an affair with the head chef of this pub and CID's desperate to question him, but he's done a runner. That's a guilty man in my book. Don't breathe a word to anybody, mind. Wouldn't want our friendly sergeant to get into trouble, would we?'

Both men shared hearty laughter.

'I'm away now, Rob. See you in a couple of hours. Can't wait to get back.'

Gus slouched past, and Jon closed the cupboard door. He was back out in the corridor minutes later, sneaking past the office and Eddie's muffled voice. He was dying to tell Wendy what he'd learned and ready to go outside when Slate and Uttley walked in.

Slate raised his arm to block Jon's path. 'Ah, Mr Windup. I'd like a few minutes of your time, please.' He gestured to Jon to step back into the bar and sit down.

'What's this all about?' Jon said.

'We now know Lord Biggin-Smythe died after the pub closed last night. Can you remind me when you finished?'

'Just after eleven.'

'And jog my memory again. Who was working with you?'

'No one. It was too quiet to justify two members of staff.'

'*Too quiet.*' Whispered words from Slate, then back to his usual boom. 'How busy were you last night?'

'I've already told you. It was dead. Like the old boy.'

'Dead, indeed. Why do you call him the old boy? Unkind, don't you think? As you know, his lordship met his death in an ugly way.'

'Well, don't look to me for sympathy. The man was a meglomeanie and I won't miss him.'

The detectives exchanged glances.

'So, Mr Windup, what you're saying is you were behind the bar on your own and had no customers when you rang the bell for last orders.'

'That's right. Except I didn't ring the bell. What's the point of ding-dong when no one's about?'

'Fancy yourself as a comedian, do you? We could always finish this interview down at the station. Funny how you're desperate to get there, except you haven't bothered making a full statement yet. How long were you on your own?'

'About half an hour. A couple of elderly gents were playing dominoes, but left around half ten.'

'You didn't see Tom Trebilcock?' Uttley piped up.

'He was supposed to be working until closing like me, but it was his baking class last night at Biggin Hall. The kitchen lights were on, so I presumed someone was about. Don't know who.'

'Who locked up?' Uttley pressed.

'I did.'

'Do your keys only lock the bar?'

'My keys are for all downstairs areas, except the annex.'

'What's the annex?'

'The cottage where Eddie, his wife, and Mr Quince live, but they've had notice to leave.'

'Who's Mr Quince and where can I find him? Need a word.'

'He'll be having his late morning nap, but Quincy won't tell you much. Not even the price of fish.'

'And why is that?'

'He's Eddie's cat.'

'Shall I make a note, sir? That you want to question a cat?'

'Do you expect me to answer that, Uttley?'

'No, sir.'

'You've already met him, chief inspector. That big, ginger cat in the cellar. Remember? The one you couldn't catch. Still haven't caught him, then?'

'No. And you didn't help, Mr Windup. What's this about notice to leave?'

'Don't know much about it. Nobody's business.'

'Well, if *you* don't know much, Mr Rutter should.'

'*He might*, but not his cat.'

Slate held Jon with stern, baggy eyes. 'One more thing, and I trust you know this much. Where were you between twelve and two on Monday night?'

'Doing last checks and going home.'

'Alone?'

'Yes.'

'Doesn't take two hours to get to Treeton,' Uttley said.

'Didn't say it took two hours. Left at twelve-fifteen after cashing up. Got home around quarter to one. In bed by one. Is that enough, or do you want all the knots and twists?'

'That'll do. Which road did you take?' Slate came at him again.

This endless stream of questions had Jon panicked. *Surely they didn't suspect him?* He knew Slate had already prodded Eddie about his living arrangements. Trying to trip him up. Now they were pulling the same stunt with him. Asking questions he'd already answered.

'Well?' Slate prodded.

'Same as always. Via Bogus Hole and Little Swell. A few tangles and twizzles in there.'

'Can anyone corroborate that?'

Jon could've slapped Uttley's brash face. 'Yes. The whopping big pothole that nearly swallowed me up.'

'A pothole isn't a person, Mr Windup.'

'I beg to differ, sergeant, and so would you if you'd heard it laughing. Potholes are pranksters. They lie in wait with malicious intent. Had a narrow escape I can tell you.'

'You still here, Jon? Oh, it's you lot again.' Eddie's smile turned into a frown.

'Need another word with you after I'm done here, Mr Rutter,' Slate said.

'Why? You've had words with me twice already.'

'And I'll have words with you thrice. This investigation isn't finished until it's finished. I'm told Biggin-Smythe gave you notice to leave and you weren't happy.'

'Maybe he didn't like the colour of my skin.'

'Describe how you felt.'

'I didn't want me and my wife thrown on the street. I was desperate. Oh, how silly of me. I've just given myself a motive for killing him.'

'How desperate?'

'Not enough to murder if that's what you mean.'

'How long had you known him? How did you get the manager's job? Seen anything shifty while working here? You know, not quite adding up? Mr Windup! Get out!'

'See you tomorrow, Ed.' Jon reached the door when Slate boomed at him. 'One more thing, Mr. Windup.' The detective strode over, raised his arm across the door, and faced Jon. 'When you went to bed, were you alone?'

'None of your business.'

'I'm investigating a murder. Everything's *my* business. Let me rephrase. Do you have a partner?'

'No. I have a housemate.'

'But you're not in a rela—'

'No. We're friends sharing a house.'

'Name?'

'Jon Marcus Windup.'

'This isn't a pantomime, sir.' Slate looked exhausted, eyes deep enough to tote luggage for a six-month cruise. 'Your housemate's name.'

'Wendy May.'

'Please, don't leave Treeton, and get into the station to make a full statement. *Soon*. By the way, where can I find this Wendy May?'

'She's behind you.'

17

Upstaged

Once upon a time, in a school production of Aladdin, Wendy May hammed it up in a glittery turban and dodgy moustache. Bellowing evil laughter and brandishing a silver cardboard sword, she cut a credible Abanazar. Nowadays, depending on her mood, the frivolity of outrageous costumes, big hair, and dire dialogue either made her giggle or balk. But Wendy loved a slice of pantomime. The theatre and the word itself. The latter hit her in a soft spot. It rolled off her tongue and left a deliciously sweet taste.

After leaving Prue to catch up with Jon, voices from the Noose had Wendy intrigued. Idling outside, she caught the tail end of Jon and Slate's battle of wills, sniggering at Jon's fastidious last word wiles. He could never say die. When Slate said "pantomime", cue the theatrics. Wendy's mischievous mode kicked in and the age-old one-liner dripped off her tongue. She couldn't resist. So far, she hadn't crossed paths with DCI Slate. About time she faced him.

Drama wasn't wise on a sweltering day. Not with a thankless audience of one baggy-eyed, dour detective and his snitching sidekick. Both itching to slither out of suits. Both gasping for a cold pint of craft ale. Still, Jon would appreciate the show. No doubt he'd shine, playing the outlandish, bewigged pantomime dame to her questionable, demure principal boy. Wendy's yen to slap on greasepaint and tread the boards still flickered.

DCI Slate swivelled around, glaring long and hard. 'Wendy May, I presume?'

'That's me, and you are?'

'Detective Chief Inspector Slate, Treeton CID.'

'Could I see your warrant card?'

Slate fished in his pocket, flashed the card, then beckoned Wendy inside. As a senior police officer, the satisfaction of having the upper hand with "difficult" members of the public was apparent. 'I believe you know this gentleman.'

Wendy plonked next to Jon and nudged him. 'Shame on you, Mr Windup. I said you'd get into trouble one day. He's always leaving the lights on, chief inspector. That's certainly a crime in my book.'

'Miss May, we are investigating a serious offence. Do you think you can manage serious?'

'Always. How can I help?'

'You can start by telling me your full name.'

'Wendy May.'

'No middle name?'

'No.'

'Date of birth?'

'Fourteenth December, nineteen eighty-two.'

'Occupation?'

'Non-practicing solicitor. Now a freelance editor, copywriter, and researcher. Also penning the first in a series of children's fantasy books. I'm looking for an antagonist and a hero. Maybe I could base two of the characters on you and your colleague. Him behind you.'

'We have another comedian, I see.'

Uttley stopped making notes, his face aglow. 'Don't you fancy being in a book, sir? Sounds exciting. I'd love to be the hero.'

'Can we concentrate on the matter at hand, sergeant?'

'Yes, sir. Sorry, sir.'

'Miss May, can you please confirm you live with Mr Windup here?'

'For my sins, I share Mr Windup's home. A temporary arrangement. Never heard of a "Mr Windup here."'

'I'll take that as a yes. Where were you between twelve last night and two this morning?'

'At home. I went to bed about half-eleven, fell asleep soon after.'

'Did you hear Mr Windup come home last night?'

'No. Like I said, I fell asleep. The next thing, the alarm's going off.'

'So, what you're telling me is you didn't hear your housemate return last night?'

Wendy's legal background had taught her that police must be thorough during an investigation. That didn't stop the urge to ask Slate if he was dim. Instead, she gave a simple reply. 'No.'

'Thank you, that's all for now, but I'll likely want to speak with you again. Please don't go anywhere. Mr Rutter, I'm ready for that thrice interview now and would appreciate your time, please.'

Wendy and Jon waved to Eddie, then went outside. Despite his ashen face, Jon's anxiety raged.

'From now on, he's DCIbrow. His big, bushy beasties are a grave problem. There's a lot going on there. All that hipping and hopping. What next? A tango or waltz, or heaving up and down and hugging in the middle? That's my bet. A rude rumba and mega monobrow. Oh, Windy, my friend. You look wan.'

'The way they go on makes me believe I did it.'

'Don't take it personally. They're only doing their job. One won't and one can't.'

'What?'

''Twas a saying of my late mother. No idea who won't and who can't.''

'Trouble is, I was alone in the bar last night. Alone in the car on the way home. Alone when I got home. Alone in bed. See where this is going?'

'Oops, and me telling Slate I didn't hear you come in last night means I've dropped you right in it. From a great height. Pooh!'

'It's not funny. Even though I didn't see a thing, I was alone. What if the real killer covered his tracks and because they're desperate for a result, the police arrest me instead? You could've said you heard me last night. We're together in this, remember?'

'Oh, cut the drama, Shakespeare. The police aren't stupid. What reason or motivation do you have? Besides, where would you get a bunch of banknotes, real or fake?'

'That's what Eddie said. Whoever did this obviously had access to a fake money printing press and a piggybank full of silver.'

'There you go then.'

'Talking of silver, some news on the coins.'

'Coins? Thought we'd done coins.'

'Yes, and no. Was on my way to tell you the latest when laughing boy got his hooks in me.'

'Are they counterfeit?'

'Don't know. Didn't swipe one. Wouldn't think so. Higher value coins, yes, but not five pence pieces. For now, looks like the Judas connection. Thirty pieces of silver for a traitor. I'll tell you the full story later.'

'You can tell me now. Off you diddle.'

Jon looked around. 'Let's get out of here before my friends won't and can't grill me again.'

'Love it. Forget characters for my fantasy stories. Slapstick's better. How about they play a pantomime horse? With dodgy eyebrows. Better still, a panto ass, or is that typecasting?'

Jon chuckled and pulled Wendy towards the car. 'We'd better move our ass. Sharpish.'

18

The Dead Wake

'Say again?' Jon could barely hear over blaring voices and clinking glasses. A stark contrast to recent days in the Noose & Gibbet.

'You and your iffy right ear. At least your Christmas present's sorted this year. Ear trumpet it is. With stereo sound.'

Jon flapped away Wendy's comment. Jokes about his hearing were a staple of the seasoned sparring partners' banter, but it was all in good taste. 'What do you expect in this din? Have a heart.'

'I have. Keep it pickled in a jar in the proving drawer. It's warm and squidgy. I'll donate the centre to you, meaning, my windy friend, you won't only have a piece of my heart, but an *ear* too. I'm kind like that.'

'You're a card, Wendy,' Prue managed a giggle.

'Been called worse.'

'With everything that's going on, I shouldn't be laughing, but you have a way of making me smile. Do you ever stop fiddling with words?'

'Stop playing with an everlasting toy? Never. Such evil isn't an option. Me and my friends go back years. The things I can do with words are unprintable. By the way, it's lovely to see you laugh. Now, Jon, back to the question. How long before Eddie's turfed out?'

'At least a fortnight, but can't be sure.'

'Where will he go?' Prue asked.

'Doesn't know, but his brother's offered to help if he's stuck. He has a mountain of stuff to store. Offered him my loft for a while.'

'That's good of you. Poor Eddie. Some landlords are cruel, even if they are dead. Who's in charge of this place now?'

'The trustees, until probate's through, and it seems the old boy's death changes nothing, Prue. Eddie's still out on his ear.'

'My, my. Ears *are* fashionable today,' Wendy said. 'The family hasn't reconsidered then?'

'No. At least not the hard-faced meanies holding the cards. Anyway, the old boy's death's thrown everything up in the air and a pub manager's fate isn't high on the priority list. Don't worry. Eddie's a tough nut. He'll sort something out.'

'Hope so. How's prep going for the annual pub quiz, Wendy? Been swotting? Not long now.'

'Comes around quick. Until this recent business, we camped in libraries for a while, didn't we, Jon?'

'Indeedy.'

Wendy swallowed a mouthful of Shiraz. 'Fancy milord shuffling off when a big event's due. Stiff as a board and no consideration. How selfish. Must get back on track with the quiz. See if Jon can top his own world record for videos watched and articles read in a month.'

'You won't believe some of the random stuff I've dug up. Did you know the world's most dangerous stretch of water's right here in Britain?'

'Really?' Prue said. 'Tell me more.'

Jon took a swig of kombucha. 'Yes. The world's big rivers have nothing on the River Wharfe in Yorkshire.'

'Get away.' Wendy wasn't convinced.

'Seriously. The Strid, near Bolton Abbey.'

'The what?'

'Strid. The River Wharfe flows through a narrow gorge, where rocks, deep water, and fast currents combine. Add mossy, steep sides and you get danger. Lots of it. The fatality rate's a hundred per cent, according to my research. Local legend says a future king of Scotland tried to jump over The Strid, but slid on the moss, banged his head, and drowned.'

'That sounds horrible,' Prue said.

'I'm sure you make these things up, Jon. How much is the Yorkshire Tourist Board paying you?' Wendy teased.

'Very funny. Okay, the Strid's claim to being the most dangerous stretch is a tad bold, but no one with any sense would walk along the edge or go swimming in it.'

'Sounds like you've been goggling a click-bait video. What's the chances of this fishy fact being a quiz question?' Wendy said.

'You never know. There are more questions than answers. Hey, Eddie, how you doing?'

Prue shook her head. 'We think it's shocking you have to move.'

'Not a lot I can do about it,' Eddie said, collecting empty glasses.

'Jon says you don't have another house sorted yet.'

'Have a couple to view. A flat in Treeton, and a cottage in Bogus Hole. We prefer to stay local because of work and such. Gina's bittersweet about the whole mess. Isn't happy about being kicked out, but is happy that we'll get away from *that ugly, noisy thing.*'

'No way to talk about the old boy,' Jon grinned.

'She means the gibbet cage. I'm not bothered either way.'

'Tell her to put a different swing on it. Could come in handy if you had a baby. No need to buy one of those musical mobile whatsits to help the kid sleep.'

Prue almost choked.

'You tell her, Jon, and I'll come visit you in hospital,' Eddie roared.

'If he's lucky enough to get there,' Wendy cautioned. 'Knowing Gina, she'll put him six feet under. Or in that ugly, noisy thing. You asked for that, Jon. Sometimes even I'm shocked at your ghoulish sense of humour.'

'Sorry, folks. Was only kidding, Ed.'

'I know, mate. Don't panic. Anyway, everything's coming to a head. We must think about Mr Quince too. Many landlords won't accept animals, even in unfurnished property. Don't know or get why. Rent's higher in the village, but there's more room in the cottage and, before you ask, neither property's owned by the Biggin-Smythes.'

'That's a relief. See what you mean about Quincy. Can't understand that so-called logic either. How long've you got?' Wendy said.

'Two weeks officially, but we're not hurrying. The old goat's gone and that could delay matters. We'll hang on. No doubt they'll send the heavies round to shift me.'

In her legal years, Wendy had dealt with her fair share of landlord and tenant law. 'Yes, hold out, and if a posse comes calling, phone the police. Without a court order, no eviction.' Wendy felt a change of subject necessary. 'Bet you're glad the cops've gone.'

'Too right. The last of the forensic team disappeared this morning but might need to come back. The locals were getting restless. I've hired new temp bar staff but am still stretched in the kitchen with the head chef AWOL.' Eddie turned to Prue.

'Don't look at me. I'm only his stepsister.'

'Still no word then? Wish he'd get in touch. He's not doing him—'

'Haven't seen this place so busy in a long time, Eddie,' Wendy butted in, sensing Prue's discomfort. ''Tis crazy. Biggin-Smythe's death and coverage in the local and national news has done wonders for the Noose. Everyone's flocking to little Honest Tor. To visit the pub where a baguette bagged a lord.'

'Visit, or nose around, Wendy? They're coming from London and up north. From east, west and everywhere in between. Might need your help if it gets any busier, Jon.'

'It's the *inn* place, for sure,' Jon said. 'Cut the groans, you lot. I'm trying to redeem myself after my last boob. Not bad for off-the-cuff wit. I'll lend a hand, Ed. Starting now. Same again, girls?'

'Orange juice for me,' Prue said.

'Still don't know where the baguette fits in,' Eddie said. 'Police haven't released that info yet, but we buy in par-baked frozen loaves to serve with food or make sandwiches. Bake them on the premises. Would make sense if it was from here. Anyway, better get on.'

Jon stood to get more drinks. 'Everyone's looking this way.'

'Not everyone, but of those who are, it's Prue they're looking at,' Wendy said.

'Why me?'

'Judging by gossip, it's the Tom connection. You're an easy target.'

'Should mind their own business.'

'In this village? More chance of Nelson getting his arm back. You should know the quaint English village rule, Prue. Everyone must know everyone else's business. To be a rural dweller, accept this essential, or go. Put up and shut up, though I doubt the real workings are as harsh.'

'Come live in Treeton, Prue.'

'No, thanks, Jon. I'm perfectly happy in the country.'

'No one would bother you in town. By the way, not everyone's pointing the finger at Tom. Some say Dickie did it or one of the old boy's other sons. Lady Lu's in the frame. Others think Eddie had good reason. There are a few suspects. Even lovable Mr Quince.'

108

'Cats are smart, but plotting and carrying out a murder? People are so dumb.' Prue's patience had long gone.

'Where is Quincy anyway?' Jon looked around for the big ginger puss.

'Fast asleep over there. Eddie must've moved the stool so no one could swipe his bed,' Wendy said.

'Don't you just love that? No matter how much noise, kitty still sleeps,' Jon said.

'But is he asleep or pretending? You know what cats are like. One ear up, one ear down,' Wendy chuckled.

'We're obsessed with ears this evening. Oh, damn, that's all I need. Claptrap Clegg,' Prue huffed.

Annie shuffled into the busy pub, threw Prue a funny look, then hunched at a table on the other side of the bar, fidgeting with a piece of paper.

'Ignore her and leave her to drool,' Wendy said. 'When she's having a go at you, she's leaving someone else alone. There's Ems, looking lost as ever. Over here!'

Emily Clarke, stylist and nail technician at the local hair and beauty salon, waved at Wendy and pushed her way through sweaty bodies. Angled locks in varying shades of pink framed a pretty face that always looked close to tears. Though lacking in common sense and academic knowledge, Emily often surprised an audience with offbeat facts. Mute and humourless or loud and witless, Emily had no in-between. She either charmed or chafed, usually the latter after downing a few drinks, taking histrionics and clueless to the extreme.

'Hey!' As usual, the glowing smile killed Emily's vacant look.

'You're welcome to join us,' Wendy said, loving the radiance and wishing the girl would beam more often. 'Stir your stumps, Prue. Make room for another.'

Emily flopped onto the cushioned bench, put her drinks down, then drummed torturous black talons on the table. 'Busy in here. What's going on?'

'The Lord Biggin-Smythe vigil. Not the best place to hold a wake, but it's apt,' Wendy said.

'Awake? Thought he was dead?'

'He is dead. *This is his fake wake.* You know, a get-together for family and friends after a funeral. Bit pointless, really. He's still chilling in the morgue. This is more a congrats to the killer, not a respectful homage to the killed. But enough of that. How are you, Ems?'

'Not bad. You lot okay?'

'In the main, yes, but Prue's worried about Tom.'

'Why? What's happened to him?'

'You haven't heard?'

'What's to hear?'

'He's chief suspect for killing milord.'

'Oh, I know that. Know he's gone missing too.'

'So why ask?' Wendy scratched her chin.

'Thought you meant something else. Did Tom do it then?'

'Don't be stupid.' Like Tom, Prue's patience was still absent.

'Sorry.'

'How's Ross?' Wendy asked. She couldn't care about Pengelly, but needed to lighten the atmosphere.

'Okay, I think, but he's been acting funny lately.' Emily sounded irritated and confused.

'Weird funny? Or fancies himself as a comedian funny?' The remark had piqued Wendy's interest.

'Weird funny. Like he's got something to hide.'

19

Birdbrain Brew

'What *is* our artful postman hiding?' Wendy's playful, acidic tone promised more. 'Can't be his ego. Couldn't disguise something that big. Tell me more, Ems.'

Emily knocked back one drink and started the second. She gritted bleached white teeth. Thrummed long, painted fingernails on the table. She looked pained. Murderous. 'No idea what he's hiding, but he's gone all moody and won't say why. When I ask, he acts like it's some big secret. And that's not all. He's suddenly interested in things men shouldn't be.'

'What, like cross-dressing?' Wendy japed.

'He's not religious.'

'No, I mean. Never mind. What's he doing?' Wendy was thankful Emily had stopped beating her talons. The noise jarred.

'Caught him sneaking from my bedroom with a pack of emery boards and my best tweezers. Never got them back.'

'Is that all? People use emery boards for lots of reasons. Tweezers too. Sorry they're your besties, but don't think that's peculiar.'

For Emily Clarke, the art of making a drama out of fresh air was a breeze. She was hammier than Jon Windup, with so much theatre Wendy craved the finale. But Jon had other ideas. Wanting an encore, he pumped up the play, and scuppered Wendy's wish.

'Maybe he wants his nails done to keep up with your standards. Cut, buffed, and painted. Something cheerful, mind, not a darker shade of black. Man, your claws are scary.' Jon's twisted face would rival Annie Clegg's freaky features.

'Very funny. So why's he sneaking around?'

'Emilentary, my dear, Miss Clarke,' Jon cracked. 'He's a sneaker. No, seriously. Don't ask me. I'm Jon Windup, not Sherlock Holmes.'

'What you going on about?'

'Jon's paraphrasing the legendary Baker Street detective, Ems. Except, Holmes never said "Elementary, my dear Watson" in any of the Conan Doyle books. Not word for word, anyway. Shall we get off this and get back to Ross? Perhaps your man's having private beauty therapy in some exclusive parlour. He's into all that male grooming stuff. Immaculate hair. The latest cycling getup. Always tanned to the hilt. He's like a Belisha beacon.'

'What's that?'

'You must've seen them while driving or walking. Black-and-white striped poles mounted on the pavement with a flashing amber globe on top to mark pedestrian crossings.'

'Named after Leslie Hore-Belisha, Minister of Transport. Sorry. Can't remember dates. Road safety measures were Belisha's thing.' Jon's knowledge of all things roady was admirable.

'Yes, I've seen them. Didn't know they had a name. So why's Ross like one? Don't get it.' Emily slugged more drink and started her nails up again.

'Because his tan's so bright, you can't miss him. That amber glow. Like a Belisha beacon. I need therapy just looking at him,' Wendy groaned.

'Is that because he's so lush, Wendy? You need help to stop your heart missing a beat?'

'Orange skin, Lycra, and excessive pride aren't things I trouble myself with, Ems. Was thinking psychotherapy.'

'Psycho? Like mad, you mean? Know that feeling too. Ross drives me mad, but I don't care. He's a dream.'

'Dear Emily, I want to live in your world. Where pixies pirouette, fairies flamenco, and Lycra-clad Belisha beacons have unparalleled pedal power. A sphere full of innocence and trusting, but sadly, dreams come in all forms. No matter. We've gone off track again. Shall we get back on the weird one? Ross and his funny doings. What else is he up to?'

'Just being sly. Not telling me anything. Awake at strange hours of the night, but not the day.' Emily's tone upped a notch.

'That's it. A vampire. Seen any bat po—?'

'Shut up, Jon, and get another round in.'

Jon's attempt at wit hit the table with a dull thud. 'More drinks it is then.'

'I'll come with you. What's your poison, Ems?'

Emily guzzled her second drink, then banged the empty bottle on the table. She looked ready to cry. 'Large G&T with ice and another one of these.' She waved the bottle in the air.

Fearing she'd launch it across the room, Jon took the bottle and looked at the label. 'The new craft beer Eddie's sampling. Everyone's talking about how strong it is. Reckon the name gives it away.'

'Birdbrain Brew,' Wendy snorted. 'Whatever next?'

'Not a brew for me,' Jon said. 'When I'm in the mood, I tweet enough, thanks very much. Number one birdbrain.'

'Chirp-chirp,' Wendy giggled. 'Same again, Prue?'

'Bottled water, thanks.'

Prue opened up the chat again when Jon and Wendy came back. 'So, no clue what your guy's been up to, Emily?'

'Nope, but I saw him running across the road to meet someone the other night. Don't know who. They went off somewhere.'

'Are you sure?' Wendy asked.

'Quite sure. I think.'

'You think you're quite sure?'

'Yes.'

'There's no think about it, Ems. You're sure or not sure. Which is it?'

'I'm sure.'

'Positive?'

'Yes. I think so.'

'Positive and think don't marry. If they ever did, there'd be major grounds for divorce.'

'Refreshment?' Jon had picked up the strain in Wendy's voice and gestured to a waiting glass of red.

'Think I'm positively sure, or is that surely positive? Who cares? Bye-bye Malbec.' A third of the wine vanished in one swill.

Emily sank a mouthful of Birdbrain Brew, glugged half of the iced G&T, then went off again. Louder this time, she ribbed Ross Pengelly. 'Anyway, I don't care where he was going or where he's been. These days, all he talks about is vodka and sex. When I do his hair, he doesn't even give me a tip. Hairdressers need tips to top up their wages.'

'Think he needs one,' Wendy said.

'One what?'

'A tip.'

'Like what?'

'Tell him vodka's better with tonic.'

'Is that supposed to be funny?'

'Not if you don't have a sense of humour. Where is he now?'

'Not sure. Seeing him later.'

'Clegg! What's this heap doing in here? Move it will you! I've nearly snapped me neck on the bleeding thing.'

'She's peddling rumours, Lenny,' Wendy said.

'Annie, I've told you before. Don't bring that pile of scrap in here. Park it outside,' Eddie scowled.

'What? For someone to steal it, Mr Manager? This village's seen enough dodgy dealings. Prue Penn! You've got some nerve showing your face in here while that brother of yours runs amok after what he's done. Lock your doors and windows. There's a madman on the loose.'

Prue refused to rise to Annie Clegg's bait. 'Think I better go. Everyone's staring.'

'Time for The Prudini Show,' Jon quipped.

'But, Jon, if she goes, Prue won't show. If that makes sense. That woman can talk about nerve. More neck than a giraffe. Hey, Annie! Ever fancied doing a bungee jump? Without the bungee.'

'You and your funny eyes should do it.'

'Me and heights don't agree, nor do I agree with your vile jabber. Now, take it and go.'

Annie made a rude gesture, then sloped off, muttering to herself.

'You and your funny eyes aren't hitting the highs, Wendy,' Jon tutted. 'The thumbs are down from folk who just don't appreciate your sparkling wit.'

''Twould seem so. Those with no sense of humour who live a stony life will never get me, or you, or even darling Prue. But I have a cure. Fancy a knees-up? Happy hour in the chapel of rest. Drinks half price. Could do with a stiff one after being here. It's quiet in there, but the vibe's always dead good. Among candles, cadavers, and formaldehyde, I can be unfunny to my heart's content.'

'What's the music like?' Jon asked.

'Nothing lively, but the place cranks out a decent cover of Danse Macabre.'

'I'm in.'

'Then off we go. Since milord's demise, 'tisn't only the creepy who flock to the Noose. Seems goons, gossips, and grumps have made a home here.' Wendy drained her wine. 'Coming, Prue? See you on the other side, Ems. Don't forget that tip.'

20

In the Hall of Monty King

'W hy did I let you drag me here?' Decked in shorts, sleeveless shirt, and the flighty cool vest, Prue withered over a bubbling hob.

On the opposite bench, Wendy blew cold air onto her scorching face and juggled a clutch of steaming pots and pans. The friends were in the community hall in beautiful Bogus Hole, sister village to Honest Tor. Bogie was the place Wendy called home, had the surging river Mell and subsequent floods not forced her to seek temporary refuge with Jon in Treeton.

'So? Remind me why we're doing this?' Prue pressed.

'Two reasons. To check out this *ghastly* man King, and to cook up some gourmet treats. You love cooking. Thought it would do you good.'

'Good? This is worse than sitting on a live wire with wet hair. MS shocks *are* shocking. Excuse the science lesson, or is it a lesson in medicine?'

'It's whatever you want it to be. Thank heaven Jon isn't here. He'd get all technical and reel off ten top facts about Alessandro Volta. Is it really that bad? Sorry, Prue. Thought you needed a distraction from the Tom business. Me and my daft ideas.'

'Some distraction. I bought this vest to help when the heat's on, but it's struggling in this hell. What on earth was I thinking? Yes, I love cooking, but I'm dying here.'

'Is that dying to tell me I can shove Michelin star cuisine up my Gordon Ramsay, second shelf on the left?'

'Something like that.'

'How rude.'

Ever since Richard Biggin-Smythe mentioned King, intrigue wouldn't leave Wendy alone. Prue was none the wiser until Tom's phone call. He'd given no name or clue, other than a brief mention of someone from his catering college days. Prue vaguely recalled a man whose name began with M. Martin? Michael? Melvyn? She couldn't remember until Wendy found Kuisine by Kingoisseur. Highbrow cookery classes owned and run by Montgomery Oliver King. *Was this the King in question?* Only one way to find out. Wendy booked two places.

Turned out, a man named Milton King was taking today's class. Wendy aimed to determine if he and Montgomery were one and the same. If not, who and where was the other?

'How are things over here?' Dressed in chef's whites, Milton greeted Prue.

'I'm flagging, but nothing to do with the recipes,' Prue huffed.

'Yes. Doubt you'll be head chef at the world's top restaurants anytime soon,' Milton chuckled. 'Not even troops on exercise would welcome your offerings.'

'Piece of cake.' Wendy's face said otherwise.

'As long as you're both enjoying yourselves, that's the way to go.' With an irritating smirk, Milton shook his head and moved onto the next workstation.

'Cheeky git. Think someone needs to belt him with a baguette,' Prue scowled.

'You devil.'

'He's been making snide remarks all afternoon. Don't remember seeing three Michelin stars next to his name.'

'Just ignore him, Prue. His problem's with himself, not you.'

'I should try not to bite so, but all this uncertainty's got me in a lather. I'm too hot!'

'Being top chef isn't why we're here, but any skills we pick up along the way'll be a bonus. The man who runs these classes could be the man Dickie mentioned. Not cheeky git Milton, of course, but there must be a connection between him and the boss.'

'But how will you find the boss?'

'Leave that to me.'

Later that day, with attempts at haute cuisine or nought cuisine behind them, Wendy and Prue finished up.

Milton King stood centre stage and clapped his hands. 'Thank you all for coming. I hope you found this afternoon's class useful.'

'We got through it in the end, didn't we, Prue?'

'That's one way of putting it.'

'Never mind. At least we tried. Anyway, must speak to the head honcho.'

The friends caught up with Milton near the exit with a tacit agreement that Wendy do the talking.

'Hello again, ladies. Hope you both enjoyed the class.' Milton had one of those sneering faces itching to be slapped. 'Yes. It was interesting. Have you been doing them long?'

'I've been working for the company for three months, but my father's been in the catering industry for years.'

'Your father?'

'Montgomery Oliver King. Proprietor of the business and owner of this hall. Doesn't teach or run the show as much these days, but keeps his hand in at the nicer spots.'

That's handy. Milton the Mocking, son of Montgomery the Misled. 'Is Montgomery cheffing at a top restaurant this afternoon, then?' Wendy's snipe harked to Milton's earlier dig at Prue.

King junior didn't swallow the scorn. Unless he didn't get it. 'No, it's his day off, but when he teaches, it's here, Treeton, or London. And he prefers Monty.'

'Sounds like *Monty*'s doing well.'

'Yes, and no.'

'Something standing in his way?'

'Dad wants to expand and go national, but his plans are on hold. He had it all mapped out. Restaurants and colleges in every major UK city and all set to go, when his intended business partner, who was also his chief investor and financial backer, pulled out.'

'Really? Shame. No chance of a U-turn with the investor?'

'Hardly. He's dead. Found in one of his own pubs in a weird state. It's all over the news. Surprised you haven't heard.'

'Don't watch the news, and papers aren't my thing. Bit of a Luddite me. Wonder why the backer pulled the plug when your father knows his onions.'

'No idea. Happened long before I came here. All I know, it was a last-minute thing. I wasn't told reasons and didn't ask questions. Dad soon forgot about it.'

'Must be great working in a family business.'

Milton shrugged his skinny shoulders. 'Depends how you look at it. Dad's a first-class chef and a ruthless businessman. Not the sort you'd want to get on the wrong side of. He doesn't muck about, but that's the best way to be. He's definitely destined for the top. Just needs to find another partner.'

'When did he buy this place?'

'A while ago. Exact dates aren't my thing. Anyway, would love to stay and chat, but I have another class soon, and desperately need food before I collapse.'

'Sorry to have kept you. I'll check out the news. See what I can find out about this pub murder. Was he a local man?'

'Not any old man. The local lord.'

'No! You mean Lord Biggin-Smythe? He who wanted to hog all the county. Who loved rattling around in his old mausoleum, thinking he could change history and looking down his nose at the great unwashed.'

'What's that?'

'Not what, Mr King. Who. The working class.'

'That's him.'

'His poor wife. She must be going through it.'

'Don't talk to me about *her*. She's hardly poor, or a wife. Must go.'

'I do hope everything works out for *Monty*. Best wishes for success. Come on, Prue. Mr King's a busy man, with a ferocious appetite.'

21

At a Crossroads

An evening snuggled in Beans & Leaves bliss gave Jon, Wendy, and Prue the chance to pick over the latest happenings. Adam said they could mull and brainstorm without interruption while he was stock-taking.

The outing to Bogus Hole and chat with Milton King had unveiled a flurry of revelations, one of which had Wendy stumped.

'Montgomery King owns the village hall. How did I miss that one?'

'Because you weren't looking for it. Why would you?' Jon sipped cappuccino from an enormous cup.

''Tis true. Sometimes you don't know what you're looking for until you find it. Milton King couldn't tell me when Monty bought the place. He was lying, of course. Came across as an evasive sort. His father must be the one who did a flit, and no one's seen for years. The one Tom knows. The King we're looking for. Loving that frothy moustache, Jon.'

Jon wiped his top lip with the back of his hand, then bit the head off a gingerbread man and fiercely chewed.

Prue sipped peppermint tea, set her cut down, and gave her opinion of Milton. 'Didn't like him, or his snide remarks. He had a smarmy face and seemed edgy.'

'He was that. A man with something to hide?' Wendy mused.

'Like fake dough, cash cigars, and shiny silver coins. You could've met the killer, girls.' Jon plunged a zingy gingerbread body into his waiting mouth.

'Wonder if he knows Ross Pengelly,' Wendy said.

'Maybe. From what you've said, don't think he liked the old boy.'

'Nor the merry widow. I'm sure she and Monty have history. Milton couldn't hide his hostility. I feel a meeting coming on.'

'How far did you get with the old boy's interview? Get that, Prue. Mixing with the elite. That's some gig.'

'You make it sound like a privilege.' Wendy started on her second espresso.

'But know it wasn't. Don't envy you.'

'I didn't get to finish the meeting. Was halfway through how milord dealt with his status as a stinking rich county squire when he cut me short. Urgent business with his tailor, summoned to fit two suits made from the new Bigsmy tweed. Afterwards, the pair went shooting before taking tea in the lounge. Oh, how super.'

'Not for the poor birds. All that blood and feathers. How can they bear to pick them up?' Prue looked close to tears.

'Gun dogs collect the spoils. Probably a pack of retrievers, spaniels, the like, although blooding is part of upper-class recreation. It's all in a day's hunt for the elite.' Jon's face twisted, as if he'd eaten something rotten.

Prue poured another tea. 'Don't want to know. Shame you didn't finish your talk, Wendy.'

'Or not. Milord's dead, but milady's still clattering around in silly heels. She loves the spotlight. She's halfway there already with all the goings-on. A well-timed piece in a choice mag and the national media will thrust her centre stage. Temptation holds no bounds. The chance for glory will prove too much. Despite being a usual suspect, she'll be in. No such thing as bad publicity. I've said it before. Lady Lu only cares about Lady Lu.'

'You're reading my mind again, Darling,' Jon drained his coffee.

'In that case, my windy friend, fancy a trip to the big house?'

22

The Big House

'Any danger of getting there in one piece, Windy, or d'you want boiled eggs and buttered soldiers in your lap? Runny yolks and all.'

Jon was a competent driver, but his cautious approach didn't always extend to country roads and routes off the beaten track.

'Maniac! Watch that pothole. It's big enough.'

'Give it up. I'm only doing ten miles an hour. Any slower and we'll be going backwards. Or stopping.'

'Stopping sounds good to me. If you want to be clever, do it on your own watch.'

'I'm *not* being clever.'

'No, you're not. You're being a plank.'

'You're all heart, Darling.'

'Whose fault's that? Gave you the middle, remember? A piece of my heart and a new ear. Made no difference. You're still mean and your hearing's still flaky.'

'Like I said, Darling. All heart.'

'You won't be showing off on a cold slab, but count me out of your death wish. I'm not ready for Albie Drew's scrubs and blades yet. Not keeping him in a job with my remains, thank you very much.'

'He's a police pathologist. Aren't post-mortems rare after car accidents? Thought you'd know—'

'I do know. Unless the accident's in mysterious circumstances, so take your must have the last word rot and shove it where a squirrel shoves its nuts.'

'Nice.' Jon's car bumped through a small pothole, then turned onto the private track leading to Biggin Hall. 'At last. A smooth road.'

'Thought as much. The private road's pristine, but the stingy old buzzard lived up to his reputation when it came to public roads. The state of that stretch before we hit this one. It's a disgrace.'

'Guess I'm nitpicking, but shouldn't that be, *is disgraceful*? You haven't tightened the sentence up. Seems the editor sleeps, after all.'

'And seems your death wish's imminent. The sentence works either way. Now, shut it, or *you'll* be sleeping. Permanently.'

'Lucky me. And lucky Albie Drew. Two dates with yours truly in a week. Anyway, we're more likely to end up dead from your distraction. I'm sure backseat-drivers account for a quarter of all road fatalities.'

'Sitting in the front? That's clever.'

'Very funny. You know what I mean. Anyway, the state of the road doesn't surprise me. Unless for his own gain, the old boy wasn't fond of pleasing the masses.'

'The local council sits in the Biggin-Smythe pocket. That family must have influence over the upkeep of the public road. Milord could've tarmacked it a million times, but helping Joe Public was beneath his high and mighty ways. Wonder if the heir apparent will stoop to assist. Of course, the conservation area thing could play a part. Wouldn't be in keeping with the character of the place, meaning inevitable potholes, puddles, and other gremlins. Your favourites.'

'Conservation, my foot. Not if I know the old boy. Or the rest of them. For the common people, skinflints all.' Jon's eyes widened and his mouth dropped as he pulled up outside Biggin Hall. Flanked by oak trees and green as far as the eye could see. 'What the—? Look at this place! It's megantic.'

'Big 'ouse,' Wendy cried, something she always said when seeing a house of whopping proportions.

'Look at those fancy turrets, and that crowned roof with its merlons and crenels. Add a moat, a drawbridge, and a few other castley bits and you've got yourself a medieval castle.'

'If it needs *castley* bits, it's not a castle, Windy. Medieval or otherwise. Castles had a keep or donjon. Battlements. Parapets. A portcullis.'

'Okay. It could be.'

'You're right. It could. With *castley* bits. New wacky word?'

'Proper wacky. How did you wangle an invitation here, Darling?'

'Easy. When I interviewed milord, I was privy to the elite's phone number and used it to my advantage. The housekeeper remembered me. Told her following the untimely death of his lordship, readers were screaming for Lady Biggin-Smythe's story. As for the mag's editor, well. She was just cock-a-hoop at the prospect of an exclusive from the heartbroken widow of such a well-respected, charitable man. May he rest in peace.'

'You cheeky scamp.'

'I nearly choked on my own drivel, but needs must. Milady will do anything for publicity and a feature in a leading mag's too tempting to pass up. She's too vain to check if my tale's true.'

'Indeedy. A proper pompositor.'

'When she heard about the exclusive, she took my call. Chatty to the point of gushing, and I intend to milk every last drop. Apart from Lucinda's pretentious ego, the only downside is her voice. Minnie Mouse on helium. Got an earful while eavesdropping t'other day, but I'll happily endure another bellyful to get to the truth. The things I do in the name of justice. Ready for the house of fun?'

'It's so green here. And that house. Can't get over the size of it. How the other half live, eh?'

'Far less than half. Rattling around in a place this size's vulgar. Countless rooms, and I doubt all used. Wonder who does the cleaning? Must be a mammoth task. And all those windows. Probably need a cherry picker to reach the highest heights.'

'Suppose it is grandiose for the sake of it. Wouldn't like to pay the bills. All the kids live here, too. Must have plenty of room to play, you know. Oh, and acres of land to hunt and shoot.'

'Please, don't.'

'Sorry.'

'The sons may thrive on blood sports, but not Antonia. She told me she hates all that and refuses to join in. Think she said Royce wasn't a fan either. Could be wrong.'

Jon clocked the swarm of CCTV cameras and motion sensor lights mounted above the doorway and windows he could see. 'Think they're paranoid?'

'Know it. Here we go. It's showtime.'

Wendy knocked, and the pair waited. Minutes later, the huge door opened, and a leathery, sullen face peered out.

'Good morning. I'm Wendy May, and this is my assistant, Jon Windup. We're here to see Lady Biggin-Smythe.'

The gaunt face looked doubtful.

'*She is expecting us.* Are you the butler?'

'Wait here,' he croaked, then slammed the door.

'Charming creature,' Wendy said. 'Reminds me of Lurch from the Addams Family. Nah, come to think of it, Lurch had charisma and was better dressed.'

The door opened again and the prickly man gestured Jon and Wendy inside.

'Butler or no butler, he could do with some manners. What happened to basic common courtesy?' Wendy whispered.

The couple followed frosty face down a long corridor into a vast hallway adorned with portraits, priceless art, and tapestries. Lined up along the walls must've been twenty suits of shining armour. Ten on each side, standing guard. Watching. Waiting.

'Some collection,' Jon whooped.

Through a doorway into a gargantuan library clad in expensive wood panels and shelving, overflowing with books and manuals. Tomes of every description. From ancient Egypt and Chinese dynasties to the world's rarest gems and centuries of landed gentry.

On one wall, a vast gallery of generations of male Biggin-Smythes. Each portrait showing that obligatory snivelling simper, dressed to kill in the family tweeds. On the adjacent wall, above an ornate fireplace, hung a colossal portrait of Lord Seymour Biggin-Smythe. Like Dickie, the eyes were mean and cold, and there was that hook for a nose too big for his face. He hadn't guzzled an ironing board, but the hairline was similar. And the stance. Dickie's father right enough. Couldn't wriggle out of that one.

At last, the butler spoke. 'Wait here.' He shuffled off without a please or thank you, head bobbing up and down like a nodding dog.

'Bony old grizzle guts,' Wendy said. 'Someone must've programmed him to speak at random.'

'Next time I want chilled beer, I'll ask him to breathe on the bottles. What a misery. I wonder if all the staff are as warm and charming.'

'Probably, but hats off to him for bringing us to this room. Don't mind waiting here. It's total bliss. Must be thousands of books.'

'They are fantastic, and look at the windows. All stained glass. Let's sit on that couch over there. Looks the best of the best.'

The couple parked on a chaise longue facing another fancy fireplace bedecked with everything needed for a roaring fire. Three baskets of logs, kindling, a huge fireguard, and two golden companion sets. Over the fireplace, three more imposing portraits glared down, daring Jon or Wendy to misbehave.

'That middle picture looks like milord, but doesn't,' Wendy said. 'Could be his daddy or grandaddy. Definitely kin. The others are from the same stock too. That lofty look gives it away. And the tweed. A Biggin-Smythe must have.'

'The old boy sure liked his armour. Another six suits here. He should've been wearing one the night he got jumped in the cellar. Missed a trick there.' Jon lowered his voice. 'Listen, when we were in the Noose yesterday, Emily said something I can't get out of my head.'

'What?'

'Shh, not so loud. About Ross and emery boards.'

Wendy peered at Jon's animated face. 'Go on,' she urged, anticipating a deeper meaning behind his simple observation.

'I often carry emery boards and tweezers in my drat pack.'

'So? Pengelly likes to carry odd things around. Your point?'

'When I found the old boy, I only saw the notes. Didn't know someone had shoved coins down his throat.'

'Don't dither, Windy. What are you driving at?'

'If I wanted to push coins down someone's throat, I'd consider using emery boards.'

'Are you serious?'

'Deadly. No pun intended. Two to keep the mouth open, one to force them down.'

'What about tweezers?'

'To grab the coins, then drop them in the mouth.'

'Sounds like a chore.'

'That's what I thought, especially in that dim cellar, but it can be done. Maybe two perps? One holding the old boy's mouth open, another flinging silver down his throat.'

'Nasty. Two's a possibility, but surely they'd use their hands. Gloved, if they had any sense. Why bother with emery boards and tweezers?'

'Wendy May?'

The squeak was unmistakable. Minnie had pattered in, and she'd OD'd on helium.

23

The Lady in Red

J on and Wendy scrambled from the seat and turned around. It was no surprise to see Lucinda Biggin-Smythe had worn her second skin into the room. Wendy couldn't believe how snug the statement scarlet dress. How high the matching heels. Dripping in jewels and ego, she teetered inches from the door.

A scary croak stuttered from Jon's throat. Something between an embarrassed cough and a strangled expletive. Smiling at the spangled vision, Wendy grabbed his arm and pulled him towards the door.

Milady's painted face, the work of expert hands, highlighted cherished features. Enormous emerald eyes shielded by heavy, long lashes fluttered and fawned. The perfect cupid's bow set off full red lips, pouting and puckering at will. The woman's entire persona stank of pleasure and wanting. Wendy turned her gaze to Lucinda's big hair. *Did a murderous mind lurk inside that tumble of golden curls? Was milady the epitome of a deadly scarlet woman?* In that getup, she looked the part.

Lucinda appraised the couple, then wrinkled her nose. 'Good morning. I'm Lucinda Daphne Biggin-Smythe, Lady of Biggin Hall and owner of the family estate.'

'Delighted to meet you,' Wendy said in a tone Jon knew meant the opposite. 'I'm Wendy May. This is my faithful assistant, Jon Windup.'

Lucinda shook Wendy's hand and ignored Jon. 'Hurry along. I'm a busy lady and don't have all day. This way.' She flung back her mane, then tottered off. Like two obedient puppies, Jon and Wendy followed until Lucinda stopped at the doorway of an opulent room lavished in beautiful objets d'art. 'This is the crystal room, one of four drawing rooms, and my favourite. Be careful here. These priceless pieces were so precious to my late husband. Such a vast collection. There wasn't room for every item. The rest's in the glass room, Seymour's favourite place to relax.'

'What's the difference between crystal and glass?' Jon probed. He knew the answer, but mischief was never far away, and putting Lucinda on the spot amused him.

She dismissed his question and invited the couple to sit on a sumptuous sofa. She chose a high-backed, winged chair and crossed her legs, swinging one leg back and forth, back and forth. The rhythmic action set Jon's nerves on edge. He wanted out.

Wendy was a divided soul. On the one hand, it was tough to clamp her tongue and not spew the words this woman had uttered on Figgy's Field. It was clear she had no time for Lord Biggin-Smythe, so her attempt to play the devoted, grieving widow was a waste of time. On the other, Wendy was adept at handling such a situation. She'd been there many times, and this was no different. Dignity. Protocol. Decorum. Etiquette. Formalities she'd choked on during her legal years at functions and dinners and balls. Promising years that turned into empty years. She'd got out at the right time. When the taste of rancid bile choked her.

Wendy sensed Jon's discomfort. He looked nervy and ready to flee. Neither would dance to Lucinda's tune. Time to stop her boastful beat. 'Who boils the kettle around here? I'd love a cup of coffee. Jon would too.'

About to retort, Lucinda held back. Better be civil if it meant having your picture splashed over a popular magazine and the national press. She signalled the housekeeper, who was hovering outside the room.

'Coffee for three.'

Wendy fished in her bag for her mini recorder to tape the interview. 'Would you credit it? I've left my notes in the car.'

Lucinda exhaled and uncrossed her legs.

Wendy sensed impatience, but had the matter under control. 'I can start without my notes, but will need them at some stage. Jon, be a sweet and grab my notebook from the car, would you?'

'The front door might be locked. If the housekeeper or butler's about, ask one of them to assist. It can be a bit funny.'

'A door that cracks jokes. Could do with a laugh,' Jon mumbled, feeling far less confident than his cheeky wisecrack hinted. So much for mischief.

'*Not funny in that way.*'

'Right.' Without giving eye contact, Jon disappeared into the hallway and retraced his steps to the entrance. He was relieved to be away from the stuffy room and, thank the stars, he was alone. He'd figure out any locks and bolts. Didn't need help. He caught the start of Lucinda's interview. That voice was beyond infuriating. The woman could squeak for hours about her life. Her dreams. Her clothes. Her shoes. Her grief. *Her. Her. Her.* Poor Wendy hated toxic company, but would do whatever it took to stoke and stroke the big ego. She'd keep Lucinda in check, even if it put her in a stinking mood. He was in for a quality evening of ripping banter when they got home.

As much as he wanted answers, Jon's temperament couldn't cope with conceit. Thankful he'd reached the heavy front door, he turned the key and edged it open. Free at last!

Jon ran to the car, then took time out to admire the stunning landscape. To bathe in green. As he pocketed the notes, a wry smile tickled his face. He had a job to do. That's why Wendy had conveniently forgotten her notes.

Given him an excuse to leave the meeting. Not only for a brief respite, but a chance to explore the big house.

24

The Big Buttinsky

B ack inside Biggin Hall, Jon veered off to the left and darted along another endless corridor, past a line of closed doors. Behind one, muffled tones reached him, despite his dodgy ear. Jon strained to hear. The voice was familiar, but he couldn't place it.

'You know how these things work. As soon as I get it, you'll have it.'

No audible reply made Jon suspect the speaker was on the telephone. He pressed his good ear to the door.

'As soon as there's news, you'll be the first to know. As always, it's been a pleasure.'

Silence, then shuffling. Jon hurried across the corridor and tried a few doors. All locked. He breathed again when one opened and he tumbled inside. A luxury executive chair, four-drawer filing cabinet, and all manner of stationery told Jon this was someone's study or office. Jon seized his chance. He closed the door, made for the cabinet, and drew a hairpin from his drat pack to probe the lock.

In a trice, Jon was in. Bumf galore. Coloured folders in red, amber, and green lined the top drawer, each one labelled. Why a traffic light system Jon didn't know, but he did know he was for the high jump if caught in the act. He sifted through the folders. Nothing to pique his nosy nose. Save for a scattering of discarded paper clips, the second and third drawers were empty. Jon yanked open the bottom drawer. Only one red folder inside, but the name in bold letters was the treasure Jon had hoped for. King Project.

Inside the outer folder, an inner holding sheets of paper in varying sizes, and a business proposal that fuelled Jon's fire. He put his phone to use, took a stack of pictures, shot a quick video, then returned the folder to the cabinet. Now to find his way back. If he played follow the squeak, he was sure to find the crystal room and that nauseating woman. Jon peeked into the corridor. Clear. He took a few quick steps before an incensed male voice stopped him.

'You there! What do you think you're doing?'

25

Lording It

Even limp lugged Jon couldn't mistake Dickie Biggin-Smythe's pretentious yap. *Was he the voice behind the door? The muffled man?* Jon turned around. There, in his finest golfing togs, stood the little sniveller himself. Brandishing a club, all pursed lips and unruly hair.

'Sorry. I was looking for the toilet, but got lost. This house is so big, but I guess that's why people call it the big house.'

Jon laughed. Dickie didn't.

'You oik! I believe you mean the lavatory, and you won't find it there. I should call the police. Commoners taking liberties. Thinking they can come in here and use the facilities. It's a beastly disgrace.'

Jon struggled to speak. This was nothing like his last run-in with Dickie. On Biggin-Smythe turf, the pampered fool had the upper hand, and it showed. Jon's gut twisted. Acid burned his chest, spread to his neck and face. He'd used his emergency gloop, had nowhere to run, and a rogue pin from his drat pack stabbed him where it shouldn't.

'It's all right, sir. He's with that freelance writer who came to interview Her Ladyship.' Housekeeper Marie tried to calm the situation.

'Writer? What are you talking about? Why wasn't I told?'

'I thought you knew, sir.'

'Why do you insist on calling me sir? Daddy's dead. I'm his heir and *alive* and now own the title of Lord Biggin-Smythe. You should address me as Your Lordship. As for that frightful woman, she's a widow and dowager. Her ladyship she is not!'

Marie's face didn't crack. She'd spent years dealing with the likes of Dickie. 'Don't you remember? Wendy May was interviewing your late father but didn't finish the interview. Your stepmother offered to fill in the gaps.'

'You mean offered to tell the world how marvellous she is? I don't regard her as my stepmother. Please, remember that. Now, show this idiot where the lavatory is, and you!' Dickie's cold eyes froze Jon. 'Don't roam around here on your own. This is a private residence, not a tourist attraction. Wait a minute. Don't I know you from somewhere? Your face is horribly familiar.' Without waiting for a reply, Dickie sped off down the corridor.

'This way, please.' Marie guided Jon to the bathroom.

'Thank you. I'll try not to get lost this time.'

'Hopefully. Take Mr Biggin-Smythe's advice and don't roam around. He has a wicked temper. His late father was the same.'

'With any luck, he'll fall into a bunker and cause a sandstorm. Thanks, again.'

Marie scuttled off and vanished into the maze. Jon splashed cold water on his face. He assumed the family reserved this basic bathroom for staff. He removed the offending pin, put it back in the pack, then made his way back to the crystal room. That woman's grating shriek picked him up and pitched him at the door. And there she sat with Wendy, enjoying more refreshments. An elaborate coffee pot, dainty jug of cream, and an empty cup sat on the expensive table. Lucinda was doing the talking. *Good old Wendy. Stroking the lady's ego.*

'About time, Jon. I asked for my notepad, not a roll of ancient Egyptian papyrus. Pour yourself a coffee. It's divine.'

'Sorry, but I needed to go. Your housekeeper was most helpful showing me where the toilet was.' Jon chuckled to himself as he poured.

'Toilet? What a dreadful word!' Lucinda's face resembled chewed-up toffee.

'Beg your pardon. The lavatory,' Jon spluttered, reeling from Lucinda's hard stare and cursing his blunder. His eyes focused on the plush carpet.

'Is your assistant always this impertinent?'

'Apologies, your ladyship. He can't even hold his knife and fork properly, but he's a good egg.'

Jon buried his discomfort and anger in the coffee cup, amazed at Wendy's detached ability to speak to this pompous creature. No doubt she'd extracted much from Lucinda, but he suspected Wendy wasn't done yet. Jon was right. She flipped the pages of her notepad and probed some more, flattery rolling off her articulate tongue like honey off a hot spoon. The rhetoric was all part of her ploy.

Minutes later, Wendy stopped recording. 'Think that's everything.'

'Most stimulating.'

'Agreed. In my line of work, I realise some don't enjoy talking about themselves, while others have a remarkable talent for it. You are the latter. An expert. What's known in the trade as a conversational narcissist. Thank you for making it easy for me to record Lady Biggin-Smythe's views on the trappings of country life. Read my article. See how I make a hollow log sing. Your voice, milady. The voice of pride. The magazine should be out in a couple of months, and I warrant circulation will escalate.'

'Wonderful, and thank you for your glowing compliments. I'm looking forward to reading. So sorry I had to rush you. So much to do. Solicitors to see. All the ghastly business in the aftermath of death. Having to keep a face when you want to crumble. You must return for a grand tour of the house and grounds. Get lots of pictures for your article?'

Jon and Wendy exchanged satisfied glances. Too tempting an opportunity to pass up. Objective accomplished.

'Tomorrow if you're not busy? Three o'clock? Show you how afternoon tea's done. In style.'

'Sounds fabulous,' Wendy lied, irked at Lucinda's smugness and conscious of another of Jon's untimely choked grunts. 'Already, my tastebuds are tingling. Jon's a genius with the camera. You serve up the wonderfully British tradition of tiny crustless sandwiches, pastries, scones, and cakes. He'll serve up a unique portfolio of the quintessential lady cocooned in her indelicate manor. I trust exceptional brews will accompany the delights? Coffee and tea?'

'Of course.'

'Then I'll slip into my best outfit in this homage to Anna, seventh Duchess of Bedford. The lady who inspired the concept of afternoon tea in eighteen forty if you didn't know.'

'Splendid. I'll tell Briggs to expect you.'

'Your butler, I presume? He'd make a fine poker player, don't you think?'

Lucinda didn't answer. She appeared fascinated by a speck on her dress. She stood, ran slender hands over her hips, and ushered Jon and Wendy from the crystal room, down the long corridor, and to the front door.

'Many thanks for your time,' Wendy smiled.

'A pleasure.' Lucinda turned to Jon. 'Make sure you have your photographer's head on, assistant. Nothing but the best for Lucinda Daphne Biggin-Smythe, lady of the manor.' Lucinda giggled like a teenager.

'Let's go, Jon,' Wendy murmured, 'the prima donna craves her next audience. Besides, I see old grizzle guts himself shuffling with intent. Wearing the death stare. Briggs, wielding misery and gloom. Until tomorrow, your lady.'

'Bye.' Lucinda tottered off, leaving Briggs to slam the door.

'Off we go, assistant,' Wendy joked. 'Try to avoid the potholes this time.'

The pair hooted as Jon pulled away from the big house.

'Did you have a nose around on your way to the loo?'

'Oh, yes. Nice place. Too easy to get lost in. Did you get what you wanted? Her lady's life story, perhaps?'

'Near enough. Did you find anything?'

'Might've done.'

'Out with it, then.'

'A little office with a filing cabinet and flimsy lock.'

'And you went foraging?'

'Would've been rude not to. Got pictures. And a video. I'm working later, but I'll send them to you.'

'Pictures of what?'

'A business proposal between the old boy, Montgomery Oliver King, and get this. Richard Biggin-Smythe.'

26

Capital and Capitals

W hile sipping tea and munching on chocolate chip cookies, Jon studied an enormous atlas. 'That's more geography covered. The capital of Afghanistan's Kabul. Ashgabat for Turkmenistan, and Astana, literally meaning "capital city" for Kazakhstan.'

'Ooh, goody. The stan clan. I'm on the edge of my seat, Columbus.' Wendy glugged a cold liquorice brew, poured another from a glass teapot, then raised her cup. 'Here's to a hotter one.'

'By the time the quiz comes around, Kaz might've changed its capital again. Was formerly Nur-Sultan, but—'

'Give it a rest, Jon. I can't *stan*d anymore.'

'Come on. I know you love the seven stans, but enough of Af, Taj, and Uz now. What's your take on the snaps I sent over?'

'Fascinating. King's culinary idea for a chain of new gastropubs bankrolled by the big cheese. A mouldy old cheese at that.'

'You could say they were cooking up a storm.'

'Hilarious. Man, did you miss your vocation.'

'Did I! So, where does icky Dickie fit in? My impression was relations between the old boy and his eldest were strained at the best of times.'

'Don't know. On the face of it, milord proposed to cough up most of the cash and Dickie'd only be a sleeping partner. If he's bringing more to the table, the proposal doesn't say what. Something's not right. Milord could've funded the deal a thousand times. Doesn't need the heir.'

'Forgot to mention that Dickie now sees himself as Lord Biggin-Smythe, not the heir apparent. Daddy's dead's what he said. And don't you forget it.'

'Pretentious clown. I'd love to know what he proposed to put into the deal.'

'Why don't we ask him? See if he's around when your new bestie gives us the grand tour.'

'Milady's no bestie of mine, cheeky. Lost count how many times I had to stop myself slapping her. Or telling her to shut up. What Tom Trebilcock sees in her, I do not know. She has no redeeming qualities, but I doubt he's looking for redemption. Reminds me of that plank, Pengelly. Only difference is she sits in the Royal Mint, and he sits in a Royal Mail van. Both are too self-absorbed for their own good.'

'But you wangled coffee from her, so not too bad.'

''Tis true, but that's more to do with my powers of persuasion. And a few fibs.'

'And you bagged afternoon tea and a tour.'

'What can I say? I've got it going on. Know how to do the do. Where would you be without me, Windy?'

'On the streets, no doubt.'

'You got that the wrong way around. It's me sleeping in your spare room, remember? Otherwise I'd be on the streets.'

'You know what I mean. You'd do the same for me. Helped me so heaps in the past. What are friends for?'

Wendy scanned through the photos Jon had sent earlier. The proposal outlined the nature of the business, projected income, and expansion. It also detailed an analysis of the market, and, crucially, the major stakeholders. 'It's clear. King needed Biggin-Smythe to front the capital.'

'Plenty of other people could've invested. Or why not apply for a loan, or re-mortgage his house?'

'I wager the amount's beyond the limits of your average high street lender. Maybe King's credit rating's kaput and he had no choice than to hold out his begging bowl. What percentage of the business would milord have if the deal had been done?'

'Seventy, with King on twenty and Dickie, ten. After his investment's paid, the old boy's stake reduces to forty, but Dickie still keeps ten.'

'Ouch! Milord stitched King up like the proverbial kipper, but that's how most venture capitalists operate. Saw plenty of that when practicing law. Investors offering vast sums, only to insist on a healthy slice of the business. Money goes to money, and moneybaggers are as economical with cash as they are with the truth. Tight-fisted. That's how they become wealthy. Unless they're born into riches.'

'Indeedy. And I'm swiping moneybaggers for Windy's Wacky Words.'

'Swipe away. How long for milord to recoup his investment?'

'The proposal says within five years.'

'Optimistic. Mind you, the man was ruthless. Noted for it. Something's jarring. I sense a crucial piece of the puzzle's lost.'

'One of your hunches?'

Wendy looked at the papers again. 'Must've missed this first time around, but King wants each new gastropub to have a theme, exploiting the local history.'

'More like milking it.'

'Yes. Starting with the Noose. The jewel in the crown and blueprint for all other pubs to follow.' Wendy cringed at the cliché.

'Really?'

'Yes, really. To accentuate the history and promote the gibbet cage. They'd replicate that theme in every pub. With the necessary variations.'

'Hang on. The old boy wanted to get without that cage.'

'Say again?'

'He wanted rid of it. Said it was an eyesore. That's one thing I do remember.'

'Yes. You mentioned that the other day when I was telling you and Prue about the Noose. We also talked about Annie Clegg's petition.'

'And now that eyesore's relevant.'

'The missing piece?'

'You don't think someone bumped off the old boy over a trivial disagreement about a gibbet cage, do you?'

'Don't know, but this could be evidence of cracks in the business relationship. Not the main missing piece, but a clue.'

'Must grab my drat pack.'

'You and that bag.'

'What time are we expected tomorrow?'

'Three on the dot. Can't be late for milady.'

'Golly, no!'

'I think more questions need answers. Hope that clown Richard Biggin-Smythe's about. What's his involvement and what does he know of daddy dearest's backing?'

'I'm hungry to know that too, but now, back to Asia. Kyrgyzstan next.' Jon revisited his beloved atlas.

'Is all this swotting necessary?'

'Life or death. To *stan*d a chance of becoming quiz champion of champions, we must get cosy with the stan clan.'

27

The Merry Widow's Tea Party

J on wore his grey suit like a straitjacket, but that didn't stop him from plundering the pleasures of a sumptuous spread. 'This is the bomb,' he muttered through a mouthful of artisan bread.

Perched beside Jon at the grand oval table in Biggin Hall's main dining room, Wendy sipped coffee from a dinky cup. Though not in her finest togs, she cut a stylish figure dressed in a knee-length black dress and modest heels. A dusting of make-up, black-and-white wide-brimmed hat, and tasteful jewellery complemented the outfit. Wendy adjusted her hat to a jaunty angle. The mad hatter within had screamed for a natty purple topper, but judicious Wendy had shushed its cries for audience. One merry widow and two kooky amateur sleuths were enough for this crackpot tea party.

Enormous bay windows overlooked pristine lawns flanked by abundant flower beds and stylish topiary. Stretching to thick woodland, what the eye could see told only one chapter of the Biggin-Smythe epic. Nestled in hundreds of acres, the big house and its natural delights were a never-ending story. Wendy and Jon knew as much from their recent visit.

Jon licked his lips and seized another tiny sandwich. The sooner he waded through the artisan bread, the sooner he'd taste the heaven of fruit-laden mini scones, rich preserves, and clotted cream. The sinful selection of petit fours and dainty French patisseries was only minutes away.

Wendy chuckled at Jon's antics. 'Put your eyes and tongue back in, Windy. You're like a pig at a trough.'

'Do you blame me? Afternoon tea on this scale'd cost a hundred quid a pop at The Ritz.' Jon took a sip of Earl Grey from his delicate teacup, popped the tiny bite into his mouth, and chewed.

'And the rest if one's also quaffing the best champagne and guzzling truffles,' Wendy scoffed in her best plummy accent.

Jon grabbed another nibble.

'Bet that bread you're stuffing was baked and delivered this morning. Nothing but the freshest, finest fare for the upper crust family.'

'See what you did there, Darling.'

'By appointment to Lord Biggin-Smythe.'

'Yes, Icky Dickie now holds that lordy title and don't you forget it.'

'Can't take him seriously, but who cares? You crack me up, Windy. Full of disdain for the gentry, but the minute they lay on a fancy spread, you go weak at the knees.'

'Clichés, Darling. Clichés.' Jon crammed in another bite.

'Now don't go dribbling down that lovely white shirt. It'll be a devil to clean. I must admit, this is quality, although crustless cucumber nosh isn't my teatime treat. I have no fear you'll polish off the lot.'

'You know me too well.'

'Just leave me a scone and the trimmings, please. See Milady's cracking her clogs to get here on time.'

'So much for joining us shortly.'

'Question. How long *is* shortly? Given the speed the housekeeper ushered us in, I thought she was ready to greet us. Thirty minutes and still no sign. As punctual as you, my windy friend. At least afternoon tea was all laid out, and you were straight in, pillaging its fiddly delights.'

'I'm not complaining. Yummy free food at the big house. It's a triumph for me either way.'

'Yes, but don't forget our mission. We're here to sleuth, not gorge.'

'I know, but I've trussed myself up like a chicken in these clothes, so I intend to enjoy every morsel and every drop. Hate wearing suits and ties. Always feel hot and bothered. You reckon all this malarkey is custom for the rich, or is Lady Lu desperate to impress?'

''Tis plain. Milord snuffs it and becomes big news. Enter Lady Lucinda Biggin-Smythe. Even in her darkest hour, her modus operandi to bleed the situation for maximum personal gain is king. Anything to upstage Milord Seymour. In the morgue or his coffin.'

'You think so?'

'Know so. The media's sniffing around. Lucinda wants her day, and her say. Who gets her ear? Those who listen, of course. Especially anyone showing her in a good light. Hence the lavish tea. Watch, listen, and learn. I've seen it all before. The merry widow's inching her way to the palm of my hand. Right where I want her. She isn't making enough noise yet. I want her singing some more.'

'If Annie Clegg's anything to go by, she will.'

'Different animal.'

'Both have big mouths.'

'But not bigger egos. Only milady owns that title.'

'Time for a scone. Want yours?'

'You go first, but leave me a smidgen, won't you?'

'Nope.' Jon chuckled, heaping the finest cherry jam and clotted cream onto a teeny fruit scone. The sweet treat disappeared in one munch. Jon loaded up another,

'I better hurry before you scoff the lot. Here's Marie.'

'Hello. Is everything to your satisfaction?'

'Lovely,' Jon mumbled, mouth brimming with pistachio macaron. He'd hit the patisserie, and how.

'Will her ladyship be much longer?' Wendy said.

'She's asked me to apologise for the delay.'

'What *is* the delay?'

'Funeral matters. All very upsetting.' Marie gave an embarrassed smile and left.

'Probably takes an hour to paint her nails,' Jon said, looking forlornly at the empty cake stands. He licked his forefinger to mop up rogue crumbs.

'Doubt she paints them. It's likely the pampered princess has an entourage of beauty therapists. Tucks, implants, and liposuction probably favour high in her regime. Bet a couple of plastic surgeons share her boudoir, armed with a vac to suck out any excess flesh to inject elsewhere. Lips. Boobs. Forehead. Not that there'll be much to hoover up. Milady's the ultimate plastic princess. Image means everything. Her key to the world.'

Wendy's words were barely out when Lucinda hurtled in, flushed and reeking of musky perfume.

'Sorry to keep you. Estate business and appointments to arrange. Anyway, here I am, ready to go.' Lucinda flicked back the enormous golden curls whipping around her face.

Wendy was quick to spot behaviour that contradicted the reckless, almost brash manner of yesterday. Lucinda appeared distracted. Her clothes, out of character. What was that hideous pink thing flapping around her body? Disguised as a dress, neither shape nor chic. Something she'd flung on in a hurry, along with white, open-toed, flat sandals, and a silly grin. At least the dress was knee-length and roomy and her sandals weren't high-rise heels on a bling binge. Convinced she'd dressed and made herself up in haste, Wendy exchanged a knowing look with Jon.

'A pleasure to see you again. Can't wait to finish our piece. Did I mention the magazine already has a huge distribution? My article will raise its profile and its readers. You'll be a celebrity. The fame you'll attract will be scandalous.'

'You did tell me, but how super marvellous to hear it again. How was afternoon tea?'

'The empty stands and teapot speak for themselves. Only a drop of coffee left.'

'Jolly good. I've ordered refills. I'll sit here beside you, and we can continue.' Lucinda eased beside Wendy and smoothed down her hair.

Jon guessed she was in toady mode to make a good impression, but Wendy suspected something, or rather someone else, was behind the buoyant mood.

'You're cheerful today, Lu. Don't mind me calling you Lu, do you? The first time we spoke, I sensed a meeting of minds. An unquestionable togetherness. That fitting feeling of being in sync.'

'Marvellous. You're a friend and all's well with the world.'

'Not that well, surely? Your husband's flat out on a cold slab while the police procrastinate. Any clue when they'll release his body for the funeral?'

'No. I understand they're still probing. Of course, I'm sad at Seymour's loss, but life goes on. How can I crumble when the family needs me?'

'I see. Before starting, I have a proposal for you. A photoshoot. Pictures of the house. The grounds. And you, of course.'

'How exciting! Me first.'

'Splendid. Come along, Jon. Take that pout off your face. No more sweet treats. Honestly, Lu, can't get the staff these days.'

Jon pulled out his mobile phone. 'I'm ready.'

'Is that it? I was expecting an expensive camera and tripod. And one of those enormous umbrellas. What about a wind machine? I thought all glamour photographers used one. I hope you know what you're doing, Mr Wind.'

'You said it, Lu. Jon *is* the wind machine.' Wendy's giggles bounced around the room.

'I'm not a glamour photographer, but I know what I'm doing. Everything's digital these days,' Jon mumbled. Playing stooge to Wendy's japes was hard work when he wanted to wring Lucinda's neck, but he must stick to the brief. The widow must talk.

'No-no, Jon. The equipment's in the boot, remember? Sorry to disappoint, but no wind machine, Lu. Don't worry. There's a fair breeze today. That will help the effect. No doubt your pictures will stun, regardless.'

'I'm so excited! Ah, the refills.'

Marie set the pots down on the table and accepted Jon and Wendy's thanks. No gratitude from Lucinda. Only a stiff nod to dismiss the housekeeper.

'Coffee, Jon?' Wendy asked, tipping a wink at her snooping friend.

'I'll nip to the car first. Hopefully, the breeze won't be too strong. Can do without nasty country niffs. There's only so much crap a man can take in one day.'

28

Rich History

'While we're waiting, I'll let you into a little secret, Lu. Being a history buff and writer means I get to do a stack of research. I know lots about Biggin Hall and the family.'

'How interesting. You're such a mine of information, Wendy, but you won't know as much as me.'

'Never. I do know the hall is centuries old and built by the first Lord Bigginsworth. At some point, the family name changed to Biggin. One lord got entangled with a Smythe. A much younger woman. A wallflower, Lu. Much like yourself. It's said her demands for honour resulted in the birth of the Biggin-Smythe surname. Can't recall the exact date when all this happened, but you'll know, of course. How many generations back?'

'Hundreds of years.'

'Impressive. I love how you just pluck the date from the air in a whisker. I believe the hall offers guided tours. Do you conduct them?'

'Heavens, no. We have paid staff to do all that.'

Jon slipped back into the dining room and helped himself to a coffee. Lucinda didn't notice, so enamoured was she faking knowledge of the Biggin-Smythe lineage. Jon decided having a gammy ear wasn't so bad after all. A man could only hack so much squeaking in a day.

'Who is that, Lu?' Wendy pointed to an immense portrait covering a section of the wall.

'That is the second Lord Bigginsworth, the first of Seymour's ancestors born here. He was a major influence.

The one who wanted to change the family name. He put everything in motion, but the name Biggin didn't come about until his son, the third Lord Bigginsworth, fulfilled his father's wish. Did you know the hall got raided many times?'

'I did. All because of the family's religion.'

'Catholic then?' Jon said.

'No, Jon. Martian,' Wendy jested.

'For its sins.' Lady Biggin-Smythe giggled.

'Priest holes?' Jon asked, animated.

'Somewhere. Probably filled in years ago. Seymour told me the family had to hide the second Lord Bigginsworth once or twice.'

'How old was he?' Wendy asked.

'Just an infant.'

'How did they keep him quiet?'

'Thick walls. Secret places. Luckily, the family was gaining power. Soon, nobody would touch them. It showed over the years. The second lord was a tyrant when he grew up. They all were.'

'Probably too much gin in their milk. Seems you have little time for the house history?'

'Depends on the topic, Wendy.'

Jon couldn't resist. 'So, remind me. Why did you marry Lord Biggin-Smythe, *multi-millionaire*?'

'Ah, here's my stepson. Good afternoon to you, Richard.'

Lucinda was polite, but Wendy detected tension.

'Good afternoon.' Dickie was equally polite, but the edge was more apparent.

'Richard, meet Wendy May. She's writing a piece about me for a top magazine. Huge dis—'

'And has she told you why she married my father?'

'I asked her why,' Jon said. 'She ignored me.'

Richard growled at Jon. 'You again. I'll be charging rent soon.'

'Richard, it's clear you haven't had your afternoon cognac. Perhaps you should retire to the crystal room for a drop,' Lucinda urged.

'It's whisky, actually, and one cannot retire when one has work to do.' Dickie stormed off.

Wendy had a feeling he wanted to be candid and was struggling to remain polite. 'The British stiff upper lip. He's drowning in it, Lu.'

'Quite. That's Richard for you. Always full of happiness and love.'

'Would it be fair to say there's agitation between you?'

'Let's just say we're not in harmony. Richard's a little boy pining for mummy.'

'Is his mother still in the picture?'

'As far as I'm aware. Speaking of pictures, where's your equipment, Mr Wind? I don't have all day to wait for you.'

'Bit of a problem there. Didn't put the tripod in the boot.'

Lucinda's glare sliced Jon in two. 'The camera and umbrella will have to do.'

'No umbrella either.'

'And the camera?'

'Pass.'

'Jon, you are an idiot. Sorry, Lu, but the photoshoot's doomed.'

'But what about my fans? You told me the readers wanted an exclusive. A story isn't a story without pretty pictures.'

'You could take a few selfies.'

'Shut up, Jon. What did I say earlier, milady? Can't get the staff. We can reschedule, but I have a deadline for this piece, and my diary's frantic for the next couple of months.'

'Please, do something. I can't let millions of readers down.'

Wendy wanted to slap Lucinda's delusional face, but performing for the sulky puss was her only option. 'Don't worry. You're in expert hands. I'm owed a few favours and will do my utmost to avoid any disappointment. I'll look to shift things around.'

'Wonderful, and if you do, I'll give a guided tour. The personal touch, no staff. That alone is worth a lot of shuffling on your part.'

'I'm honoured. I'm hoping to postpone a big meeting tomorrow,' Wendy lied, itching to shuffle milady into the nearest septic tank. 'We could do the shoot if you're free. Arrive in the morning, around nine, and snap as many *pretty pictures* as you can muster.'

'Yes, I'm free!' Lucinda squealed, jumping up and down.

Wendy turned away from the intense self-absorption. From the scary pink sack billowing around Lucinda's body. A powerful gust, and she'd take off. *Mercy me. This child was hard work.* 'How long will the tour take?'

'An hour. I can't offer longer. I'm a busy lady.'

'It's a date. See you tomorrow. Come along, Jon.' Wendy turned to leave, then doubled back. 'Out of interest, does Richard get on with his real mother?'

'Yes. Better than he ever did with his father.'

29

Say Cheese!

The big house had never seen such a dazzling commotion, so said Lady Biggin-Smythe. And she was the essence of it all. The stuff dreams were made of. In bespoke designs and exclusive fabrics, skyscraper stilettos and jewels galore, Lucinda posed and preened. Standing. Sitting. Pouting. Prancing. Wherever the lens pointed, she was at its end.

'I'm loving this, Wendy,' she gurgled, the painted face adopting an alluring, faraway look. The very expression that likely enchanted milord as his self-obsessed intended sharpened her claws and sank them in. 'Your camera's wonderful. And all the little extras too. Simply marvellous.'

'So it should be,' Jon huffed. 'Had to go to—'

'A little moodier, Lu,' Wendy cut in. 'Give your fans what they want. The grieving widow. The mournful, lonely lady, nursing a broken heart.'

Lucinda didn't need to know about Wendy and Jon's escapades yesterday evening. How they'd dashed to buy equipment to satisfy an ego. Wendy had dipped into her savings for camera, tripod, and two umbrellas. She'd drawn the line at a wind machine. She could always kidnap Annie Clegg. Enough wind there to power the UK. No! Not the slobbering she-devil. A nasty blot on the landscape.

Another outfit change gave Jon time to photograph the house and grounds from outside. He'd already shot many rooms indoors, with and without the lady of the manor.

For this round of cheese, Lucinda swaggered into the crystal room, dressed in a baby blue number dotted in little white daisies. Matching sandals hugged her feet.

'I hope you're getting lots of shots, Mr Wind.'

'*Windup*, and yes, I am.'

'Windup. Gosh, what a funny name,' Lucinda tittered.

'So I've been told. I'm used to it.'

'Could never get used to that frightful name. Wendy, we'll break for lunch soon. You can finish your interview while he takes pictures of the house, then I'll give you a personal tour of the grounds.'

'Sounds good to me. Jon?'

'What's for lunch?'

'Wait and see,' Lucinda said.

'By the way, think your butler photobombed a couple of shots,' Jon snorted.

'What! That will never do. I'll have words with him.'

'Don't worry, Lu. We edit out any nasty bits, and that includes bellyaching butlers called Briggs. Airbrushing's a wonderful thing. Not that it's needed where you're concerned. You're a camera's dream.'

'Always have been. Ah, a little refreshment. Set the drinks down, Marie, then go. There's nothing for you here. Get ready with your camera, Mr Wind. I'm in a model mood.'

Jon prepared for another round of shots, fuming at Lucinda's sad attempt at humour. He could stomach no more. If she was in a model mood, his mood was murderous. He had a vision of landing her with an artisan baguette and cheering on the Sowers as they carted her off to join the old boy. Two puffed-up pompositors. May they rot in peace.

After two hours of a vain-fuelled photoshoot and enough cheese to cover the Moon, Jon and Wendy were ready for the funny farm. Lucinda headed to her luxury suite of rooms to shower and change. Marie escorted the house guests to sit down for lunch. On the menu, an exquisite mushroom and tarragon soup starter. Then succulent roasted vegetable salad served with crusty petit pains and creamy Cornish butter. Tea, coffee, filtered water, and freshly squeezed orange juice accompanied the meal. Butler Briggs did the silver service honours. He even cracked a smile. Marie bustled here and there. Keeping house as a housekeeper should.

The meal was scrumptious, the room air-conditioned, but, after the morning's arduous task, Jon and Wendy craved a cool shower and a change of clothes. Wendy had worn a flowing, colourful boho dress and strappy kitten-heeled sandals but longed to climb into combats, t-shirt, and a pair of comfy trainers. She also wanted to swap an enormous sunhat for a humble baseball cap. She couldn't believe she'd worn another dress. Wearing two in as many days wasn't done. Even in her legal years, she'd favoured trousers. Acceptable in the office. Frowned upon in court.

Jon was in khaki cargo pants, Eye of Horus t-shirt, and olive hiking boots. Sweating buckets and ready to kill, he needed to lie down in a darkened room. Briggs stood at the door on guard. Jon didn't care for his grumpy visage.

'She's doing my head in,' Jon muttered to Wendy. 'As you know, the Eye of Horus is an Egyptian concept and symbol. Represents well-being, healing, and protection. That's why I put this top on. To save me from that snooty Lu Brush. She treats me like a servant, and if she calls me Mr Wind once more, I *will* blow. Like a tornado.'

'Lu Brush!' Wendy went off in a fit of giggles. 'Not much longer. The interview. The tour. Then off we go. Get a few more snaps while she's in the chair. Unless you want to push off soon and I'll come back another day. Alone. Wouldn't blame you.'

'You're all right. Let's do it all today.'

'Good call. Don't fancy another helping of conceited crowing. That woman's voice brings on convulsions.'

'Finding the going tough?'

'With the helium queen. Always.'

'What are you hoping to get from the interview?'

'More like what I'm going to give.'

'Give? I'm not with you.'

'Rope. Enough for milady to hang herself.'

30

Model Subject

Never off-the-peg, nor always a fashionista, one thing was plain. Lady Lucinda Biggin-Smythe loved dressing up. Jon and Wendy had lived and breathed six outfit changes and would soon choke on the seventh. Who knew how many frightful frocks lurked with intent in Lu's whopping walk-in wardrobes? She was obvious ad nauseum. The only constant was change.

In a formal, grey pin-striped suit, Lucinda sashayed into the glass room, hair tamed, and whirled into a chignon. By her standards, the shoes were sensible to complement the suit. The only visible jewellery, dainty sapphire earrings. There was no overpowering scent. No make-up trowelled on her smooth face. She had Marie pour oolong tea, serve Jon and Wendy organic coffee, then perched on an impressive, winged chair. The glass room wore its objets d'art well. Slightly smaller than the crystal room, but as opulent, there was little contrast between the two. The same don't-touch vibe. Identical furniture, shapes, and textures. Plush carpet, deep enough to lose your feet in. The colour scheme was uniform. The decor parallel, right down to the whopping family portraits and prissy, petite coffee cups Jon and Wendy deemed pointless. Jon was already on his fourth, but still hadn't wet his whistle.

'I thought this room the ideal place for the interview,' Lucinda said. 'Remember, I told you this was Seymour's favourite drawing room? He housed the rest of his wonderful collection here. How I miss him.'

'Course you do,' Wendy fibbed, and so the interview started.

Still camera high, with the promise of another shoot when Jon and Wendy could accommodate, Lucinda wasted no time in painting herself as a victim. Born into wealth. Well-educated and wanting for nothing, her father's bankruptcy left the family Fanshaw destitute. 'It was beastly having to move from a mansion to a cottage.'

'Downsizing. To how many bedrooms?'

'Five.'

'From how many?'

'Twelve. Can you imagine the terrible time I had?'

'Simply dreadful, I'm sure,' Wendy yawned, seeing only an entitled whiner. Never grateful. Always wanting more. A woman as greedy as her late husband, and just as lifeless.

Lucinda's eternal grumbles reminded Wendy of Annie Clegg's bellyaching. Forever finding fault. She spent half her time griping about Seymour, but, with begrudged charm and much patience, Wendy encouraged her to open up about all areas of her life. Despite the odd digression, Lu eventually got to her nuptials.

'I don't mind admitting I married for convenience, status, and money. Anything but love. I simply couldn't give up the lifestyle I was born into. When Daddy went bankrupt, going without for months was beastly. It traumatised me. Luxury is everything, and I wanted that on a bigger scale. What is love, anyway?'

'I agree. That silly little thing called love ranks a poor second to untold riches and money-money-money.'

'It was clear Seymour needed a strong woman in his life. You must take pity on certain men. The needy types. Seymour had the money, but I was his strength. Of course, I wanted his wealth. A title. His devotion. And I wanted fun, but not with an old man who only cared about the family name and being a sir and lord.'

'Fancy talking like that about the old boy.' Once again, Jon was behind the lens, snapping pictures. Until now, he hadn't spoken, but couldn't resist a dig at Seymour. Or his self-obsessed widow.

'Off you go to take a few shots of the house, Jon. You don't need to know the intricacies of Lu's indiscretion. Understandable, of course. Who wants to be with a wizened old fuddy duddy insisting on elitism and preserving time-honoured traditions? Out with the old wrinkly.'

Wendy knew from Jon's stride he was thankful for liberation. Poor soul must be pining for home, his beloved computer, and a decent mug of coffee. With gentle prodding, she delved further into Lu's infidelities. 'You had many affairs?'

'Yes. Strictly off the record, of course. A beautiful young woman must have outlets, Wendy.'

'Who and what were your outlets?' Wendy coaxed, hoping for an admission of Lu's dalliance with Tom.

Lucinda wouldn't yield. Instead, she rambled on. Extolling her virtues. Pity-partying about the injustice of how much she'd suffered when daddy disgraced the family. 'Now that Seymour's gone, I'm still suffering,' she snivelled.

Wendy was heading off to nodland when the name King slapped her in the face. She shifted in her seat, arched her back, then drenched her dry mouth with water. Next, a long swig of coffee. 'Wasn't King a former business partner of Seymour?'

'How did you know that?' Lucinda's eyes and tone held suspicion.

'You mentioned him yesterday,' Wendy lied.

Lucinda laughed. 'Of course, how silly of me. Nasty fellow. Had this idea for a chain of gastropubs, starting with the Noose and Gibbet. There was another deal in the air, too. With a new company to supply quality bread to all pubs. King wanted Seymour to front both deals and put up all the cash.' She held her teacup, crooked little finger poised mid-air.

Wendy shushed a groan. That old myth of extending the pinky to appear elegant and regal smacked of snobbery. *One should avoid, Lucinda. It's pretentious.* 'What did Seymour think of King and his proposal?'

'Enthusiastic, at first. He usually was with any new face or project, but something put him off. He didn't share everything with me, you know. I was just his wife.'

'I believe they had an argument over the gibbet cage. Your husband hated it, but King wanted it to stay. Local rumour.'

'Yes, and the rumour's true about the fallout. Monty wanted every pub to have a theme, but Seymour wasn't keen.'

'Is that why Seymour withdrew his interest?' Wendy hit on Lu's use of King's first name.

'There may have been other reasons, but like I said, I'm only his wife.'

'I think there's something you're not telling me, Lucinda. Did you and Mr King—'

'All right, you win. Seymour's gone, so what harm can it do? I had a brief fling with Monty. Now there's a man who knows how to treat a lady.'

'Not such a nasty fellow after all, then? What happened? Did Seymour find out?'

'Yes. He was livid. How dare anybody mow on his lawn, never mind a prospective business partner, or however he put it.'

'What about Monty?'

Lucinda looked solemn. 'He called it off. I suppose it was my fault. If Seymour hadn't found out, he and Monty would've been business partners and Seymour would still be alive.'

'Are you implying King killed your husband?'

'After Seymour called the whole thing off, King tried to salvage the deal. I heard him shout, "Surely, you won't let some idiot cloud your judgment." To think I was only an object to him. Seymour was unmoved. The damage was done. I remember King roaring something like, "You'll regret this, you old miser. Revenge is mine." That's where the nasty fellow bit comes in. The threat in his voice. I genuinely believed he would do something bad to Seymour. And what he said about me. The audacity.' Lucinda dabbed at sobbing eyes with a lace handkerchief, voice breaking.

The tearful performance didn't dupe Wendy. During her legal years, she'd waded through oceans of insincere sorrow. This was one of those occasions where the crocodile protesteth too much.

'Do you know where King is now?'

'Last I know, he lives in Berkshire, has an office in London, and does his cookery classes all over.'

'Do you know where his home and office are?'

'No, we always met up here or in hotels. Anyway, I think it's time to show you the house and grounds. The air in some of these rooms gets a little stale. Nothing like natural freshness to clear the senses.'

'I'm looking forward to the tour. Jon is too. I'll nip out and tell him.'

Wendy caught up with Jon outside. 'Ready for a tour of the house and grounds?'

'Indeedy. How did the interview go?'

'She didn't mention Tom, but the King revelations were a bonus. I'll fill you in later with all the grubby gossip.'

'How did you get her to talk?'

'Easy. With a woman as obvious as Lucinda, it only takes a camera.'

31

Malice in Wonderland

B ack inside the manor, a squabble at the far end of the long hallway caught Jon and Wendy's attention. Minutes later, decked out in obligatory tweed, Dickie charged up and ran into Jon.

'Are you here again? First a wrangle with that beastly woman, then a run-in with the irritating oik. What a bind. Get out of my way.' Dickie pushed past Jon, scowled at Wendy, and headed to the door.

'What's eating that fool?' Wendy hissed.

'This way,' Lucinda gestured.

Jon and Wendy hurried down the corridor and caught up with stony-faced Lucinda in an expansive room draped in landscapes, seascapes, portraits, and tapestries. More exquisite René Lalique glass adorned heavy pieces of priceless furniture, all resting on a highly polished floor.

'This is the great hall,' Lucinda boasted. 'Spectacular, yes? More finery in here.'

'More armour too,' Jon said. 'This place is crammed with the stuff.'

'You and Dickie were having words, Lu. Is everything all right?' The disagreement didn't bother Wendy, but what caused it could be helpful to Windy & Darling's cause.

'Just Richard being Richard. Come, let's change the subject. Talking about that bore makes frightfully dull conversation. Time to see the grounds.'

'What about upstairs? Bet it's amazing up there,' said Jon.

'Off limits, I'm afraid. Some things are sacred. Just the outside today. It's better that way.' Lucinda ushered the couple to the front door, then addressed Jon as she would a lapdog. 'Be a good boy and open the door.'

'Do as you're told now, Jon,' Wendy aped, squeezing his hand, and stemming the urge to tear down milady's vile humiliation.

Jon, poor soul, was torn between staying, going, or turning to killing. And not softly. Wendy knew his sulky face veiled bubbling anger. He opened the door, muttering disapproval.

'There's a lot to see, so we must be quick. No more than an hour. I have an urgent meeting later and can't be late. One moment.' Lucinda barked into her phone.

Minutes later, a young man arrived in a golf buggy. He looked as happy to be here as Jon. Lucinda sat upfront, Wendy and Jon scrambled in the back. The vehicle sped off, navigating a series of criss-crossing paths winding through the extensive grounds.

'This is impressive,' Wendy called, relieved that driver Sam had slowed down to allow an appreciation of the estate's natural beauty.

'Centuries of history here,' Lucinda said.

'The gardens are stunning, and I love that oak. Must be ancient.'

'We have Gordon and his team to thank. Sam's one of the team. All keeping the land in marvellous condition. The oak's over five-hundred-years-old. Right, Sam?'

'Yes, my lady,' Sam grunted.

Apart from the occasional comment from Lucinda, the tour continued in silence, until she shrieked, 'Stop! We'll get out here.' Lucinda gestured to Jon and Wendy to view the magnificence of the walled garden. 'The pièce de résistance. Isn't it beautiful?' Lucinda gushed.

'Breathtaking,' Wendy said, and she meant it. A horticulturist's dream. Precise patterns. Plants and flowers in meticulous symmetry. Even a maze.

'Back in the nineteenth century, Seymour's great-great-grandfather installed heating to protect his collection of exotic plants. It was rather basic, but did the job. Exotics need warmth, you know.'

Jon had to rain on Lucinda's droning screech. 'Well, exotics do. The word sort of gives it away. You say the heating was basic, but, for its day, a cutting-edge system. The eighteen hundreds. A fascinating time for invention and innovation and—'

'Back to the buggy.'

Jon didn't bother with a comeback. Lu Brush wouldn't appreciate his last word.

'Carry on, Sam. Slowly does it.'

Thankfully, Jon couldn't hear properly when the buggy was in motion. He welcomed anything to drown out that terror. As they passed the walled garden and slowed, Wendy spotted Dickie and two other men near a garage. Once again, Dickie was shouting, and waving his arms at a man in working clothes. A younger man, also wearing tweed, ushered the worker away but continued the exchange.

'Bet you can hear them in London,' Jon said.

'Richard's such an embarrassment. I do wish he was more like Royce.'

'That's Royce?' Wendy said.

'Yes. The youngest child, but more level-headed and patient than Richard. Shame he's like the others, too. Loyal to his real mum.'

'That's how he rolls,' Jon quipped. 'Sorry. Couldn't resist.'

'Behave, Jon. Her ladyship doesn't share your silly sense of humour. Any more howlers like that and I'll disown you. If you must tell jokes, get some new material.' She winked at Jon and gave a sly smile. 'Any thoughts on what the boys were bickering about, Lu?'

'Couldn't say, but there's a lot of that going on lately.'

'How did Royce take his daddy's death?'

'Goodness knows. He doesn't talk to me. Speed up, Sam. Can't be late for my appointment.'

Sam reached the big house, where Antonia Biggin-Smythe, dressed in jeans, tee, and trainers, was saying goodbye to someone on the phone. She carried a croquet mallet and scowled when she saw the buggy. Lucinda made a face, giving Jon and Wendy the impression of strained relations.

'Antonia. What are you doing with that?' Lucinda's greeting was curt.

The girl equalled, if not bettered, her stepmother's reception. 'What does one usually do with a croquet mallet? Two things come to mind. Smash it over someone's head or play a game of croquet. What will it be?'

'Don't be funny.'

Antonia ignored the reply. 'Wendy!'

'Hello. You're looking well. I've been on such an adventure. 'Tis like I slipped down a rabbit hole into wonderland's madness. My purple topper would've been the perfect foil, after all. Do flamingos or hedgehogs lurk? Are playing cards ready to double up as soldiers and croquet hoops? Where's the king?'

'The king is dead. Long live the king.'

'And the rest?'

'Nothing like that. Not quite the adventure. The Queen of Hearts is here, and we all know what she was about.'

'You know each other?' Lucinda couldn't hide her confusion.

'What are you doing here, Wendy?' Antonia stole the conversation.

'Interviewing me for an exclusive magazine spread,' Lucinda said.

'You mean Daddy's story. You've wasted no time in filling the void.'

Jon couldn't stop himself. 'Bet you wouldn't jump in his grave so soon.'

'Off with your head, Mr Windup,' Wendy joked. 'Comments like that are treasonous. Far worse than painting the roses red.'

Lucinda glared at Jon, then turned on Antonia, her tone venomous. 'And you were always Daddy's little girl. Pity he didn't know how you despised being a Biggin-Smythe and a rebel at that. He saw no wrong in you, but had he known what you were up to, he would've cut your allowance and all privileges. If you wish to point blame, I can do the same. I know what you're doing. You should be ashamed.'

Wendy and Jon looked at each other. What was all this? A daily prescription of family squabbles. Another surety with the Biggin-Smythe household. Lots of history and many secrets.

Antonia didn't rise to Lucinda's baiting. 'How are you, Wendy?'

'Good, thanks. Lu kindly treated me and Jon to afternoon tea yesterday. Today it's a photoshoot, lunch, and a personal tour of the grounds.'

'No surprise. She's desperate to make an impression. Anything for fame and fortune.'

'And frippery,' Wendy added, 'don't be frugal with frippery.'

'Sorry, I can't stay to listen to this nonsense. I have an appointment with my solicitor to discuss probate matters. I'm sure he'll give good news. Like this house is now mine, so you'd better hold your tongue, young lady.' Dressing Antonia down gave smug Lucinda a buzz. She smiled and turned to Wendy. 'If you need anything else, please let me know. Must change.'

Wendy watched her scurry away. 'Tell me, Antonia, have you always loved the queen of hearts?'

'Always.'

'I'm paying lip service to her put downs and insults, of course. And that screech she calls eloquent. It's destroying me. And Jon.'

'If Lady Lu inherits this place, what about you and the others, Antonia?' Jon said.

'She thinks she'll own this place outright, but she's in for a shock. Daddy made provision for us all. That means our beautiful friendship will remain intact.'

'Sure it will,' Wendy grinned. 'Must be national family quarrel day. We passed Richard and Royce having a to-do earlier. Richard appeared to be arguing with a staff member first.'

'No surprise there. He's been uptight for a while, even before Daddy's death. Like a child who's broken his favourite toy.'

Jon recalled the business proposal naming Richard as a sleeping partner. No doubt the heir apparent was bitter. Or disappointed, it hadn't come to fruition.

Lucinda reappeared in cream linen trousers, black turtleneck jumper, and a camel-coloured jacket. Her eighth clothes change of the day. Appropriate for high society. No labels. No logos. Sensible shoes again, the only visible bling, stylish diamond earrings. Wendy assumed diamonds. Milady Lu wasn't the rhinestone type. Nasty imitations would not do. Lucinda didn't speak, simply made her way to her gleaming red sports car and whizzed past, jarring Jon from his reflection.

'Wow, she's in a hurry.'

'Where there's a will, there's a relative,' said Wendy.

'George is back from London,' Antonia said. 'He's calling me over. Won't be long.'

171

'Second eldest son, and not a bad egg, I've heard,' Wendy said.

Antonia returned, wearing a puzzled look. 'That's odd.'

'What is?' Wendy said.

'George says he saw Lucinda turning right towards Tor.'

'So?'

'If she's going to see the solicitor, that's the wrong way. He's in Treeton. She should've turned left.'

'Maybe she had to go to the village first,' said Jon.

'When she's in a hurry with no time for detours?' Antonia stressed. 'I'll tell you something, but keep it quiet. I've been seeing someone from the village and was there a few days ago.'

'Who's the lucky guy?' Wendy said.

'His name's Duncan. He's lovely. Anyway, I was leaving his house when I saw Lucinda. The last person I want to see ever. If she saw me and Dunc together, I'd never hear the end of it. *The daughter of Lord Biggin-Smythe with a commoner*. She's not fussed, of course, but we don't get on as you know, so she'd love to make trouble. Anyway, I hid behind a bush before she saw me.'

'I suspect she's seen you and Dunc. The remark she made about knowing what you were about. What was she doing near his house?' asked Wendy.

'Making a big effort to be sneaky. She kept looking over her shoulder, even parked down the road. At the time, I thought nothing of it. More concerned about her not seeing me. She's been acting strange. Even before Daddy's death.'

'Do you know where she was going?'

'Maybe to her cottage. Daddy bought it while he was still married to Mummy. Lucinda thinks it's all a big secret. How dumb.'

'A cottage deep in the woods. That's a turnup for us, Windy,' Wendy said.

'I saw a man there once. Don't know who he is or what she's up to.' Antonia shrugged.

Wendy ran her hand down her face. 'No guarantee, but I have a pretty good idea.'

32

If You Go Down to the Woods Today

'Slow down, Windy. We're hugging the wood. Feels like I'm in a bleeding psychedelic tree tunnel. Everything's spinning.'

'Don't want to lose her.'

'If Antonia's right, we know where Lu's going. And we have directions. Hold back. She mustn't spot us. Meh. I feel ill.'

Jon eased off the accelerator. Riding shotgun on Treetonshire's winding country roads needed cast iron guts, and Wendy hadn't brought a sick sack. Jon snaked up a gentle gradient. A woodland glade, breaking the country drive through farm fields and tall hedges.

Antonia had told Jon and Wendy all about Lucinda's secret cottage. A gift from Lord Biggin-Smythe when he started doing the old sneaky with his new lover. No one was supposed to know, but Antonia had eavesdropped on many private conversations. Stealth was her strong point. Easy when you're the only girl and the invisible child.

'The old boy bought the place to have a secret love nest away from his wife. Dirty old dog.'

'And you, kamikaze kid. Watch the blasted trees!'

When Jon knew he was beaten, saying nothing was wise. Having the last word routine would only infuriate. Best apologise and say no more. The flash of a vehicle slowed him down.

'Her car, I think.'

'Caution.'

Jon crawled up a small hill and clocked Lucinda's shiny red toy, minus the lady. Further down the road was a gap in the hedge and a wooden gate. A signpost showed a public footpath.

'She couldn't have been there long. Must've taken the footpath,' Jon said. He slammed on the brake, then steered the car into the entrance to Figgis's Farm.

'Mercy me. 'Tis a miracle you're let loose on the roads. Patience, Albie. Won't be long. Scrub down your finest slab and get ready to carve.'

'Oops. Country roads.'

'When alone, you can drive as you please, but a little thought for your passenger wouldn't go amiss.'

Jon halted the car on a verge. He looked sheepish.

'Are we okay parking here, Windy?'

'We won't be long. If anyone has a go, you can make up one of your credible stories. After all, you're a writer.'

The friends headed back to the public footpath.

'Any sign of milady?'

'No.'

'Where does this path lead?'

'Back to Tor, passing Summerbee's Farm and Acorn Cottages on the way. Don't quote me, though. I haven't walked the full trail.' Jon opened the gate.

'Antonia says the house's near here.'

'Pretty close to Ross Pengelly's place, then.'

'Yes. The devil only knows what she sees in him. Kept quiet when she talked of some guy called Duncan. Had an inkling it was Pengelly all along. Poor old Emily.'

'Don't get me started.'

'Wonder why Lu's parked on the road. That's suspicious in itself.'

'Doesn't want anyone to see her car outside the house? Must have something to hide.'

The couple followed the footpath, skirting the edge of a wheatfield and a thicket of trees encircling the field. There was still no sign of Lucinda.

'She had quite a head start,' said Jon.

'She could've turned off. Keep your eyes peeled for any sidetracks.'

Jon scanned the path and the trees ahead, but there were no gaps. As they neared the corner of the field, the trail disappeared deep into the wood.

'We go through the wood, but I think there's another field on the other side,' said Jon. 'Isn't nature beautiful? Yesterday we had a tea party. Now we're at a tree party. There's oak, beech, and sycamore, all having fun, and here comes gatecrasher, holly.'

'Loving your quirky imagination.'

'Hope I don't rip this t-shirt. It's one of my best.'

'Didn't protect you from milady's toxic tongue.'

'I'll forgive the eye. This is beautiful. The perfect place to walk on a hot summer's day. Nothing better than a natural leafy canopy to keep you cool.'

''Tis so. Trees. Extraordinary plants. Nourishing. Diverse. Beautiful homes for wildlife. And the only place Annie Clegg's hair makes sense. *Look at that.* Some idiot's hung a poo bag on that baby oak. What's with some dog owners? Why swing it when you should pick it up and bin it?'

Jon shook his head. 'Never mind, let sleeping dogs lie. This is more let non-sleeping dogs' poop lie. Why bother bagging it up if you intend to hang it on a tree, or dump at the side of the path? Never fathomed that out.'

'Me neither, but there could be a method to the madness. Suppose there's less chance of someone treading in it. I love dogs and they're only doing what comes naturally. Most dog owners are responsible, but there's always one. Or more. Even with bins around, it's the old decorate the tree madness. Hello, what's this?'

Jon and Wendy cleared the dense woodland. On their right, sheep and horses grazed on a divided field, but the wooden fence and big gate commanded Wendy's attention.

'Wonder where that leads?' Jon said.

Wendy scanned the horizon. 'I'm back in Wonderland again, but this could be it. The rear entrance to Lu's secret nest.'

'Shall we check it out?'

'To the gate, my fearless friend.'

'Drat. It's padlocked.'

'Better do your magic. Don't call your little pouch *drat pack* for nothing.'

Jon fished for a hairpin in his little bag of magic to work on the lock. Seconds later, it sprang and slipped open. He unbolted the gate. 'Eureka,' he whispered.

'Don't let anyone say you're completely useless.'

'As if.' Jon held open the gate. 'You know this technically constitutes breaking an entry.'

'Oh, shush. The merry widow could be harbouring the prime suspect in a murder investigation here. Slate'll thank us.'

'Just as well Prue's not around. Doubt she'd be tickled by your last comment.'

'I meant no harm. Prue's no fan of Lucinda and would back us. Must look in on her later.'

Jon replaced the padlock. 'Done my best to make it look like no one's tampered. With a bit of luck, Lady Lu'll think she didn't lock up properly.'

'Nice one. Come on, Windy. We're onto something here.'

33

The Kilted Killer

A narrow tree-lined path opened onto an oval lawn and a riot of flowerbeds flanked by lofty pine hedges. A charming back garden to the stunning two-storey, thatched-roof cottage standing proudly amid a superb collection of shrubs. Wendy eyed an enormous rhododendron, its red flowers randomly scattered.

Jon gazed at the house. 'It's big. And beautiful.'

'The business. Typical Lu. Everything oversized and exaggerated. Careful now. Don't want to be seen. We'll duck behind the rhodo. The flowering season's over, but the shrubby bit'll make a suitable cover. We'll squiz through a gap. And keep your roar down.'

'Bet this rhodo looks amazing when it's in flower.'

'Gorgeous, but never mind that now. What can you see?'

'Not much. Can make out the house. Wish I had binoculars. Hang on a second.'

'What is it?'

'Lady Lu. In the kitchen.'

'Doing what?'

'Washing her hands, I think.'

'Riveting.'

'At least we know it's her place. The old boy was well taken with her. He's spared no expense on this place.'

'Some men are easily led. And he was years older, remember? Some might say he didn't stand a chance. Others might say she's nothing but a pretentious gold digger. I say, couldn't care less about the toxic pair, dead or alive. It's Tom I'm bothered about. A clown he may be, but doubt he's a killer. I feel a need to help him, and Prue, of course.'

'Hold it. She's coming out.'

'What's she doing?'

'Fawning over the garden. Smarming because she knows she owns a fabulous country hideaway and didn't pay a penny for it.'

'Your voice, you nut. It carries. Smarming?'

'Wacky word.'

'What she's doing now?'

'Staring at the back of the garden. Frowning. Oh, hell. Could be nabbed here.'

Wendy squeezed in beside Jon and pulled a face. 'What the heck's she wearing? It's like that pink thing she had on the other day. Only longer. And lemon. Bet it cost a packet. Bare feet too. And bling free.'

'Are you coming out?' Lucinda said. 'The geraniums look marvellous. My gardeners are doing a splendid job and rightly so. I pay them enough. I'll have one of them give the garden a good sweep next time.'

'Who's she talking to?'

'Him.'

Wendy gawked at the tall, handsome man who'd strolled out to take Lucinda in his arms. He looked freshly showered in bathrobe and flip-flops, damp dark hair slightly spiked. 'Well, I'll eat my chef's hat. 'Tis that damned, elusive Tom Trebilcock.'

'Boom. Bingo. The kilt.'

'Blast your big mouth, and curse this stupid hat.'

'What you doing down there, Darling? Having a nap?'

'Lost my balance. These sandals are killing me, my skin's itching, and there's a crick in me neck.'

'Better uncrick it then,' Jon hooted.

'What was that?' Lucinda said.

'Could be a magpie or crow,' replied Tom.

'Awful creatures.'

'Never mind that. Where were we?'

'Time for your next photoshoot, Lady Lu.' Jon's phone snapped a few shots of the snuggled-up pair. 'Proper movie mush this. Where's the popcorn?'

'Like a couple of love-struck teenagers. Would make a good romcom, and we provide the comic relief.'

'So, Mr T, this is where you've been hiding. Keeping us all guessing while you're shacked up with the old boy's widow.' Jon tutted and shook his head.

'Pass me a bucket.'

'*There's a hole in my bucket, dear Darling, a hole.*'

'*Then mend it, dear Windy, mend it.*'

'Crikey. Did you see that?' Jon said.

'*Did I.* Pushing Tom away after all the moony looks? What's going on?'

'Listen.'

'I could get into trouble for holding a fugitive, Tom.' Lucinda's squeak had an accusing lilt.

'You doubt my innocence?'

'The police case is compelling, and you definitely had the motive.'

'I'm shocked you'd say that.'

'I remember Seymour speaking as fondly of you as you did and do of him.'

'Sarcasm doesn't suit you, my lovely Lu.'

'I can't protect you forever, Tom. And won't. Especially if the police come calling.'

'All I ask is that you wait a little while longer. You know how I'm fixed. You must.'

Tom pulled Lucinda towards him. Jon and Wendy saw her melt into his embrace before the giggling pair linked fingers and returned to the cottage. The back door closed, and they faded from sight.

'She's easily swayed,' Jon said.

'Far as I can see, he's the same.'

'What do you think, then?'

''Twill all come out in the wash, for sure.'

'Time to go?'

'Nothing to hang around for. And these dummies are coming off. They're not even that high. How milady wears stilts, I do not know.' Wendy yanked off her sandals and adjusted her hat. 'Barefoot and Bigfoot go walkabout. Come on, Windy.'

'Bare feet are great for grounding, but careful any nasties don't jump you.'

'With the amount of apple cider vinegar I drown my trotters in? That's a lot of acid. All I can say to any nasties is happy tripping.'

The couple hurried down the path and onto the public walkway. Wendy slipped her sandals back on. Jon locked the gate.

'Two questions, Darling. Do we tell Prue we've found her fugitive brother? And do we tell the police?'

34

The Big Flapple

D id you know there's a piece of England in New York?' Jon reeled off another quirky quiz snip while washing down jackfruit chilli with a smooth Merlot.

Wendy ate and drank with her feet in a bowl of warm water, organic, raw ACV, and pink Himalayan salt. 'After yesterday's little escapade, my tootsies are screaming. This is their third soak. Corns and bunions keep away. What's that you say about New York? Sounds like another fishy fact.'

'Nothing fishy about it. There's a bit of Bristol in the Big Apple.'

'How so?'

'How's a fascinating story. During World War Two, American supply ships arrived in Bristol. After unloading their cargo, they needed something to weigh the ships for the return journey, otherwise they'd capsize.'

'Captivating stuff. Keep sailing.'

There were times Jon didn't know if Wendy was being serious or sarcastic. He looked at her face, plumped for neither, and carried on. 'Thanks to the Luftwaffe bombing Bristol, a ton of rubble lay around. The Americans helped themselves, took it home to New York, and dumped it in the East River. That's how Waterside Plaza and the surrounding land came to be.'

'Don't get it.'

'They dumped so much rubble, eventually, it stuck out of the river.'

'Why dump?'

'To build on it. Limited building land meant Bristol's boulders came in handy. The same sort of thing happens in Hong Kong. Skyscrapers galore.'

'Who knew?'

'This food's delicious. Your bread might be a car crash, but your chilli's in top gear. And thankfully, mine's not flaming hot. Bet yours is fiery.'

'Like a furnace.'

'Thought so. How you stomach blistering hot food I'll never know. Would kill my gut. Yours is lined with asbestos.' Jon wolfed another forkful.

'You never had such good food before I moved in. What will you do when I go?'

'What indeed. Bore myself silly eating beans on toast or homemade lentil soup. Even soup won't taste the same without your yum veggie stock. Anyway, photo time.'

'You're on.'

Jon scrolled to the pictures of Tom and Lucinda on his phone. 'Something just occurred to me.'

'What something?'

'Tom's car. We didn't look at the front of that cottage and if there's isn't a garage, I doubt he'd park his car outside for all to see.'

'It's probably in a lockup. Hell, there must be dozens on the Biggin-Smythe estate. It's big enough.'

'Perhaps Antonia could have a nosy around.'

'I'll ask her, but we must be careful. I suspect if the car's on the estate, only Lucinda and Tom know. Surely, Lu's cottage has a garage. A house that size. If Dickie suspects anything amiss, he'll waste no time in shopping Tom to the police, or using a spot of blackmail. The new lord'll consider his skin more precious than the dowager's. He's one to watch.'

'Assuming he knows about the love nest, of course.'

'Even if he doesn't, the police would question her, and she'd probably give the game away. Anything to save her own neck. These pictures are fab. You're a dab hand with the camera.'

'Thanks. You're not so bad yourself. By the way, you didn't say whether we should go to the police? And what about Prue?'

'Doubtful whether we should tell either. Tom might be playing the twin role of secret lover and runaway, but my gut says there's more to this, and my gut rarely lies. The business proposal. King. And not to mention Dickie's involvement and strange behaviour yesterday.'

'Yes. Lord Richard's quite the pompositor. You reckon he's involved?'

'I'm convinced his dirty little mitts are in this whole nasty business. Right up to his pompous eyeballs. Don't know how, but he and King are connected. We must find that connection.'

'Think it'll take more than a business proposal to link them. As far as everyone's concerned, said business never got off the ground. Perhaps we should leave this to the experts.'

'Seriously? Call yourself a sleuth.'

'Amateur sleuth. Think we should tell the police about the proposal. Say we saw Dickie acting suspiciously. Surely, they have a duty to investigate all leads.'

'In your little idealistic world, yes. In the real world, those with money, status, and power are the law and the real law won't touch them.'

'Are you saying Treeton Constabulary's corrupt?'

'Could be. I'm not saying all police forces or officers are immoral, far from it, but rotten apples hang from every tree and money talks all languages. Milord probably had the police in his pocket. He only has to pay off the chief constable and the entire force follows suit.'

'The police'll find Tom. Eventually. He can't stay cooped up in that house forever. We owe it to Prue to help.'

'Okay. For Prue's sake, we'll tell the police about our visit to the big house, but don't hold your breath.'

'Should tell Prue, too.'

'I'm reluctant.'

'Why? She's worried sick.'

'Yes, but MS and stress don't marry. Nothing marries with stress. Prue won't sit on the news. She'll insist on seeing Tom. Given her fragile state, that could prove disastrous.'

'As things stand, I imagine Tom won't want company other than his lover. What's the lesser of two evils then? Tell her or not? Stress either way.'

'That, my windy friend, is the rub.'

35

Supercilious Supercilium

F or Jon Windup, Treeton Police Station was becoming a habit. This was his second visit in a week. When DCI Slate asked him to make a formal statement, he promised Jon a cup of tea. Jon was still waiting. Maybe the force would be with him today and serve one up.

'I'm not optimistic,' Wendy said. 'Let's see if won't and can't are game for listening. Promising doesn't look promising.'

'We won't know unless we try.'

Wendy pressed the outside buzzer, and automatic doors hissed open into a stark white reception area. Cold. Clinical. To the right, a booth and counter, but no receptionist.

'Welcoming not,' said Jon, pushing a button on the counter. 'Was like this the other day.'

A desk sergeant shuffled through the door, expression blank. His crumpled face reminded Wendy of a wet paper bag. His manner was just wet.

'How can I help?' the officer said.

'Wendy May and Jon Windup to see DCI Slate. I arranged an appointment this morning.'

'Right.' The sergeant put a call through and gestured to the seats. 'He'll be with you shortly.' Without waiting for a response, he disappeared back through the door.

'Think he's seen his backside and doesn't like the look of it,' Wendy gibed.

'He's not the officer I saw the other day. Wouldn't last long in TV cop shows.'

'About as long as my laughter from one of your daft jokes.'

'Your knocks crack me up. Splitting my sides.'

'Anytime.'

'Wonder how long we'll have to wait.'

'No idea. Reminds me of the doctor's surgery, except there's no sign here saying notify reception if you've been waiting over thirty minutes.'

Jon unpocketed his phone. 'Gives me time to see what lovelies the web has today.'

'Things that'll help win the quiz, hopefully.'

'I'll see what I can do. I'm a sucker for odd facts.'

'You mean fishy facts.'

'Whatever you say.'

Jon foraged the net while Wendy mulled over yesterday's events. *Was Tom Trebilcock guilty or innocent?* The former, of course, so why had doubts crept in? *Did he bump off milord? Was he planning to run off with Lucinda to start a new life?* Life insurance, false passports, and new identities weighed on Wendy's mind. Images of Prue's anxious face brought her back to reality, cemented by DCI Slate's baggy eyes and bushy brows looming her way.

'Miss May. Mr Windup. This way.'

DCI Slate went to a secure door, punched in a code and invited Jon and Wendy into the heart of Treeton Police Station. Down a corridor, then another, and into an interview room with a lone table and six cheap chairs. Looking as slick as ever in a grey pin-striped suit, black tie, and pristine hair, DS Uttley sat at the desk. Slate plonked down beside him and asked Jon and Wendy to sit opposite. He smoothed back his crowning glory and fixed his steely glare Wendy's way.

'Well, Miss May. You said seeing me was important.'

'Yes. Wanted to let you know I interviewed the late Lord Biggin-Smythe for an article I'm writing for a highbrow mag. As luck wouldn't have it, he met his maker before I'd finished. His widow stepped into the breach and volunteered to help me complete it.'

'Did she now?'

'She did. Such a selfless act, don't you think? Most helpful. Prattled on about herself for the duration, but useful, anyway. Then there was the photosho—'

'I don't wish to be rude, but I have a pile of work to plough through, and would appreciate you getting to the point.' Slate's eyebrows had warmed up and were on the move.

Wendy pressed her tongue to the roof of her mouth, stifling the urge to giggle.

'Get on with it.'

'Sorry, chief inspector. While at Biggin Hall, we saw a business proposal.'

'So?'

The rise and fall of Slate's eyebrows compensated for his irritating impatience. He wasn't aware his supercilious waltzing heroes warmed Wendy's heart, curbing her assertive tongue.

'Well? What did this proposal say?'

'A three-way deal between his lordship, eldest son, Richard, and a former associate called King, who was quite the antagonistic. Jon has pictures of the document on his phone.'

'The family said nothing of this.'

'Knowing how to charm people and rub egos helps. In fact, it's true that police often suspect family when there's a murder. I don't think that's changed since I retired from legal practice.'

'Yes, but not always the case. What's your point?'

Jon put in his theory. 'Isn't it obvious, sir? We saw a business proposal between the old boy, his son, and King. Long story short. Mr King had the expertise, but not the money. Enter his lordship to bankroll the deal. When said proposal fell through, King threatened the old boy. I'm no crime expert, but something tells me that if this King fellow's shady, and his funding options limited, well, you know what I mean. And that's not all. The old boy and his son weren't the best of friends, yet here they are, proposing a proposal. Richard Biggin-Smythe gets a ten percent stake bringing nothing to the table, and when we were there, he was acting all weird and—'

'My, my, we are slow at getting from A to B today. I'm still waiting for the obvious. Theory's all very well, but you must back it up with proof. Where's your proof, Mr Windup?' DCI Slate looked at his watch and groaned.

'Cut the cackle, Jon. You don't half go on. Sorry, chief inspector. What Jon's trying to say is, this King fellow should be your chief suspect.'

'Oh, really? I'll be the judge of that. Look, I appreciate Mr Trebilcock's your friend, but all evidence points in his direction. His disappearance compounds all suspicion.'

Jon was indignant. 'You don't honestly think Tom had access to lots of money just so he could stick it in the old boy's mouth, do you? Surely you know that's mad?'

'Wouldn't be difficult to obtain cash from the pub.'

'He doesn't handle cash, and the Noose doesn't keep much money lying around.'

'Well, it's possible Thomas Trebilcock wasn't acting alone. According to village gossip, he is—how to put this delicately—quite thick with the deceased's widow. With or without her help, he had ways to get the money.'

Jon knew Biggin-Smythe had cash stuffed in his mouth. He also knew at least one note was fake, but couldn't let it slip. Surely Slate would know about counterfeit money from forensics. Something didn't square. Time to improvise. 'I've seen a few stories in the local news about a rise in forgeries. That's a possibility.'

Careful, Windy. Wendy gaped as Slate's brows danced a rude rumba deserving of an encore. Meeting in the middle, parting, then embracing again in a passionate monobrow above his twitching nose.

Oblivious, Jon went on. 'Maybe Tom's disappeared because on the face of it, the evidence points to him, but he knows he's innocent and just needs time to identify the real killer? Have you thought of that?'

'You should come and work for CID, Mr Windup. With your wild theories, we'll solve every case in no time. I've never heard anything so ridiculous in my life. Sillier than your story about, what was it, aniseed gloop. Still no chocolate on the horizon?'

'No,' Jon sulked, 'and my theory isn't silly. Not when you *really* think about it.'

'I don't have time to *really* think about it unless there's something you're not telling me. Perhaps you know of Mr Trebilcock's whereabouts. I could have you both arrested for obstructing a police investigation, and, don't forget, Mr Windup, you were on your own that night in the pub. You could always make another statement. Here. Now.'

'Does that go with tea?' Jon quipped, ouching at Wendy's sharp elbow in his ribs.

'Far from us to tell you how to do your job, chief inspector. We know forces are stretched and you're under pressure. We're only trying to help. Don't want to see a miscarriage of justice.'

'That's right, Miss May. Having worked in the legal profession for many years, you of all people will know the law's only interested in facts. So many innocents would be behind bars if convicted on speculation alone. The CPS wants concrete. Definite. I'll need something more solid than a mere business proposal and some strange goings-on at the Biggin-Smythe manor.'

'Will you at least look at the proposal? I've taken time to print it for you. New ink.' Wendy pushed the document Slate's way.

'Okay. When I have time. Now, if you'll excuse me, I'm a very busy man. I'll have someone show you out. Come along, Uttley. Work to do.'

The senior officers disappeared, leaving a constable to escort Jon and Wendy to the main entrance. Outside, in the car, the pair reflected.

'Told you, Windy. Complete waste of time.'

'We had to try. Didn't like the way he took that printout. Bet it went straight in the shredder. And I still didn't get me tea.'

'Will you stop rambling on about tea! There's bags of tea back home. Literally.'

'Tea-rific. I don't understand the reluctance to investigate King and the old boy's family.'

'Get the feeling something else's going on here.'

'Like what?'

'Who knows? Could be getting cynical as I'm getting older, but instinct tells me the police are afraid to investigate milord and his offspring. See Slate flinch when you mentioned counterfeiting?'

'Yeah. Didn't like that, did he?'

'And what was Uttley doing? Said bog all. Neither use nor ornament.'

'There to make sure the recording recorded. Going back to the old boy and his offspring, are we talking genuine fear of investigating or a bit of good, old-fashioned corruption?'

'Both. Especially the latter.'

'Really? You think Slate was taking backhanders from BS? Is still taking them from Dickie or Lu Brush?'

'Don't think he's the type. He might be a pain in the proverbial at times, and those brows of his are smug as well as hilarious, but something tells me he's an honest man and good at his job. Someone from above could be working his strings. Tying his hands.'

'Interesting. That means the chief constable's taking backhanders and ordering Slate to leave the family alone. What about King, though?'

'It's just a feeling, Jon. I could be totally off the mark. You know what police forces are like nowadays. Desperate for results to justify their funding when budgets are slashed to kingdom come.'

'In other words, they'll turn a blind eye to justice as long as they succeed. So, where does that leave us?'

'In the lap of the gods, and Prue Penn.'

36

Cruel to be Kind

F or the third time in five minutes, shaking fingers forced Prue to put down her cup. Since Wendy's revelations about Tom and Lucinda, her expression was part relief, part troubled.

'We couldn't believe it, but it's no surprise he'd be with her. Me and Jon agonised over telling you and decided we must.'

'I should have known, but how did you find out about the cottage?'

'Antonia said she'd seen Lu in the area. Her house isn't far from Pengelly's place.'

'Ross Pengelly?'

'The dude himself. He and Antonia are having a fling, although, as a cover, Antonia calls him Duncan. Can you imagine the furore if Dickie found out? The late lord's daughter fooling around with the local postie.'

'Poor Emily.'

'And poor Antonia. I'm sure neither girl knows about Pengelly's playing, but it's their business. Anyway, Antonia's doing the old sneaky to avoid being seen, and who does she chance upon doing the same? Milady Lu. Antonia put two and two together and came up trumps.'

'Anyway, we saw Lady Lu and Tom in the garden, doing, well, you know.'

'Kissing's the word Jon's looking for.'

'Yes. That. And holding hands. And whispering sweet nothings, and—'

'Questioning his innocence,' Wendy cut in.

'She did that?' asked Prue.

'Yes. He maintains it, but milady made it clear she'll not protect him forever. In fact, she said she'd drop him in it if the law comes sniffing.'

'What a horror. What does Tom see in her?'

'Ego. Pride. Getting one over his boss who's festering in the morgue. Still no news of the funeral. Coroner won't release the body until the inquest's satisfied. Maybe Tom's in love. Those gooey looks say something. Pity him if he is. Lu's made it clear she only cares about herself.' Wendy recalled the interview and photoshoot, and milady's lust to be the centre of attention, at any cost.

'At least she's honest. Most two-faced people aren't,' said Jon.

'True, but that's like serving poison in a jewelled cup. Looks inviting, but you'll die if you drink it.'

'What should we do?'

Prue's face concerned Wendy. 'Has Tom called you again?'

'No, and when I try to call him, I get voicemail.'

'Probably used the phone once and got rid. Calls traced and so on.'

'But what about Tom?' Prue shrieked.

'Go easy, Prue. If you confront him, there's a good chance he'll bolt. If it's true, he's getting evidence to nail the real killer, he'll want to keep a low profile, especially as the police are looking for him.'

'The thing is, the cops'll find that place sooner or later, so Tom'll have to move on, anyway. At least we know where he is, for now,' said Jon. He picked up his tenth caramel wafer and munched.

Wendy wrung her hands. 'It's a tricky one. Stop yapping, Jon. You're doing your pig at a trough act again, only not as cute.'

'Oink-oink. We should tell Prue about our visit to the cop shop,' Jon said.

Prue's eyes bored into Wendy. 'You went to the police?'

'Not to drop Tom in it,' Jon assured.

'Not at all,' Wendy seconded. 'To divert attention away from Tom.'

'And how did you do that?' Prue was dubious.

'At the big house, Jon found a business proposal between milord, Dickie, and Montgomery Oliver King, who's surely Milton's father. Our man. The deal was for a chain of gastropubs, taking advantage of the local history. The other day outside the Noose, when Slate and Dickie were talking, I overheard Dickie mention a *ghastly fellow* called King. He said things had turned nasty when daddy dearest reneged on the deal. Unpleasantries, was what he said. What he didn't say was that his name also featured in the proposal. I wanted to check out King, hence the cookery class with Milton.

'According to the proposal, milord was financing the project, but there were snags. He wanted to change the Noose's name and remove the gibbet cage, but King said no. This disagreement and subsequent argument turned out to be the final straw, and the whole plan collapsed. And, wait for it, King and Lucinda Biggin-Smythe were having an affair.'

Prue's mouth dropped open. 'Oh, my, his lordship knew how to pick them, didn't he? That woman has no scruples.'

'She doesn't, and it's doubtful whether Tom'll last much longer, either.'

'I took pictures of the proposal to show DCI Slate. Told him he should investigate King and Dickie,' Jon said.

'What did he say?'

'Apart from telling us he didn't like being told how to do his job, both him and Uttley were unmoved. It's made us suspicious. I mean, where would Tom get a bundle of money? Real or otherwise. I pointed that out to the pair of them. If you ask me, they're afraid to investigate because someone's taking bribes.'

'What? Poor Tom. Is there no hope?'

'Well, there is. Sort of. If we can find concrete evidence to show to the police, linking Monty King and Dickie, then they'll have no choice but to follow up.'

'And what if we don't find any evidence?'

'We will, Prue. Enough suspicious goings-on over at the big house to suggest something's amiss and I have an ally in Antonia, remember?'

'Of course.'

'Even though daddy doted on his daughter, there was no love lost between them. She has the same feelings towards Dickie and Lucinda. She's one of the decent few in that whole rotten family and won't want to see a miscarriage of justice.'

'Hope so.'

Wendy took Prue's hand. 'Don't worry, we'll find the killer and why he or she's framed Tom.'

'Thank you.'

'What are friends for?'

'And Tom? I know where he is now.'

'I'd stay away, but something tells me you won't let it be. I've known you too long. Please, be careful.'

37

Chagachino Choux-Choux

Jon and Wendy's early morning visit to Prue left them hankering for coffee. In the ambience of Beans & Leaves, Adam invited them to sample his new concoction. Chagachino, a blend of chaga mushroom powder, cinnamon, and vanilla, swirled into a frothy cappuccino. Fascinated, the couple watched Adam's skilful hands work mushroom magic. A dusting of chocolate sprinkles, chaga, cocoa, or all three brought the quirky brew to life.

Jon's resistance to dessert paradise didn't last, eyes widening as Adam plated six toffee profiteroles drenched in gooey salted caramel and topped with butterscotch shavings. Wendy refused sin. Her sweet mood had deserted her.

A handful of locals sat in the cafe, mainly near the windows to people watch. Jon and Wendy chose a corner window seat, but gawking wasn't on their agenda. As long as they kept their voices low, they'd be out of earshot.

'Did we do the right thing, Darling?' Jon chomped on airy choux pastry filled with toffee cream and dripping in sticky salted caramel.

'We had to. For Prue's sake. Couldn't have kept that chipping away.'

'Think she'll go to the cottage?'

'I've known her long enough to suspect she won't stay put. Clearing Tom's name and silencing doubters is vital. Pity we couldn't screw Annie Clegg's jaws shut, and clamp old Jemima for good measure. Enjoying yourself,

Windy?' Jon's antics around confection never failed to amuse Wendy.

Adam bustled to the table for a quick chat. 'How's it all going?'

'It's good, but it's not right,' Jon said. 'The police are doing a great job of reminding me I was alone on the night of the murder, but things could be worse. At least I'm not the chief suspect, nor am I getting evicted. That reminds me, I'm working this afternoon. Let's say hello to Eddie before we go home, Wendy.'

'Let's. Another new apron, Adam? You're as reckless with your pinnies as I am with my hats. That makes how many?'

'Twenty odd, and I could never be that reckless. How's Prue? Haven't seen her lately.'

'Not good. The police keep hounding her. I'm surprised there isn't a marked car outside her home permanently. Or glowering Annie Clegg and that old rattletrap, Jemima.'

'Police could be staking her house in an unmarked car. Couldn't unmark Jemima, though.'

'Thankfully, police don't have the resources, Jon. This coffee's a winner, Adam. Chagachino not only tastes delicious, it's a tonic for the soul.'

'I agree. Never thought medicinal mushroom powder in coffee would be my thing, but it's hitting all the right notes.'

'Thanks. I'll give it a couple of weeks. If it proves popular, I'll roll it out. I'll try a non-dairy mix too, with raw cacao powder, unsweetened cocoa, and dark chocolate nibs. Endless possibilities. I've three other blends in mind. Still have to perfect the recipes, but named after the mushroom powders I intend using.'

'Which are?' Wendy said.

'Liolatte. Lion's mane latte. Reishice. Iced flat white using reishi. And cordycano. That's cordyceps Americano.'

'Clever names. Loving the idea and can't wait to taste,' Wendy said.

'Tell Prue I'm asking after her. She'll have to try one of my new inventions.' The cafe's little bell jingled, and Adam turned to greet Barbara Mardell, parish and church archivist.

Wendy leaned across the table. 'Hope police resources stay limited, Jon. Dear Prue doesn't need more stress.'

38

Tombstone

J on and Wendy waved to Adam, then popped into Half-Baked to buy a couple of bonkers buns for an early lunch on the hoof. They headed to the Noose in Jon's car, the morning sun in a cloudless blue sky smiling down as they chugged up heart attack hill.

'Is there another reason you're going to see Eddie?' Wendy asked.

'Need a spare set of keys for the pub. I've left mine at home. Ed's house-hunting this afternoon, so I'm closing up again. Want to see how he's doing, too. Being evicted's not easy. I should know. Been through it twice. Oh, and any excuse to say hello to Mr Quince.'

'You have a real soft spot for that cat, don't you?'

'How can you tell?'

'Moony eyes and gaga face give the game away. Must admit, I can't resist saying hello to the big fella, too. You should get a cat.'

'Funny you should say that. I've been thinking about it. Must go to the animal shelter sometime and find a furry friend to rehome. Right now, I'll have to find a home for the car. The pub's still drawing crowds. Even at this hour.'

'See if you can park next door. I want a nose around the cemetery, anyway. Hunt down Patcheye Peg's grave. I'll come say hi to Eddie when I'm done.'

'I'll nose with you. After all, my hooter's big enough.'

'Not on the Cyrano de Bergerac scale, Jon, although, like him, you do lack self-confidence. Guess you mean because of your love for snooping? Won't argue there. You have a mega schnoz for that.'

'That's me. The meddler.'

'Then let's meddle. Onwards to the hilltop where the yew trees grow.'

Alone in their thoughts, but united in their quest to nail the truth, Jon and Wendy threaded through headstones of varying colour, shape, and size. One epitaph caught Jon's eye.

'*About time the worms had me over for supper,*' he roared. 'What sort of memorial's that for a loved one?'

Wendy collapsed in a fit of giggles. 'Me's an objective personal pronoun. Bet Archie Wood chose his own inscription. Had a dark sense of humour, like you.'

'Indeedy, and even in a graveyard, the editor's dead right.'

'You and your daft jokes. At least there's humour in a tiptoe through the tombstones.'

In a bank of heat, the couple picked their way uphill until a cluster of gnarled, ancient yews halted Wendy's steps.

'They cut Peg down from the gibbet cage and buried him under a yew, so history says. From what I recall, they laid a few rogues and rascals to rest here. We're standing on Honest Tor's very own Boot Hill.'

'In all my research, I've never found out why it's called Boot Hill. Do you know?'

'It's a common name for any burial place of those who died with their boots on. Peg fits the bill. Scout around, Windy. Holler if you get a whiff of our pickled pirate.'

Jon took off to the left and Wendy headed right, dodging sunken graves, and broken, weather-beaten headstones. She wanted names and dates. Most were illegible, although a handful showed dates between 1700-1750.

'Over here, Jon.'

Jon's long legs were soon at Wendy's side. 'Result?'

'Not exactly. There's a tiny clue from a few stones in the first half of the eighteenth century, but no names. I've looked at records in the library and village hall, but must search the church and parish archives. Seeing Barbara Mardell earlier must've been an omen. I'll have a word with her. Don't know why I haven't before. Guess you had no luck?'

'You guess right. Are we done here?'

'For now, but I have a funny feeling I've just walked on Peg's grave.'

39

Spooked!

B ack at the Noose, punters still poured into the pub that had claimed a lord. There was no police presence, but the local constabulary could always choose stealth if they wished.

'Still mobbed,' Jon said.

'Anna's on her own behind the bar. She's going some.'

'Bless her. I'll have a quick chat with Eddie, take you home, then back for my shift. It'll be a busy one. Hey, Anna. Where's Ed?'

'Hi, Jon. He's in the cellar, checking the kegs. A problem with the ale.'

'Cheers. I'll wait for him.'

'Biggin-Smythe's ghost wreaking havoc?' Wendy chuckled.

'That's all we need.'

Eddie appeared, looking troubled.

'How you doing, Ed? Forgot my keys. Need a spare set.'

Eddie delved into his pocket. 'There you go. Look after them.'

'You look worried,' Wendy said. 'Keg issues?'

'No problem there. The problem's with a couple of heavies.'

'Don't tell me they're putting pressure on you to leave.'

'I'm telling you. BS's been dead all of five minutes, but I still have to go. It's as if his ghost's calling the shots. My problem is the deal was always casual. I live here and manage. Don't pay rent, so technically, don't have a leg to stand on. Believe that's how it works.'

'You'd think the old boy's death would put other plans on hold. What's the rush?' Jon demanded.

'You'd think, wouldn't you? But BS management's just as ruthless as the family. Rumour has it Dickie's assumed command of the empire.'

'That makes sense, I suppose. He is the eldest son. How long've you got?' asked Jon.

'Want me out in a month. So, no house, no job.'

'You're kidding. They can't do that!' Jon was furious.

'That's what the heavies said.'

Wendy cut in. 'Despite the informal arrangement, there are rules for evicting tenants. You will have some protection. The Biggin-Smythe clan think they're above the law, but they're not. If you have any paperwork, *anything* to help your case, let me see it.'

'I can handle them, but Gina's struggling. Her tears are killing me.'

'I'll look into it for you. Easy said, I know, but try not to worry.'

'Thanks, Wendy. Appreciate your help. Anyway, whatever happens, a new home's a must. Any problems tonight, Jon, get me on the mobile. Any drinks?'

'I'm working later, so just an orange juice, thanks,' Jon said.

'Small red for me.'

'Can we eat our lunch in the beer garden? Went to Half-Baked intending to eat in the car, but Wendy fancied a wine and now we're both hungry.'

'No worries. I'll get your drinks. On the house.'

Jon and Wendy found a shaded spot outside and unpacked their lunch. Jon had chosen veggie lasagne on multigrain. Wendy plumped for an organic almond butter and red jalapeno bagel.

'That management team's a nasty bunch,' Jon said, juggling mischievous cherry tomatoes, courgette, and mozzarella. 'And this is delicious, but messy.'

'Looks it. I'm more determined now, Windy. We must find out what's going on. Dickie Boy's up to no good. Who *is* this Monty King, and what's he all about? And is that son of his one to watch? As for Lu, there's more to her than wacky heels and outrageous clothes. Yes, Tom's a buffoon, but we can't let him take the rap for something he didn't do. Slate may have his mitts tied, but we don't.' Wendy raised her glass. 'To Windy and Darling's free hands. The hands of justice.'

'I'll drink to that,' Jon enthused, clinking his glass with hers.

40

Thigh's the Limit

Feeling the pain of uncertainty, Prue Penn fidgeted in her living room. Thwarted by MS nasties, she'd shaken off the fervent temptation to look for Lucinda's cottage. Now she battled the triggered effects. Spasticity muscle spasms tightened her calves and moved up her legs. Secondary fatigue screamed rest.

MS was a contrary character. Though sunshine was important, sultry weather could worsen symptoms. Turning to nature, and Grandad's old deck chair, was often the stressbuster Prue needed. As long as she didn't stay out too long. Wearing thin shorts and a vest top, Prue slipped on a cooling bandana, then hobbled in flip-flops to her favourite spot in the back garden.

Naturally green-fingered, Prue did a remarkable job managing the front and rear plots, but certain tasks needed extra hands. Enter keen gardeners, Lenny and Frank. When not knocking dominoes in the Noose, or clubbing the bunker to death at Pheasant's Acre Golf Club, both were happy to help. In their retirement, horticulture kept them out of mischief.

Brambles faced south, and though the sun was hot, it wasn't unkind. The enchanting burble of the Mell and sublime melody of an English country summer sent Prue's low spirits packing as she drifted to her castle in the air.

'Hey, Prue. Fabby day, isn't it?' The girly tone pulled Prue from her reverie.

'Hi, Ems, what are you doing around here? Thought you'd be working today.'

'Day off. Going to Ross's later. I'm cooking for him.'

Prue knew Antonia was also seeing Ross, and neither girlfriend knew about the other. She also knew it would devastate poor Emily if she found out Ross was a cheating rat. Prue didn't know how Antonia would react to his two-timing. She understood her to be the resilient type. Even so, who wants their man fooling around? She'd been there and would wish it on no one. Though Prue had a mind to, she wasn't about to tell Emily of the cad's capers. 'What's on the menu for dinner?'

'Chicken thigs in breadcrumbs. Ross loves them with chips.'

'Adventurous eater then,' Prue said. 'I've cooked and baked for years and confess I've never heard of chicken thigs. Do you have a recipe? Or a picture?'

'I'll show you.'

Emily came into the garden, opened her little shopping bag, and looked puzzled when Prue burst out laughing. 'Oh, Emily, you do make me giggle, even if it's unintentional. They're chicken *thighs*. Like the thighs at the top of your own legs.

'Oh.' Emily's face stayed blank. 'It's good to see you laugh. You looked so sad before.'

'I'm okay.' Prue was still sniggering at Emily's blunder. 'This condition can be brutal, but I never let it win. I've lots to be thankful for.'

'You poor thing. Is there anything I can do?'

Some people loved others fussing over them. Prue wasn't some people. She despised pity, rejected special treatment, and looked only for dignity and respect. Sadly, Emily didn't get it, and threw her arms around Prue. She meant well and for that, Prue was grateful. A mad idea came to her.

'Actually, there is something you could do for me, Ems.'

'Anything.'

'When are you seeing Ross?'

'I'm going to his place after I've seen my friends.'

'You couldn't give me a lift, could you? There's a really lovely walk near his home and I fancy a mooch.'

'It's so nice there. You'll have to show me. We could walk together.'

'Yes, but some other time. You're cooking for Ross and won't want to be late.'

Emily was a lovely girl, but a known gossip. Not in Annie Clegg's league, but still not one to confide in. At all costs, Prue must protect what she knew. Lucinda's secret grove would stay secret.

'I'm going to the pub for food. See you in an hour?'

'Okay. Just knock for me when you're done. I'm sure a brisk walk will do me and my thigs a lot of good.'

41

Backpedal

When Wendy May fought for a cause, Jon Windup knew she couldn't be moved. After lunch and drinks, Jon noted her unblinking eyes staring into nothing. The mouth set in a determined line. That dogged look screaming, "I'm in a quandary, but this tenacious soul won't let go!" And Wendy wouldn't. Especially if a situation could destroy those she cared about, even if she knew she was beat before she started. Ever the gambler, Wendy took risks Jon would never consider. Gutsy. Assured. Compassionate. She'd carry on. Brave defeat her own way.

'Don't worry, Darling. It's a trek to Lady Lu's cottage. I know Prue's desperate to see Tom, but—'

'You're right, my windy friend. And you're a poet and didn't know it.'

'At least I try.'

'A trek, I know. I also know Prue's wilful.'

'Surely, she wouldn't walk all that way by herself. She'd never make it. She'd need a lift. Or taxi.'

'Tricky location to describe to a taxi driver.'

'Prue isn't stupid.'

'That's what troubles me. Come on, let's go.'

On their way out, Emily swung into the Noose. She waved and whooped at Jon and Wendy, then greeted her waiting girlfriends with a screech.

'Hi, Ems, what you up to?' Wendy said.

'Meeting the girls for food. Just seen Prue in her garden.'

'Enjoying the sun, was she? It's good for her, as long as it doesn't get too hot.'

'She was on about some new walk near Ross's place.'

'She kept that one quiet. I love a good country walk and if it's new, she can count me in. Did she say anything else?' Wendy knew the answer to the pointless question.

'Asked if I could give her a lift later when I head to Ross's. I'm going to cook for him. Chicken and chips. Must go.' Emily dashed off. Soon, a bevy of excited female voices and crazy cackles pierced the lounge.

'How long before you start your shift, Jon?'

'About an hour. Just enough time to take you home and come back.'

'Damn.'

'What's up?'

'I should've stayed with Prue. I'm going round there.'

'I'm working until close, remember?'

'I'll worry about that later. If need be, I'll borrow your car and come back for you, but it's crucial you drop me off.' Wendy pulled out her phone.

Though troubled, Jon quickly conceded. He knew Wendy wasn't in a quibbling mood. 'No point in arguing when your mind's made up.'

'Argue all you like. I'm not listening.'

42

Helpers, Hedges, and Hopes

For the nth time, Prue checked her watch. Fingers, clumsy. Head shaking, back and forth. 'Emily should've been here by now.'

'She will be. Keep calm. Stress doesn't pay.'

'You'd feel the same, Wendy, but I'm glad of your company. Hunting down Tom on my own isn't a good idea. Thanks for insisting on being by my side.'

'Always.' Wendy admired the vivid flowers and shrubs in Prue's vibrant garden. 'Lenny's done a fantastic job with the borders, and Frank's a dab hand with his whittling. I love that little wheelbarrow, even if wibbly wobbly wheels make it skew-whiff. Adds to the charm.'

'Both men are too kind, helping as they do. It makes me smile seeing all the colours and shapes for each season of the year. Forsythia and rhododendron in spring. Buddleia and sunflowers in summer, and in autumn, ah, Emily. Thank goodness.'

'Told you she'd be here,' Wendy chirped. 'Your smile's brighter than the sun, Ems. What's twinkling you?'

'I'm so excited. Me and Ross are back on track. I'm all filled up with fabby food, and it's a lovely day. Couldn't be better.'

'Happy days.'

'More than happy, Wendy. Didn't know you were coming along.'

'Can't leave Prue to explore all the best walks alone. I'll keep an eye on her. A good walk should shoo away any pain in her thigs.'

Emily didn't twig Wendy's jest. The same way she hadn't twigged Prue's earlier. Wendy agreed with Jon and concluded it had nothing to do with euphoria. He said Emily just wasn't a twigger. Prue turned her head to hide her giggles. *Wendy May. What a devil. But what an angel.*

'Better go. I'm late and don't want to upset Ross.'

Wendy slid into the back of Emily's car, letting Prue ride shotgun. Soon they were winding up a narrow country road, lost between a pair of hedges that went on and on. Wendy looked over her shoulder, expecting to see a marked police car trailing them, but the road was empty.

'Your driving's shocking, Emily,' Wendy tutted.

'What's wrong with it?'

'Any faster and we'll be hugging the hedges. These twisty roads are notorious for accidents. Think it's best to drive like a nun on a Sunday.'

'Is she always a backseat driver, Prue? What's a nun on a Sunday got to do with anything?'

'Imagine nuns always drive carefully, but even more so on a rest day. And don't refer to me in the third person. I am here.'

'But you are the third person. In the back.' Emily looked puzzled.

'It's a grammar thing, Ems. Concentrate on the road and not Wendy's nitpicking.'

'I've already told Jon I'm not ready to go just yet. Now I'm telling you.'

'Sorry. I know I'm fast sometimes and it's not good on these roads, but I can't be late for Ross.'

'Even if it means killing yourself, or a couple of passengers? Especially this old, confused biddy? So how is Mr Pengelly? Still swiping emery boards?' Wendy said.

'No. He's over that now.'

'Back to normal.' Prue said.

'When was Ross Pengelly ever normal?' scoffed Wendy. 'With respect, an aversion to the arts, a peacock mentality, and skin the colour of a Belisha beacon globe are the trappings of a philistine, surely.'

'Leave him alone. He's amazing!' Emily pouted.

'Oops. Think I've touched a nerve. Better change the subject, quick.'

'Good idea, Wendy. Don't the wheat fields look lovely this time of year?'

'Sure they do, Prue, if I could see them. I'm hedged in.'

'Yes, silly me.'

'Ross *is* still acting strange, but I'm sure it's nothing.'

'Thought we'd changed the subject,' said Prue.

'What's nothing?' Wendy pressed.

'Not sure, but when he starts with his funny ways, the first thing that comes to mind is he might be seeing someone else. What do you think?'

Wendy couldn't confirm Emily's thoughts. Telling her the truth would slay the girl. 'He's probably a closet trainspotter and too embarrassed to admit it. Jon belongs to a group obsessed with roads and just joined another bunch bonkers about maps. He's a proper anorak. One of his nicknames is Mapman. Fits both the roads and maps malarkey. Would you like me to ask if he could map your man's sneaky movements, Ems?'

'Isn't a closet a wardrobe? How can someone spot trains in a wardrobe, and what've anoraks to do with roads or maps?'

'Yes, a wardrobe, and forget the rest,' Wendy laughed.

The mood had lightened, and the trio continued in silence, admiring the scenery, or what they could see of it. Occasionally, a lone oak or sycamore defeated the hedge wall, but hedges still ruled okay.

'So, where's this path?' Emily eventually asked.

'Should be near Ross's place. We'll get out when you reach his house. You have to go through some fields.' Wendy made it up as she went along.

'Okay.'

The weather had turned, the sky no longer a brilliant blue, but a sombre grey. 'Trust our rotten luck for a change in the weather. The sun's in a huff and flung his hat to hell. Wish I'd brought me brolly.'

'We're here.' Emily pulled up outside a lone cottage nestled between a wheat field and woodland.

'What a gorgeous spot! Ross's one lucky man. No wonder he's in such a state about the eviction,' Prue said.

'Isn't it cute? It's called The Barn. Don't know why. It's not a barn.'

'Would've been originally before its conversion to a house,' Wendy said. 'Just as well, it's no longer a barn, or Mr Pengelly could find himself in new living quarters. He's a bit of an animal, I hear. Or is that hogwash?'

Emily's frosty look silenced Wendy's jesting. 'Just kidding,' Wendy lied. Emily wasn't to blame for the bighead that was Ross Pengelly, even if she wore blinkers.

'Thanks for the lift. Give Ross our best,' said Prue.

Wendy didn't join the Pengelly tribute club. Prue's sentiment was enough. The pair watched Emily scurry down the footpath, then Prue turned to Wendy.

'You really don't like our dear postman, do you? The atmosphere bites when his name's mentioned. '

'I'd put it stronger, but I don't do hate. That craves energy and I've better things to expend my joules on. You know me. Strive to avoid negative people, but if one gets me, I let fly. Pengelly makes me soar. He's a slug. Doing the dirty on Ems and the same to Antonia. Too much swagger, too little modesty, and there's something about him I just can't get. It'll come. That conversation outside the Noose was clear. He's not milord's number one fan. I don't trust him.'

'Do you think he's a suspect?'

'Could be. Motive. Time. Opportunity. It's all there, and Emily told us he's been acting funny. Like I said, that something will come, and when it does, clarity.'

'Where to now?'

'We could've got out at the entrance to the pathway, but mustn't let dipsy know where we're going. Ems is a sweet, but can't be trusted to keep her trap shut.' Wendy beckoned Prue to follow her back down the road.

'Did you see the look she gave you when you called Ross an animal?'

'Couldn't miss it. 'Tis the truth. In fact, that's an insult to any animal.'

'Oh, Wendy. You can be a right meanie when you want to be,' Prue chuckled.

'What can I say? I have a big heart. Just no time for idiots, fakers, and cheating sexists.'

'Do you think he plays around because Ems isn't the brightest girl and prefers Antonia because she's smart?'

'Prue Penn! Think you've outmeaned me. That's a definite entry for Windy's Wacky Words. I think he plays around because he can. He'll control Ems as long as she lets him. And Antonia? She's from a wealthy family and he'll use that to his advantage. Mr Pengelly says I'm old and confused, but you can't fox the unfoxable. I swallowed the vixen long before him.

'Anyway, must get my bearings. Let me think. We approached from the rear, but Jon had to pick the lock on the gate. Then, he put it back, as he didn't want to arouse suspicion. According to his map, there should be a lane leading off to the left nearby. That should take us right to the house.'

'Lead on.'

In silence, Wendy and Prue walked down the country road. Soon the hedges and farm fields gave way to woodland on both sides and, sure enough, a small dirt track led off to the left. Blocking the track was a fancy wrought-iron gate emblazoned with its name: *Owls Nest*. Next to the gate, a post box.

Prue looked uncertain. 'Is this it? That post box looks like no one's used it for years.'

'There's only one way to find out if this is the one.'

Wendy pushed the gate, but it didn't move. Pulling had the same effect.

'Damn, it's locked. Where's Jon when you need him?'

'What now?'

Wendy examined the gate. 'You'd think this fancy cottage would have a mechanised gate. It is part of the Biggin-Smythe estate, after all. I'm not complaining about the height though. Any taller'd be a struggle. How does climbing grab you, Prue?'

'It doesn't.'

'Shame Jon has to work this afternoon, but not to worry. Wait here and I'll have a look. Be as quick as I can. Text if anyone comes.'

'But what if Tom's there? Or her?'

'Those tyre marks look pretty fresh. We might've missed the merry widow. As for Tom, who knows? Could still be there. Could've moved on. If I were on the run, wouldn't want to hang around the same spot too long.'

'Are you sure about this? She could do us for trespassing.'

'Don't panic, you'll be fine. 'Tis me going asnooping. 'Twill be me who gets done if there's doing to do. I'm not scared. I'll ham it up. Just say I got lost. Anyhow, Lucinda's banking on me to stroke her ego. She won't want to miss out on the classy mag spread. Displaying her charms. Telling her story. Those stilts'll need a double page at least. Wonder if she has hammertoe or bunions? If she doesn't have lumps and bumps now, she will when she's older. Or corns. Heels that high must do damage. Right. I'm going in.'

'Please, be careful.'

'You, my friend, are a born worrier, and warrior, but thanks for your kindness.' Wendy saluted, then climbed over the gate.

43

Owl's Nest

W endy trekked up the winding dirt track through the trees. The trunks and thick canopies concealed the way, making it difficult to gauge the cottage's location. On the flip side, the trunks made excellent cover, allowing her to dart from tree to tree on the approach.

Eventually, the driveway opened out into a clearing and looming in front, the impressive two-storey cottage. The occasional hoot made an apt name for the house. *Owl's Nest*. At the front, an immaculate garden, with pristine lawn, pretty little flowers all in a row, and a freshly mown lawn.

Wendy tuned in to silence. No cars outside. No sign of life. Even the hooting had stopped. None of the windows appeared open. She edged around the side to the back garden. The lawn looked tidier, and Wendy knew it had also seen a mower. She peered through the kitchen window. Clean and neat, as if no one had been there for days. The place looked and felt deserted.

A locked back door. It wasn't unusual to find unlocked doors in the countryside, but milady was neither the trusting nor careless type. Neither was Tom Trebilcock. Wendy headed to the front and gazed in through the lounge window. Again, no activity. She tried the front door handle. Locked. She peered through the letterbox at an empty hallway. Knocked on the door, then again, louder this time. Nothing. Angered by thoughts of Prue, anxious, desperate, and waiting for news, Wendy yelled through the letterbox.

'Tom. Can you hear me? Tom!' The stubborn sound of silence irked. 'Tom, it's Wendy. Open up. Prue's here with me. For pity's sake, I know you're there. Open the door!'

Frustrated, Wendy stumbled backwards and gaped at the cottage. All she could hear was birdsong, the occasional hoot, and an aircraft. She looked at the big sky. At lifting grey, blue patches creeping in, and clumps of cotton cloud. The throb of helicopter blades was unmistakable, the aircraft's low altitude and circling unnerving. Wendy took off, dashing along the driveway back to a panicked Prue.

'Wendy, you were gone ages. I was worried.'

'Sorry. I walked around the house. Had to be doubly sure.'

'Did you see him?'

'No.'

'Anybody?'

'Like the Marie Celeste. No doors or windows open. All silent, apart from the birds and the owl. Even yelled through the letterbox, not that it would've made a difference.' Prue looked close to breaking. Wendy threw an arm around her shoulders. She could kill that idiot Tom. 'We won't give up.'

'That chopper's been circling for a while.'

'Wouldn't surprise me if it's the police.'

'Funny you should say that.'

'Why?'

'When you were gone, a man pulled up in a car and asked me if I was all right?'

'What type of car?'

'Not sure. It wasn't a police car, but the driver was wearing a suit. There was something official about him.'

'Did he say anything else?'

'Asked me what I was doing here.'

'What did you say?'

'Said I was fine. Just having a rest and this gate seemed the perfect place. I didn't tell him about my condition. Not broadcasting that to strangers.'

'And then?'

'He seemed satisfied but reminded me the driveway behind was private property and the owner might take exception to me leaning on the gate. Then he drove off.'

'Strange.'

'I don't like it here. Can we go, please?'

'I don't like it either. That chopper's making me edgy. By the way, are you up for doing a bit of walking?'

Prue was about to answer when a car stopped, and a voice rang out.

'Well-well-well. Fancy seeing you here.'

44

Clean Slate

Wendy would know that voice in a vacuum. She swung around to face her suited friends, iBrow and strut. One wore the baggy default glower. The other, his stock wise guy smirk.

'What brings you out to this lonely spot, Miss May?' Slate appeared animated. A striking interrobang.

Wendy hoped for an eyebrow jive, but they weren't talking. 'Dodging boredom and how with a bracing walk, chief inspector. Exercise and country air work wonders for the soul.'

'Here? I'm no expert on country walks, but surely there are far better places to stroll than a winding road with tall hedges. It's hardly pedestrian friendly.'

'Not a stroll. A bracing walk. We like a challenge.'

'And where did you spring from?' Uttley's question startled Prue.

'What do you mean?' Prue stammered.

'A colleague reported seeing you. Sorry, didn't catch your name.'

'Prue Penn, and you didn't ask.'

'He had a chat with you earlier. You told him you were having a rest. He told you the gate you were leaning on was private property. You didn't mention *her*.'

'Who's *her*, sergeant? And did Prue have to mention me?' Wendy didn't care for Uttley's irritating, rude manner. Until now, Wendy hadn't given Uttley a mark, but his oafish behaviour warranted an apostrophe.

'Seems logical.'

'Nothing logical about it. Prue wanted a rest. I carried on walking, then returned. Since when was it illegal for two friends to enjoy a country walk?'

'It isn't, but is if you're obstructing or tampering with a police investigation.'

'I'm not sure I like your tone, chief inspector. Strolling in the sticks is hardly obstructing HM Constabulary.'

'I appreciate you may not know that the gate behind you leads to a house we believe harbours the chief suspect in a murder investigation. If I'm not mistaken, I understand you're related to that suspect, Miss Penn. As for you, Miss May, I trust you weren't somewhere you shouldn't have been.'

A couple of marked police vehicles pulled up and two teams of uniformed officers scrambled out. Within seconds, they'd scaled the gate and were sprinting towards Owl's Nest.

'Whether our prime suspect is still in hiding remains to be seen.' Slate's brows were off again.

Wendy ignored his slack face. She knew the owls had flown and there was nobody home, but she also knew Prue's stress levels had hit detonate. 'I assume you have a warrant?'

'That's no concern of yours.'

'I know of many instances where police have broken doors down, smashed windows, and gone on a rampage with no warrant. No harm in asking a civilised question.'

'If you don't like my tone, I certainly don't like yours.'

A voice crackled on Slate's radio. After a brief exchange of words, he turned to face Wendy and Prue.

'Uttley, take over here. I want statements from this pair. Come with me, ladies.'

'Do what?' said Wendy.

'This area's now a crime scene. Your presence and refusing to cooperate is suspicious, especially as you're related to the man we're after, Miss Penn.'

'He hasn't done anything,' Prue wailed.

'Absconding isn't the action of an innocent man, nor is keeping that man's whereabouts quiet. I want those statements. Either get into the car willingly or I'll arrest you both.'

45

Statements and Sympathy

E arly evening, down in Treeton police station, Prue waited in reception for Wendy to surface. It was clocking two hours since marked cars had whisked the friends off. In separate interview rooms, each had given a recorded statement.

Prue's distress was palpable. She advised Uttley about her condition and he treated her cordially. With gentle nudging, she confessed she'd heard about Lady Biggin-Smythe's country cottage in passing. It wasn't a lie. She said it was only natural to assume Tom might be there if the rumours about him and Lucinda were true.

Wendy emerged from her interview, twisting her bright orange cap between irritated fingers. It looked crumpled and miserable. The women embraced, both hungry, fatigued, and thirsty.

'What an ordeal! Can't wait to get home. Are you okay, Wendy?'

'Not the best, but at least it's over. I've been worried about you. Jon's place isn't far, but I'll call a taxi.'

'Good idea. Don't think I could face walking after that.'

'Come on, let's get out of here.'

Away from the stuffy station, breathing in the pleasure of the cool evening air, Prue spoke again. 'Had to tell them we were looking for Tom. They're not stupid.'

'That's fine. My footprints are all around that cottage, anyway. Would've been pointless to deny I'd been snooping. Said we'd heard a rumour about her cottage being near Pengelly's place. You were adamant you were going to explore, so I thought it best to go with you. Said I wandered around the house, saw nobody home, and came back to the gate.'

'Were they okay with that?'

'Seemed to be. Think there's no love lost between Slate and the aristos, especially milord and the merry widow. In fact, he came over as quite sympathetic.'

'Slate took your statement?'

'Of course. I'm a real dahlink and have that devastating effect on men. He has a soft spot for me. Either that or he likes to remind me who's boss. Must be the latter because his brows didn't perform in the interview. Fresh from the country, thought they'd do a line dance or hoedown, but they were out of puff.' Wendy pulled on her mangled cap and tutted.

'Oh, Wendy, you're a scream. Anyway, what did Slate say?'

'Warned me to keep away and let the police do their job. Expected nothing less, but he was full of disdain for the Biggin-Smythe clan. Something's not right. Like Slate wants to investigate the family, but can't. Don't know. Can't explain it. I mentioned Pengelly's pending eviction. That vibe won't go away. Can't explain that either.'

Prue reached out to Wendy. 'If there's anyone who can sort this out, it's you. And Jon. Windy and Darling. Team Awesome. Thanks for your friendship today.'

'Always. That's my phone pinging. Message from Jon. Must be on his break. Asking how I'm doing, and do I need a lift back to Treeton?'

Prue chuckled. 'Poor old Jon, missing out on all the fun. He's clueless about what's happened this afternoon.'

'Won't be clueless too long. I'm sure he'll be glad that he doesn't have to rush all the way to Treeton and back.'

'Do you think he'll give me a lift back to Tor?'

'I should have asked Slate to drive you, but never mind. I think we both need cheering up following our ordeal today.'

'Definitely.'

'Tell you what, you have my room and I'll kip on the settee. No doubt Jon'll be tired when he gets in. He'll drive us to Tor tomorrow morning. If she agrees, I'll have a word with Antonia.'

'How can she help?'

'Don't know yet, but she told us about milady's country retreat and must know a lot more. She's earwigged on many cosy chats. My gut's leading me to the Biggin-Smythe estate. Think that's the next piece of the puzzle. Speaking of guts, mine thinks my throat's been cut. Taxi. Food. Drink. Shower. Sleep. In that order.'

46

Jon le Taxi

A nimated chat and laughter filled Jon's car as he, Wendy, and Prue travelled to Honest Tor after a simple breakfast.

'Typical. I have to work, and you two get all the excitement, although not the type you wanted or needed.'

After his shift in the Noose, Jon hadn't returned home until the early hours and crashed within minutes. He didn't know Prue had stayed over until he showed for breakfast. Wendy briefed him on the latest.

'I appreciate the lift home, Jon, and for letting me stay last night.' Anxiety had lessened, but Prue couldn't help fidgeting in the passenger seat.

'You're welcome. Since Wendy sold her car to pay enormous renovation bills, I'm your taxi. Wendy's taxi. Anyone's taxi. Should install a meter,' Jon joked.

'You make quite the chauffeur, and thanks for letting me drive sometimes. Milady's article should fetch a wedge and voilà. A new motor for me. Hopefully. In the meantime, my windy friend, you're Jon le Taxi.'

'Happy to help. Being interrogated is no fun. Been there. Don't fancy going again. The view was awful.'

'Wasn't really an interrogation. Just giving statements. No arrests. No Spanish Inquisition. A few sticky questions and the odd disapproving look,' said Prue.

'Bet you got the "let us do our job" speech. Heard that a few times. As if they're incapable of doing it.'

'Rings a bell. Just wish they'd investigate other leads and stop picking on Tom.'

'Trouble is, Slate's right. Running away from the law doesn't look good. Hope this business to nail the real culprit comes up trumps, otherwise Tom's going down.'

'Have you met the driver, Prue? Introducing Mr Mel O'Drama, whose gaffes put faux pas to shame. Fluffs. Howlers. Bloopers. Blunders. You name it, he'll spew a miscue. He loves a dollop of theatre. Brings quality ham to any proceedings. In fact, tragedy's his middle name.'

'Thought I was Jon le Taxi? Blame my size elevens. Yeti feet always muck up. Sorry, Prue.'

'Don't worry. It's all my fault. If we hadn't gone up there, the police wouldn't have collared us. Wendy tried to warn me.'

'The cops figured it out for themselves. They were bound to hit on milady's cottage. Probably been hunting for days. Slate's heard the rumours about her association with Tom. The rest's child's play, so to speak.'

'Seems that way, Wendy.'

'Tom would've moved on, anyway. Couldn't hang around there forever,' Wendy said.

'Where do you think he's gone?'

'No idea, Jon, but milady knows more than she's letting on.'

'Reckon he's hiding on the family estate?' Prue said.

'A possibility.'

'Lu Brush told us the family was catholic. Remember, Wendy? Bet the big house has priest holes and secret rooms and passageways. She reckoned they'd been filled in, but I think she's filling us in. With rubbish.'

'A serious probability,' Wendy agreed.

'How would we know if Tom's in a priest hole or some other hidey hole? That woman won't tell us, will she?' Prue said.

'Wouldn't bank on her keeping quiet. She confessed her affair with Monty King to me, something she kept hidden from the police. Speaking of which, I think another cookery class calls. Where Papa King's head chef. Not his offspring.'

'Must we?' Prue screwed up her face.

'No, but if King can spill just one drop, we must drink. Anything and everything to clear Tom's name, though I could kill him for putting you through this pain.'

'Wendy makes a valid point, Prue.'

'She does,' Prue agreed.

'That's settled then. I'll track down the class. Get wired for Monty.'

47

The Plot Thickens

E ddie dished up full veggie breakfasts to Jon and Wendy. They'd only had toast and coffee and were still hungry. 'Hear you had fun and games up at Peck's Wood yesterday, Wendy?'

'Damn those woodpeckers. Always telling tales. Imagine the entire village knows by now.' Wendy smiled thanks to Will for the round of toast, coffee, and orange juice. She watched him scurry back towards the kitchen, looking dejected.

'Treeton Police can't muscle into our little corner of the world without it making a fuss. That's how village life works. If anyone didn't know before, they will now.'

'Bet Annie's gone into full spin with this one. Wearing out poor Jemima while slobbering the latest to anyone who cares to listen. The pedalling peddler.'

Eddie curled his lip. 'That woman never stops.'

'She ruined my chance of a chagachino this morning,' Wendy grumbled. 'Soon as we spotted her in Beans and Leaves, we did off to escape the gunge and grilling.'

'Oh, well. Adam's loss's our gain,' Eddie laughed.

'This tastes lovely, Ed. Bet Will'll make head chef in no time.'

'Right now, he is head chef, Jon, and, unless there's a miracle, can't see Tom working here again. In that case, the role's permanent for Will. He's not happy about it. Thinks he's too young to take on the responsibility. Said this morning, he was making this his last day, but no sign of his notice yet.'

'Poor Will. And poor Tom.' Jon dipped buttered toast into the runny egg and gobbled it up before yolk dribbled down his chin.

'He might be innocent, like you say, but in the meantime, that doesn't help me. Will's a fine chef, though, and the agency guy's doing okay.'

'Any more hassle from the heavies, Eddie?'

'Nope. But they'll be back, Wendy. If I could pinch some of your valuable time later today, I'd be so grateful.'

'No problem. This afternoon's good. Tell me, who's doing all the fancy swan napkins around here? Never seen them before.'

'We buy them in.'

'Already folded?'

'Just like that. About the heavies. I knock off at four.'

'Okay. We'll have a chat when you're finished.'

'You're a star. See you then.' Eddie sloped off.

'What do you make of that, Windy? Buying in swan napkins. Since when? And Eddie went all funny. He couldn't wait to get away. What's he hiding? My instinct's grumbling again.'

'You and your gut, but I know what you mean. A bit suspect. Did you speak to Antonia?'

'Yes.' Wendy poured another coffee, then picked at her food. 'It's all blown up at the big house. Milady's gone missing, and Dickie's in a rage.'

'Again! What's up this time?'

'Something to do with a locked garage and missing keys. Dickie believes Lucinda has them. Antonia wants to meet us tomorrow. Okay?'

'You bet. Can't wait to hear the latest instalment.'

'I'll spend some time with Prue after breakfast and see Eddie later. One more thing.'

'What's that?'

'Antonia said milord made a second will, but got himself killed before signing it.'

48

Where There's a Will

It hadn't struck noon, but Antonia Biggin-Smythe was already on her second glass of chilled Chardonnay and her third round of small talk. She'd worn out shoes, handbags, and make-up, and now her upcoming holiday took centre stage.

Jon and Wendy ordered another pot of coffee. Wendy was in no mood for more tomfoolery. Like the wayward escapee, her patience had fled.

'Stop messing about, Antonia. Forget the Hawaiian hula and give us the Dickie quickiestep.'

'Sorry to leave you hanging. Must say, thanks for seeing me. Needed to get away from home. It's heavy at the best of times, but now it's an asylum.'

'That bad?'

'I'm used to my darling brother being a spoiled, entitled brat, but he's outdoing himself lately with his vicious tantrums.'

'Hasn't Dickie always been touched?'

'Can always count on you to say what you feel, Wendy,' Antonia laughed.

'What's up with him now?'

'Extremely edgy. Eggshell territory. We're all avoiding him. He's furious about a locked garage and incensed because no one knows where the keys are.'

'No spares?' Jon asked.

'Don't know. As far as I'm aware, ground staff look after keys. We keep our cars in separate garages.'

'What's in that garage?'

'Gardening equipment.'

'So, why's Dickie going ape because he can't get in? Why does he want gardening tools? Hang on, we saw him arguing with a gardener the other day.' Jon's mind whirred into overdrive.

'That's right. Is that why they clashed, I wonder?' said Wendy.

'Maybe our fugitive's parked his car there.'

'Exactly. Tom's car must be inside, and milady's swiped the keys.'

'Still doesn't explain Dickie's behaviour,' Antonia stressed, guzzling a mouthful of Chardonnay.

'I know. There must be an explanation, and the only way to find out is to open that garage,' Jon raved.

'Which brings us to our next question. Presumably, only milady can open the garage. What's happened to her?'

'Missing for twenty-four hours. Nobody knows where she is.'

'Take it you heard about yesterday?' Wendy said.

'Yes. All the staff are talking about the police raiding Lucinda's cottage. Estate and village life can be humdrum, so people get excited at nothing, although for some it's a big deal.'

'Were you the only one who knew about her second home?'

'Doubt it, Wendy, but she doesn't tell me her secrets and I don't tell her mine.'

'Thought as much the other day.'

'Exactly.'

'Well, it's obvious what's happened. The police suspected Lu of hiding a fugitive and found out about the cottage,' said Wendy.

'But Tom wasn't there.'

'Yes, but forensics would have ripped that house apart and found something. You mentioned your father's will?'

'I went with George and Royce to see the solicitor yesterday.'

'Where was Dickie?' said Jon.

'Don't know. Don't care. The solicitor was glad he wasn't with us. Doesn't like him either. Can't think of anyone who does. We talked through the formalities and the solicitor just dropped the new will into the conversation. Daddy had it drawn up, but didn't sign it. Null and void, apparently.'

Wendy was agog. In her legal years, she'd cuddled probate law, but had never given it a loving bear hug. Regardless, she knew enough to know the importance of this development. Signed or not. 'Why a new will?'

'Two major differences.'

'Which are?'

'He cut out Richard and Lucinda.'

'That's interesting. Why?'

'The solicitor wouldn't say. I suspect Daddy didn't tell him. That was his way. Everything was cloak and dagger.'

'How do you feel about it, Antonia?' Wendy was more than curious.

'Shocked, I guess. I don't give two hoots for Richard, and the same goes for me and the queen. Obviously, Daddy had the same idea. His son was an overgrown child. His wife played around and swept everyone else under the carpet.'

'Told you Lu Brush was a great name,' Jon roared. 'A broom for all rooms. Swept everyone under the carpet. That's classic.'

'Antonia's being serious here, Jon,' Wendy said, struggling to keep a straight face. 'It's quality, yes, but cut the toilet humour and pull yourself together.'

'Sorry. Carry on,' Jon muttered, almost choking as he fought to suppress laughter.

'Richard's still my brother, so not sure why Daddy would want to disinherit him. As for Lucinda, Daddy idolised her, or so it seemed.'

'Clearly oblivious to her womanly wiles,' said Jon.

'Or was he? I think your father knew a lot more than he let on,' said Wendy.

'Wow. You reckon he knew about Tom and was plotting against her all along?'

'Yes, and probably knew about her fling with King, too. Divorce would bring scandal and shame, and Seymour Biggin-Smythe had to preserve the family reputation. I wager that's what swung his decision. To cancel the business proposal with King and cut Lucinda out of his will. Dickie's another matter, but he fits in to this web somewhere. Is he the fly?'

'So you know all about the affair? I guessed ages ago. This new will business is making sense. Daddy always had a ruthless streak and played his cards close to his chest.'

'Who would've inherited his title under the new will?' Wendy said.

'You'll know that title usually passes to the eldest son, but Daddy wanted George to be his successor.'

'Well, that's that. Unless we get anything on him, Dickie's lord and master,' Wendy huffed.

'What about Lu Brush?' Jon said.

'She's been acting like the boss, but Richard insists on calling her the dowager. I don't know all the protocol.'

'Nor me, Antonia. I think Lucinda keeps her title until Dickie marries. His wife would then become Lady Biggin-Smythe and Lu would be the dowager. Imagine there'll be a wing of Biggin-Hall or a cottage on the estate. Not the one your father bought for his naughties. But who in their right mind would marry Dickie? What does the will say?'

'There was generous provision in the first will, which is still the official one. An equal split of the estate between the children and widow. Ownership of the house passes to the eldest child, and you're right, Wendy. She gets the dower house. It's early days, and probate's far from settled, but Richard's doing everything possible to expedite her departure.'

'And she's doing everything to resist. She didn't strike me as a pushover. This changes everything. Do the police know about the second will?'

'Yes. Our solicitor mentioned it to the chief. He said the proposed change was important even though Daddy didn't sign it.'

Jon scratched his chin. 'It's possible the police think Lu Brush, with Tom's help, killed your father before he could sign his new will. She must've found out he was planning to make changes and be out in the cold if he did. Makes Tom's disappearance look worse than ever. I'm glad Prue's not here. This doesn't look good.'

'Nope. Nor explains where Dickie comes in,' said Wendy.

'Could be in cahoots with Lu Brush. All this animosity's just a front.'

'Besides the solicitor and your father, who knew about the proposed change to the will?' Wendy said.

'I don't know. It's easy for things to slip. Besides, Richard's good at keeping tabs on people, and the queen of hearts can always work her charm.'

'And if all else fails, a backhander or two'll always grease the wheels,' Jon said. 'What do we do now?'

'Pray. If you like,' Wendy said.

Jon's face twisted. '*Things aren't that bad*.'

Wendy's phone rang. 'Hi, Prue. Slow down. You what? When did he? We're coming over.'

'What?' Jon probed.

'Tom called.'

49

Hell's Heart

'He tells me not to worry, but how can I not?' Prue wept. 'This is driving me insane. Can't cope anymore.'

Prue's chronic anxiety aggravated air hunger that could lead to hyperventilation. If it happened, the correct breathing technique calmed her.

Wendy held Prue's hand. 'Better?'

'Yes, thanks.'

'If you're up to it and want to tell us what Tom said, that's fine. But don't push yourself. It can wait.'

Prue took a long drink of cool water. 'I'll tell you the gist. He said he was sure I'd know what happened at Peck's Wood. He was at the cottage briefly. Said I'd find out Biggin-Smythe made a second will that doesn't include Richard or Lucinda, but the old goat snuffed it before he could sign. He knows it looks bad. Puts Lucinda in the frame and we'd all think he helped her kill. He wishes he'd kept away from Lucinda, but he swears he didn't murder his lordship. Said he's having to lie even lower than before. Must go right into hell's heart. That's the only way he can make the police see the truth. Whatever that means.'

'Blimey. Tom certainly has a flair for the dramatic. He should team up with Jon. They'd put Shakespeare to shame.'

Despite the situation, Prue managed a smile. '*What does it all mean, Wendy?*'

'Wish I knew, but I don't.'

Until now, Antonia had only been a spectator. Now she spoke. 'See? The new will was supposed to be confidential, but it got out anyway.'

'I suppose you think Tom helped Lucinda kill your dad?' Prue accused.

Antonia said nothing.

'You must admit, this all puts a bad spin on things,' said Jon.

'He has a point,' Wendy agreed.

'I thought you were my friends.' Prue sulked.

'Oh, Prue. We are. I'm sure there's a rational explanation. There are a few suspects on the list and no concrete evidence pointing to anyone.'

Jon scratched his head, then nipped at his chin. 'Think we'll need to go away and think about this new development. My head can't take it in right now. Like an ancient, blurred map I can't read.'

'I'll stay with Prue. I'm hoping for a gab with Barbara Mardell, too. While I'm digging deep into parish archives, you could dig deep into a certain lockup on a certain estate. Okay to take Antonia home and do that, Jon le Taxi?' Wendy flashed a sneaky grin.

'No worries. I rather liked the afternoon tea there.'

'Doubt there'll be sweeties. You've had your fill, mate, unless Lu piles up the patisserie.'

'Pity. I won't bother asking her. Let me know if you need a lift back to Treeton.'

'Will do. I'll call Barbara. See if she'll let me dive for pearls of wisdom. If I can get any traction on this mad affair, it'll be an epiphany. Get me and my drama giving Mr Histrionics a run for his money.'

'You'll never upstage me,' Jon objected. 'Hope you feel well soon, Prue. Don't forget, we're with you on this.'

'I'm better now, thanks. Sorry about snapping at you all. Just wish this nightmare was over.'

'It's understandable. This saga's enough to push anyone over the edge, never mind close to it,' Wendy said.

Jon gestured to Antonia. 'Better go. Leave these two ladies in peace.'

'Give my best to Lu, Windy!'

'If she's there.'

50

The Lockup

O n route to the big house, Jon and Antonia sat in comfortable silence. Naturally shy, Jon wasn't a fan of small talk, refusing to fill the hush with what he deemed meaningless conversation. Outgoing, Antonia felt the same. Instead, they admired the picturesque scenery. Clipped hedges flanking the road. Wheatfields and lush pastures. Hills rolling as far as the eye could see. There was a gentle breeze, the sun struggling to poke through the bank of moving cloud. When it eventually smiled, a thought struck Jon.

'Will Dickie be around today?'

'Don't know, Mr Windup. He never tells me what he's doing. Why do you ask?'

'If he's not about, I wouldn't mind having a look at that garage. Wendy was angling at me having a nose.'

'But it's locked.'

'That's a glass half-empty way of looking at it. You never know. I could have a way of releasing the lock.' Jon's expression was pure mischief.

'That's intriguing. Wendy said you had a few tricks.'

'No guarantee, mind. I can only try.'

'I'll speak to Marie. If anyone knows about Richard, she will.'

'Great. Could you also ask if she's seen Lu Brush? Wouldn't mind asking her a thing or two.'

'I will,' Antonia giggled.

When he reached Biggin Hall, Jon once again marvelled at the sheer size, the beautiful architecture, and the phenomenal grounds. He headed to the front door, but Antonia grabbed his arm.

'Not that way. According to darling Richard, that door's for the plebs. He's such an idiot. He uses it himself. We all do.' Antonia didn't hide her disdain.

'I forgot the landed gentry has doors for all occasions. During one of his puffed-up lectures on wealth, titles, and power, your dad told us plebs from the Noose about the upstairs-downstairs logistics. Sorry to bring it up, but he had a way of getting under people's skin.'

'Don't remind me. Apologies for all the pomp.'

'Don't be. You're not to blame.'

Inside the big house, the couple stood in an entrance vestibule leading into a hallway. Antonia escorted Jon to a reception room. Thankfully, no crystal or glass allowed.

'How many lounges does this place have?'

'You probably know, but we don't say lounge. Lounges are for hotels, or something stupid like that. This is a drawing room. The blue room to be present and correct.'

'Would never guess,' Jon smirked. 'It's all blue.'

'You'd get along with my younger brother, Royce, Mr Windup. He's on my wavelength.'

'Thanks. I'll keep that in mind.'

'Wait here. I'll find Marie.'

'What happens if someone comes?'

'Just tell them you're my guest.'

'Got it.'

Jon followed Antonia's exit, then looked around. Blue décor. Blue furniture and furnishings. Blue rug. A sea of blue ornaments with fancy white decoration. From a clock to a plant pot to a collection of urns and jugs. The room was a lot smaller than the one Lucinda chose for her interview. Maybe used less, hence the reason Antonia had picked it. Like other areas of the house, enormous portraits and a fireplace adorned the walls. There was no full suit of armour, but there was a striking glass cabinet housing a trio of polished medieval helmets.

Antonia returned with a smile. 'Good news. Marie said Richard left about ten and no one's seen him since. His main car's not in the garage. The one he uses for business.'

'Brilliant. But what about Lu Brush?'

'Still no sign. Guess she's fallen down the rabbit hole.'

'Hope she stays there. Where's this lockup?'

'Back the way we came.'

'After you.'

The pair hurried to the gardener's outbuildings, Antonia surprising Jon with her preference for walking. He knew others in the family would have insisted on a chauffeur-driven ride in a buggy. Maybe not Royce.

'You're not enamoured with the grand life, are you Antonia?'

'I'm very grateful for my upbringing, Mr Windup, but often despair. We're all human and should be kind to one another, but that isn't always the way with the elite. The custom and ceremony is tiresome. The inequality, ugly.'

'Yes. As Wendy says, we all came into the world the same way. We'll go the same way too.'

'Precisely.'

'It's refreshing to hear someone of your ilk talk the way you do.'

'Like I said, we're all human.'

'Is it true the family's more or less a big, glorified boys' club?'

'That's fair. It was for Daddy. Richard's the same, especially when he holds shooting and hunting weekends for his silly friends. Both men and women. So irritating. So cruel.'

'Not your thing.'

'No, Mr Windup.'

'Please, call me Jon.'

'Thanks. I will.'

The couple passed an assortment of outbuildings, rounded a corner, then reached a row of lockups.

'We use these buildings for storing equipment, heavy machinery, and sundries.'

'Suppose all that grass must be cut. Gardening hundreds of acres must be like shovelling snow when it's snowing. A never-ending job.'

'Yes. Something like that. Here we are.'

Jon now faced two heavy wooden doors, bound by a padlock. 'Perfect. I could've been in bother with a mortice lock. Hope no one's around.'

'Don't worry. Ground staff will thank you if you can open this building.'

'Let's do it, then.' Jon unpocketed his pack and fished for a hairpin to work the padlock. 'Drat!' he rasped.

'Problem?'

'This one's awkward, but hopefully … got you, you scamp.' Jon removed the padlock and heaved. The left door refused to budge. After a hefty tug, the right one shifted and fully opened. He examined the left door. 'So, that's why it wouldn't give. It's bolted to the ground, but I'll soon fix that.' Jon lifted the heavy bolts and shoved the left side open.

Antonia peered inside. 'There's a car in here. I've never seen it before.'

'I have. It's Tom Trebilcock's.'

51

The Treasury

A n Aladdin's cave of chaos and clutter. That's what Jon and Antonia faced. Shelves holding old paint cans, brushes, and emulsion trays. A snarl of tree ties, twine, and plant wires. A crumpled paper trail. Old coats and shoes and bag upon bag of all kinds of everything.

'What a mess,' Jon huffed. 'Thought I was untidy. If Wendy was here, she'd have a fit. Hello. What's this?'

Other than Tom's car, there was little else of substance in the lockup, until Jon's big hooter stumbled upon an unlocked cupboard. Wide eyes spied two bin bags, a laptop, and a printer. Jon untied one bag, winded at the contents. A genuine scam paper trail.

'Now we know why the heir's in a rage. Tom's seized Dickie's dirty dough den and sinful stepmummy's pocketed the key.'

'Must be a fortune there,' Antonia shrieked, ready to rummage in the bag and grab a handful of notes.

'Hold up! Something tells me they're fake. Wish I had a pair of gloves.' Jon took out his mobile phone, widened the opening of the bag, and took pictures. He switched on the torch, whooping at the bundles of £50 notes, then crouched down to examine them.

'Can't touch, but I'm sure these are forgeries. Just like those rammed in the old boy's … your dad's mouth.' The nickname had slipped out unchecked.

Antonia couldn't decide whether to laugh or cry. She moved to the door. 'Let's go outside.'

Out in the open air, Jon cursed his clanger. 'The sun's playing chase with the clouds,' he said lamely.

Antonia may not have seen eye to eye with her father, but best reserve "the old boy" for Wendy, Eddie, and those who got it. Jon was sure Slate got it too, even though the chief inspector had chided him for being disrespectful. Antonia's next words tapped into Jon's thoughts.

'Should we call the police? This is the last thing the family needs, so soon after Daddy's death.'

'Indeedy. Trouble is, Dickie'll deny knowledge of dud banknotes. Unless he's been careless and handled them with bare hands, it's his word against whoever wants to point the finger. He'll probably claim they belong to Tom Treblicock, and with Tom's car in the garage and wanted for your dad's death, things don't look good for him to start with.'

'And you've handled the lock and we've both been inside.'

'Exactly. I was working alone in the pub the night of the killing, so the police haven't ruled me out as a suspect. Good idea to keep this quiet for now.'

'What about the doors?'

'I'll put the lock back on, make it look like we've never been here. Must text Wendy first though.'

Jon readied to type a message when a burly hand grabbed his arm. 'Not so fast.'

52

Goons and Guns

J on had never seen a shotgun at close range, let alone kiss the barrel. Antonia had seen all sorts of guns, but not by choice. Being part of family Biggin-Smythe, meant it was tricky avoiding the trappings of blood sports and shooters. Jon was sure this man, in grubby overalls and hobnail boots, was the one Dickie had argued with when he and Wendy toured the grounds.

'Jones. What on earth are you doing?' Antonia yelled.

'Get in there, the pair of you. In! I won't say it again.'

The nervy pair stumbled backwards into the lockup.

'Jones! What is the meaning of this? Put that gun down. Immediately.'

'You've seen everything in here. I can't let you leave.'

'Seen what?'

It was clear Jones didn't know what to do. 'Move if you dare,' he said, fishing in his pocket for a small two-way radio. While the shotgun kept his captives in check, he spoke into the machine. Jon and Antonia caught little of the exchange, only the words "found the stuff" and "but we've got a problem."

'His Lordship's on his way,' Jones said, smugly.

'You mean Richard. He isn't his lordship yet. Let us go, Jones, and I'll pretend this never happened.'

'Too late for that now.'

'For heaven's sake.'

'Get back. I'm warning you.'

'It's no good, Antonia. We're at his mercy.' Jon's anxiety hit silent mode.

53

The Comic Relief

D*on't know what he's wearing, but thank the stars he is.* Dickie Biggin-Smythe looked ridiculous at the best of times, but right now, Jon saluted the comic relief.

Standing in Bigsmy Tweed, shotgun cocked over his arm, Dickie had pushed his trousers into long socks and pulled his flat cap over jug ears. His nose seemed to have grown, his eyes were meaner, but his voice hadn't changed. It still snivelled.

'What's all this? My annoying baby sister and that irritating oik who can't keep away.'

'Ready to bully the birds, brother? Thought you were away on business,' said Antonia.

'You thought wrong.'

'Caught them coming out of the lockup. Must've seen everything.'

'How did you get in through locked doors? I presume this car belongs to that fellow the police are hunting for.'

Jon found his voice. 'So that's what was up the other day. Your stuff was in here, but you couldn't get in.'

'Will you be quiet! Quite frankly, I don't care how you got in. In fact, you've done me a favour, now the dowager's AWOL. She must've secured the lock, but you buggers have given me quite a headache. Let's see now.' Dickie paced the ground, scratching his head.

'Indecisive as ever,' Antonia whispered to Jon.

Eventually, Dickie spoke to Jones. 'Take the equipment and cash, and this time, put it in a safe place. Understood?'

Used to submission, Jones didn't question. He grabbed both bags and dragged them outside, came back for the laptop and printer, then did off with his spoils.

'And now I've dealt with him, there's the little problem of the beastly sister and the common oik. You can stay here until I decide what to do. Who knows? Maybe I'll call the police,' he chortled.

'Richard! You can't do this.'

'Lord Richard, you stupid girl. And you're wrong. I can and am.'

'You won't get away with this.'

'Don't be an ass. Women have no clout in my family,' Dickie roared. 'Hand over your phones. Won't have you ruining my plans.'

54

Lockdown

'Well, this is just great.' Jon's Yeti feet pounded the concrete floor. 'Lockdown in a lockup. No windows or light, and no one around to help. Even my drat pack's redundant.'

'I should've asked Marie to tell me when Richard came home. He's so sneaky, he probably went in through a priest hole.' Voice rueful, Antonia was close to tears.

'It's not your fault. If he's that sneaky, he probably came straight here without telling anyone. That's if he's been away on business. A priest hole, you say? That's odd. Lu Brush sa—'

'One or two, still in use. Some filled in. Never mind that. What are we going to do?'

'Let me think. Surely, the ground staff will come along at some stage?'

'I hope so. Don't know their rota.'

'If Dickie used the same padlock to secure the garage, then we know only one person has the key, and she's keeping a low profile.'

'Then how will Richard let us out?'

'Perhaps he intends us to stay in here for all eternity. Unless, of course, he's used his own padlock, or he knows where Lu Brush's hiding.'

Antonia couldn't raise a smile. 'All eternity? That's a bit dramatic. For now, we're stuck here. For how much longer, I don't know.'

'Just humour me and don't worry. We'll get out of here somehow. What do you think Dickie will do now we've found him out?'

'Couldn't say. One thing I do know, he's the most indecisive man ever. The last person you want in an emergency.'

'*This is an emergency.*'

'Richard needs an entire morning just to decide what socks to wear.'

'That bad?'

'Worse.'

'Well, he should've taken all day. Those ones he's wearing are scary. Think he'll phone the police?'

'He might. Tell them he's found Tom's car and make up a story about our involvement. On the other hand, he might not want police snooping around. No telling what he's stashed around here.'

'If he doesn't draw attention to himself or his tools of the trade, the police'll only be interested in the car. However, they might want to do a thorough search. They'll need a warrant, and for some reason, the law's scared of your family.'

'Richard's a coward at heart. I have a feeling he won't take any chances. He'll sleep on it and decide tomorrow, but that doesn't help us. He'll have the last laugh knowing we're spending the night here.'

'Someone must come. Even if they can't unlock the door, they could call the fire brigade or police. Free us using bolt cutters.'

'If he doesn't want police around, it's likely he's given ground staff the rest of the day off.'

'That's just brilliant! You didn't tell anyone you were coming up here?'

'No. Less said the better. What about Wendy?'

'She knows I gave you a lift and suggested I do a bit of snooping, but that's it. She's not stupid. If I'm gone for hours with no contact, she'll twig something's up. Wendy has superb instinct.'

'That's reassuring.'

'Sorry, Antonia, this is all my fault. It was me who wanted to look around. I could never resist a locked door.'

'It's happened, so nothing we can do. Guess I was curious, too.'

'The tummy rumbles are here. I'm peckish.' Jon grumbled at the depressing thought. He hoped acid wouldn't burn. He had no gloop.

'I'm thirsty. And need the loo.'

Jon's anxiety was escalating. He cursed his big nose. Insatiable curiosity had landed him in right in it. 'Locked doors. Windowless. No way of getting out of here.'

'Better start yelling then.'

'Shh. Listen.'

To Jon, the clicking noise could only mean one thing. He'd even trained his iffy ear to recognise the sublime sound. The left garage door flew open, light flooded in, and a familiar face peered around the door.

55

Liberation

N ever thought I'd be happy to see you!' Antonia couldn't believe she'd uttered the unutterable. Such was the power of euphoria.

Standing in the lockup's doorway, frantic eyes darting from Antonia to Jon, Lucinda Biggin-Smythe looked furious. 'I am not so happy that you and your friend have snooped into things you know nothing about. Hold on. You're Wendy's assistant. Mr Wind.'

'For the last time, it's Windup. Come on, Antonia. Let's get out of here.'

Lucinda stepped outside. Jon and Antonia followed.

'So, now you know.'

'Know what?' Jon said.

'Don't play games.'

'I know Tom Trebilcock's car's in there. Know the two of you are having an affair. Also know he's been hiding in your cottage, his sister's distraught, and that you both had no time for your husband and wanted him gone.'

'And you think we killed him? Well, you're wrong.'

'Where did you spring from, Lucinda?' Antonia wanted answers.

'Your friend's right. Everything he says about me and Tom, but we had nothing to do with your father's death, Antonia. It's ridiculous to suggest we wanted him gone. I came here today to check on Tom's car, but heard Richard's voice and had to postpone. I always knew that scoundrel was up to something. Seymour suspected foul play too, but Richard always covered his tracks. With your help, we'll get him. When I said, "now you know," I meant you know about his escapades. Give me a moment.' Lucinda went back inside the lockup to check Tom's car, then came out and secured the doors.

'I thought the police feared you lot,' Jon said.

Lucinda ignored Jon. 'If we had a watertight case, the police may arrest Richard to find out what he's up to. One Biggin-Smythe rule you may not know states if the current lord or his successor disgraces himself in the eyes of the family, he loses his title right. If Richard *is* breaking the law, that's definitely disgracing himself.'

'Interesting, but we don't know if he is,' Jon lied. 'Don't suppose there's any chance of getting my phone back?'

'Knowing Richard, he'll have thrown the phones away out of spite. Or put them down somewhere and forgotten where,' said Antonia.

'Wonder if he's still about?'

'No idea. He's quite the fickle man these days. Here one minute, gone the next,' said Lucinda.

'Which brings us to the million-dollar question. Where is Tom Treblicock?' Jon pushed.

Lucinda said nothing.

'His car's parked in that lockup. Is he hiding here? Everyone, including the police, thinks he killed Lord Biggin-Smythe. I'm sure he's innocent. Even though he could have aided you in—'

'I beg your pardon?'

'You know your late husband made a second will, excluding you and Richard, don't you?'

Lucinda paled, but remained silent.

'So, you do know. You'll also know your husband didn't sign the will.'

Lucinda nodded.

'Surely everyone knows by now,' said Antonia.

'So, it's possible the police might think you, or Richard, or both of you might have … you know.'

'Murdered Seymour.'

'Yes. The police could already be onto you, but I'm convinced they're reluctant to come here. If I didn't know better, I'd say corruption. Know anything about that Lady Biggin-Smythe?'

'My late husband had a lot of influence in many circles. He and Chief Constable Bowden were both members of the Treeton yacht club. Other than that, I know nothing.'

'Is that so?' Jon wasn't buying.

'Oh, come on. Daddy wouldn't have kept the entire family fortune for philanthropic purposes. You remember what he used to say? *The Biggin-Smythe family is above the law.*'

Lucinda ignored Antonia and maintained a hard face. 'I'd love to stay and chat, but I must be somewhere. I'm taking a risk being here and talking to you. Richard could've seen me. He has eyes and ears all over the place.'

'Where's Tom? In a priest hole? One that hasn't been filled in?' asked Jon.

'I don't know.'

'Don't believe you,' Jon said in a sing-song tone.

Lucinda leaned forward and whispered. 'I don't know where, only that he's somewhere safe. He won't tell me. Now, I must go.' She hurried away.

'Start talking, lady, or an innocent man's going to prison,' Jon bawled.

56

Finding Nelly

B arbara Mardell was a gem and scholar. Wendy's knowledge of the past was admirable, but who better than the church-cum-parish archivist to help her dig deeper into the annals of Treetonshire. Wendy's past excavation had intrigued, and she wanted more fascinating local history. Especially background about the villages, inns, and their notorious clientele. She hoped Barbara could tell her more about Patcheye Peg, even help her locate his grave.

Babs's overall knowledge of Treet was exemplary, but her main interest focused on four villages on Treeton's periphery. Honest Tor was one village, and Babs's stories were about to knock Wendy's learning into a cocked hat.

While Jon did a sneaky beaky at the big house, and Rector Hall shepherded his flock in Little Swell, Barbara invited Wendy to the church. Nestled in the vestry, the pair sipped Kenyan coffee and munched on one of Prue's persuasive Persian lemon cakes.

Wendy's time of interest was early to mid-eighteenth century, give or take a few years either side. With that in mind, Babs had stacked bundles of records onto two trestle tables, including a hard-backed book written and illustrated by local historians, Lottie Carr and Si Dobson. *Not So Sweet Treet, Cads & Crimes in the 1700s*, was a comprehensive chronicle of treachery and treason in eighteenth-century Treetonshire. A journey of grisly goings-on and the grislier penalties paid.

Two pairs of white gloves sat on the table. 'For handling fragile papers and registers. Please wear them to preserve the documents.'

'Of course,' Wendy agreed, dazed by the sheer volume of files and folders, but eager to get stuck in. She'd ask questions first. Maybe that would yield answers and save trawling time. 'Do you know the story of Patcheye Peg?'

'I do. Scandalous, mysterious cad, smuggler, and part-time highwayman. In the day, famous as a pirate captain. Ladies' man, philanderer and hedonist, who often stole other men's women and laughed about it too. Noted for having more than one mistress at the same time. A girl in every inn, although Sal Hoskins from the Noose and Gibbet was his favourite. Expect you know how the Noose got its name.'

'Yes. 'Tis a fascinating history, and because of its celebrated history and grisly star attraction, the pub's kept its name.'

'Peg came to a bad end in the gibbet cage. Many said the show-off deserved all he got. He was also known as Peacock Patcheye Peg, because of the swagger.'

'I knew all of that, apart from the peacock bit. He hated authority. Treated the law with contempt. I'm liked to find his resting place and real name. Understand he's buried in this graveyard. I can't pin down a record of his birth. Do you know?'

'No one knew his name, only his alias. His parents were obscure, too, though the archives say his father sweated for silver in the same way. A corsair and smuggler. A peacock, like his son, and definitely as proud. Called himself Peg too.'

'Patcheye made his name during the Golden Age of Piracy. A dashing dandy. Only on land, of course. At sea he would've worn plain old mariner's togs. Hardy gear for blustery gusts and wild waters. I read pirates got fancied up at their execution. Unless they died at sea, then it was burial overboard. He didn't have a gammy eye either. He loved attention and wore the patch as a fashion statement. It probably thrilled the ladies. Like men today with their six-pack, toned biceps, and tan, fake or no. Did Peg's father also wear a patch?'

'No idea. It's likely. They were both show-offs and Casanovas.'

'Peg certainly lived life on the edge. He was a looker. That's why tales about him are romanticised. Any clue why father and son had the name Peg?'

'At that time, people had a fondness for making an alias from letters of their surname, but there's no evidence to endorse that theory. Without knowing real names, determining a person's existence is a tough task. Parents rarely registered a child's birth. No law to say they must. I'd start by searching from seventeen hundred up to Peg's death around seventeen thirty-five. I believe he was mid-thirties when murdered by Edward Hoskins. Then gibbeted.'

'Nasty Ned. The man who ended Peg and his philandering ways. Didn't know Peg's death day, and he was so young.'

'The perils of flirting with danger.'

'So, is he buried in this graveyard? The research I've done says so, but thought I'd check with you.'

'That's the history. On the hilltop, under a yew.'

'Could you show me?'

'Would love to, Wendy, but my body grumps at hills and rugged ground. Norman Spall should be up there today. He might be able to help. I'll brew another pot of coffee if your stomach can cope.'

'Always.'

'Don't forget the gloves, thanks.' Barbara bustled from the vestry.

Daunted by the task ahead, but keen to get going, Wendy heeded Barbara's advice and slipped on a pair of gloves. She located the births, deaths, and marriages files and opened the births. Barbara returned with more coffee and left Wendy scouring for a couple of hours. Back mid-afternoon, she invited Wendy to rest her eyes and eat a late lunch. In a corner of the vestry, they both tucked into sandwiches and salad dressed in a delicious vinaigrette.

'Any luck with the archives?' Barbara asked.

'Nothing. Like you said, a tough task. I'm finding the search exciting, but it's frustrating not being able to pin down anything concrete. I'll stay another hour, then I must go. Top lunch, by the way. And the dressing's superb. Can I have the recipe?'

'Yes, of course. Wish I could help more with the research, but I'm in the dark, too. Have you looked at the local history book? And the sketches in the archives? If nothing else, you'll get an eyeful of infamous debonair devils who made Treetonshire history.'

'I'll do that. Could be a pleasing way to end a fruitless search. Thanks.'

After lunch, Barbara cleared away, gifted Wendy a jug of iced water and a glass of fresh orange juice, and left her wading through pictures.

Archived sketches showed scarred, one-legged, or one-armed desperados. Men and women. Dressed down or to the nines. 'Spot on, Babs. This is one grim gallery,' Wendy muttered, paying close attention to any rogue wearing an eyepatch.

Halfway through her forage, Wendy clocked an image that had her sitting upright. She blew out a fervid whistle. Male. Age, she couldn't say. And though the face was vaguely familiar, it was the stance that drew her in. *Where had she seen it before? In her search weeks ago? Was that it?* Wendy gaped at the dapper pirate, set to make his mark on Treetonshire, all spiffed up in bright ribbons, ruffles, velvet, and silk. On his legs hung fancy breeches tapering into ribboned stockings. On his head, perched a tricorne hat. A cutlass swung at his left hip, and for sure, he had a pistol or two tucked away in the folds and gathers of his florid body sash. *Why did the expression and posture jolt? Even with the patch?* Beneath the drawing, a caption: Patcheye Peg, date unknown.

Yes, Peg, if the sketch's anything to go by, you *were* a looker. But still no name. Wendy sighed. After another half hour's research, she gave up combing records. At least she'd found her man, and Barbara had spilled a few arresting facts. Not a bad few hours' work. Wendy finished the juice and water, then stacked the files and papers.

Barbara scurried in. 'More refreshments?'

'No. That's me done in here. I'll take a walk uphill. Looking forward to having a chat with the yews and my back and legs'll love the exercise. Thanks for your time and kindness. I appreciate your help.'

'You're welcome. Thank Prue for the lovely cake. Enjoy the view. Bye, Wendy.'

'Bye.'

The glorious weather and tired legs made for a strenuous trek to the top of the hill, but Wendy made it and took Barbara's advice. Enjoyed the view. Then she spied the blot on the landscape. Annie Clegg's male match, gravedigger, Norman "Spanker" Spall, and his faithful shovel scuttling towards her in a blast of hot air and huffs.

His nickname hailed from schooldays, when he picked on younger, weaker kids. A loudmouth bully, too handy with his fists. He married a girl he longed to control, but Jessie Nesbit was neither meek, nor mild, and Norman soon learned he'd met his nemesis. Local rumour said she was handier with her fists than him, and she did the spanking. Often. Served him right for being a thug in his youth, Jessie said. Wendy agreed.

Norman dug his spade into the earth and leaned on the handle. 'You looking for a grave?'

Despite his wife being the boss, he still kept that comical public tough-guy image.

'Can't imagine I'd be looking for anything else, Mr Spall. Certainly not a UFO. Me and my friend tried to find the plot recently, but had no luck. Finding it's of grave importance, my mate said. So, I've come back.'

'With your sharp tongue and wit, I see. Who is it you're looking for? Not much about this graveyard I don't know.'

'I can believe that.'

'Been digging here and tidying up for years. Well?'

'An ancient grave, and I don't know the deceased's name, only his alias. A pirate called Patcheye Peg. Allegedly buried on the hill under a yew tree around seventeen thirty-five. Locals cut him down from the gibbet cage. Finding him's a faint hope, but I'm the positive type.'

'Know him well. His grave, I mean. This way.'

Wendy followed Norman to the hill's crest, stopping when he did under the intricate labyrinth of the branches of an old yew.

'My boss said they buried a famous local pirate here. Called him Patcheye Peg.'

'That's a gift. Do you think your boss would talk to me?'

'Have a hard job. He's dead. I dug his grave. All you'll get's that broken headstone lying on the ground. It's well-worn, but if you look closely, you can see bits of a name and date. Anyway, better get home. Can't be late for the wife.'

'No. Or you'll be digging your own grave.'

Norman hoisted the shovel over his shoulder and trundled downhill.

'Wait up, Mr Spall! Did your boss have any clue of the name on the headstone?' It was a long shot.

'No guarantee, but he thought George Pengelly. A real poser who loved himself. Who knows? Could be related to that puffed-up postie. Same surname goes years back. He wants to watch out or he'll go the same way. That sort often come to a nasty end.' Norman resumed his lope down the bank.

Wendy recalled Barbara's explanation of making an alias from a surname. Pengelly to Peg. That worked. She remembered the sketch. The stance. The look. The flamboyant threads. Could be, or was, an ancestor of Ross Pengelly? Wendy was no nelly. Instinct told her there was no question. The pirate lived on.

57

Trading Tales

'Where've you been? Was ready to call out the sniffer dogs.' Wendy greeted Jon at Prue's door, more relieved than angry.

'Sorry. You wouldn't credit the afternoon me and Antonia've had.'

Jon told of his lockup antics. 'If jolly Jones hadn't cocked his trigger, I would've sent you a message, but Dickie nicked our phones. We were locked up. In a lockup! Or locked down. Same thing. Couldn't believe it when Lu Brush appeared. Our unlikely saviour. She admitted her affair with Tom, but still won't say where he is. I warned her, but she wouldn't give. And that voice of hers was driving me nuts. Sorry, Prue. I did my best. Antonia kindly let me use the loo and gave me a cold drink. As luck would have it, Dickie boy had dumped our phones on a table before he went shooting. Couldn't message you. Battery was dead. Dickie's nothing but a pumped-up pompositor. Saying that, I'm pretty pumped myself. The sleuth done good.'

'He did, and thank goodness you're in one piece. I thought our rum do the other day was bad enough. Trust you to go one better.'

'Not just the last word, Darling. The last deed. Think I need a drink.'

'Best get back to Treeton. How do you feel, Prue?'

'Wish I knew where Tom was, but at least that woman's owned up to her fling with him. I'm going for a rest. As always, Wendy, you've been the best distraction, thanks. Go home. If I need you, I'll call.'

'Be sure to do that. I'll call later, anyway.'

'No worries. Speak soon.' Prue hugged Wendy and kissed her cheek. 'Thank you, my friend. You mean the world to me.'

Wendy drew back and wiped away a lone tear. 'Always. So, Windy, you're bursting with news. And your sleuthing buddy did good, too. I have my own scoop. Ready to go?'

'Think you'd better drive.'

'Feel better?'

'Much, thanks.' Jon had polished off one glass of red and was pouring another.

'You've had a terrible fright. Fancy that goon pulling a gun on you.'

'Could've been unloaded, but we weren't taking any chances. Would've paid to see Dickie's face when he found out we were no longer holed up in that scabby old lockup. Although not *that* scabby. Not for a lockup.'

'And how's Antonia?'

'A little shaken, but she's a toughie. Said she was going to visit her friend in Norfolk. She'd asked *Dunc* if she could stay with him, but it wasn't convenient. No surprise there. Oh, and I can see why the old boy and his ancestors were averse to women.'

'Why?'

'Afraid of the fairer sex. I bet Antonia's real mother's strong. She strikes me as being the assertive type. Like you. I can picture the old boy and that idiot Dickie mouthing off in the gentleman's club about how a woman should know her place.'

'Dickie said he and mummy have a jolly decent relationship. She's a brick, don't you know? He's probably terrified of her. Chauvinistic upper-class men and their archaic beliefs. Mind you, Pengelly isn't blue blood, and he's a neanderthal. Anyway, back to the matter in hand. Milady's appearance was well-timed.'

'Yes, but it wasn't a coincidence. Somehow, she knew we were there. She's had suspicions about Dickie for a while. *I have suspicions about her.* Reckon the big house's full of hidey holes. Even tunnels. Houses that big always had secret hideaways. Aristocrats were fussy about escape routes. Still are for all I know.'

'Lucinda gave no clues about Tom?'

'No. Completely guarded. She went pale when I mentioned the second will. Could be bluffing, of course. I know she and the old boy weren't the happiest couple in the world, but did she snuff him or have him snuffed? She has a smarmy face and a hard streak, but that doesn't make her a killer. She doesn't look like a killer.'

'What does a killer look like? What about Dickie boy?'

'Get the impression, although well-educated and academic, he's not too smart. So indecisive. And his dress sense! I won't make the world's next top male model, but Dickie doesn't need the outfit. He's already a clown.'

'The type who doesn't know whether he wants the loo or a haircut?'

'That's him,' Jon laughed. 'Jolly Jones jumps to his command. He could've bumped off the old boy on Dickie's orders. I don't know. The motive's there.'

''Tis for many who wanted to end milord's days. All suspects had the motive and could've done it. Even Mr Quince. If only he could talk.'

'You're right. I still have this image of Eddie and that big, padded envelope. He clams up sometimes and I don't know why. One more thing. Lucinda said Seymour was a member of Treeton Yacht Club. Chief Constable Bowden, too.'

'The dirty scent of corruption's in the air, but how our peacock postie fits in, I do not know. Have doubtful doubts about that man, and after today's findings, doubtful doubts are shifting to definite definites. Don't know why he doesn't square, but I'm sure it has nothing to do with fake tan and Lycra.'

58

Up the Junction

After a late dinner, Jon and Wendy migrated to the living room. Sipping red wine. Mulling the day's events.

'Okay, Windy. If Dickie was nicked and found guilty of whatever, the title of lord would go to brother George. He's the next son down. A spare.'

'And George gets on better with Lu Brush, Darling.'

'Every time you say that I giggle so much it hurts,' Wendy sniggered. 'Regardless of whether Lu or Dickie are guilty, she'd certainly benefit from the heir's absence. I believe she rescued you not as a kind gesture, but because she wants our help. Nothing like being manipulated into doing someone's dirty work.'

'You mean we're the pawns to her queen?'

'I like your chess analogy.'

'It's apt. She's wealthy. We're the plebs.'

'Speak for yourself. I'm no pleb. Milady's always thinking of her own skin. We know that.'

'Pleb or not, changes nothing. We still think Tom's innocent, or is that me speaking for myself again?'

'This time, you *can* speak for me. Like that bleeding gibbet cage, I've been swaying and swinging but I've come to a stop.'

'What about Pengelly?'

'Like I said, I'm stuck. Right now, he's the proverbial square peg in a round hole. Strange how a few weeks ago, Prue asked for a brief history about the Noose. I obliged, throwing in a notable memoir of the dandy Patcheye Peg with no clue that under our noses, his swaggering kinsman lived and breathed. Uncanny how the pair have similar traits, but dissimilar characters. Explains why I have a soft spot for the pirate and a sore spot for the postie, though.'

'So, what's the next step?'

'With Antonia off to Norfolk, Tom still AWOL, and Lu muted, a visit to the big house's out of the question. That leaves Monty. He's my man.'

'King?'

'He's the only Monty I know. Me and Prue are off to another cookery class, and this time he's in charge.'

'How do you know?'

'Said so on his website, *and* we paid extra for the privilege. If I've been had, there'll be skin and hair flying.'

'Where's the class? Tor, Bogus Hole, or Treeton?'

'None of the above.'

'Where then?'

'Old London town. Inside the belly of the beast itself. I'm ready for King and the Big Smoke. Question is, are they ready for me?'

59

Old London Town

On a scorching early August day, the bustling London underground wasn't the best place to be. Jon dropped Wendy and Prue at Treeton Station, and they travelled to London Paddington before hitting the tube. After much shuffling and weaving on a tightly packed airless train, Prue found a seat. Wendy had to stand near her. Heading for Knightsbridge via the Bakerloo and Piccadilly lines, a trickle of cool air occasionally wafted their way. But the confined atmosphere was taxing. Especially for Prue.

'Not long now,' Wendy said.

'Hope so. Can't stand much more of this.'

'Jon said to come this way, but looking at the map, we could've walked across Hyde Park rather than tubing. I'm no expert, but it probs takes the same time. We'll go back that way. I'll swipe a soapbox and rant for England at Speaker's Corner. A reasonable rant, of course. You can swipe an icebox and chill.'

'I've always wanted to see the Serpentine.'

'You're on. We'll have a splash. Cool you down.'

Wendy pictured the long ascent from the underground tracks to surface level and hoped their destination wouldn't be too busy. Thankfully, when they changed trains, the switch was fairly smooth.

Before they'd set off, Jon'd told them a quirky fact. To prevent overcrowding during busy periods, on descent and ascent, commuters must take the longer route. On the first descent, Prue struggled. Even with fully functioning escalators, Wendy feared the ascent would be challenging. Prue considered such issues a small price to pay and remained resolute, the desire to help Tom driving her on.

'Next stop's ours,' Wendy said.

'Yay,' Prue beamed as the tube pulled into the station and ground to a halt.

Wendy quickly got her bearings when she stepped off onto the platform. 'Follow me,' she said, looking for exit signs. The friends followed the corridor and escalators to surface level, the ascent painless.

'That wasn't too bad. Thought it'd be harder,' Prue said.

'Good to hear. It's funny how going down's harder than going up.'

'Yes. MS's a weird old thing.'

Wendy looked up and down the lively street.

'Are we near Harrods?' Prue said.

'Believe so. If we have time, maybe do some shopping?'

'Sounds lovely. Before or after your reasonable rant?'

'Well, now. There's a teaser,' Wendy chuckled. 'Depends what mood King puts me in. This is a classy part of town. Lots of five-star hotels. We cross over here and head down Sloane Street. King's place's somewhere on the right.'

'How far?'

'Ten minutes or so.'

The pair headed down Sloane Street, passed a series of side streets, then gardens on the left side. To a crossroads and onto Pont Street.

'Not far now,' said Wendy.

'I love red brick facades.'

'Me too. London has some fine buildings. Get out of town! This blue plaque on the wall says Lillie Langtry once lived here.'

'The actress?'

'Can't think of another. Stumbling upon that info has parallels to why we're here.'

'How?'

'Lillie was the mistress of the Prince of Wales, later King Edward the Seventh. Our man's a King, and enjoys dabbling with the ladies too.'

'What a charmer,' said Prue, her tone anything but.

'Keep a lid on it, friend. We're here.'

60

From a Jack to a King

N ear the exit, in a vast room fitted with sophisticated portable cooking stations, Wendy and Prue waited for Montgomery Oliver King. Kuisine by Kingoisseur had gone to a lot of trouble. And rightly so, given the cost of today's class. Hiring a function room here would cost a mint. The location. The ambience. The grandeur. Despite Biggin-Smythe reneging on their deal, King must be doing all right.

Thankfully, the girls had booked as a couple and saved a few quid. Wendy had used another chunk of cash to treat her and Prue to dinner at a nearby restaurant, then an overnight stay in a lower-cost hotel. Wendy's savings just about stretched, but she couldn't justify paying a grand a night plus in this hotel. After much searching, she'd found a decent place close to Hyde Park. Though steep, the cost of a twin room was half the price of this gaffe. It also catered for Prue's diet and made a nifty starting point for a spot of sightseeing and shopping tomorrow. That soapbox in Speaker's Corner was getting warmer and the iconic Serpentine's lifting lilt sang a cool melody.

At precisely one, Wendy spied a tall, sandy-haired man dressed in chef's whites entering the room. Exuding natural charisma, the slim figure carried himself with air and grace. Wendy grabbed Prue's arm. 'That must be King. Look at that swagger.'

Prue stared hard. 'He's lush. Can see why Lady Lu succumbed.'

'Blimey, thought you weren't interested in blokes. Word is, he was a Jack the Lad in his youth. A cocky show-off. Another Ross Pengelly. I'd wait before you swoon. He might not be so *luursh* up close. And try not to stare. It's uncouth.'

Prue blushed and composed herself. 'Sorry, but from what I can see, he's a dish. Don't you think? He doesn't look like a killer. Quite the opposite, in fact.'

'What does a killer look like? Said the same thing to Jon about milady. Always watch the handsome charmers, Prue. Most of all, don't forget why we're here. We're helping Tom, remember?'

'I haven't forgotten, silly. He's my brother. What are we making?'

'Chocolate. Working with. Not making.'

'You should've brought Jon. He'd be in heaven.'

'Pfft. He wouldn't do any baking. Just wolf enough chocolate to coat The Shard.'

'That bad?'

'Worse.'

'So, we've come all this way to make a chocolate cake? For four hours?'

'Not just any old chocolate cake. Sachertorte. A famous Viennese speciality, invented by Franz Sacher in the nineteenth century for some Prince whose name escapes me. But we've gone one better. Rubbing shoulders with a king, and that's our prime reason for being in old London town. Pin back your ears. Looks like the monarch's ready to address his subjects.'

King greeted the class of twenty-four bakers behind twelve workstations. Wendy and Prue were near the back, but the room's acoustics made his voice loud and clear.

'Ladies. Gentleman. Good afternoon and welcome to Kingoisseur. You lucky people have the privilege of a lesson with the master and, make no mistake, you're in for a rare treat. Here stands a man blessed with years of experience, unparalleled excellence, sublime skills, and a smile to melt Antarctica. Montgomery Oliver King, Chef Extraordinaire. Call me Monty.'

'Call him twit with a capital T,' Wendy whispered to Prue.

'He might be handsome, but is he full of himself, or what?'

'Definitely full of himself. Neither looks nor sounds like a what. He's the "I love me, who do you love" type.'

King gave a potted history of himself and his company, then a series of cooking anecdotes. A swellhead, but in fairness he'd grafted hard to build his company from nothing. Now here he stood in front of adoring fans, hosting cookery classes in one of London's top hotels. The venue was a stage, and he loved it.

He counted down to start the class, and everyone started prepping. Wendy and Prue knew their way around scales, measuring spoons, and cake tins and had their ingredients ready in no time.

'King's on his way down, Wendy.'

'Calm yourself, woman. Keep your eyes off the smooth operator and more on making a smooth cake batter.'

'Hello, lovely ladies. How are you getting on?'

With his clipped accent and smarm, King cut an impressive dash. If she had a mind to let it ruffle her, Wendy knew he'd waste no time in trying to conquer. He was that type. Wendy didn't have a mind, nor a desire to applaud the knave at work, but she'd play her part, and hoped his guile wouldn't suck Prue in.

'We're winning,' Wendy said, ready to test King. Stuff the Sachertorte. She wasn't here just to crack eggs. 'Not the best, but why reach the top when there's nowhere to go but down?'

King ignored Wendy's remark and checked their progress, his face iced with a show of indifferent expressions. 'I've seen worse.'

'Can't tell if that's complimentary or critical,' Wendy snapped.

'Please excuse my sense of humour, ladies. Things don't look bad at all. Carry on this way and you'll have a fine torte on your hands. My register tells me your names are Wendy and Prue. Who's who and where are you from?'

'I'm Wendy. This is Prue. We're from Treetonshire.'

'Delighted to meet you. You're a long way from home.'

'We'd fly to the moon and back for a chance to shine with the Michelin man. That's stars. Not tyres. Same company.'

'It is, and thank you. I hope you're not disappointed. From Treetonshire, you say? A county hogging the headlines recently. Some wealthy man murdered?'

Wendy could be both actor and audience and, much like Lucinda, Monty King craved the latter. Time to switch character mode. 'That's right. The stinking rich Lord Seymour Biggin-Smythe. There's a hot rumour that you and *some wealthy man* were planning to launch a business together. Right or wrong?'

King fanned away Wendy's comment as if beating off a pesky flea. 'Right, but that was years ago. Big plans for a chain of gastropubs, but he changed his mind. Not to worry. These things happen.'

'Wouldn't have anything to do with you canoodling with his consort, would it?'

King's square jaw hit the ground before the words left Wendy's mouth. He picked it from the floor and fixed it back on his face. 'Sorry?'

'Another popular rumour doing the rounds.'

'You don't say much, Prue.'

'Not when I'm baking,' Prue said, feeling a foolish rush of warmth flooding her cheeks.

'Normally, she won't shut up, Monty, but put her anywhere near food and she's super focused.'

'I can see she's enjoying herself.'

At last, Prue found her voice. 'I think you know my brother.'

'Do I?'

'He went to the catering college where you were a lecturer.'

'Again, years ago. What's his name?'

'Tom. Tom Trebilcock.'

Wendy didn't take her eyes off King's face. For a moment, she traced a troubled look before he regained composure.

'Sorry. Don't remember.'

'That's odd. He remembers you.'

'Then he has an enviable memory. There were so many students back in the day. I was and still am very ambitious. My focus was on teaching and helping trainees pass exams. I can't recall names or faces. Not then. Not now. Anyway, keep up the good work.' King moved onto the next table, where a married couple wrestled with chocolate and cake tins.

'Something you said, Prue?' Wendy laughed.

'He knew I was tongue tied. Landed myself right in it.'

'Wouldn't worry. You won't be the first, nor the last.'

'But how to get him to confess? You seem immune to his charm.'

'He doesn't impress me, nor do his eyebrows. I'd pay good money to watch Slate's brows jig and jive, but Monty's don't do the do. I admit he has charisma. If you're into that old silver-tongued slime.'

'He nearly dropped when you mentioned Lady Lu.'

'I know. Wanted to see how he'd react. He didn't disappoint.'

'Couldn't wait to change the subject. Did you buy that bit about Tom?'

'Swear he's hiding something. Who knows? We're desperate for answers, but shouldn't clutch at anything just because. We better get on, Madame Penn. Our torte won't make itself. By the way, just as well you left the ferrets at home. You'll have more than a flushed face if King cops a flash of the fulsome front.'

The class ended at five. As the room emptied, Wendy collared King. Despite a few tricky questions earlier, the radiant smile hadn't left his face.

'Ladies! Congratulations to you and your triumphant torte. Sacher would be proud.'

'It was a blast,' Prue smiled.

'Sorry if I embarrassed you with the Lady Biggin-Smythe talk, Monty. Village gossip's second nature to rural types.'

'Apology accepted, but not needed. I knew her, of course, but only through her husband. I knew of her reputation as a predator. Some would say, why not, with a husband thirty years older. Don't know if she's still on the hunt now he's gone. Don't think she married for love. If you know what I mean.'

'I do. Lucinda Daphne Biggin-Smythe doesn't come cheap.'

'You know her?'

'Interviewed her recently for an article about country life. Started with his lordship, but someone craved a murderous plot twist and bumped him off. The grieving widow had to step into the breach. I didn't have to twist her arm.'

'Are you being sarcastic?'

'Me, sir? How rude.'

Prue saw this lighthearted moment as another chance to probe King. 'So, you definitely don't remember my brother?'

'Afraid not. Like I said, catering college was a long time ago. Over the years, I've met and worked with dozens of people. Too many.'

'Is your chain of gastropubs dead in the water?' Wendy asked.

'For now. I thought the investment was good, but we can't always have what we want. Biggin-Smythe insisted on running the show. Dictating everything. I wanted each pub to have a special theme, capitalising on its history, starting with the Noose and Gibbet in Honest Tor. That was the jewel in the crown.'

'Or the body in the cage?'

'Can't get better than that. His lordship hated the name and concept and set about changing it. No doubt wanted the pub named after him and a new sign with his pompous face on it.'

'Sounds like you had no time for him.'

'I didn't kill him before you ask. But it was only a matter of time before someone did.'

'What do you mean?'

'He had many enemies. Noted for changing his mind at the last minute. Over the years, he let many people down. I got off lightly.'

'How so?'

'He wasn't the easiest person to work with, but if he'd loaned the cash, I'd have thirty national outlets by now. In business, one must put personal feelings aside. I understand he wasn't much of a father. Wouldn't shock me if one of his kids killed him. Especially Richard. Met him twice. Worse than his father. At least old Seymour knew how to run a business, but Richard relied on others to keep bailing him out. Especially daddy. Spoiled, privileged brat.'

'Attended one of your cookery classes, did he?'

'Sorry?'

'In your speech earlier, you said we had the privilege of meeting you. Is that why Richard was privileged?'

'*You* are razor sharp. I'm sure you know my angle.'

'Lucinda thought Richard was going to be a partner in your business.'

'That's news to me. I wonder what the old man was planning? Would touch nothing if it didn't turn a profit. There was always a catch, but maybe he was mellowing. Who knows?'

'So you knew nothing about the Richard connection?'

'No. You know more, it seems. Are you sure you pair aren't working for the police?'

'I'm a freelance editor and writer, and Prue's my part-time assistant.'

'That explains it. Interesting angle. Sorry, but time runs away, and I must eat. It would be a pleasure to see you again. Why don't we meet? I'm sure your readers would love to hear my side of the story. Would certainly throw a spanner in the works, so to speak. Call me.' It was an order, not a request. King thrust his business card at Wendy, then ushered her and Prue out of the room.

The friends headed to the foyer, both eager to escape the stuffy surroundings.

'That man is what Jon would call a proper pompositor. I call him a twit, a nit, and a lying—'

'I've got the message,' Prue laughed.

'King may still be a knave, but is he a killer? It's usually the most likely who are the most unlikely. If that makes sense. Are you still gaga?'

'No. I'm taking a leaf out of your book.'

'That's the spirit. We'll give this triumphant torte to one of the homeless at the tube. You don't eat dairy, I'm not big on chocolate cake, and if we don't get rid, the damn thing'll melt, anyway. We'll throw in the tin too.

'Twill come in handy for a collection pan. I'm looking forward to dinn … no, it can't be. It is. *It is.*'

'What is?'

'Who not what. Clattering her way towards us in a bubble of bling and helium. Watch what you say.' Wendy doffed her red fedora. 'Good afternoon.'

The sight of Wendy had Lucinda Biggin-Smythe in a fluster. 'Wendy May. How lovely to see you.' Words tumbled out in that nauseating squawk. 'No Mr Wind?'

'Jon's back in the country. Today I'm with my other assistant and good friend. Meet Prue Penn.'

'Hello.'

'She's. Tom's. Sister.' Wendy's words were precise. Deliberate.

Lucinda blanched. Prue fumed but said nothing.

'What are you doing in London, Wendy? Here? Now?'

'You sound nettled, Lu. As if I don't belong in five-star finery. More your stomping ground, yes?'

'Of course not. I'm surprised to see you, that's all. You didn't say why you're here.'

'I suspect my reasons are similar to yours. Sorry. Must dash. Have a date with a pauper nursing a torte sweet tooth.'

61

Dead End

During a rare spell of quiet in the Noose & Gibbet, Jon and Wendy enjoyed a cool drink. Jon had just finished a shift and was dying to hear about Wendy's exploits in the capital.

'You said what? You've gasted my flabber!'

Wendy's boldness often staggered Jon, but listening to her dissect the flesh and bones of her "entertaining" London trip left him dumbstruck.

'Come on, Jon. You should know me by now.'

'But fancy just coming out with it. I wouldn't dare.'

'What can I say? Sit on the fence and get a numb bum and splinters. Or take the problem and wring it by the scruff of the neck. King denied any association with Lu, but he'll relent. Eventually. I wager he likes a challenge, and the last word. Like you. Except he's nothing like you.'

'From what you say, he sounds like a proper pompositor. You also said you don't know if he's the type who'd kill, then be all charm and smiles, next to the corpse. But isn't it the charming ones you have to watch?'

'Not always, but you have a point. I said I don't know if he's the type. The jury's still out.'

'Hope Prue didn't find the trip exhausting.'

'She wasn't too bad. You have a superb knowledge of the London Underground, but it's likely we could've hoofed it to our stop in the same time.'

'What? How?'

'Walking across Hyde Park. The tube goes around it.'

'You mean Mapman got it wrong? Must look at a detailed map of London and not just the underground.'

'Think you did the right thing. Walking might've been too much for Prue. Getting to the class, then having an MS flare-up? Not the best.'

'So why bring it up?'

'To keep Mapman on his toes. I know how you love nailing your charts. Giving feedback is the perfect excuse for you to spend hours in your cartographer's chair and hone your skills. But, I digress. Our hotel was near Hyde Park, so we had a lovely walk there yesterday. Sat for a while. Enjoyed the ambience. Took in the Serpentine, but not Speaker's Corner. Shame. I had more than enough ammo for a reasonable rant. Perched on my soapbox, basking in free speech and sunshine. More sightseeing and shopping, had a meal at the hotel, then back to the station, homeward bound.'

'Sounds like a great trip, with drama thrown in for good measure. Pity I wasn't there to see King's face when you made that quip about him and Lu Brush.'

'Haven't got to the second best part yet. King gave me his business card. Wants to meet when I'm free.'

'But he isn't your type.'

'Not meet in that sense. Three failed engagements and still single tell me I don't have a type. If that's King's angle, he better stop fishing. He's wasting his time. Wouldn't entertain the idea. The smoothie's too slimy, in every which way.'

'I get it. He's not your dish of the day. So, what's his game, you reckon?'

'Told him about the article I'd written. He completely misunderstood what the piece's all about and wants readers to hear his side of the story. Barging into my exclusive. "Call me," he said. Gave me no choice in the matter. Nothing endearing. The front of the man.'

'Definitely cocky. What did you say?'

'He escorted me and Prue off the premises before I had a chance to speak.'

'If him giving you his business card's the second best part, what's the first?'

'The glitzy merry widow. Close your mouth, Jon, before King reels you in. We were near the exit, and in Lu walks, wearing so much make-up, I swear I could hear war drums. Immaculate hair and nails. The vital second skin and heels—in that heat, I ask you—and a whopping great hat, with a brim so wide, it nearly wiped me out. To say she was shocked to see me's an understatement. *Her* flabber was definitely gasted. And her face when I introduced Prue as Tom's sister. The paint didn't crack, and how she stayed upright on her props, I do not know. Have to hand it to Prue. She was sublime. Kept her cool, though she was raging inside.'

'Where did Lu Brush go?'

'Don't know, but she was edgy as hell. Asked what I was doing in London. What I was doing at that hotel. Told her I suspected we were both there for similar reasons. Then me and Prue left.'

'Think she was there to see King?'

'Who else? Don't believe in coincidence, Jon.'

'Will you take him up on his offer?'

'Already left a voicemail.'

'You're dead keen.'

'Yes, Keen to question. We've hit a dead end and must do a U-turn. Tom's still missing. We're still clueless. Montgomery King may not be a killer, but he's a something and I intend to find out what.'

62

Swansong

E ddie Rutter had many qualities, but none more
fetching than his smile. Generous, warm, it sang
from the heart, radiating vitality from big brown eyes that
glowed and giggled in beautiful black skin. Of late, Ed
had found no reason to smile, but today, he grinned like a
fool, almost skipping to greet Jon and Wendy. He set
down more drinks and pulled up a stool.

'Someone's had a pick-me-up. So good to see you like
this. Have the henchmen changed their minds and said
you can stay?' Wendy was curious.

'No. They still want us out, but we've found a cottage
in Bogus Hole. Just on the market yesterday. How's that
for luck?' Eddie couldn't stop grinning.

'Fantastic news! That's my haunt, and I'll be back
there soon when work on my cottage's done. Bet you're
relieved. And Gina too.'

'Can't tell you how much. That's not all. I've put in
for the manager's job at the village pub, and for Gina to
do housekeeping. No dodgy aristos in sight. Keep it to
yourselves for now. With my rubbish luck, don't want to
jinx the outcome. Prefer not to let the Biggin-Smythes or
their goons know either. Had enough of that lot.'

'Don't worry, we'll keep it zipped. We've missed that
crushing smile. By the way, how's things going with the
running of this place?'

'The heavies have backed off. As far as I know,
Richard Biggin-Smythe's in charge, but he's dealing with
other things.'

Jon's head jerked at Dickie's name. 'Wonder what?'

'Yes, Jon. Your little adventure at the big house's no secret. Maybe we should organise a lock in here as well.'

'Wasn't funny. If Lu Brush hadn't shown her face, I could still be holed up in that bleeding garage.'

'Did you call the police?'

'No.'

'Why not?'

'Because I believe the Biggin-Smythes have the law in their pocket, or that's how I see it. Must be some truth in it. They won't follow any alternative leads for the old boy's death. They're convinced it's Tom, even though the evidence says otherwise.'

'Doesn't surprise me. You've seen how they've treated me and Gina. Probably been getting away with murder for years. Maybe centuries.'

'That'll be right. By the way, Tom and Lady Lu's affair is real as real can be. No rumour, but you didn't hear it from us.'

'Knew Tom had an eye for the ladies, but … well, it's his life. The sooner he gets back here, the better. Will can't hold the fort forever and good agency chefs are hard to find.'

'Hey, all. What's happening?' Flaunting his fabulous, dressed in shorts, tight vest, and the latest trainers, Ross Pengelly sauntered up, Emily in tow.

'Hi, Ross. How you doing?' Eddie smiled.

'All good. Been to London.'

'Poor London,' Wendy quipped.

'Could say the same. Hear you were there, too.'

'Yes, I was there. At a cooking class with a friend.'

'You went all the way to London to learn to cook? Must be mad,' Ross sneered.

'I know how to cook. Me and Prue went to a special baking class, courtesy of Kuisine by Kingoisseur. Fancier than your usual chicken thigs and chips. With or without breadcrumbs.'

'Kingoss what?'

'Kingoisseur.'

'Never heard of it. Sounds boring.'

'Depends on your perception of boredom. Every one of us has a diversion in life. Don't all go in for spray tans and leery Lycra. Or switch tonic for sex.'

'I've got a suntan. Don't need spray in this heat, you silly old—'

'How was London, Ross?' Eddie cut in. The spiky atmosphere had stolen his glow.

'Had a great time, although Ems spent too much time in shops. Waiting around got boring, but that's girls for you. Think you might be turning into a girl, Eddie. Spotted you doing the dishes, and I kept quiet. Then saw you doing them again. No. Never. You're lowering the tone. Giving men a bad name. Isn't that right, ex-copper? Are you in favour of men doing a woman's work?'

'Mr Pengelly, this isn't the Dickensian age, where the weak little woman should know her place. Under the master's thumb and do as you're told, or off to the asylum you go. According to studies, men are heading for extinction. Won't be long before they're obsolete. Like fax machines. The only place you'll spot them will be in a museum, next to the dinosaurs. Men of a certain type, anyway. Your sort. Prehistoric. It's time you were in a cultured environment. On second thoughts, no. That *would* lower the tone.'

'Boring.'

'Is boring your word of the day?'

Ross ignored Wendy and carried on with his tale.

'Wonder why he stays with Emily,' Jon whispered to Wendy. 'Get the impression he's more into Antonia.'

'He's a particular breed, Jon. The cavalier kind that likes to have his Sachertorte and eat it. A control freak, too. As long as Emily dances to his tune, he'll pull her strings. No doubt the thrill of being caught has him enraptured.'

'Hey, you,' Ross hollered to Wendy.

'Who is this person, people?'

'Have a question for you.'

'If you want an answer, don't bawl at me like a market trader selling cheap tat. It's crude.'

'Did you go on that new walk the other day?'

Wendy detected contempt. 'Walk? I know of no walk.'

'Ems told me you and that Prue were going on a new walk near my house. I always knew you two were trouble. You must know what I'm talking about.'

'And you must be wrong.'

'Are you trying to tell me you didn't know about her ladyship's secret hideaway?'

'I'm not *trying* to tell you. I am telling you.'

'Come on, Ross,' Emily said lamely, 'they were just having a walk. No harm in that.'

'Did I ask you?'

Wendy and Jon shared a glance. Poor Emily. She had no idea she was simply a pawn in Ross's devious, cruel game. Antonia, too. Goodness knows how many others he'd wronged along the way. Nasties didn't always get their due.

'Won't be long,' Emily excused herself.

Wendy couldn't resist. 'Sounds like our fabulous capital bored you senseless, Mr Pengelly.'

'Not really. It was a laugh. Highlight for me was food in the Hard Rock Cafe. Wouldn't let Emily stop that. She can't cook to save her life. Useless!'

'Do I detect trouble in paradise? Problems in your relationship?'

'No, and keep your nose out of my business.'

'With your other flame absent on her first jolly of the season, guess Emily'll have to do. Here she comes.' Wendy detected the awkward shift in Pengelly's stance.

'I don't feel well, Ems. Too much sun. Think I need a lie down and some tlc.'

'Poor thing. Are you all right?' Emily moved towards Pengelly, arms outstretched.

'What did I just say? And none of your silly hugs. Need a word before I go, Ed. Got something for you. Over here.' Pengelly grabbed Emily's hand and pulled her towards the exit.

What followed had Wendy and Jon baffled. Pengelly handed Eddie two big brown envelopes, slapped him on the back, then marched Emily out of the Noose. Eddie raised his hands in triumph, punched the air, then vanished.

'Feathers ruffled and more mysterious packages. It's all in a day's work for Windy and Darling,' Jon said. 'You had Pengelly good and proper.'

'His ego needed taking down.'

'What's doing with Ed? It's all very cryptic. Not sure where he's gone. Heading for his office, maybe?'

Minutes later, Eddie was back. So was the beam. Bigger than before. 'Friends, you are both a pleasure to be around. By the way, who's the other flame you were referring to, Wendy?'

'Antonia Biggin-Smythe.'

'Blimey. Ross doesn't do things by half. Probably using her to curry favour with the family.'

'Because of the eviction, you mean? That thought's crossed our minds. Antonia's absence has likely peed him right off. He treats women like batteries. Use and dispose,' Jon said.

'Emily worships the ground the skunk walks on. So sad. One day she'll find out. She'll be heartbroken, but get over him and count her blessings she got rid. As for

Pengelly, what goes around doesn't always come around. Sadder still. It's that old rough justice thing. But enough of that, Eddie. The spotlight's on you. Two big brown envelopes. Raised hands. An air punch. And a smile to knock our socks off. What's the story?'

'That's why Jon calls you hawkeye. He says you never miss a trick.'

'Or eagle eye. Same difference, Ed,' Jon agreed.

'I'm an editor. A sharp eye's critical, and don't change the subject. It's obvious you've had good news, but I won't push it, if you—'

'All right. All right. Been offered the manager's job at the Brock and Sett in Bogus Hole. Start in two months. I had my interview a few days ago, but from what I make out, it was a done deal just with my application. Gina's landed the job as housekeeper. She'll be buzzing when I tell her. She's out shopping and in for two surprises when she gets back.'

Wendy wasn't a hugger, but this was one of those moments when she made an exception. 'Congratulations. I'm thrilled for you.'

'Put it there, mate,' Jon praised, shaking Eddie's hand and doing the bromance big hug, back-slapping bit.

'And the other surprise? Must have something to do with that envelope you're cuddling,' Wendy said.

'Yes. Promise not to laugh.' Eddie removed an A4 sheet of embossed cream paper and showed it to Jon and Wendy. 'Passed my origami test.'

It was Wendy's turn to catch flies. 'So you're the fancy napkin folder making swans and roses. I even spotted a bishop's mitre. You fibber. You told us you bought them in folded.'

'It was only a little white lie. Felt silly saying I was doing a paper folding course. Remember that package you asked me about, Jon? That was the test paper, but I couldn't let on. Have this thing about jinxing. You're not the only geek around here. I can now call myself a proper anorak. Origami. Who would've thought? It's great for hand-eye and mental concentration and motor skills. Fantastic brain exercise, too, and I need it.' Eddie laughed long and loud.

'You're a dark horse, Eddie. We knew you were up to something, but it had nothing to do with paper folding.'

'You thought I'd bumped off BS, didn't you?'

'Won't lie. Me and Jon had our suspicions. Sorry.'

'Fair enough. I'll admit to thinking Jon was in the frame. You're not, are you?'

'*Not*. Let's toast your success.'

'Hear-hear. A sterling job, Eddie,' Wendy said.

'Thanks. Not long to manage this place, then I'm off.'

'Yes. The next few weeks'll be your swansong.'

'Especially now you're a master origamist. Even got a new wacky word out of it,' Jon grinned.

The trio raised their glasses to toast. Then came a ping.

'Voicemail. One mo.' Wendy listened to the message and snorted. 'He's keen.'

'Who?'

'Montgomery King.'

63

Angels and Demons

In the tranquil ambience of the Noose & Gibbet's beer garden, Wendy called Monty King. As she talked, she eyed the root of ill will and murder. The clanging eyesore that was the grisly gibbet cage. Was King a killer? An accessory? Or just the man who'd had his head turned by a temptress wife and the misfortune to fall out with her husband, the richest, most powerful man in Treet?

Wendy's call took less than three minutes. The deed was done. She settled back in the Noose and drained her glass. Jon surreptitiously faffed with his drat pack, and Eddie was back behind the bar serving customers.

'What?' Jon said, feeling Wendy's eyes boring into him.

'King wants to meet tomorrow night at the Brock and Sett.'

'In Bogus Hole?'

'Know of no other. His son has a cooking class in the hall, but he isn't well, poor lamb, so daddy's filling in. King said, I quote, "Villages aren't my thing, you know, but I'll do it for the business." What rubbish. He and Pengelly should compete for the title of who can spew the most tosh in sixty seconds. 'Twould be a close-run thing.'

'That's a turn up for the books.'

'Recipe books?'

'You're quick, Darling. Nearly as good as me.'

'Want to know what he said or not?'

'Indeedy.'

'Told him I live in Treeton. Didn't go into the renovation. He suggested we meet at the Brock after the cooking class. Said he has some explosive stuff for my piece. He's keen to tear into milord and his family.'

'After getting shafted by the old boy, what better way to get revenge? The pen's mightier than the sword.'

'That old chestnut.'

'Wonder what he's got to say about the spiffing Biggin-Smythe brigade? If his material's as explosive as he says, will you include it in your article?'

'Depends. Could prompt a chat with the mag's editor. Printed media's all about increasing circulation and I've always said people love gossip. The juicier the better. If it has the potential to up sales and readers, the ed'll jump on it. He banks on scandal to increase circulation. Give him a generous payout too. Not that he needs it. Neither does milady, but that didn't stop her from begging to be centre stage. I'll use my wedge to pay the excess on the insurance and buy a new motor.'

'Sounds like a plan.'

'Think we should tell Emily about pants-down-Pengelly?'

'You're a scream, Windy. Good handle, though. I'm torn between what's necessary and what's kind. She'll be devastated when she finds out. If we tell her, she'll likely blame us for ruining her happiness. If we don't, we'll be saddled with a guilty conscience. Damned if we do. Damned if we don't. Pengelly's such an arrogant oaf, he'll hang himself with his own rope. That way, Ems'll know what a loser he is without our help. Antonia too. Fingers crossed, he drops himself sooner rather than later.'

'His sort always do.'

'Now, to the quiz. Preparations going as planned?'

'With all the fun and games, I'd forgotten about it, but here's a rub. When I was doing my shift, an elderly chap came into the Noose and said angels are really demons.'

'Is this one of your fishy facts?'

'It might be fishy, but it's not mine.'

'What was his point?'

'Can't remember how it started exactly. A group of punters yakking about the works of Anthony Gormley and talking about that sculpture of his up in the northeast. The Angel of the North. This chap had had a few, but as soon as he heard "angel" he started wittering on about how angels were terrifying. Thomas Aquinas, and some other fifth century fella with a longer name than Biggin-Smythe, are to blame.'

'Angels. Terrifying? How many had he had?'

'A few, or a few too many. Anyway, he went on about angels with four heads. One head was a man. One a lion. The third an ox. The fourth, also an ox.'

'You heard it here first, people. Looks like an elderly chappie's usurped the king of fishy facts.'

'If you think that's funny, he went on about an angel looking like a wheel within a wheel. And it had eyes.'

'Oh, come on. What baloney. Or not. Maybe he's an angel. A terrifying, sinister winged cherub, who had a score to settle with milord from way back, and settle he did. What about this for a theory? He *is* Biggin-Smythe, and the man you thought you saw in the cellar *wasn't* the man you thought you saw. Imagine that, Windy.'

'I'm only telling you what the old buffer said.'

'No doubt he insisted it was a circular argument or made his point in a roundabout way.'

'Clever. I like it.'

'Watch out. You're in danger of being usurped as the king of wit, too. Did your friend say anything else?'

'I'll always be the king of wittiness, thank you very much. As for the soothsayer, think he said it's all in the Book of Ezekiel, or something like that. Religion isn't my thing, so I tuned out at that point. He must've rambled on another half hour or so. Felt like an eternity and no one was listening.'

'Poor you. The joys of pulling pints. Maybe it's an omen and there'll be an angelic question in the quiz final. Hold up. I have a message.' Wendy scrabbled for her phone. 'From Prue.'

'Is she all right?'

'Fine. Just saying she had a fab time in London, but she's exhausted. Okay if we check in before heading back to Treeton?'

'No worries. Speaking of King, you never told me what you did with your Sachertorte. You didn't eat it.'

'We didn't, but a homeless couple did.'

'After all that work, you gave it away!'

'I was doing my bit for charity.'

'Charity begins at home.'

'Don't sulk. I'll make you a triple choccy cake soon. Right now, a date with the devil's top of my agenda. The game's afoot, Windy.'

64

The Bogie Man

From the outside, the cottage looked idyllic. The perfect country escape, where nature beguiled, and peace reigned. On the inside, a different story. When the Mell burst its banks in torrential rainstorms, flood damage devastated the interior of *Sakura*. The entire cottage needed gutting. Works were ongoing, and Wendy still didn't know when she could move back in.

At least the scaffolding was down and the pastoral charm that seduced and conquered five years gone shone brighter than the August sun. An insurance payout had rescued her plight, but Wendy doubted the company would insure again. The perils of living near a river. Or, in her case, the woes of one luckless lass.

Wendy moved on. Time to kill in Bogie's delightful clutch of quaint and practical stores. A poke around the antique shop, a catch-up in the gift studio, then a meander around the market. Seemed forever since she'd tromped the village's cobbles and it wasn't long before Wendy's feet danced upon the worn stones. She let Bogie's swaying rhythm wrap its loving arms around her, basking in the warm, happy hug. Bogus Hole hadn't lost its soul. For that, Wendy was grateful.

At noon, Wendy strolled by Dorky's pond before indulging in the Japanese picnic she'd prepared. Among a landscape of trees and blooms, she feasted on vegetable, umeboshi, and finger lime sushi rolls drizzled with tamari and sesame ponzu, then a yuzu panna cotta and satsuma syrup. Savouring the last decadent mouthful, Wendy breathed in Bogie's aura. It felt so good to be back home.

After clearing up, she headed to Beans & Leaves to enjoy a cup of lemon ginger tea. The brew was one of Wendy's herbal favourites. Unfortunately, dynamic tea queen, Kate Brown, was in Treeton today, so no chance of a natter but Wendy asked staff to pass on well wishes.

She'd arranged to meet King at the Brock & Sett at seven sharp. She knew the local watering hole well. It was the hub of village life, and would soon have a new manager. Origami king, Eddie Rutter.

King. What was he about? She recalled Milton King saying his father owned the village hall. Unlike its little sister, Honest Tor, much of Bogus Hole had the luxury of escaping Seymour Biggin-Smythe's grabbing hands. The miser had failed to put his stamp on the village and being thwarted wasn't well received. Bogie was bigger than Tor. A bigger area meant a greater heist. A greater heist meant a fatter profit. If Dickie had his way, he'd change the situation, but, for now, King was the proud owner of something his would-not-be partner hadn't snatched. One-upmanship in its subtlest form.

At six, Wendy arrived at the Brock. Like the Noose, it was busy at mealtimes and weekends, but fairly quiet during the week. Unlike the Noose, it had kept one half of its coaching inn status, offering overnight accommodation for two-footers, though no stabling for four. She'd elected to come alone, figuring King would open up more if it was just the two of them. Jon was working. The Noose was hosting its weekly quiz, but tonight, it would miss Windy & Darling. Determined to leave Bogus Hole with something, Wendy's meeting with King took precedence. Jon had dropped Wendy off before starting his shift. She planned to return in a taxi, but not back to Treeton. She'd promised to spend time with Prue, who was enduring the chronic effects of bad stress overload, but insisted she didn't wish to be a killjoy and preferred to spend this evening alone.

Save for two couples and barman, Mike, the Brock was empty.

'Hello, stranger. Haven't seen you in a while. You're looking well.' Mike greeted Wendy with a warm smile.

'Yes, it's good to be back. You're looking well too. You know I'm living in Treeton while my cottage's renovated after flood damage.'

Mike gave a compassionate nod. In varying degrees, the destruction had touched many residents. Wendy's hit had been worse than most. She ordered a small glass of red and said she was meeting someone to finish an article she was writing. The pair chatted a while, then Wendy took a window seat overlooking Dorky's pond.

What the hell was she doing here? Dressed in her best, and hatless, for pity's sake. If justice, or an urge to help Prue and Tom weren't in the mix, she'd have nothing to do with this mad affair. Would've scarpered King and his doings long ago. Wendy sipped at her wine. Minutes ticked, the witching hour neared, and apprehension grew. *There must be another way.* She pushed back her chair and readied to leave.

'We meet again, lovely lady,' the tone flattered.

Wendy jolted at the voice. She hadn't seen King approaching. 'Do you always sneak up on people?'

He slid into a chair. 'Sincere apologies. Didn't mean to frighten you. I assume that's red wine. I'll get you another.'

'I prefer to—'

King was up and away, cutting Wendy off mid-speech and back soon with a large glass of red and scotch on the rocks.

He raised his glass. 'Cheers. A good malt puts me in the mood like nothing else. No driving tonight. I'm staying here. For a village inn, the rooms are incredibly comfortable. The food's decent, too. I have a liking for the breakfast. Chef does a tasty eggs Benedict with a dash of seasoning. How do you like yours?'

'How do I like my what?'

'Eggs.'

'With respect, Mr King—'

'Monty, please.'

'With respect, Monty, I'm writing a magazine piece, not a recipe book. I'm here to talk about you, not eggs.'

'Apologies. I'll rewind. When we spoke on the phone, it sounded like you know a lot about Bogus Hole. Have you spent a lot of time here?'

'I have a cottage here, but am living with a friend while it's under renovation.'

'Your friend from the cookery class? Can't remember her name.'

The truth or a fib? 'Yes. And it's Prue.'

'That's her. Was your cottage damaged by the floods? Where in the village?'

'Gutted. How do you know about the floods?' Wendy ignored King's second question.

'I'm familiar with Bogie. I own the hall and lease part of it to the local council.'

'Nice.'

'You say you didn't come here to talk about eggs? I guess you don't want small talk either, even from the man with the scintillating personality,' King laughed.

'No. We can talk about your doomed business deal with Seymour Biggin-Smythe.'

King looked around the room. Mike had vanished, presumably out the back or to change the kegs, and a couple sat in one corner in deep conversation. The other couple had gone.

'Here's the news. Seymour Biggin-Smythe wasn't just a filthy rich aristocrat. He had his dirty fingers in many pies, and not the finest. Most were above board, but a few were—'

'Illegal?'

'Got it. Goodness me, you're sharp.'

King had said something similar in London. In the same patronising, provocative tone. He sensed Wendy's objection and was quick to apologise.

'I'm sorry. That remark was a tad condescending.'

Ever the chameleon, it was clear King thought he could wipe the unguarded comment with more flattery. His manner infuriated Wendy, but strengthened her resolve. She kept her smile, determined not to let him get under her skin. If her charm wavered, he might be less willing to dish the dirt. She'd met his type before. The Ross Pengelly mentality. Big mouth. Bigger ego. She must play to her audience. Invite him to play, too. Though aware of the platitude, if one knew what buttons to press, sorts such as King had trouble keeping secrets. Wendy would press his buttons. And fast.

'That mouth of yours could get you into trouble, Monty. Bet it has before.'

King laughed. Wendy guessed he wasn't used to people talking back. Especially women. Or had he seen her remark as innuendo and wanted more? If so, she had it covered.

'So, Lord Biggin-Smythe was up to no good?' Wendy fluttered her eyelashes, the smile, coy, the pout, outrageous.

'Yes. Had a penchant for overseas investment. We're not just talking about offshore accounts. He liked to invest in unsavoury companies.'

'Unsavoury?'

'You know the type. Companies masquerading as bona fide, but just a front for illegal activities.'

Yes, Wendy knew the type. She'd been there before, but she wanted King to blow the gaff. 'Explain.'

'Drugs. Weapons. Money laundering. Offshore investments. You name it. Any kind of contraband. Didn't bother him, so long as he made a quick buck. *Profit.* Another of his forenames.'

'I see.'

'You sound sceptical.'

'Thought he only made his money buying property and fleecing tenants,' Wendy lied.

'That's the popular image.'

'If I'm to write anything damning in my feature, I'd need hard evidence. Do these companies have British offices or trade on the Stock Exchange?'

'Some do, some don't.' King sipped a second whisky and ran his tongue over moist lips.

Wendy started on her third glass of red. The big glass. She'd have no more. 'Is that all you have? I'll lose my credibility if making unsubstantiated claims. And land myself and the mag's editor in a vigorous libel suit. You surely didn't lure me all the way to Bogus Hole just to say Milord Biggin-Smythe made a handful of poor investments, but not tell me who, why, or when.'

'It's vague, I know, but my contacts swear he was up to no good. And you didn't need luring.'

Wendy wouldn't bite. 'And you can't reveal your contacts? Confidentiality, and so on.'

'That's the gist of it.'

'You're not giving me much here.'

'There's more.'

'Sounds promising.'

'I was whetting your appetite,' King smiled mischievously.

''Tis a naughty thing to do, Mr King. If there's more, don't hide it.'

'Seymour's business dealings were just the tip. Inconsequential if you ask me. If I were you, I'd be concentrating on the eldest son and the family's relationship with the police.'

'This had better be good.'

'It is. For some years, Richard Biggin-Smythe's run a counterfeit money-making operation. He thinks his father didn't know, but he did.'

Wendy thought of Jon and Antonia in the lockup and their unwitting discovery of Dickie's fake money scheme. She decided not to share that with King. *If he knew, why had he not shared his findings with the police?*

'Seymour cared little for Richard, you know. Wasn't bothered by his shady escapades, but was bothered about him bringing the family name into disrepute. He moved mountains to protect the image. Richard isn't too sharp, and Seymour worried he'd eventually trip himself up. That's why it surprised me when you mentioned Richard in the business proposal.'

'Lucinda Biggin-Smythe was adamant Richard's name was there.'

'Like I said, news to me. You have very interesting eyes,' King crooned.

'Yes. A condition called heterochromia. Affects less than one per cent of the world's population, I believe. Do you prefer the blue one? Or green?'

'Tough call. They're individually beautiful and together, quite devastating. Would look better still watching champagne fizzing somewhere more comfortable. It is getting late.'

'Do you want to hear something you don't want to hear? Unlike Richard's name in the proposal? Something that isn't news to you?'

'Cryptic.'

'You had a fling with Lucinda Biggin-Smythe.'

'Did I?'

'Don't deny it.'

'All right, you win. But I wasn't the first.'

'Nor the last. You mentioned the police.'

'Seymour and the chief constable were old friends. Went to the same yachting club, I believe. In short, the Biggin-Smythe family's in league with the police. A liaison that probably goes back generations. That's why I'm reluctant to involve the authorities. If that's what you're thinking.'

'I am.'

'Talking would be pointless. The police are paid to look the other way. The family can do what they like. That chief constable's the king of corruption. Oh, and there's one more thing. Your friend said I knew her brother. Well, it turns out—'

Making a beeline for their table, a man's voice stopped King mid-flow.

'Hello, Miss May. Fancy seeing you here.'

'A pleasure, Dave.' Wendy was polite, but inwardly seething at the interruption. *King had mentioned Tom.*

'See you're moving in high circles these days. You want to watch him. Can't trust these business types.' Dave grunted at King.

'Monty, this is Dave, the foreman for my house renovation. You must excuse his sense of humour. Always said he was a character. Late finish, Dave? Popped in for a pint or six?' Wendy noted it was almost ten.

Dave gave a quick update on the work, then talked about the construction industry, football, and cricket. Wendy endured the rambling, but in the nicest way, wished he'd go.

'If you don't mind, we were talking,' King sniped. 'I have an early start tomorrow and haven't finished my story. I'm off to the gents and expect you'll be gone when I return.'

'What's his problem, then?' Dave grumbled.

You, Dave. You're the problem. Wendy wanted to curse, but couldn't cause a scene. Dave was just being Dave. A sociable man. A joker. A life and soul of the party type. Regretfully, on this occasion, he'd broken up the party. Wendy hoped King would spill his guts about Tom. It would be something to tell Prue. Light in the shadow of too much gloom.

'You want to watch him,' Dave repeated. 'Did some work on the village hall and still waiting for him to cough up the cash. Dodgy sort. Stay well clear.'

'Thanks for the advice.'

'Don't mention it, Miss May. I'm off for a pint.'

King strutted back to the table, armed with more drinks. 'I waited until he'd gone. What an awful man. Where were we?'

'Prue's brother,' Wendy said, eyeing the drinks and hiding a sneer. King was so obvious.

'Ah, yes. Prue's brother. Shall we continue this discussion somewhere cosier? The rooms here are good.'

'So you said.'

'And I'll say it again. We don't want everyone being privy to our conversation. Why don't we move on, slip into something less stuffy and share a bottle of bubbles? I love the pinstripes and boots, but somewhat formal, don't you think? As the temperature rises, the interview will get more intense. I'm sure we could make beautiful music together. Come along. I know you want to.'

Wendy wanted all right. Wanted to know what King knew about Tom. To learn more about his dealings with the Biggin-Smythes and his affair with Lucinda. She didn't want to sample the lothario's flattery, play hot tonsil tennis, or know the colour of his smalls, nor the contours of his bones. She wanted out. Now.

'Mr King, just so there's no misunderstanding. I have neither the time nor inclination to engage in any activity that involves shedding my clothes and making anything, never mind music. You're no Mozart, and if boozing me up's your intention, forget it.'

Wendy praised the shade of sickly grey clouding Montgomery King's face. He couldn't speak. Could barely move. She pushed back her chair and stood up.

'Why, sir, you're flabbergasted. Must say that emotion's earned its stripes this week. Just so you know, I prefer my eggs unfertilised, can pay my own way, and while you may not be, I'm well done. Mercifully, not by you.' Laughing at King's bewildered face, Wendy threw down a tenner and left.

Waiting for a taxi, Wendy considered the past few hours. Unlike her charming cottage, the bogie man hadn't seduced and conquered. She'd turned the tables, and he'd given much, though nothing about Tom. That aside, it was clear King was a man who fell for feminine guile. Every time. The type that never learned.

'You still here, Miss May?' Dave loomed out of the shadows.

'Going soon. Waiting for my taxi.'

'Whatever you said to that creep in there didn't go down well. He's smashing around the place like a five-year-old who wants sweeties and been told no. He better pay what he owes me. Goodnight, Miss May.'

'Night, Dave. And thanks.'

So big was Wendy's triumphant smile she feared her face would split in two. King's disclosure was a step forward for Windy & Darling. She wasn't such an unlucky wretch after all.

65

The Starry Night

B ack in Honest Tor, Prue took a taxi. Deep breathing often restored a level of calm, but edginess remained, and she couldn't settle.

How Ross Pengelly had got her number, she didn't know. All she knew was he'd seen Tom, who'd asked Ross to pass on a message. Meet at the Noose & Gibbet at midnight. Prue was anxious to see her brother. To know he was well. To ask questions that had burned for days. She thought the time and place unusual, but this could be her only chance to get the answers she craved. Tom must have given Ross her number. All was legit. She would go.

As the taxi climbed heart attack hill, Prue admired how breathtaking Tor looked at night. The novelty of its beauty had never waned. In rural parts, the night sky dazzled. Unlike towns or cities, no artificial light streaming upwards to pollute purity. Tonight, a waxing crescent moon danced in a clear sky, caressed by stars in their millions shimmering in a sumptuous, vast velvet cushion.

Would Tom be at the Noose or had Ross Pengelly sent her on a wild goose chase? The number of times he and Wendy had exchanged barbs made the theory plausible, but she'd risk anything to see her brother. Brushing aside her jitters, Prue let the starry night eclipse the hesitant mood as the taxi crested the hill.

The driver turned right and stopped at St. Mark's church. Prue paid and thanked him, then watched the vehicle head back to Treeton. Aided by trekking poles and a small torch, she made her way along the dark road past

Eddie's cottage. She had strict instructions to come alone. Tom knew he was taking a massive risk, Ross said, and secrecy was key. Any deviation and the meeting was off.

Prue reached the Noose. A faint light filtered through the window blinds. Go to the rear entrance, then through the wrought-iron gate into the beer garden. Following the brief, she turned left, pocketed her torch, then opened the gate. In the hush, the squeak might as well've been an orchestra. Using her trusty poles to navigate, Prue edged into the beer garden and inched her way to the double back doors. A thin strip of light illuminated part of the decking and wooden tables. Funny how sinister the seating looked in the dead of night. Anxiety was back.

"Wait in the garden until Tom comes," Ross had said, but Prue was tired of waiting and couldn't resist the strange lure, inviting her in. From the kitchen, she heard tense, muffled voices and leaned against an enormous dresser, where she could see but not be seen. Listening, but not hearing. The voices were low, hard to identify. Soon, anger took over. *Who was arguing? Where was Tom?*

A voice demanded more money or else. Rattled at the threat, a hissed snarl made it clear blackmail was a fool's game and if the law came calling, there'd be another murder to crack. Voices upped a notch. Prue sensed there were three, perhaps four, people in the kitchen, but she couldn't pick out who. *Was one Biggin-Smythe's killer? And what about Tom? Had he got himself mixed up with this lot? How?*

Prue wished she hadn't come. Her legs cramped, her feet burned, and she struggled to keep her balance. Dizziness waxed and waned. Vision became erratic. This was a dangerous place to be. A thud, then all was quiet. She didn't know what to do. Didn't want to go further inside, nor did she want to leave. It wasn't only the wranglers having a battle of wills. In her desperation to see Tom, she had her own conflict. Now, she recognised one voice and was almost sure of another.

The side kitchen door opened. Prue ducked down, her vision slightly obscured, but still able to make out two hooded figures lugging something onto the decking. There was enough light from the open kitchen to see movement, but not enough to make out faces. Prue peeled away from the dresser's side and stood up unsteadily, watching their journey across the grass. The hoods stopped at the gibbet cage. *Surely not. A corpse? Or someone still alive?*

A raised, flailing hand brought two swift, heavy blows down on the prone form. Busy fingers got to work, then the two figures bolted through the gate. All was calm, save for the creaking of the cage and the pitiful body hanging there. Prue silenced a horrified gasp. It looked male. Of robust build. *Tom's build.*

Prue had no choice. She must know the truth. Confront what horror swung there. She risked being seen, but logic had escaped her. Stumbling forth, she braced herself to focus. To reach inside the cage. This time, she couldn't choke back the cry, nor control crippling body spasms or numbness ravaging her feet.

Draped in the starry night, before the scream answered her brain, fatigue overwhelmed, and blindness came quick. Prey to the darkness, so dark she thought she'd never see light again, Prue and her trusty poles hit the ground.

66

The Sunless Morning

W endy rose at six, reflecting on last night's meeting with King. Some of his revelations carried weight. The rest, nothing she didn't already know.

Again, she cursed Dave's intrusion. Not his fault, but he'd butted in when talk was coming to a boil. Wendy knew King was lying when he said he couldn't remember Tom, but didn't want to make waves in front of Prue. Last night, she was warming King up and he was ready to deliver. What, she didn't know, but she'd sensed an important something, and Dave the rave had scuppered the moment. Clearly, King had a yen to peddle gratuitous smut. He failed. No surprise he was bashing around the Brock in a tantrum. Pity Wendy hadn't seen it, but her imagination was such she might as well have been there.

Dave's invasion wasn't a complete washout. He'd told Wendy about the job he'd done on the village hall. Said King hadn't paid him. *Dodgy man. Stay well clear.* King's charisma may work at disarming and keeping creditors at bay, but, unless they were dim, they'd lose patience. Eventually. No doubt the smoothie had a zillion excuses to avoid coughing up the readies. One big, bottomless bag of schmooze.

Though too short, Wendy cherished last night's restful, sweet sleep. She was grateful for Jon's hospitality, but his thunderous snoring was neither sociable nor funny. She likened him to a pneumatic drill powering through her bedroom wall. Thank goodness she'd invested in an oscillating fan and heavy-duty earplugs to drown out the drone. Here, at the blissful Brambles, she had no issues with fizzing, wheezing, and snuffling.

Prue was an early riser, but lately, sleep hadn't come easy. Her bedroom door was closed and there was no sound of stirring. Wendy left her to sleep, padded to the kitchen, and opened the blinds. A sunless, stormy sky, with no break in thick rolls of grey cloud. Tor needed a shift in the weather to cool it down. Bring on the rain.

Wendy had just sat down with a huge mug of coffee when an urgent thump on the front door jarred her from her seat. Still in her dressing gown, she hurried to see who was making the unwanted din. Expecting the police— who else would knock the door down at stupid o'clock— it alarmed Wendy to see Emily struggling to breathe.

'Ems, what's to do? It's —'

'Horrible, Wendy. Horrible!' Emily stammered.

Not even Lucinda could trump that shriek, and what could better the red-eyed, twisted blob that was Emily's face, Wendy did not know. Peering at Wendy through tortured eyes, Emily's shaking hands pawed at grotesque features, pulling her face back into shape. *For Heaven's sake, what had made her so?*

Before nebby villagers could get an eye and earful, Wendy ushered Emily inside and sat her down at the kitchen table. She took the girl's hands. 'Ems. Breathe easy, and tell me what's happened.'

A gurgle. A low moan. Then. 'Ross. In that cage. *He's dead.*' A banshee couldn't top Emily's harrowing wail.

67

Dead as a Dodo

There were many things Wendy expected to hear. Ross Pengelly dead in that cage wasn't one. Emily may not be making any sense, nor telling the truth, but that wasn't important. Wendy knew the girl was in deep shock. Pale skin, enlarged pupils, and shallow, rapid breathing gave the game away. As did wild, staring eyes, cold, clammy hands, and a never-ending stream of guttural guff. Emily needed help. Now!

While waiting for the ambulance, Wendy did her best to calm the gibbering wreck. Despite the commotion, there was still no sign of Prue. Emily's torment would've woken the entire village as she weaved and squawked her way across the cobblestones. Yet Prue hadn't surfaced and that was odd. When paramedics finally carted Emily off to hospital, Wendy knocked on Prue's bedroom door. No response. She knocked again. Silence.

'Prue! Open up.'

The door stayed closed, no answer from beyond. Wendy eased it open and snuck in. An empty bed that hadn't been slept in. A closed window. A sense the room had seen no one for hours. An uneasy prickle stung Wendy's skin. *Had Prue gone out this morning or in the night?* Unlikely. Wendy would've heard movement. On her return from Bogie last night, she'd sipped another glass of red and contemplated the bittersweet evening. The quiet cottage led her to assume Prue had had an early night. It was out of character for her to go off alone. *Did*

309

Prue's absence have anything to do with Tom? Had she gone walking?

Wendy grabbed a cold coffee from the fridge and quickly dressed. A hike up heart attack hill didn't appeal, but dithering wasn't an option. She pulled on a cap, gathered a few essentials, and took off to the Noose & Gibbet. No sun, but muggy, still. Wendy hadn't contacted Jon. He wasn't working until this afternoon and would likely be in the land of nod, snoring for England. Once she knew the scoop, she'd call.

When Wendy reached the Noose, there was no sign of life. Apart from the screamed, garbled tidings that Ross Pengelly was hanging dead, she hadn't had an intelligible squeak out of Emily. There was only one cage around here. Wendy ignored the front entrance and dashed up the no through road beside the left gable end. At the top, where hedges shouted dead end, sat Emily's little white car. Parked askew and dangerously close to dense bushes, as if she were on a mission and didn't give two hoots about safe parking. The car was unlocked.

To Wendy's right was the big, wrought-iron gate leading into the beer garden. Slightly ajar, Wendy pushed it open and edged onto the paving stones surrounding a grassed square bordered with vivid flowers.

'Over here!'

Wendy swung around to her right. Looking lost and waving like a madman, Eddie Rutter sat at a table on the decking. Though she should've known better, Wendy couldn't stop herself from turning her head left, to look at the gibbet cage and the wretched body hanging there. In her legal years, when on call, she'd seen a few corpses eyeball to eyeball. The ugly side of her calling. The heinous nature of people. Scores of pictures, too. Snapshots. Video footage. Diverse media that was equally disturbing and never forgettable.

Wendy trudged to the decking and gave Eddie a wry smile. He didn't smile back. He'd lined up four empty espresso cups on the table and drank from a fifth. No surprise he was bouncing. Wendy sat opposite and took Eddie's hand. She'd never seen him tremble so. Even when he'd spoken of the pending eviction and the stinking time the heavies were giving him and Gina, she couldn't recall a quiver. Years of heavy bar work had made him a physically strong man, but physique and feeling were poles apart. What he'd seen had got him emotionally. Right in a soft spot.

'What the hell happened, Eddie?' Wendy didn't ask if he was okay. The redundant question people often asked in dire situations. He was far from okay and what had gone on was anyone's guess.

'Came in usual time for the early morning shift. You know the drill. Jon's done it often enough. Went in through the main door. Didn't hear the alarm. Thought the system was kaput, and I needed an engineer. Headed to the kitchen and saw the back doors open. Sensed something was up. Jon was last in after the quiz, and he's manic about door and window checks.'

'That's his OCD. Then?'

'Came out here. Saw that in the cage. Went to check and … nearly spewed. Horrifying. Couldn't believe it. Emily turned up at the gate, mad as hell. Yelling like a crazy. Demanding to know where Ross was. Said she saw him coming here last night and knew he was cheating on her. Said the pair of us were hiding his dirty little secret and she saw how matey we were in the Noose the other day. Shaking hands. Hugging. All that bromance stuff. She came right into the garden, then saw what I'd just seen. Even went up to the cage and just stood there, staring. Then she started howling. Terrifying noises like I've never heard. Then she took off.'

'She came to Prue's in severe shock. I couldn't get any sense out of her. Called an ambulance and she's off to hospital. You haven't seen Prue, have you?'

'No. Jon's on his way. Need help this morning. Police are on their way. Whoever did this must've disconnected the CCTV and sensor lights. Same thing happened when BS was done in. The killer had keys too. Couldn't get in without them. Come to think of it, BS's keys haven't been found. Can I get you a coffee?'

'Thanks, but I'll pass. Must find Prue. How long will Jon be? My phone's died and he may be trying to get me.'

'Should be here soon. Go home, Wendy. You look tired. And distressed.'

'Let Jon know you've seen me. Ask him to message. I'll charge my phone when I get back to Brambles. Take care, friend.' As raindrops fell, threatening a deluge, Wendy kissed Eddie's cheek and dashed off through the gate. She kept her eyes straight ahead.

So, someone had done for dude Pengelly. Karma *had* wreaked revenge. Not the best way to go, but nothing her old, confused mind should dwell on. Her chief concern was Prue. And Emily, too. Pengelly dead. Prue missing. Monty King in Bogie. Wendy's gut wasn't old and confused.

The game's afoot, Darling.

68

The Fallout

B ack at Brambles, Wendy put on her rational head. She charged her phone—no word from Jon—and changed into dry clothes. Focus needed coffee, and it wasn't long before she sat with a giant cup of number 8 reasoning recent events.

So, Ross Pengelly was gone. Didn't need his own rope to hang himself. Someone had done it for him. Turned out her last barb with him in the Noose was *his* swansong and Eddie was still singing. Granted, he wasn't crooning earlier. Could hardly crank out a tune when a dropped body was swinging a few feet away. How many more killings? Biggin-Smythe was one thing, and yes, Pengelly was a two-timing rake and deserved his dues, but like this? Bizarre how he'd gone the same way as Patcheye Peg. That old devil called instinct gave Wendy a hard shove. Pushing. Driving. Brewing up a notion.

Wendy parked the theory. She'd come back to it later. Right now, her head only had time for Prue. What of her? There was nothing for it but to go on a hunt. She'd visit all their favourite haunts and treasured walks. Search and scour and keep on foraging until she found her dear friend.

On her way down heart attack hill, when the cloudburst brought torrential rain, Wendy had seen police on their way to the Noose. She considered going back to put her oar in, but finding Prue was her priority. She hadn't seen Jon. Nothing strange there. No one could accuse him of being Mr Punctuality.

The second strident thumping at the front door came as no surprise. Wendy knew it was the law. She was right. A drenched Slate and Uttley, accompanied by two paramedics.

'You certainly get about, Miss May,' Slate said.

'Come into the kitchen,' Wendy signalled. 'Coffee?'

'No.'

Wendy sensed Slate spoke for everyone. 'What's going on?'

'There's been an incident.'

'You could say that. An ambulance took Emily Clarke to hospital. She was in a terrible state. Her boyfriend's dead, but you'll know that. Why are paramedics here?'

'I've spoken to Eddie Rutter. He tells me you were at the Noose earlier. Medics have treated him for shock. I thought you might need the same.'

'I'm shocked, yes, but not on Emily's level. I've seen many nasty things in my life, chief inspector. What I saw looked grisly, but I'm not a sightseer and didn't stare.'

'Unlike Mr Windup. He was doing a lot of staring. Funny how he always shows up near a corpse.'

'Nothing funny about it. Jon wasn't supposed to be working this morning. Eddie called him in. Had to. I haven't seen Jon. We'll speak later. Right now, I'm concerned about Prue. I can't find her.' Wendy's voice wavered.

Slate gestured to a chair. 'I think you should sit down.'

'Why?'

'Please. Sit down.'

Wendy sensed the urgency and slumped into a chair. 'Prue?'

'We've found her body.'

69

Cagey Situation

Wendy May wasn't often lost for words. She was an editor. A writer. A woman of letters. But Slate's announcement tied her tongue. Left her mouth hanging open. Reality hit hard.

DS Uttley flipped open his notepad and scribbled.

'She's alive, but lucky to be so,' Slate said.

Energy rushed up Wendy's body. She checked the urge to scream and lash out. Relief. It was the sweetest thing. 'Where is she?'

'Hospital. It was Mr Windup who found her sprawled semi-conscious in the bushes behind the gibbet cage. Don't know how long she'd been there. He arrived at the Noose just before us and, thankfully, left us to do our job. At first, I thought Miss Penn was dead, but I found a weak pulse and an ambulance whisked her off soon after. Eddie Rutter hadn't seen her. Nor you. All in all, an eventful morning.'

'You could say that.'

'Are you up to a few questions? Not a full statement, but I'll need one soon.'

'I'll do what I can. Don't know why Prue would be at the Noose.'

'That's a shame. I hoped you'd tell me.' Slate's tone was grim.

'Couldn't say. Only knew she was gone this morning. Thought she was asleep, but when she didn't show I checked her room and nothing. Her bed was made. The room felt so empty, like no one had been there for hours.'

'Is it normal for her to sleep late?'

'If she's having a turn, yes. You know she has MS?'

'Yes. Is that why you're staying with her?'

'As you'll appreciate, she's been through the motions in the last few days. Still going through them. This situation with Tom has caused so much bad stress and worsened her condition.'

'I see.'

'Prue deals with life well, but doesn't go out alone much. Certainly not at night. She's still adapting to a serious condition. A new lifestyle and diet. Fatigue is one of the biggest snags. When I came home last night, I presumed she'd had an early night.'

'Where had you been?'

'The Brock and Sett. In Bogus Hole.'

'And were you alone or in company?'

Though intrusive, Wendy knew Slate was doing what detectives were trained and paid to do. Prying. Probing. Casting suspicion. All part of a copper's remit.

'In company.'

'Does this company have a name or names?'

Wendy hesitated. *Should she say who she was with? What did she have to hide?* 'Montgomery King.'

Slate's face shone, waking up his bushy beasties.

'The King you've mentioned before?'

'The very same.'

'Odd choice of company, if you don't mind me saying.'

'I don't. I was sort of interviewing him.'

'Sort of?'

'It was his idea. I'm sure I told you about my unfinished interview with Lord Biggin-Smythe and the meeting with his widow to complete my magazine article. King was up from London, holding one of his famed cookery classes in Bogie, and we had a chat. He ended up gatecrashing my story and telling his own. It wouldn't win any Oscars. Or increase readership.'

Wendy didn't divulge her primary reason for meeting King. She knew Slate wouldn't relish her and Jon dabbling further into Biggin-Smythe's murder. Slate's face suggested he guessed why she'd met him, but he said nothing.

'Thanks for satisfying my curiosity. I know what you're thinking. King comes to Treetonshire and there's a murder the same night. A coincidence, I'm sure, but we have a duty to follow all leads and will do so. We'll speak to King. He's likely gone back to London, so it's a job for the Met. I'll call them back at the station. So? Who do you know who had it in for Ross Pengelly, or Prue Penn?'

'For Pengelly, where do you start? His postal round covered at least ten villages. There'll be a long list of doers from here to Old Farrow. Pengelly was a cocky so-and-so. Always rubbing people up the wrong way. Thought he was Adonis. No, scrub that. He wouldn't know who Adonis was. Let's say vanity and him were more than close. I could never grasp what Emily saw in him. He was cheating on her. Who knows, maybe she found out and did for him, though given the state she was in, I doubt it. As for Prue, I don't understand. Can't think of anyone who'd want to harm her.' Wendy watched Uttley's hand dancing across his notebook in time with Slate's skipping brows.

'That's all very interesting. You don't know who Pengelly was cheating with?'

'Antonia Biggin-Smythe.'

'So, a visit to the grand estate's on the cards.'

Wendy couldn't tell if Slate's face showed puzzlement, curiosity, or frustration. She decided on the latter.

'Antonia's staying with a friend in Norfolk.' The sentence was out before Wendy could hold it.

'How do you know?'

It was pointless not to tell. 'There was an incident on the *grand estate.*'

'An incident?'

Wendy explained how Jon and Antonia stumbled upon Richard Biggin-Smythe's counterfeit money operation. Their lockdown in a lockup and rescue by Lu.

'You know a lot about the goings-on around here. That's some story, and no one thought to tell the police?'

'Considered it pointless. Richard would've moved his equipment, but …'

'I'm waiting.'

'There's a rumour going around that the Biggin-Smythes have the police in their pocket. They certainly have the wealth, and you know what they say. Money is power. And power has influence.'

Slate and Uttley exchanged glances, but said nothing. They didn't need to. Wendy knew from Slate's face. A look lasting long enough for Wendy to think *gotcha. That's what I'm talking about.*

'I have no clue,' Slate coughed. 'Rest assured, the police investigate all crimes without prejudice.'

Slate failed to convince Wendy. 'Just telling you what I've heard. Don't shoot the messenger and all.'

'Thanks again, Miss May. I'd like you to come to the station and make a full statement. Once I've looked into matters further. I'll be in touch. You will be all right? Is there anyone we can call?'

'I'm fine, thanks.'

'Good. We'll see ourselves out.'

Slate and Uttley got up to go. Wendy followed, anyway.

Slate turned around. 'One more thing. Leave the investigating to the professionals, please.'

'Sure thing, Columbo.'

Slate made no reply and scurried to the front gate, Uttley not far behind. Slate hadn't admitted it, but Wendy knew. *Treetonshire Constabulary had been bought.*

70

Cordon Blue

F resh from the crime scene, Jon met Wendy outside
the Noose and Gibbet. Sealed off to the public for the
second time in as many months, it once again drew a
curious crowd.

'What was Prue doing here last night?' Jon said.

'No idea,' Wendy whispered, doing her damnedest to
be strong, while underneath she was fading. Not just
because she cared so much about Prue, but because guilt
stung. She should've known something was amiss when
Prue insisted on being alone, despite flaring symptoms.
Had she not gone to meet the sleazy Montgomery King,
she could've stopped Prue from making a lousy decision.
Or accompanied her if she was adamant. Either way,
Wendy had let her dear friend down and remorse was raw.

Again, the sulky Sowers and their trusty trolley were
ready to bag a body. Eyes watched with the same macabre
anticipation as weeks ago. Even the cheers and applause
were comparable. As usual, Pengelly was fashionably
late. A dedicated follower, even in death.

'Typical postman,' Figgy Figgis growled. 'Never on
time.'

'Pengelly sure loved a van,' Jon said. 'Bye-bye, Royal
Mail van. Hello, cadavan and the sham tan. The old
morgue mobile's seeing some action lately. Oops.
Shouldn't speak ill of the dead.'

'Never understood that philosophy. Does anyone
speak well of dead despots, warmongers, or lowlifes? If

someone's a rotter while alive, why hypocrisy when dead? Death doesn't change a person's character.'

'That's true, but you know how bigoted some people are. Oh, no!'

Wendy followed Jon's eyes and pointed finger and saw what he was seeing. A huffing, puffing Annie Clegg, pushing Jemima uphill. Where the taxing hilltop ended, the tireless foghorn started.

'Hear the village postie's dead, and Prue Penn's in a bit of a lather,' Annie rattled. The odious overbite had taken charge.

'News spreads like a flood in these parts,' Jon said.

'And dribble still drips,' Wendy sniped.

Annie gestured to the Sowers. 'Those two miseries are at it again. Like vultures preying on carrion. Won't see that postie gussied up no more. Swapped his bright orange tan for a dull black bag. Never liked that Ross Penwally. Heard he liked to put it about, so to speak. As for Penn, that's what you get for shielding the kilted killer.'

Annie's malice any day incensed Wendy. And today, if left unchecked, that vicious tongue would happily turn Wendy into a killer. 'His name was Pengelly, and he won't be "putting it about" anymore. As for Prue, you'd be "in a bit of a lather" if someone walloped you over the head. Considering the amount of drivel you spout, think it's already happened. You've lost it, woman. On your bike, and get back to the funny farm. Go on. Be gone. Before someone whacks and gibbets you and leaves you hanging in that cage for the crows to peck at.'

'No need to be rude.'

Annie scuttled off to mingle with a group of nosy parkers gathered behind the cordon. Daytrippers on a tour of Tor, the grisly old gibbet cage being the star attraction. Perfect for those who loved a morbid life. They'd picked a fine day for it. The cage's new lodger still rested at will. Nobody knew what was holding him up, but it was clear the delay didn't amuse the Sowers. Unlike other tourists who visited Tor's focal point, this latest grim happening stopped big beaks from getting up close and personal. Didn't stop wagging tongues, though. Nor the cackle of giggles and titters.

'Did Slate say Prue was hit on the head, Wendy?' Jon asked.

'He believed so. Sprawled in the bushes. Semi-conscious. A rolling pin nearby. Seems logical, but don't know for sure. You never mentioned a rolling pin.'

'Didn't see it. I'd only just found Prue when the cops turned up. Uniform first, then Uttley, who secured the scene, and Slate minutes after. Ed told me you'd just gone. Reckon I was parking up while you were on your way down heart attack hill. Hope she hasn't been hit with a rolling pin. So much damage. Head trauma, the like.' Jon looked across at Annie and her new besties. 'Honestly, some people love revelling in other people's grief. Look at that bunch of old crows,' he sniped.

'And with her rake on a break and the big wooden spoon standing in, Tor's meanest old crow's stirring them up. That's what I call a murder.'

'What?'

'A murder. The collective term for crows.'

'Got you. A killing or a crowd of corvidae.'

'It's apt for today. Annie's venom and all.'

'You're not wrong.'

'But we'll see it as a beautiful word for the scientific name. Thanks, Windy.'

'You're welcome.'

Behind the cordon, wearing the obligatory white suit and overshoes, Wendy spotted Albie Drew in deep discussion with DS Uttley. Slate wasn't around. 'Wonder if Albie knows anything.'

'Wait until Muttley scarpers and we'll ask.'

When Uttley headed back to the Noose, Wendy called out. 'Got a minute, Albie?'

Albie lifted the barrier tape and greeted the couple. His professional air never wavered, but Wendy detected a mess of emotions behind his eyes. Stress. Anxiety. Fatigue. Disgust. She knew that frazzled look well. In the last two years of her legal career, she'd worn it daily. DCI Slate wore it too. In this game, untold disorders were standard. The evils of evil.

'How's Prue?'

Albie shook his head. 'You know what happened?'

'Slate assumed someone hit her with a blunt instrument. A rolling pin, maybe?'

'No. She took a minor blow to the back of the head. Any head injury's cause for concern, but that isn't what felled her.'

'What then?'

'An MS relapse. No surprise, with all that's going on. Reckon it's been building for weeks and came to a head early this morning. Someone struck, but it was a glancing knock. Ironically, it's likely the relapse saved her life. I'll know more when I look in on her later. You know my background as a doctor before I got into pathology. And my fondness for Prue means I've sort of taken over. Fighting her corner. The whole thing's wicked.'

Wendy touched Albie's shoulder, eyes burning as she held back tears. 'Please, let me know if you hear anything.'

'I will. Better go. Must keep the gruesome twosome happy, and the sooner I get the postie on the slab, the sooner the coroner completes his inquest.' Albie moved off, back to his corpse.

'What a turn-up. Prue having a relapse. And likely it saved her life. That's incredible, but I still can't understand what she was doing here, and why anyone'd want to harm her. Somebody tried. Just doesn't make sense.'

'Does life? I wish I'd stayed with her last night. Part of me feels responsible for this horror. She's still had a relapse, and I wasn't there to support her.'

'You're not to blame. She could've sneaked out while you were sleeping. Last night was out of character for her. She was determined and nothing was going to stop her.'

'The only thing that could have that pull is Tom. He *must've* been there.'

'And the probability of him harming his sister is about as likely as likely isn't.'

'Remote as the sun. Distance wise.'

'So who do we think did for Prue and Pengelly?'

'That's the burner. I was no Pengelly fan, but did he deserve this?'

'Some might say he had it coming.'

'Some might. Poor Emily's devastated. As for Antonia, don't know if she's back, or knows he's dead.'

'Someone from the estate or Tor's likely told her. She has a few friends here. Nothing stays contained in these parts.' Jon peered at Annie and her friends, still in animated conversation. 'Look at that lot. Aren't people nosy?'

'Says the world's chief meddler.'

'Must meddle to be a sleuth, Darling. So, what about King? Can't be a coincidence he was in Bogus Hole last night. Then a murder and attempted murder down the road. We suspect his involvement in the old boy's death. What about the young man? Very fishy.'

'My take too. I told Slate.'

'Think he'll follow up?'

'He should, but King'll cover his tracks. That's if the police investigate at all.'

'Surely Slate won't think Tom injured his sister. He'll realise someone else's in the frame?'

'You'd think. Call it instinct, but when he interviewed me, I saw something in his eyes.'

'What did you see?'

'Like he knows where he should look, but can't. Or won't. There's a reason.'

'Like his hands are tied?'

'With a tourniquet, and that can only mean one thing.'

'A bent copper.'

'Right ballpark. To quote you, Windy, "it's good, but it's not right."'

'Okay. Not Slate, but someone else.'

'Correct. Slate's clean.'

'Like what you did there. Clean slate. You and your wordplay.'

'Thank you. I'm sure Slate's the honest type, but certain suits or uniforms may be corrupt.'

'The old boy knew the chief constable. Went to the same yachting club.'

'And the chief wears a uniform. Could explain why the force is ignoring the family, but doesn't explain King.'

'Unless there's a connection between King and the family.'

'King knew about Dickie's fake money operation, and the tension between him and milord. Knew a fair bit about milord too.'

'Hi there,' Eddie greeted Jon and Wendy.

'You look better than you did earlier,' Wendy said.

'Feel better too, thanks. Not what you want to see when you turn up for work.'

'Know the feeling, Ed. Been there with the old boy. Guess my shift's cancelled again?'

'You guess right.'

'I'll say. The way things are going, the whole pub'll end up in the bleeding gibbet cage,' Wendy agreed.

'Doesn't bother me. I'm leaving anyway.'

'Wish I was going to work in the Brock.'

'Don't worry, Jon. I'll send plenty of shifts your way, even if you think I'm a killer.'

'Thanks in advance, even if you think the same of me.'

Despite the despair, the trio managed a giggle.

Eddie spied DS Uttley. 'Must find out how long they'll have the Noose out of action. See you later.'

'Come on, Darling, let's go. Nothing much doing here. Leave the gossips gossiping. We'll call the hospital. See how Prue's doing.'

As Jon's car navigated the downward slope, Wendy spied a red sports car parked at the foot of the hill. The driver watched them pass, enormous shades and hat a feeble disguise. Lucinda Biggin-Smythe fooled no one.

71

Solemn Reflection

J on and Wendy sat down to their evening meal, tuning into the deafening sound of silence. Both toyed with vegetable teriyaki seasoned with sesame and wasabi. Both sipped yuzu sake. After a call to Treeton General Hospital, their much-loved weekly Japanese experience had fallen flat.

Severely blurred vision. Nausea. Crippling body spasms. Reduced mobility. Prue's relapse had left her in a sorry state. A steroid drip to reduce inflammation would, hopefully, shorten the relapse and put her back into recovery. Nothing Jon or Wendy could do other than send warm wishes and let medics do their jobs.

Jon broke the silence to lighten the mood. 'Your teriyaki puts the cherry in blossom.'

'Thanks.'

'Still feeling guilty? I'm sure she'll pull through. Doctors say she would've relapsed anyway and, if hit on the head harder, it could've been fatal. She's in the best place, Wendy. Keep the faith.'

''Tis true, I feel guilty, and know things could be much worse, but what's happened has made me more determined to stop this ugly violence. For Prue and Tom's sake, we must crack this case.'

'I'll drink to that.' Jon clinked his glass with Wendy's. 'Pity Dave barged into the Brock when he did. A proper stumblebum.'

Wendy managed a smile at the wacky word. 'King was about to reveal something, then Dave steams in. Perhaps the Sacher king felt uncomfortable at the London class, but was willing to talk last night. He was certainly willing to do something, but he got told.'

'Indeedy. Imagine he wasn't eggstatic when you said no to whisking up an omelette with him. Left him proper scrambled, you did.'

'Daft Jokes Jon, I salute you. They get sillier, but right now, I'm grateful for your batty japes.'

'DJJ at your service. Think King'll meet you again?'

'After I wrung him out and wiped the floor with him last night? If he's into dominance, he might want more of the same. Whatever his motive, I doubt I've heard the last of him. One thing's certain. King didn't travel into the sticks just to meet me. His presence in Bogie and Pengelly's death weren't a coincidence.'

'Remind me why he was in Bogie.'

'Doing a cooking class at the village hall. He owns the hall, remember? Said he was covering for his son, who'd taken ill. A likely story. According to Dave, King doesn't like paying bills.'

'How so?'

'Owes Dave for work done on the village hall, but our friend King isn't easy to pin down. Surprised Dave didn't kick off in the Brock. Odd. Remember how you found Biggin-Smythe? A broken baguette and cash. Deadly dough, of course. Whether King's mixed up in this as killer, conspirator, or just an innocent bystander, money must be the motive. And that foolish thing called pride.'

'Got it, and we reckon King is mixed up somehow, but don't know that somehow.'

'Don't discount Dickie. His name's in the business proposal. King denied it, but that's no surprise. Fake notes in milord's mouth. A counterfeit money operation. Lord Dickie's more than tricky.'

'You think there's a connection?'

'Must be. King's a natural born liar. Who knows what else he's hiding? But that doesn't make him a killer. Oh, I don't know, Windy. We're out of our depth here.'

'That's your phone.'

'If it's another one of those stupid scam calls asking if I've been in an accident that wasn't my fault, I'll hit the roof. I don't have time for that rubbish.'

Wendy vanished, then reappeared, mystified. 'It was Lucinda.'

'Really? Has she been in an accident that wasn't her fault?'

'Ha! No accident, but an interesting development.'

'Well, come on.'

'She wouldn't say, but wants to meet me as soon as. Something to do with milord's diary.'

'The old boy kept a diary? What for?'

'Didn't go into details, but said she has news. Says it's *frightfully important*. For her or the article I don't know, but she *simply must tell me*.'

'Where does she want to meet? After my ordeal the other day, I'm in no hurry to go back to the big bad house.'

Wendy suppressed a chuckle 'At her cottage. Must be worried about prying eyes and ears. Surprised she wants to see me again after our encounter in London. I wasn't the warmest soul.'

'Very cloak and dagger. Wonder what she has to say for herself.'

'This time tomorrow, you'll wonder no more. We meet in the morning.'

72

Deadlock

H ammering at Jon's front door disturbed a flood of breakfast table musings. Cursing, Wendy put her head in her hands.

'Who the hell's that on a Saturday morning?' Irritated curiosity spiked Jon's tone.

'That's a copper's knock,' Wendy said.

Jon slurped a mouthful of coffee, bit into another toasted peanut butter sandwich, and hurried to the door.

'Morning, Mr Windup,' DCI Slate greeted, barging past Jon into the hallway. Uttley tagged behind.

'Come in, why don't you?' Jon mumbled through a nutty mouthful. He gulped down the mulch and went back into the kitchen.

'Any chance you could knock the door down next time, chief inspector? Jon's been after a new one for months. Something a little more upmarket to cause a stir. Big brass knobs and knockers, and you can foot the bill.'

'Good morning, Miss May. Ever the comedian.'

'I'm a riot, no question. What can I do for you?'

'It's Mr Windup we want, but as you're here—'

'Me? Is this about the other night?'

'Just routine. Like before, we're asking everybody who works in the Noose where they were between ten pm and three am.'

'I was behind the bar. Not on my own, I'm pleased to say. It was our weekly quiz night. Then home.'

'You were behind the bar until three?' Uttley said.

'The bar closed at ten-thirty. I left an hour or so later after drinking-up and cashing-up. Can't remember the exact time.' Jon remained polite, despite wanting to shove Uttley's flippant question down his throat.

'Yes. Remember time wasn't your thing. And how many people at the quiz night?'

'About twenty or so. It's always fun, but a few get competitive. Me and Wendy normally take part, but I was working, and Wendy had a prior engagement.'

Slate turned to Wendy and flashed a stony look. His eyes were at their baggiest. Brows still slumbered. 'Yes, a date with Montgomery King. I had a chat with the staff and guests at the Brock and Sett. The barman said King retired to his bedroom shortly after you left. He also said the front door's locked at night and makes an almighty creaking when opened. Someone would've heard if King had sneaked out and back in. Turns out nobody did.'

'Could've snuck out another way.'

'That's true, but the guest staying next door to King said she heard snoring from around eleven and again at one when it woke her up. She said it was like trying to sleep next to a power saw.'

'I know the feeling, though Jon's more pneumatic drill. What are you saying, chief inspector?'

'What I'm saying is the probability of Mr King leaving his room in the Brock and Sett and coming to the Noose and Gibbet is somewhere between zero and never.'

'What time did Pengelly drop? If you don't mind me asking.'

Slate and Uttley looked at one another.

'Don't mind you asking, Miss May, but hope you don't mind me telling you that's privileged information. Not for the public. Yet.'

'Understood, chief inspector. Thank you.'

'One more thing, Mr Windup. What did you do after you left the Noose and Gibbet?'

'The same thing I do every night after closing. Went straight home. Same way as before. Nice relaxing drive down the country lanes to Treeton. Got home around twelve-thirty and straight to bed. Didn't find out what happened until the following morning, when—'

'Thank you, Mr Windup, that'll be all. I'll leave you to your breakfast. Don't forget that statement, Miss May. I'll be in touch if there's anything else. And remember, please leave the investigation to us. We'll see ourselves out.'

Wendy blew out a sigh. 'Shame he wouldn't spill what we wanted, though he gave a time window. Between ten pm and three am, he said. That's something. Of course, the police can lead you into a trap. Say one thing, but mean another. That window may be bogus to trip you up.'

'Can't fox the wind, Darling.'

'I'm not sad to see the back of them, but am happy that Slate's brows eventually put on a decent floorshow. A tango today. All abstract and angles.'

'Must have a proper look next time. I never notice them.'

'I've programmed my eyes. Can't help myself.'

'Cheers to quiz night, otherwise I'd have been on my own again in the Noose.'

'Don't think he suspects you. Anyway, better get going. Meeting milady in an hour.'

73

Diary of the Dead

'Hope another trip to see Lu Brush's worth the effort.' Jon focused on the narrow country lane flanked by tall beech hedges.

'She sounded urgent. Mind you, milady and self-indulgence go hand in hand, so don't have high hopes. Good thing is, you have no work for a while. Imagine police'll keep the Noose closed for a couple of days.'

'Probably. I'm due a bit of time off soon, too. Now, where's that opening?'

Jon's car pulled into a wooden section and the entrance to Lucinda's country hideaway. The gate was open. Turning off the road, he slowed to a crawl up the stone driveway. The charming cottage loomed. Lu's red sports car stood outside.

'Well, here we are again, and this time we get to see inside. How exciting!'

'Is that sarcasm, Windy?'

'Mostly, but my big snout wants to see what it's like. After all, we only saw the garden last time.'

'I saw the front too, remember? Milady's here to greet us. What she has to say must be pressing.'

Jon looked in his wing mirror and groaned. He got out to join Wendy beside the car.

'Thank you for coming. A little late, but at least you're here.' Lucinda turned and headed inside, a cue for Jon and Wendy to follow.

'Even when we're doing her a favour, she has attitude,' Jon whispered, miffed at the remark.

'Ignore her. Attitude's a cover. Maybe she's feeling cornered and vulnerable because there's nowhere to run. If I'm wrong, I know ignoring her kind'll pee her off more than biting ever will. Put your teeth away, Jaws.'

Lucinda invited the couple to sit on an enormous fabric sofa. 'Help yourselves to refreshments and patisserie.'

'Don't mind if I do,' Jon said, seizing a vanilla millefeuille and two mini red velvet cakes.

'Your call smacked of urgency,' Wendy said, pouring coffee for herself and Jon.

'Yes, I wanted to show you this.' Lucinda took a sip of tea, then held up a diary 'I understand you saw Monty King the other night.'

The sight of Lu's crooked pinky finger irked Wendy. 'Never fails to amuse how quickly news travels around these parts. Yet, milord still lies in state and the police haven't collared whoever bagged him. Proves my point, for the zillionth time, that people can't get enough of gossip.'

Wendy's straight-talking had Jon nursing a severe coughing fit.

'Take more water with it, Jon. Told you swilling it neat always has this effect on you. No word from the coroner or police about release of Seymour's body, Lu?'

'Nothing.'

'Uh-huh. So, what do you make of Mr King begging to see me?'

'That man knows no bounds. No doubt he was trying to impress you.'

'Meaning?'

'Do you know what his name was in college? In fact, most of his life?'

'Thankfully, I didn't know him in college. Didn't know him at all before this mess. Your point?'

'It was Chess.'

'You've lost me.'

'His name. I thought a lady of your literary talent would've spotted the irony.'

'With respect, Lu, I'm in no mood for riddles. A dear friend of mine's in hospital and I have little time to waste. I came here to see your late husband's diary.'

'And you will, but stay with me. Can I ask who the dear friend is?'

'Prue Penn. You remember Prue? Tom's sister. She was with me in London. As you won't say where he is, perhaps you'd be good enough to tell him his sister's in a bad way. Now, where were we?'

Lucinda's face paled beneath heavy powder and paint. 'King's alias. Chess.'

'And? Still don't get your angle. Apart from the fact that the king's a piece in a game of chess.'

'You don't play, then?'

'No, but I have an idea how it goes. Will you please get to the point?' Wendy poured more coffee.

'I don't play either. Chess was a pursuit of Seymour's. There are more important things than stupid games.'

'You sure of that? The way you have me hanging suggests you have a passion for all games. What am I doing here?'

'Stay with me, Wendy. You know chess is a game of strategy—'

'I've played before,' Jon said, stuffing more pastries.

Lucinda cast a series of thunderous looks Jon's way. Wendy wished she had the camera handy to snap such priceless daggers.

Jon carried on, oblivious. 'Guess you want to talk about the pawns? Are you implying that King sees life as one big chessboard? Will happily sacrifice people— pawns—for his own benefit?'

'I don't imply. I tell.'

Jon despaired at Lucinda's tiresome haughtiness, but at least she'd cracked the egg. Add a pinch of seasoning and Wendy would cook the omelette.

'He sees you as a pawn, Wendy. As he does everybody. Including my late husband and even me when I was stupid enough to fall for his charm.'

'No fear of that happening to me. The man reeks of shallow and sludge.'

'Be careful. I felt the same way when I first met him, but he has an uncanny ability to worm his way in—'

'Men like that don't interest me, Lu. Full of fibs, flattery, and futility. Try saying that when you've had a few gins. Except I don't drink gin.'

For the first time, Lucinda giggled. 'King was trying to manipulate you. He knew you'd be curious and thought he'd dangle a carrot.'

'Given his conduct and blarney when I met him, that's a fitting analogy. He was dangling something, but I didn't bite. He said Dickie ran a counterfeit money operation, which I already knew, and was about to talk about Tom when he was rudely interrupted.'

'He and Tom were at catering school together. Monty was the lecturer.'

'So Prue tells me. When I first mentioned college days to King, he said he couldn't remember Tom.'

'He was lying. They knew each other. Friends at first, as lecturer and student often are, and both competitive. Too competitive. It didn't stop at cuisine either. The final straw came when Tom stole Monty's girlfriend. She was a lot younger. Monty's trophy. I believe she was a student. Tom muscling in was the ultimate humiliation. Tom was young and stupid and only cared about getting one over his teacher. There was no forgiveness.'

'Tom did the same thing with you. One over milord. His boss. Another silly act. King and Seymour can each claim the title of brainless. Both sucked in by feminine guile. A male weakness, for sure. Sorry, Jon.'

'No. Not the same thing at all. Tom loves me, and rightly so. I'm a prize catch. He's a lucky fellow. Monty's still trying to get even with him,' Lucinda insisted.

'To the extent of framing Tom for a couple of murders?'

'Monty King's ruthless. He'll stop at nothing if his ego, pride, and reputation are on the line.'

'Can think of a few people like that. Did Tom tell you about King's ruthless ways?'

'Yes.'

'You know where he is, don't you?'

'He swore me to secrecy.'

'He was here.'

'For a short while. He left before the police broke my door down.'

'Ross Pengelly lived near,' Jon said.

'And now he's living in the morgue,' Wendy said. 'Wonder how long he'll chill before pushing up daisies. Maybe he'll be cremated. Go the same way as my dough on a bad day.'

Jon stopped chomping and laughing at Wendy's gags. Time to make himself heard. 'Perhaps Pengelly had something to do with the goings-on. Saw Tom, opened his trap and boom, police swoop like vultures. Then he ends up dead. Funny that.'

'Funny what?' Lucinda said.

'Nothing.'

'Are you insinuating Tom had something to do with Mr Pengelly's death? Don't you think he's in enough trouble?'

'You're the one who's keeping his whereabouts secret. And I'm not insinuating. Speculating, that's all.'

'Keep your speculation, Mr Wind. I don't want to hear it.'

'*Up.* Wind. *Up*. How many more times!'

'Silly name. Nearly as bad as Seymour, which brings me to my late husband's diary.'

'At last we get to the reason I'm here,' Wendy cheered.

Lucinda read from several diary entries describing Lord Biggin-Smythe's concerns about King. A thorn in his side that wouldn't go away. He felt that unless there was an alternative solution, he'd have to invest after all or settle financially. Either way, King was backing him into a corner.

'After Monty hounded him, Seymour arranged a meeting at the Noose and Gibbet. Monty wouldn't accept termination of the business proposal. Made life hell for Seymour. Monty has connections. Wanted revenge. Call it blackmail, if you will.'

'Did milord discuss this with you?'

'Seymour always played his cards close to his chest, especially where business was concerned. But I knew the matter troubled him. I sensed something bad was going to happen. Tried to put him off going out that night, but he wouldn't listen. Perhaps if I'd insisted.'

'You can't blame yourself, Lu. He'd made his mind up.'

'But I do. If I hadn't had an affair with Monty, maybe he and Seymour would be business partners, and Seymour would still be alive.'

'Perhaps. But you said King has criminal connections.'

'Yes. It wasn't just my affair that killed the deal. Seymour didn't like Monty's background. If profit was concerned, Seymour would sometimes turn a blind eye to sinister happenings, but even he'd stop at certain things. There were rumours that Monty had made people permanently disappear.'

'That bad?'

'Yes. Willing to murder to silence or remove his enemies.'

'Brings a whole new meaning to checkmate,' said Jon.

'Let me recap. King was blackmailing milord. That's why they met at the Noose and Gibbet that night?'

'According to the diary.'

'Except Seymour met his death there. Because he wasn't willing to negotiate, or King had the intention to kill all along. The mens rea, Lu.'

'What's that?'

'Not up on your Latin?'

'No. What is it?'

'The guilty mind.'

'Have you told the police?' Jon said.

'No. I've just found Seymour's diary. He'd locked it away in a desk drawer in his study. Tom helped me with the lock.'

'Tom's been in the big house? And seen that diary?' Jon probed.

Lucinda ignored the question.

Wendy adopted her advocate's tone. The stern pitch once used in court, and still used to silence show-offs and spite. 'You know the police'll pin this all on Tom. For reasons that aren't clear, unless pushed, they won't investigate King, nor go to Biggin Hall or search the grounds.'

Lucinda remained silent.

'I don't know how close milord and the chief constable were, but there'll be a gross miscarriage of justice, unless we do something about the status quo. For pity's sake, do your duty.'

'There's always been an understanding between the Biggin-Smythes and the police. Goes back centuries.'

'In other words, money's power,' said Jon.

'If you want to put it that way.'

'And with Dickie up to no good, he'll be more determined than ever to keep the law off the estate.'

'So, milord was in bed with the chief constable. Metaphorically speaking. That works. Has Dickie officially taken over as head of the family and running of the estate?' Wendy probed.

'Yes, though he shouldn't have. Probate isn't complete. Once it is, he'll banish me to the dower house. At least I have this place.'

'And a lot more besides. Despite your indiscretions, your late husband was a generous man.'

'Quite. If only there was a way to persuade the police to investigate Richard and Monty.'

'Resignation or removal of the chief constable. That's the only way. Slim chance. There'd have to be evidence of money exchanging hands between the chief and milord. Or Dickie.'

'I've checked our joint account, but there's nothing suspicious. Seymour had several private accounts. Offshore. So does Richard.'

'It's up to us. I think DCI Slate suspects King but can't act because his hands are tied.'

'Okay let's piece this together,' said Jon. 'The old boy went to meet King at the Noose and Gibbet to sort the mess he'd got himself into. Despite blackmail, he vowed not to bow to King's demands.'

'Could've been someone else there. On King's payroll,' Wendy said. 'Pengelly? He must fit in somewhere.'

'And of course, Tom,' Jon went on. 'In the wrong place at the wrong time.'

'But why would Tom be there? He was at the big house with the bakers. Where did he go after? Prue thought he probably came to see you, Lucinda. Did he?'

'Yes, but not for long. He said he had to go to the Noose to check a few things before work the next day. He was quite vague.'

'Maybe King got Tom there under false pretences. Either way, Tom's presence was vital. King planned to murder milord. And the "someone else" did the dirty deed. King wanted to frame Tom as revenge for stealing his girlfriend and stripping his male pride. Would look like Seymour had found out about the affair and come to the Noose to confront Tom. They had a fight. Milord lost. Panicked, and knowing the police and the village would assume he'd set out to kill, Tom had no choice but to run and lie low.' Wendy stopped to look directly at Lucinda. 'Was Seymour aware of your affair with Tom?'

'Yes.'

'Does he make reference in his diary?'

'Yes.'

'How did he feel about it? More importantly, what was he going to do about it?'

Lucinda couldn't speak.

'This is crucial. Two murders, and—'

'Seymour was very clever. He always knew. When you marry someone thirty years younger, there'll always be *that* risk. His words. More or less.'

'You haven't answered my question.'

'He was bogged down with Monty. Intended to solve that problem first, then deal with me. Like the rest of our marriage, I always came second after business.'

'How did he feel when he found out about your affair with King?'

'Livid, but he forgave me. Not because he's soft, but like all the lords before him, he wanted to protect the family's reputation. That was paramount. Scandal, and what it could do to the family's honour, terrified Seymour. Divorce was unthinkable. The biggest shame of all. My affair with Tom, the head chef of a country pub, was a scandal he wanted to hide.'

'Suggesting he intended to confront Tom. Maybe before he met King,' said Jon.

'Don't know when,' Lucinda said.

'And that leaves the same problem as before,' said Wendy. 'The police won't humour our theory.'

'Richard Biggin-Smythe could be involved. Why else would the police be unwilling to pursue King, but continue to hound Tom? Dickie and King must be connected,' Jon offered.

'What do you think of this hunch?' said Wendy. 'King and Dickie, in collusion. King takes care of milord, and Dickie gives King what he wants. Investment in his business and a stake in return.'

'Dickie and the old boy always had a strained relationship, but patricide?' Jon was agog.

'Anything's possible with the most powerful family in Treetonshire,' Wendy said. 'Wouldn't put anything past Dickie. He acts the clown, but his big, red nose far from fits that hook on his face. A shyster. Like father. Like son.'

'And I should know what the family's all about,' agreed Lucinda.

'It's not as if Dickie would carry out the deed himself,' Wendy said.

Lucinda paled further at the thought her stepson could be involved in his father's murder.

'Do you remember the business proposal between King, Seymour, and Dickie?' asked Jon.

Wendy showed Lucinda the document on her phone.

'Surely corroborates some of our theory,' said Jon.

'Seymour prepared that proposal. According to his diary, he included Dickie in the deal. Not out of kindness, but in the hope his illicit business dealings would surface.

He was wary of King and what he could do, but if someone else found out, perhaps they'd investigate.'

'And here we are. Never thought we'd end up doing milord's bidding.'

'One could see the diary entries as him writing his own obituary. Hello? Wonder who wants me?' Wendy fished for her phone. 'Would you believe it? A ping from King. This man can't resist my charm. Either that or he's a masochist. Or has a score to settle. Before you tell me I'm a pawn, Lu, he knows his place with me. I left him in no doubt. That hasn't changed.'

'What does he want?' Jon said.

'To meet again.'

74

The Message

'She never said where Tom is. Conveniently forgot,' Jon lamented as he drove away from Lucinda's cottage.

'Getting that ping from King made me forget to ask her again. Damn him and his message.'

'She knows where he is. Protecting him.'

'Of course she is.'

'She says he's been to the big house. Reckon he's still there? Must be secret passageways, or an underground room somewhere. You know, like a nuclear fallout shelter. The old boy or his daddy definitely had the money. Either for protection during World War Two, or the Cold War.'

'Did you hear Lu say no plans yet to release milord's body? Funny that. Could swear I spotted a pair of shiny silver tap shoes ready to dance on his grave. She's saving the six-inch bling for the wake.'

Jon laughed out loud. 'Wouldn't surprise me.'

'We must find something to pin on King. Something concrete police can't ignore.'

'Why does he want to meet?'

'Who knows?'

'At the Brock again?'

'Nope. His office.'

'In London?'

'I'm not sure.'

'Meaning?'

'A lot of companies often have a flashy London address.'

'Meaning?'

'Let me explain. A company rents a small space in the capital and registers the address at Companies House. However, most trading's done—'

'On an industrial estate somewhere that isn't London.'

'You're not so dim after all, Windy.'

'Only on dimdays. Where's King's unofficial premises, then?'

'In Treeton. A small business park near the hospital.'

'I know of that place. Speaking of hospitals, we must check on Prue.'

'Don't worry, we will. Can we stop at her house? I feel bound to look after it while she's laid up.'

'No problem.'

Jon parked outside Brambles. Thunderstorms had cleared and cooled the air, but today was another muggy one. Wendy often commented on the temperature in Jon's car, only to hear the usual whine about the rubbish air con. The last time Jon had the system checked, he'd spent a fortune, only for it to play up again. When Wendy suggested he get another car, Jon gave his default answer. "I'll have to go away and think about it."

'Wonder how Emily's doing?' Jon said.

'She's gone to stay with her folks.'

Jon shook his head. 'Nice girl, shame about the gullibility. Pengelly and his cheap charm. We'll struggle to find anyone as devastated about his death as Emily is.'

'Antonia won't be.' Wendy stuck her head around the living room door. A red light flashed on the landline telephone base unit. 'Message for Prue. I'm sure she won't mind me listening.'

Wendy pushed the button next to the number display. An automated voice advised one new message and no old. She gasped as the machine played.

'This is for Prue's friends. Listen, record, then delete.' Jon's eyes opened wide. 'That's Tom.'

75

Prime Suspect

Two bloodhound brains couldn't resist another peek at the crime scene. The Noose was still a hive of police activity, a group of villagers watching from behind the cordon.

'No Atom Annie,' Jon said.

'Don't get comfy. The village scold won't stay away too long. It's early. She's probs slurping coffee and sponge cake through her overbite and wittering to anyone who'll listen. *Poor Adam*. Where's Eddie, I wonder?'

'Having a day out with his wife and her family. Told me the sooner he gets away from this place, the better.'

'Any clue when you'll get back to work?'

'Tomorrow. Like before, police'll let management in, but the public and staff must wait another day.'

'Spotted Albie's car up the road. Must be doing more scouting around. He has a vested interest in Prue and wants swift justice. Need to see him. He'll have a good idea what's happening, and news of Prue, hopefully.' Wendy scanned the area beyond the cordon. A couple of uniformed officers guarding the entrance to the Noose, but otherwise, scarce activity. 'He must be inside.'

'Shame we can't walk up and ask to see him.'

'Any further thoughts on Tom's message?'

'Plenty. Know I can't stop thinking about it.'

'We'll have another listen in the car.'

Each had recorded Tom's message on their phone. In the cemetery car park, Wendy replayed the potent words.

"Lucinda told me about Prue. She's also heard rumours in the village. I knew about it from the paper. Being prime suspect means I can't visit Prue or call to see how she is.

"Lord BS knew about my affair with Lucinda. A few days before his murder, he came to the Noose and told me I was finished. Both with his wife and as head chef. I had one week to get out. There were people in the pub who would've heard raised voices. Some may even have heard what we said. I was on borrowed time.

"One of my old lecturers from catering college approached me soon after. Montgomery King was the last person I expected to hear from. Told me he wanted to bury the hatchet. Knew about BS's threats and wanted to discuss a profitable business deal with me. He'd had similar chats with BS, but wasn't happy with the greedy terms and withdrew his interest. He arranged to meet me at the Noose the night BS was killed. I was taking the baking class at Biggin Hall and couldn't meet until after hours. I was late getting there. When I went into the pub, the cellar door was open. Heard faint voices and listened at the door.

"The voices got louder. I recognised all but one. Biggin-Smythe, King, and Ross Pengelly. Heard a scuffle and King shouted something like, you thieving toff, you've ruined my plans and even poached my bread contract. Think he meant the company who supplies the pub's bread. Dough by Artie San. Sounded like BS had made a deal with them because he was furious at King for pulling out of the business proposal.

"Anyway, I heard footsteps and hid in a cleaning cupboard. King said, no time to hang him in the cage. Let's go. When the coast was clear, I went into the cellar and saw BS propped up dead against the barrels. There was money on the floor and in his mouth. I didn't touch anything.

"I've seen BS's diary and now know he pulled out of the deal with King. It's likely King was recording all our calls and keeping my texts. He knew of my affair with Lucinda and had set out to frame me. I don't know how he got my number, but there's a mole somewhere. Stupid me. Never thought about that. Only cared about getting my own back on BS. An affair with his wife wasn't enough. I wanted to rub his nose in it. I knew those three thugs were killers, but the police would wrongly assume I'd done it. It would be my word against them. Had no choice. Get out of there quickly and go to ground.

"I'm trying to get evidence to prove King's guilt. I'm sure Richard Biggin-Smythe's involved. Me and Lucinda know BS paid the police to look the other way and Richard's pulling strings now. I tried to be clever. Contacted Ross Pengelly and told him I had CCTV incriminating him in the murder. Told him to meet me at the Noose or he'd be sorry. It was an empty threat. CCTV only covers the public area, but that doesn't matter. I wanted Pengelly to panic and planned to blackmail him into confessing. I underestimated him.

"Pengelly called my bluff, and I think he lured Prue to the Noose. She wouldn't have gone on her own. Must've told her I'd be there. Also think King decided Pengelly was a liability and planned to get rid. He couldn't risk witnesses, and that did it for Prue. I reckon King or someone else wanted to leave her for dead. They couldn't know MS would save her skin. The paper says Prue doesn't know what's going on because she's still in shock. The coppers haven't spoken to her. It's all my fault. Pengelly must've told King, and the two of them turned my blackmail plan on its head. Pengelly had to pay, too. Now the police'll think I'm a double murderer, or treble if anything happens to Prue. I'm so ashamed of everything, but I can't risk coming out of hiding until I have the proof to nail those swines.

"I can't go to King's head office to uncover all his secrets, but you can."

'Powerful stuff,' Jon said. 'You sure you still want to meet King?'

'Not scared of him.'

'Perhaps you should be, Darling. He's a dangerous man.'

'King wants the temperature to rise. I'll pepper him with questions. Like most people of his ilk, King's a coward. Went on a date with a bloke like him. Didn't know he was all bull, but soon latched on to his not-so-charming ways. Ended up having a right old ding-dong with him. For my trouble, he threw a glass of red wine at me, but at least I got a drink out of him. Moral of the story, Windy? Men like King must be stopped. He's not even pond life. Some like it hot, Windy, but can Monty stand the heat?'

Wendy heard a tap on the window and wound it down. 'Hi, Babs. How are you?'

'Glad I caught you. Have a few updates on the archives. Are you interested?'

'Always. Are you free Monday, about eleven?'

'See you in the vestry,' Barbara smiled.

The couple walked back to the cordon.

'Oh, sweet. Here's my man. Hi, Albie. Any news?'

'Sorry, Wendy. Nothing different from what you already know. The more I think about it, the angrier I get. Had Prue not had that relapse, this tragedy could've been a different story. Still no consolation when she's pumped full of steroids and unable to see or talk properly. It's a waiting game. We're just following the usual formalities and procedures.'

'What about Pengelly? Are you allowed to tell us anything?' asked Jon.

Albie looked around. Uniformed officers were out of eye and earshot and there was no one else about.

'Struck by a blunt instrument several times. The first blow from behind suggesting he didn't see it coming. Then there were blows to the head and body. The rolling pin was definitely the culprit. Whoever did it had one intention. The first blow would've stunned Pengelly and by the time he regained his senses, if at all, his killer was on him again. No chance to put up a struggle. Cause of death, strangulation by hanging.'

Jon and Wendy shook their heads. Whoever did for Pengelly had a savage mind.

'Told you King was dangerous,' Jon mumbled.

'If it was him. What about fingerprints and DNA, Albie?'

'No fingerprints. The killer wore gloves, but there was a trace of saliva on the corpse. We're analysing.'

'Keep us updated if you hear anything about Prue.'

'You'll be the first to know. Sorry, better go. Slate won't be happy if he catches me talking to the public, especially you pair.'

'Why? Do we have a special place in his heart?'

'Something like that. Among other things, he calls you the comedians.'

'Been called worse. I won't let on what we call him, and that bigmouth sidekick of his'd give Annie Clegg a run for her money. At least me and Jon are memorable. Like legends. And that's a result. Thanks, Albie. You're a gem. Take care.'

Albie darted back to the crime scene. Moments later, a car pulled up and two suits got out. Jon and Wendy recognised Slate and Uttley, ducking under the cordon and dashing into the pub.

'They're in a hurry. Must be getting twitchy or there's an urgent development,' said Wendy.

'Yes, so urgent they didn't see us.'

'That's our cue to get out of here.'

'We need to have a chat.'

'After listening to that message again, I don't understand why Tom hasn't been to the police. Is he trying to deflect blame onto others? He wouldn't hurt Prue, but there's still a chance that him and Lucinda could've cooked up a plan to bump off milord. Thought I was sure of his innocence. Not so sure now. Still too many question marks and King's the biggest of the lot.'

'It's a tough one. So, how about that chat?'

'About what, Windy?'

'Where we go from here.'

76

Finding Ned

'Remind me why we're here, Wendy?' Jon wasn't a religious man, but he admired church architecture. The elegance and grandiose, reaching into the sky. St. Mark's church was no exception.

'One of these days, you'll actually listen. Barbara told me she'd updated the parish archives and was I interested in taking another peek. I am interested. That's why we're here.'

'Right.'

'Are you going to stare at the windows all day or are you coming in?'

'All right, all right,' Jon muttered, trailing Wendy through the heavy double doors and to the vestry.

'Hello.' Barbara greeted with a smile.

'Hi. Here, like I said. Brought along my curious friend, too. Curious about the windows, anyway.'

Barbara beckoned the couple to sit. She'd provided tea, coffee and a selection of biscuits. 'Eat as many as you like. I have a stack more nearing their best before date. Must polish them off.'

'Don't mind if I do,' Jon said, scooping up a handful of chocolate wafers. The moth to the flame.

'Nothing for me. I have things to be getting on with,' Barbara said.

Wendy poured two coffees. 'Watch the crumbs, Jon. You'll have our chief recorder on the warpath. So, what's new, Babs?'

'The updates are in this green box file. It's all self-explanatory, but if you need clarification, come and find me. There's hand gel and paper towels to clean sticky fingers. And don't forget church archive rules.' Barbara pointed to the table, then disappeared.

Wendy pulled on a pair of white gloves. 'You must wear these. Barbara'll skin your bones if you mark or stain her records.'

Jon cleaned his hands, drained his coffee, and donned the other pair. 'I'll have more biscuits later. You love history, don't you? How long have you been a fan?'

'Always. Let's have a nose.' Wendy took the papers from the file. 'These logs are all about Edward Hoskins, aka Nasty Ned. Says he was probably born in the last decade of the sixteen hundreds. There was no legal requirement to register births, so the date's sketchy. Hanged around seventeen thirty-five for the murder of Patcheye Peg, who we now know could be one George Pengelly, and spared the gibbet cage. What did I say about injustice? Going on since time immemorial.'

'No wonder you quit the legal sector. Even now, injustice and corruption rule.'

'Still and always will.' Wendy took off the gloves, gulped the rest of her coffee, and pushed the cup to the far end of the table. She pulled the gloves back on, then studied another section of notes. One page showed a sketch of a man. Wendy gave a loud cheer and Jon looked up. 'Look here. The one and only Nasty Ned, date unknown. Fantastic!'

'That's what he looked like,' Jon said.

'According to the artist, but with the excellent recorded description and the amount of detail in this picture, I'd say it's likely to be a quality representation.'

'What a horrible face. He looks a proper meanie. The sort who'd nick all your biscuits and come back for more.'

'Trust you,' Wendy laughed. 'His face and name suit, right enough. He wasn't known for his charming personality. There's something unsettling about him, and I don't just mean the nasty face.'

'Hold on,' Jon said, 'I've found something here about Edward Hoskins. Okay. He only had one child, but there were other kids on his siblings' side. Shall I read on and tell you when I'm done?'

'Please, and I'll do the same. Then I'll look at the green box records.'

The vestry fell silent as Jon and Wendy scanned and searched. Finally, Jon clapped his gloved hands.

'Found something you should like, Wendy.'

'It's all fascinating, but there are snips and gems that really sing to me. What've you got?'

'Been reading about the Hoskins family. In eighteen seventy-four, a descendant of Ned, one Jacob Hoskins, married Elizabeth Dawkins. They had two sons. The first, Edward, changed his full name. Probably because of the family history and its bad reputation. Had the same name as Nasty Ned. Bet he cursed his parents.'

'Go on,' Wendy fizzed.

'He wanted something that would give his family a fresh nod while maintaining a subtle nod to the past. In the surname anyway. Thus, Edward Hos*kins*, son of Jacob and Elizabeth, became Montague *King*.'

'Get away!' Wendy was agog.

'And listen to this! The last known male descendent of Nasty Ned once lived in nearby Bogus Hole. *Montgomery Oliver King*.'

'An age-old feud?'

'Looks like it.'

77

A Sorry State

P rue looked helpless, asleep among a tangle of tubes and wires. An acute relapse, doctors said. Wendy wasn't an expert on relapsing remitting MS, but knew symptoms had to be severe to warrant a hospital stay. Both she and Jon were in a sombre mood, unable to get why anyone would want to inflict harm on Prue, whose only crime was to be in the wrong place at the wrong time.

'This is why I'm not afraid of King,' Wendy whispered to Jon.

Jon could only nod his head in sorrow.

'Whoever's behind all this madness must face justice. If King's responsible, it's our responsibility to make sure he answers for his wrongs. I won't rest until that slimy brute's behind bars. And anyone else he's dragged along for the ride.'

'The doctors are optimistic, Wendy. Said Prue's a true fighter and shouldn't have too long a stay in here. At the moment, she looks pitiful, but what do I know? You're definitely meeting King, then?'

'No question.'

'Suppose you'll need a lift.'

'If you wouldn't mind.'

'The least I can do. So, when's the big meeting?'

'Tomorrow. Nine am.'

'What are you hoping to find out?'

'I don't know until I find it. With any luck, something implicating him.'

The pair stood silent for the rest of their visit, except for the odd comment about hospital sounds, smells, and general ambience. They left via the concourse and stopped at the cafe.

'Laughable,' Wendy snorted.

'What is?'

'This cafe. What chance does humanity have when you have that bang in the middle of a hospital?'

'Looks normal to me.'

'Normal? Doctors and nurses preach to stop smoking. Reduce alcohol intake. Exercise more. Eat less fat and sugar. And you better have your five-a-day or else. Meanwhile, here, in the bosom of the last bastion of human health, lurks a greasy spoon. Look at the menu. Bacon rolls. Hamburger and chips. Sausage, beans, and chips. Chips with everything. And all fried-fried-fried. There's double-fried and triple-fried chips, too. Now, that's healthy and then some. Wonder how many people see the irony of a hospital selling junk food?'

'At least there's a side salad with the burger and chips.'

'Or something that passes as side salad. Wilted, wet lettuce, squashed tomatoes, and soggy cucumber straight from a plastic packet is many things, but salad, it ain't. I'd say a tasteless, pointless excuse to make a fat-laden heart attack on a plate look wholesome. You are what you eat, health gurus say. Yikes! Blast it, Jon. This could've been the reasonable rant I didn't give at Speaker's Corner. You get my point?'

'Indeedy. The shop's not much better. Pre-packed sandwiches, crisps, chocolate, and sugary soft drinks. Don't get me wrong, I love crisps and chocolate, not that I eat them much these days, but hospitals should promote healthier choices. There's also a fast-food drive-thru a stone's throw from here. I mean, who gives planning permission for fast food next to a hospital? If you ask me, it's all messed up.

'Planning permission's a mere formality to a multi-million conglomerate. Money exchanges hands and permission's granted.'

'Yes, it's funny how money talks.'

'In every language. An unfortunate truth, but don't get me started on greed and corruption. I'll need a damn big soapbox and a lot of spare hours. Anyway, let's go before your sweet tooth gets the better of you. Temptation's wicked.' Wendy took Jon's arm, and they headed to the car park.

'Regarding tomorrow. Hope you know what you're doing, Darling.'

'So do I, Windy. So do I.'

78

Industrial Disease

'Small business park? It's massive!' Named after the huge redwood at the entrance, Jon drove aimlessly around Sequoia Business and Industrial Park, grumbling and growling. 'Did your friend give you directions?'

'Unit eighty-five. And he's *not* my friend.'

'That's handy. There's a site map over there.' Jon stopped next to a double sign. The left side displayed a list of businesses and unit numbers. The right was a map of the industrial estate showing the location of the units.

'There it is. Kingoisseur, and how to get there. Perfect.'

Jon eased the accelerator, and the car crept forward. According to the map, his destination was on the opposite side of the estate. Follow the main road for a couple of minutes, then navigate a series of side roads. Turn right twice, left twice, and King's unit should be on the right. Jon prided himself on his map-reading and sense of direction. No need for satellite navigation.

'Lots of empty units,' Jon observed, gliding past ghostly buildings.

'Yes, and if the cost of electricity keeps rising, we could see more.'

'Gloomy times ahead.'

'Not for King. His business's booming.'

'Did he give any clues to whet your appetite?'

'Not his style. He's like you, Windy, except he isn't. He's a painful prima donna. A dramatic diva, keeping folk in suspense and dazzling them with mystery. Honestly, if

I wanted histrionics, I'd go to the theatre, or check out local am-dram.'

'And am-dram performs in Bogus Hole village hall. Owned by the one and only—'

'Montgomery Oliver King. Can't get away from the man.'

'Okay, joking apart. I've taken two rights, now looking for the first left. He would have to choose a unit that takes forever to reach. Got it!'

'You must learn the art of patience, my windy friend.'

'The second left's coming up.' A sign showed a no through road, but the area housed units 80–100.

'This must be it here. Slow down.'

Jon stopped outside unit 85. 'Are you sure? Not much to look at, is it?'

They exited Jon's car and stood in front of a prefabricated, grey metal building. No insignia, except for a small brass sign next to a pair of double doors. There was a small car park outside, separated from the road by a metal fence and open gate.

Wendy looked puzzled. 'I expected more from him of the scintillating conversation. Not the trappings of a flamboyant businessman.'

'Maybe he's worried the local kids will swipe his cakes if he advertises his presence.'

'Behave, Jon. You coming in? After all, 'tis the Windy and Darling show.'

Jon smiled his agreement. 'At least I'm not trussed up in a silly suit and tie. Casual clothes mean comfort. Lead on.'

Jon followed Wendy to the front door. To the right, a small sign: Kuisine by Kingoisseur. For deliveries, please ring the bell.

'We're hardly a delivery.'

'We're delivering ourselves. Besides, King's expecting us, or rather me. He'll get double trouble.'

Wendy pushed the bell. Neither she nor Jon saw the CCTV camera on the roof trained on them. Recording their presence. Their every move. Moments later, they heard bolts unlocking, then a key turning.

The doors opened and a burly, dark-haired man stared their way. His eyes were cold. Menacing. His voice, more irritated than aggressive. 'Yes?'

Wendy felt uncomfortable, but remained calm. 'Is this Kuisine by Kingoisseur? I'm here to see Montgomery King. He's expecting me.'

'And you are?'

'Wendy May. This is my assistant, Jon Windup.'

The man looked the pair up and down, then replied in the same irritable tone. 'Oh, yes. Mr King's expecting you. Come in.'

Once inside, the man closed and locked the doors, then applied the bolts. Turning, he gestured Jon and Wendy to follow. 'This way.' His irritated tone unnerved.

Without looking around, he strode down the corridor, knowing the visitors had no choice but to trail him. There was nowhere else to go.

79

Unit 85

Down a bright corridor, Jon and Wendy traipsed, passing a series of glass and wooden doors on either side. They peered through glass windows. Dimly lit rooms housed benches, cooking equipment, and boxes.

'Is everyone off work? It's really quiet around here,' Jon said as they moved down the corridor.

Their guide said nothing. Instead, he focused on the corridor in front, as if the visitors weren't there.

'Don't like it, Windy, it's creepy,' Wendy murmured. 'Glad you're with me. Wouldn't fancy being here on my own.'

'No. Something's not right.'

At the far end of the corridor, the burly man unlocked a huge metal door and led them into a smaller corridor. Another wing of the factory. From beyond, they heard a radio blaring. Other than their guide, the sound was the first sign of life since arriving. There was a door on the right and a pair of double doors in front.

The man beckoned to a door. 'In here,' he barked in the same irritated tone.

Jon and Wendy went inside a small office, with a desk, huge swivel chair, and filing cabinet. Shelving all around, and a table laid with a teapot, coffee pot, and assorted sweet treats. In the chair, appraising Monty King.

'Good morning, Wendy. I see you've brought company.' King turned down the radio.

'Yes. My assistant, Jon Windup. He was busy when we last met, but had free time today and thought he'd tag along. Hope you don't mind.'

'Don't mind at all. Tea or coffee? Afraid it's not the Biggin Hall afternoon tea experience, but I'm told we serve a mean brew. I use the finest ground coffee. Only choice beans. How's your interview going, by the way? You have quite a reputation around the villages. Sounds like you've really won the lady's trust. That's a top achievement, if you know what I mean.'

Wendy didn't know what King was getting at, but played it cool. 'Coffee for me, thanks. Jon?'

'The same.'

'Don't just stand there, Gareth. Do the honours. Fetch a couple of chairs and three coffees, then back to work.'

'Yes, boss.'

'Any problems locating the unit?' King asked.

'Not at all. Jon's a wiz at finding his way around. Easy to get lost around here, though, if you're not careful.'

'True. Doesn't look big from the outside, but once you get onto the estate, there are so many units that look identical.'

'Quite a few derelict ones,' Jon said. 'Vacant, too.'

'Yes. A growing trend that'll worsen unless the current economic situation improves.'

Gareth brought a pot of coffee and three cups, deposited them on King's desk, then marched from the room to get chairs. He thrust them inside the room and left. Jon and Wendy heard stomping footsteps in the corridor, then doors open and close. Jon wondered if Gareth had gone through the double doors. Wendy waited until King poured before facing him.

'Tell me, Monty, is your assistant always so pleasant?'

King laughed. 'Don't mind Gareth. He's harmless. He isn't a people person, but he's a grafter, and dedicated. Hard to find loyalty these days.'

Wendy detected a slight ominous tone and wasn't sure whether to feel unsettled or humoured by the remark.

'Anyway, I'm sure you didn't come here for small talk, did you? I remember you're the sort who likes to knuckle down.'

Wendy grabbed two coffees and handed one to Jon. She was ready. 'That's right. You were on the verge of telling me about Tom Trebilcock before Dave interrupted the other night.'

King's charm evaporated. 'Yes. My friend Dave. And the elusive Tom. I certainly knew Mr Trebilcock.'

Wendy remembered Lucinda's words. Above all, Tom's message held fast. She must look for chinks in King's armour. 'You don't remember him fondly?'

'He was a student. I was his lecturer. Pupil and teacher should be friends. Makes for a lot more learning. A better relationship. I thought Tom was that friend, except he turned out to be a sly, duplicitous snake.'

'Phew! With so much venom in one sentence, you're not far off a reptile yourself. He stole your girlfriend. Is that right?'

'I presume Lucinda Biggin-Smythe told you. Easy to see why she and Tom got together. Bad attracts bad. Good luck to the pair of them.'

'Yes, she told me. Is it true?'

'Yes, but it all happened a long time ago. The girl wasn't exactly the love of my life—'

'But Tom dared to steal her from you. Your queen, Monty. This is how the board sees it. Though able to move anywhere, as long as her path's free, your queen chooses not to. She wants the gallant knight to take her. With a compelling advantage, the knight moves in on her, right under the king's nose. Check. Marooned, the king has nowhere to go. No square open to him. The triumphant knight takes the king, crushes his pride, and steals the queen. Checkmate.'

'So, you can play chess. Well done.'

'I don't play. Just know a little about the game, that's all. Let's go back to it. After seizure, the king wants payback. Right, Monty?'

'Is that how you see me? A silly little boy intent on revenge?'

'The thought crossed my mind. Men have gone to war over less.'

'How do you put up with her?' King asked Jon, feigning laughter.

'You get used to it. Besides, she has a point. Us men love to see how high we can pee up the wall. The silly things we do to get one up over each other. Most of us grow out of that phase in school—'

'And some never grow out of it,' Wendy chided.

King studied Wendy. 'What happened with Tom hurt at the time, but if you think I'm some juvenile moron intent on revenge—'

'I thought it worth mentioning. Always better to hear it from the horse's mouth.'

King sipped coffee. The painted smile had never left his face.

'Is there a toilet in here?' Jon broke the silence.

'Yes. Back down the corridor, to your left. You passed it on your way in.'

'Thanks. Excuse me.' Jon darted into the corridor.

Wendy smiled to herself. She knew Jon's toilet excuse was code for "Going to explore."

'Curious individual,' said King.

'Curious is good, Monty. Jon's witty, full of facts, and a dab hand at getting me about.'

'I'm sure. How's your friend?'

'Friend?'

'The one you were with in London?'

Wendy's jaw hit the ground at the same speed King's had when she mentioned his liaison with Lucinda. She didn't lose composure. The audacity. To ask how Prue was when he was likely mixed up in the whole rotten business.

'Are you all right?'

'I'm fine, but Prue isn't. She was the victim of a recent assault.'

'How terrible! Sorry to hear. Is she okay?'

'Depends what you mean by okay? Her memory's foggy, and her legs are seeking directions from a scarred, inflamed brain. Other than that, she's breathing and ready to run the London marathon in a couple of weeks.'

'What happened?'

Was this a cruel game or was King a genuinely innocent party? 'Attacked by some thug in the local pub's beer garden. The postman, too. Except he died, then got strung up in the gibbet cage. Nasty affair. Prue has a serious neurological condition. Whether the assailant knew is irrelevant. A lowlife cares zip for such trivia.' Wendy refused to tell the full story.

King shook his head. 'What is this world coming to? And here's me thinking country life's a breeze. First Lord Biggin-Smythe. Then, the postman, you say, and your friend, too. All at the Noose.'

'The first two are of no consequence. Milord Biggin-Smythe. A man with grabbing hands and a lover of corruption. As for Pengelly, how can you take a man who wears luminous Lycra and dresses in scary orange skin seriously? I wasn't his number one fan. Nor was he mine. He didn't even know about Marley's ghost. Now, that's what I call a dull skull. My friend's another matter.'

'What's the connection, I wonder?'

King's indifference broke any uncertainty in Wendy's mind. Those last off-hand words. She wanted to scream. *You're the connection, Monty, but won't admit it.* Over the years, Wendy had met many strains of vile. The evil, yet blase. Scum, who never flinched. The greedy and corrupt. Charming yet fake. Monty King was a ragbag of every strain. A special kind of sociopath.

His buttons pulsated, flashing the brightest red. "Push! Push," they screamed.

'I don't know the connection, but know the police think Tom's responsible.'

'Trebilcock? Hurt his sister? What kind of lowlife would do that? You don't think he's guilty, do you?'

'No, I don't.'

'Any thoughts on who?'

Wendy didn't answer.

'You must have an inkling. An astute woman like yourself.'

Dream on, Monty. 'Not a clue.'

'You think it was me, don't you?'

80

Cupboard Love

Heading down the bright corridor, the sheer number of lights bemused Jon. It was plain that utility costs didn't concern King. Or maybe, as Wendy said, he was all show, but loved to swank. In that case, he was no better than the old boy and his family.

Jon found the gents. Always best to know where they were, even when not needed. In stark contrast to what he'd seen in the corridor, King was frugal when lighting the facilities. Perhaps he had a lavish convenience near his office and only his workers had to tolerate such sparsity. Jon wondered how things were going now Wendy was alone with King. She had a knack of wheedling info from troublesome people, and her magic worked best without an audience. Allowing her space was Jon's second reason for leaving.

He looked up and down the corridor. In the distance, the front door. Shut fast and bolted. Behind, the door leading to the wing housing King's office. No trace of Gareth. He'd skulked back to his hornet's nest.

With loyal drat pack poised, Jon passed four doors, and tried each one. They all opened. Either King was lax about security, or there was nothing of consequence in these rooms. That didn't stop Jon Windup. He deftly explored. Poking and prodding here and there. But he was right. Nothing of consequence. Room one, a kitchen full of cooking apparatus, and cupboards revealing more equipment. Disappointed, Jon left. Rooms two, three, and four struck the same chord. *How many gadgets did one man need?*

Jon tuned into his echoing footsteps and tiptoed down the corridor. Door number five. Unlike the others, this one had no window. The door didn't budge, arousing Jon's curiosity. *Something of consequence beyond?*

He pulled a hairpin from his pack and worked on the heavy-duty mortice lock. It wouldn't give. He reached into the pack again to grab his mini screwdriver. With the combined effort of both tools, Jon freed and turned the lock. *Two. That's how many gadgets a man needs.* Jon was in, but knew he wouldn't have long. Pretending to visit the loo wouldn't wash if he delayed further. Hopefully, Wendy was disarming King with mush, mischief, and wisdom.

He peered into the darkened room at a small space. Like a cupboard, without a door, packed to the rafters with boxes. Jon was about to back out into the corridor when loose flaps on one box drew his attention. Unable to resist, he switched on the light, ripped open the box and gaped inside.

So much money. Piles of the stuff. 'What the ...?' Jon whistled, puffing out his cheeks.

Driven to probe further, he dipped into the box, so absorbed the heavy hand slapping his shoulder almost killed him.

81

Stalemate

'Well, Miss May, did I or not?' King laughed. 'I'm itching to know what conclusion the legal eagle turned writer, editor, and private investigator's drawn.'

Wendy detected and ignored the arrogant sneer in King's laughter. His manner was more jovial than threatening, but better go easy.

'In all of those occupations, the job is to ask or infer questions or lines of enquiry, which could, or can be—how to put it—awkward.'

'You sound like the police. All official. You need your pin-stripe suit. Isn't that classic courtroom garb? Not convinced jeans, t-shirt, flat cap, and trainers cut it.'

Wendy ignored the dig. Plainly still sore after their recent meeting. 'Solicitors, writers, and police usually want the same outcome, Monty. Unless one's a tabloid journalist. In that case, it's about making money by printing any old nonsense to feed the gossips.'

'You still haven't answered my question.'

'So, I will. You were party to a proposed business deal that ended up trashed. Your potential business partner ends up dead. Found in bizarre circumstances in the local pub. The prime suspect attended your catering college. There's history there.

'The arrogant village postman meets his death—at the same pub, but not in the same place—and an innocent woman's hit and left for dead. On the night one man's hanged, and one woman's abandoned in the dark, you just happen to be staying in Bogus Hole. Meeting me, no less, spouting so much guff it was pitiful.

'If you were a copper, or in my case, a writer and inquisitive soul with a legal background, wouldn't you be asking some awkward questions? Here's another teaser for you. Why would you want to meet me again? We hardly parted on good terms. Did you want to tell more of your story to include in my article?'

King pondered Wendy's words. 'I see your angle. I would be inclined to ask the same awkward questions if in your shoes.'

'You understand my predicament.'

'I do.'

'And what say you, Monty?'

'You want answers so, I'll give. I have nothing to hide. I told DCI Slate when he questioned me. Didn't leave my room all night. If I'd crept out for a nocturnal jaunt, the old, creaking floor would've woken the entire inn.'

''Tis possible you might've—' Wendy stopped, cursing the vibration in her jacket pocket. *Bleeding mobile phones.* Normally, she would apologise, continue the conversation, and look at the message later. But instinct told her it was important. And it was. From Albie Drew.

'Sorry about this. Please, excuse me.'

'Everything all right?'

'It's my mother. She rarely messages, so it must be important.'

Wendy read the message, then read it again. Forensics had analysed DNA in the saliva sample from Ross Pengelly's corpse. They'd cross-referenced it with various police databases. Until today, Wendy would've thought nothing of the name from police records, but it immediately caught her attention. Gareth Thompson. *King's surly, burly assistant was a Gareth.* Wendy didn't believe in coincidence.

Albie had also scanned Gareth's profile and thought it worth mentioning that police once arrested him and his crony for a minor offence. The crime itself wasn't important. His sidekick was. Montgomery Oliver King.

'You look pale, Wendy.'

'My mother's had to go into hospital,' Wendy lied. Her mother had passed years ago, and Wendy could hear and see the dear woman now. Tutting at the fib. Shaking her head at Wendy's ferocious appetite for justice. Crossing her fingers and hoping her daughter could wriggle out of this pickle and get back on safe ground.

'Oh, dear. Sorry to hear. Anything I can do?'

'No. I'm sure Jon'll take me to see her. She lives in Northumberland. Quite a trek.'

'It is. No worries. Speaking of Jon, he's been ages. Hope he's okay.'

'He won't appreciate me saying this, but he sometimes has an iffy stomach. He'll be happy for a break from my banter, too. Like you said. *How does he put up with me?* He'll be along soon. Won't want to miss all the fun.'

King broke the awkward silence. 'Where were we? You were making a point abo—'

'You know what? I've lost my train of thought. That message has thrown me off. I'll wait for Jon.'

'As you wish.'

'One moment. It's quite the day for messages.' King glanced at his phone, frowning at the screen.

'Problem?' Wendy knew from King's expression it was more than that.

'Excuse me. I'm wanted in the warehouse.'

King hoofed out of the office before Wendy could catch her breath.

82

Boxed in

'How did you get in here? This door's locked.' Gareth's tone had turned. No longer irritated, but incensed at finding Jon with his hand in the purse.

A cardboard box and dodgy ear had been Jon's undoing. He'd plundered the box's contents, oblivious to sounds of footsteps approaching. Caught red-handed, rifling through confidential data he wasn't supposed to see. *Damn King's henchman!* Jon knew he must stay composed. Difficult when panic was rising, and a strapping lackey blocked his path.

'The door wasn't locked. Thought I'd just have a peek inside. No harm done,' Jon said.

'You shouldn't be in here. We have a little problem, don't we?'

This time, Jon's iffy ear didn't fail him. Urgent footsteps in the corridor. Then the door swung open and King blasted in.

'Mr Windup. It appears you're somewhere you shouldn't be. Seen things you shouldn't have. As Gareth says, we have a little problem.'

'Saw nothing of interest. Just some paper. Means nothing to me.'

'Come, come. I'm sure you saw more than that.'

'What, exactly? Yes. A box full of banknotes. Big deal. You're not the first business to keep money on the premises and won't be the last. Bit foolish if you ask me, but that's your concern, not mine. Unless the money's counterfeit. Dickie Biggin-Smythe has a counterfeit operation on the go. Appears you do too. Can't be a coincidence.'

King's clapping was slow and precise. 'Well done, but this isn't the best place to talk, so we'll go somewhere more desirable. Wendy must be missing you. She said you'd be gone a long time.'

King gestured for them to leave. Something in his voice suggested to Jon it wouldn't be a good idea to refuse. He led Jon down the corridor, ordering Gareth to take up the rear. Jon cursed his anxiety. He'd blabbered too much, and this time he wasn't facing Slate. He wished Slate was here now. With or without dancing eyebrows. Even Uttley's smug mug would be a gift from the gods.

Jon turned to look behind him, then stumbled forwards, swallowing sour bile. Not again! The image of Gareth clutching something to his chest convinced Jon he could soon be looking down the barrel of a gun.

83

Think Inside the Box

'Move! Over there, where I can see you.' King shoved Jon into his office, then closed and locked the door.

Like a wayward schoolkid, Jon stood in a corner of the room, hands behind his back. Behind him, a small cylindrical box doubled as a wastebin.

Wendy knew something had narked King no end. She looked at Jon. 'What's up?'

'I'll tell you what's up. Your meddling assistant took it in his head to explore a lot more than water closets. Gareth caught him snooping. In a room that should be locked. When I find out who left that door open, they'll be sorry.' King glared at Gareth.

Wendy knew Jon had picked the lock. She also knew King and his stooge weren't the sort to mess with. Her only way to calm the situation was making light of it. 'Naughty, naughty, Jon. I've warned you about sticking your big nose where you shouldn't.'

'This is serious. He didn't just stumble into some random room.'

'Not random? Jon?'

'Found a load of boxes. One with a stack of fake money inside. Guess the rest were the same. You can see why Mr King thinks that's a problem.'

Tense silence followed. Wendy cursed Jon's curiosity, then remembered their reason for being here. King wanted to meet. She accepted. Jon had tagged along. This was not a social visit. For anyone.

Eventually, King spoke. 'I'm still curious about how you got in there, Mr Windup. A master lock picker, perhaps? Nosy types often are.'

'Well, that's just *rubbish*,' Jon scoffed, shuffling his feet and tapping the box bin with one heel.

'We'll see. Search him, Gareth.'

Jon couldn't object. His tongue had stuck to the roof of his mouth and nausea swamped him. He didn't want Gareth anywhere near, never mind frisking him. *Would he find his stash? Did he have a gun? If so, would he use it?*

For a big man, Gareth quickly jumped to order, rugged, swift hands searching Jon from head to toe. Jon endured the humiliation. Wendy didn't speak. They were in enough trouble, and revving up sarcasm or wisecracks would only fuel a flammable fix. From Jon's pockets, Gareth pulled a mobile phone, half a packet of mints, a pack of tissues, and half a bottle of pink liquid. He placed the items on the table. 'That's it, boss.'

King inspected. He pushed aside the mints and tissues, then picked up the bottle and frowned. 'What is this?'

'Medication for acid reflux. I call it gloop. That's the aniseed flavour. Taste it if you like. It won't harm you.'

'I'm aware of that, Mr Windup. Why carry it around?'

Jon had an acute sense of déjà vu. 'Reflux can hit anytime and the burn's very painful. Have gloop, will travel. Better to be safe than sorry.' Jon's attempt at humour fell flat.

King picked up Jon's phone. 'That's a bit of luck. Same model as mine. We'll do a bit of snooping of our own, Gareth. Thank you for the pleasure, Mr Windup. I want your phone, too, lady. Would love to know how you spend your social time.'

Wendy didn't argue. Not in a tinderbox where unwanted wit was doomed to ignite. She held out her phone. Gareth snatched it with a snarl.

'Your passcode, Mr … shh, what's that?'

The sound of doors opening and closing in the corridor alerted King. Footsteps stopped outside, then someone tried the office door. Hammering followed. The same thought struck Jon and Wendy. *Police. Slate's heavy hand.* For both, seeing iBrow and strut would be the sweetest relief.

King smoothed back his hair, unlocked the door, and greeted the suited visitor with obscure emotion.

84

A Prickly Pair

'I believe you know my business partner, Richard Biggin-Smythe. And you're more than acquainted with this unlikely pair, Richard.'

'Your message said urgent. I see why.' Richard sneered at Jon. 'If it isn't that frightful oik and the dowager's beastly ally. One's a nosy peasant. The other, a libellous writer. A commoner too, of course. What have they been up to now?'

'Sneaking without consent. He found the merchandise,' said King.

'Oh.'

'Is that all you can say?'

'What would you like me to say?'

Not a smooth partnership, Wendy observed, taking in King's posture. His heated glower.

'What should we do?' Richard asked.

'Nothing rash for starters,' said King.

'Keeping that for the main course, then?' Jon's ill-timed wit hit the floor.

'Forgot to say we have a comedian in our midst, Richard. Tell me, Miss May. Is your assistant always this irritating?'

So much for wanting to still the waters. 'Always, but irritation usually blossoms into a vast, intelligent mind.'

'Fascinating. Well, two can play that game. I don't do rash, but whatever I do, you can be sure I always save the best for dessert.'

'Sweet. Once a chef, always a chef.'

King ignored Wendy. 'I'll leave you pair to direct your farce to the cold room. You'll get as much back from that as you will from me. In the meantime, a present for you, Mr Windup.' King pushed Jon's belongings across the table. 'Leave the phones.'

Jon pocketed his jumble and moved back to the corner.

King crooked his forefinger. 'Time to go. This way.'

Jon and Wendy stayed put.

'Don't be silly,' King jeered. 'You don't want to make Gareth an extremely unhappy man.'

Gareth seized both mobiles from the table, then pulled a gun from inside his jacket.

'Better do as we're told, Windy.'

Jon's reply was a humble smile. He was right. Gareth was armed. No matter what size the firearm, he didn't want another barrel tucked under his chin.

King led the fearful pair back into the corridor, Dickie and Gareth not far behind. Instead of leading them to where Jon had unearthed the counterfeit money, King opened the double doors to the warehouse. Past more boxes, and a loading area next to an impressive steel door. The type that opened vertically. The warehouse was cold, but it wasn't the chill making Jon and Wendy shiver. King led them to another door.

'Let's see if vast intelligence can escape this,' King scoffed, holding the door open. Inside was shrouded in darkness.

'Not the five-star luxury of London, but I'm sure you'll both be snug on the hard, damp floor. It's wintry in there, and the pitch dark's a bonus. Fancy yourselves as private eyes? Why don't you play find the light switch?'

'How much longer? I'm tired of waiting. Let's get down to business.'

'One minute. I want phone passcodes. Pop them into your notes, Richard. Gareth can't do it while holding a gun with a cocked hammer.'

Dickie noted the codes and couldn't resist one final jibe. 'Bad luck, you bores. Must say, it will be rather a bind sealed up in a cold, murky room. And nothing to help you escape. This is all terribly amusing. Serves you right for complicating matters.'

'I have what I want,' King growled. 'Now, get inside, the pair of you.'

Jon and Wendy crept into the gloom. The door slammed, hurling them into pitch, and a key turned in the lock, walling them in silence.

85

Think Outside the Box

'**S**hould've gone to the toilet before I picked that lock. But if you don't want to go, you don't want to go, do you?'

'That's what happens when you gulp coffee. Should've sipped and savoured, like I did. Slowly does it, Windy. Don't think about it. The feeling will go.'

'Doesn't help now, but I'll keep that in mind for when I get out of here. If I get out of here. It's a maze this place. A proper network of passages and doors, but we're in a fix and it needs unfixing.'

The pair kept their voices low in case listening ears pricked outside.

'I need a drink.'

'At this hour?'

'The hour's unimportant. Anyway, not an alcoholic drink. A cotton mouth drink.'

'Such as?'

'Water.'

'The best, and we're lucky enough to have it on tap.'

'Not in here.'

'I meant as a nation.'

'Are you winding me up?'

'Always.'

'Any clue where the light switch is? Slimeball said we could play a game to find it. Condescending creep.'

Jon and Wendy's jail had no windows. The only sliver of light filtered through the bottom of the secured door.

'Hold on,' Jon said.

Wendy heard him scuffling around and mumbling. Doing his routine theatre. With extra ham and relish.

'Got it. Thanks, David Misell. You're a lifesaver.' Jon beamed at the small circle of light bobbing up and down. 'Better switch it off. Save the batteries.'

'Who's David Misell? And where did you get that torch?' Wendy said, baffled.

'Misell was a British inventor who invented the flashlight in America in the late nineteenth century. When the idea made its way to Britain, it was called the electric torch. As always, I'm going off my research. This little beauty's my handy mini torch. Powerful for its size. Now, where did I get it? Yeah. That hardware store in Craggy Bank Street. That place has some super gadgets, by golly.'

'No, you clown. I want to know where you got it. Not where you got it. Get it?'

'Again, Darling. Without the gobbledegook.'

'That goon frisked you. Where was your mini torch? And don't tell me you had it stuffed down your sock because he gave your legs a good old rubdown.'

'It was in my drat pack. Along with a few other whatnots and widgets. I wouldn't tell him to his face, but that goon didn't get frisky enough.'

'Of course. Before the search, you must've dropped the drat pack in the box behind you. That's where the foot shuffle and heel tap came in. Except the gormless goon and his bighead boss didn't twig. Nifty stuff, Windy. When did you lift it back out?'

'When King was looking at the phones and you had him wrapped in knots. Sleight of hand, Darling.' Jon switched the torch on again, shining it under a few shelves. 'And what a bonus. I've found the light switch.'

The room flooded with strong light as Jon and Wendy blinked and looked around.

'That's better,' Wendy said, pinching her nose to silence imminent sneezes.

Little more than a cupboard, the room had many wall cabinets and a series of wires leading to the ceiling from the ground.

'Think we're stuck in a utility room. These boxes must house meters and circuit breakers.'

'Don't make it, Jon.'

'Make what?'

'One of your daft comments about electricity.'

'What, like it's shocking and isn't giving me a buzz?'

'Two for the price of one,' Wendy groaned. She looked around the windowless room. At the electricity boxes, the door, then back at Jon. Jest and banter were a cover. She was scared. Bone scared. 'What do you think'll happen?'

'They're criminals, and we've witnessed their operation. What do sorts normally do when you uncover something you're not supposed to?'

'I know. I worked in the field long enough.'

'Remember what Lu Brush said about King? He can make people disappear. Already has. Could do the same with us.'

'I remember,' Wendy spluttered, slapping her hand over her mouth.

'King told us he's not the rash type. If they do anything here, they'd have bodies to get rid of. A gun would leave blood and guts, so they'd need a big clean-up oper—'

'Cut the graphics, Jon.'

'Sorry. Look, I don't know what's going to happen, and don't want to find out either. We must get out of here. Can't phone for help. King took our mobiles.'

Wendy sensed Jon's growing anxiety. And fear. Teamwork was vital to get them out of this mess they'd got themselves into. 'He took my spare phone and has the passcode, but won't find anything apart from a few pictures of fungus and a recipe for bubble and squeak.

He's a chef. That should please him. I have my main phone here. Can't use it though. Battery's dead.'

'That's a bummer. So's the number I gave Dickie boy. They'll have to crack the code.'

'Knew it was false when you said it. You're a wrong'un, Windy. So, what's in your bag of tricks today? Apart from the torch. Any hairpins for the lock?'

'A couple.' Jon slipped the torch back in the drat pack, then fiddled around for his hero. He made to insert the hairpin, then turned to Wendy.

'What's wrong?'

'Excellent idea to pick the lock. One little snag.'

'What now?'

'There's no lock.'

'*What?*'

'Look.'

Wendy stared forlornly at the door, standing sentinel between them and freedom. 'You can't be serious.'

'There must be a keyhole on the outside, but not on the inside. Perfect if you want to impound a pair of snoopers who've just uncovered the tip of your dodgy operation. It's good, but it's not right.'

'What are we going to do?'

Jon looked grim. 'I can't go away, but I'll have to think about it.'

'Well, think fast, Windy. Our lives depend on it.'

86

Box Clever

'What else did you see in that cupboard? You were gone awhile. Said you found money, but unless you were bathing in the stuff, don't know what took you so long.'

Jon was still debating how to escape their prison, but results weren't coming. Claustrophobia had surfaced, and hello again, anxiety. Wendy decided the best thing to distract him was to talk.

'Didn't only find piles of fake money, Darling. Found another proposal. Like the one at Biggin Hall, only different.'

'That doesn't make sense. How can something be the same when it's different?'

'Shush. Took pictures on my phone, but don't have that now, so I'm trying to remember what it said. It was an annex to the original. Something about thirty outlets and that bread company Tom mentioned in his message.'

'Dough by Artisan? Think that's what he said.'

'That's the one. They were all set to supply bread for every pub, but the old boy must've made them a better offer and cut King out. BS was brutal. Not only did King get a big, fat no-no to dough for his investment, he got another one to the baked stuff. It's said bread's the staff of life. Not for the old boy. For him, it was deadly all around. See what greed does, Darling?'

'Dough is foe. In London, King talked about thirty outlets. Did so again in Bogie. Went clean over my head, but now you've found that annex, it makes sense. Thirty silver coins. Thirty new outlets. Not Judas money like you first thought, although that parallel still works. To King, milord was Judas. As was Tom, back in college years ago. What about the piles of fake money you found? You saw the same in that lockup at Biggin Hall.'

'Yes. Dickie must've moved it here after me and Antonia found it.'

'King despises the Biggin-Smythes. Why help Richard?'

'From what you've told me, King's a baked Alaska. Warm and gooey on the outside. Cold and calculating inside. Not that a baked Alaska's calculating, but you get the gist. No love lost between King and the old boy. And Richard. That was clear when we saw them together. King's using him. Has an ulterior motive.'

'Using Richard to get the money milord would've invested had their business venture gone ahead? Remember what Lucinda said about King and chess?'

'He's the king. Richard's the pawn. King to Biggin-Smythe, and checkmate.'

'And don't forget how King used Pengelly. The dude was a marked man from the get-go. Now we're marked and must get out of here, Windy.'

'I'm thinking.'

'Well, think faster,' Wendy hissed.

'What do you think I'm doing? Shush, will you! Can't think straight with you wittering on.'

'Sorry. Know you're doing your best.'

Jon looked at the electrical boxes, then around the room again. Struck by an idea, he rubbed his head, then his chin.

'When he locked us in, did you hear that loud click?'

'Yes. Couldn't miss it.'

'Good.'

'Why good?'

'Got a hunch. By law, modern workplaces must have certain provisions in place in case of fire. Health and safety and all that.'

'Your point?'

'Let's say there's a fire in a warehouse or factory, and a need to get everyone out safely. Locked doors don't work. Can't get out through locked doors.'

'That makes sense. Unless you're a magician.'

'All main doors have magnetic locks. So, in the event of emergency, they're designed to unlock, or something like that. Not entirely sure, but I believe they're rigged to a central system.'

'What are you saying? We start a fire?'

'No, nothing that drastic. Besides, I can't see a smoke detector in here.'

'What then?'

'I'm no expert, and not even sure if all the doors would unlock if the fire alarm went off, but I have a feeling that one thing will make all the doors open.'

'You know what I say about going with the gut. Come on. Don't keep me in suspense.'

'I'm a gonk for not thinking of this before. It makes perfect sense. The one thing that's sure to work is a power outage.'

'I've heard of this design before. Explain more.'

'In the event of a power cut, doors have a built-in fail-safe. If the power goes down, every door opens. Think about it. There's a blazing fire, lots of choking smoke, and none of the doors'll open. That's enough to give health and safety a lifetime hernia. But with the fail-safe, all doors are designed to open, giving people a chance to get out. Aids the emergency services, too. Look what's here. Everything we need to try out my theory.' Jon gestured to the cabinets.

'Well, don't just stand there with your finger up your beak, Windy. Get saving.'

Jon set his pin to work on the biggest locked cabinet and heard a click. 'Woo-hoo. Circuit breakers galore.' He probed a big red switch. 'One potential snag. King might have a backup power source to stop the locks from failing. We're gambling he doesn't. But wait a minute. Gotcha.'

'What is it?'

'It's all here. Master and auxiliary switches, backup lighting, the lot. Brace yourself. The light'll go out when I flick the master and auxiliary switches. If that bunch are still on the premises, they'll know what's going on. No backup lights if I flick both.'

Wendy faltered. King and his goons weren't a pleasing thought. 'Is this a good idea?'

'What's the alternative? Wait here and see what nasty surprise King has in store?'

'No contest. Flick 'em.'

87

Cut to the Chase

P lunged into darkness, Jon and Wendy heard a click.
The jolt of a metal bolt. For a moment, the pair stood
immobilised.

'Try the door.'

Wendy pushed. The door opened with little effort.
'Windy. You're a genius.'

'So I've been told. My Nobel prize awaits, but first
let's get out of here.'

Wendy leaned into the warehouse and listened. She
expected to hear footsteps, but only eerie silence rushed
her way. 'Looks and sounds like we're in luck. Can't hear
a thing. Our captors must be on a jaunt. Better scram
before they get back.'

The couple dashed across the warehouse towards the
double doors leading into the corridor housing King's
office. The main entrance loomed.

'Hope the door's opened,' Jon said, reaching out, then
stepping back as the door swung open.

'Going somewhere?' Dull eyes stared. Rough hands
yanked the door shut.

The corridor was dark, but dim light filtered through
windowed doors. Enough to make out the silhouette of
Gareth and his gun.

'The boss was sure you wouldn't get out, but left me
here just in case. So, you tripped the locks? Clever.'

'So I'm told, but it's easy with breaker boxes,' Jon
retaliated.

'Don't wind him up,' Wendy hissed.

'You should listen to your friend.'

Gareth's gun fixed on the twitchy couple. No one spoke. Not the brightest spark, Wendy suspected he wasn't sure what to do. Left on guard, the last thing he expected was having to deal with a couple of runaways.

'Right. Back to the office. Any games, and I *will* fire. Now, move!'

A cautious walk up the corridor towards the office. A gun trained on them the whole time. Jon and Wendy's luck had flown.

Gareth waved his gun at the office door. 'In!'

The pair scuttled inside and sat down.

'What'll happen to us?' Wendy said.

'That's for the boss to decide.' Gareth's tone was wooden.

Another silence, then footsteps in the corridor.

'That'll be the boss.'

Wendy swore she heard glee in Gareth's voice. A psychotic thug. No stranger to getting thrills when watching people suffer. He fixed stony eyes on the opening door, but it wasn't King who stepped into the room.

88

Tough Toff

'No lights? What's going on here?' Richard Biggin-Smythe's rage was more comical than aggressive. He didn't need a clown's get-up.

'Because this pair tripped the mains so they could escape. Thanks to me, they didn't get past the front door,' Gareth bragged.

'Jolly good show. Knew it was a good idea to leave you on guard.'

'That was my idea,' Gareth barked. He clearly had no time for the privileged.

'Matters not. Well, don't just stand there. Switch the power on. We can't have Mr King returning to a dark office.'

Gareth resented taking orders from Dickie, but King wanted it that way. 'Have you got a gun?'

'No. Do I need one?'

'Yes. To keep watch.'

'Leave yours.'

Gareth handed his pistol over. 'Won't be long.'

'Wonderful. Learned how to shoot before I could walk, you know. Daddy bought me a shotgun for my thirteenth birthday. For countryside pursuits. I often have shooting parties with my chums. Had one today, but had to cancel because of this ghastly business. Couldn't watch the rugger either. Such a bind!'

Gareth took off mid-boast.

Wendy reviewed the situation. She no longer practiced advocacy, but the desire to cross-examine when necessary burned still. Lawyer's guile. 'You know King's using you, milord? He wants your inheritance and'll stop at nothing to get it.'

'Don't be absurd. I shall do what Daddy could and should have done.'

'What's that?'

'Invest in a sound business opportunity, but go one better and own the company, even after King repays the capital. I'll do what Daddy didn't do. Own Treetonshire, then rename it Bigginshire. He failed. Not me. I *will* succeed and more.'

'Do you think King will settle for you being his boss? He's a user. Not a loser. He'll find ways of digging up the dirt and leave you floundering.'

For someone who could give Annie Clegg a run for her money in the gibbering stakes, Dickie Biggin-Smythe was unusually quiet.

'What do you get out of this again?' Wendy persisted.

'I'll own a multi-million pound enterprise.'

'Did you and King kill your daddy for his money?'

'We did nothing of the sort, and I'll have my lawyer get you for such beastly slander!'

'A simple yes or no'll suffice.'

'Is she always this mean?' Richard asked Jon.

'Not mean. Isn't afraid to speak out, that's all.'

'Or ask thorny questions. What's wrong, milord? Is the big, bad writer giving you the jitters? Libellous, eh?'

'Wendy used to be a lawyer, you know. Knows all about slander, libel, and that sort of thing.' Jon voiced.

'That doesn't impress me.'

'Shall we get off this track and get back to King? Lucinda told me his nickname's Chess,' Wendy said.

'What has that woman to do with this?'

'Everything. She and King had a little tryst, but you know that. My point? King sees everything as one big game of chess. On his giant board, he *is* king and everyone else is a pawn. You are one.'

Light suddenly came to life in the office and down the corridor.

'King's using you. Used Lucinda, too. To grease the wheels. Give him inside knowledge. When the deal between King and your daddy soured, it wasn't simply revenge for Seymour Biggin-Smythe. He wanted to prove who wielded the most power, and it wasn't Montgomery Oliver King.' Wendy was relentless.

'So, what's the deal, Richard? King takes care of your father, and, in return, you give him the money he needs for his new venture?' Jon chipped in. 'Of course, and no father means you inherit the title of Lord Biggin-Smythe, take control of the estate, and even send the woman you despise packing.'

'Will never know what Daddy saw in her. She ran the show, and he let her.'

Wendy turned the screw. 'It's all coming out now. Daddy was clever. He knew everything. Lu's affair with Tom Trebilcock. Her affair with King. Your shady business dealings. It's all in his diary. He had to go.'

Richard blanched. It was clear he knew nothing about the diary. 'Did the dowager tell you that?'

Wendy ignored Dickie's bleating. 'The stumbling block here is the family's reputation, milord.'

'My family?'

'Yes. The Biggin-Smythes. Seymour was terrified of scandal. His will states that anyone bringing the family into disrepute is out. Conspiracy to murder fits that dynamic. No money. No title. And a long prison sentence. Is that what you want? We know King ordered Ross Pengelly to kill your daddy, but when Pengelly's threats and demands became excessive, King ordered Gareth to shut him up. Pengelly's taste for piracy runs in his family. Extortion. Looting. Murdering. But King's goon was careless. He left DNA at the crime scene. In my book, that's one big snag. The police are building their case as we speak.'

Richard looked startled, then smugness returned. 'That's all very interesting, but they won't touch me.'

'Why?'

'For generations, my family has enjoyed a longstanding arrangement with the police. The chief constable's a close friend. The law leaves us alone and in return, the chief enjoys the fine life.'

'Thought as much. It's sinful what money can buy, but only if there's no change in the hierarchy. Beware the police and crime commissioner, milord. Power to remove or force the resignation of a chief constable. It's happened before.'

'Fascinating, but utterly irrelevant. Sounds like a riddle to me, and riddles are for children.'

''Tis no riddle.'

Gareth stomped into the office and demanded his gun. 'I've secured the front door. Nobody gets in or out without my say-so. A word in private, Mr Biggin-Smythe. And you pair, don't try anything stupid.'

89

Pocket Proof

While Dickie and Gareth conspired in the corridor, Jon and Wendy did the same in the office. Time was against them.

'Logged the conversation with Dickie on my pocket recorder. Just hope the mike picked up enough detail.'

'Nice one, Darling. How did you switch it on when his attention was on us the whole time?'

Wendy tapped her nose. 'Except it wasn't. He isn't as attentive as you think. Hush. They're coming back.'

'Should tie and gag you both, but I'll wait for the boss. He can decide,' Gareth snapped.

'King won't get away with this,' Wendy said.

'Make as much noise as you want. No one can hear you. If it wasn't for strict orders, I'd deal with you myself. No waiting.'

'When did King say he'd be back?' Dickie said.

'Thought he told you.'

'He didn't. Said he has appointments. Wants to appear as normal as possible to the outside world. If he didn't follow his schedule, people would suspect. Goodness knows when he'll be back. An hour? Several hours? In the meantime, we must keep guard.'

'Agreed. They can stay in here. I'll stand by the door. Keep an eye on them. No circuit breakers in the office, but I don't trust these two. They've fooled us before. They won't a second time.'

'Jolly good. Sounds like a plan.'

'Empty your pockets on the table,' Gareth barked.

Jon didn't hesitate. He flung his belongings down. Wendy unpocketed a small pot of cherry lip balm and a notepad and pen. She'd stuffed her main phone down the back of her trousers and hoped Gareth wouldn't frisk her. Her right hook wasn't up to combat today.

Gareth inspected Jon's drat pack, laughed, and shook his head. 'Won't help you this time,' he snarled, pocketing the jumble and the other items left on the table. He waved a hefty paw at Dickie, and they thudded into the corridor.

Wendy waited until the door clicked and moved her jaw from side to side. 'Drat! Locked up again and no pack to the rescue. Get us out of this one, Windy!'

90

Turning Turtle

Jon studied the secure double-glazed windows. Even if he could smash them without making a din, outside was only a courtyard in the middle of the complex. No escape there. He was aware of the CCTV camera. *Probably hooked up to the computer sitting on King's desk.*

'Sleight of hand's one thing, but I'm no Houdini. Can't walk through walls. He didn't do that, of course. Went through a trapdoor in the floor.'

'Is that your expert opinion, Windy?'

'Yep. And no trapdoor here.'

Wendy looked around and blew out her cheeks in exasperation. 'Guess we'll have to sit this one out.'

'Wish we had our phones. Could brush up on our quiz knowledge.'

'How about we could call the police?'

'That as well.'

Jon looked around again. 'Thinking about the quiz takes my mind off all this.'

'You're a loon, Windy. Then again, if we get out and there's a question about how to get escape from a locked office, we'll win champion of champions.'

'Hilarious. We're not going anywhere, anytime soon. Thought it might help pass the time, that's all.'

'We can do bog all without phones.'

'Good point. At least I tried.'

Silence fell. Frustration intensified. It was no use. Even if Jon's bag of tricks hadn't fallen into Gareth's hands, the gruesome goon stood guard outside.

'Hope Prue's okay.' Wendy sat down before she fell down.

'Me too.'

'Don't forget. She's why we're here. And Tom, of course, despite my past see-sawing about his innocence.'

'I haven't forgotten.'

Silence fell again, but not for long. The door opened, and Dickie Biggin-Smythe inched in. 'What exactly has the dowager told you?'

Wendy seized her chance to sow more dubious seeds. 'Everything. She has proof of your daddy's special relationship with the chief constable and handed the evidence to Tom Trebilcock. He's informed the police. You think you have the law in your pocket, but DCI Slate's loyalty is to duty, not his corrupt boss. Remember the police and crime commissioner? And remember, King will always have the upper hand. He knows too much about you, and will use at his discretion. Twisting words. Digging the knife in. Is that your desire? A peasant having the edge?' While convincing, Wendy's robust address was only speculation.

Dickie's eyes darted from left to right. He licked his fingers and tapped the top of his head to tame strands of rogue hair. As usual, they disobeyed. Dickie stamped his feet, swallowing hard. 'Damn that beastly bitch!'

Got you. Wendy's victory speared the air.

'Detectives?'

'On their way, and expecting dangerous criminals. A fun day out for armed response.'

'If I help you, surely the police will look at me favourably?'

'It's a good start.'

'Then we must go.'

'Where's the other guy?' Jon asked.

'In the warehouse. I'm supposed to keep watch until he returns. Hurry up!'

'Our phones and stuff?'

'Gareth has them.'

'Never mind that, Windy. Come on.'

The trio hurtled down the corridor to the main entrance, and they launched into the car park. Deserted, save for Jon's car.

'Faster, faster,' Wendy urged.

Too late. A white van pulled in, blocking the exit. An unknown male driver exited, then stood sentry, muscular arms folded. The passenger door opened, and a second male climbed down. The familiar slim, suited figure and cavalier face said it all. King.

91

Checkmate!

'Off on an outing?' Like his tone, King's face spat and threatened. 'I had the same idea, so I brought Chuck along. He and Gareth will keep you company on your jolly jaunt, but first, back inside. Where's Gareth, Richard?'

'In the warehouse.'

Wendy appraised the situation. She was sure King knew Dickie had switched allegiance. It was written all over his smug mug. What game was he playing now? Why did he want them back inside?

Jon also weighed things up and concluded nothing other than resignation would do. The thug now standing guard was of Gareth's build, and Jon was in no mood to quibble with two brawny beasts. Not today, thanks.

Like kids on a school trip, they trooped back to King's office in single file, King bringing up the rear, holding a shooter.

'Sit down. Richard, up front here with me and message Gareth. Tell him I want to see him. Now! Wendy May. Your phone intrigues me. You said you'd received a message from your mother. You lied. There are no messages. Anywhere. No recent phone calls. No contacts. When I looked, all I saw were quiz apps, pictures of mushrooms, and a recipe for bubble and squeak. For a lady of business and a gregarious woman, your phone carries a severe lack of data.'

'That's not a crime. I delete content regularly. And what can I say? I'm a fungus fan. So, you didn't like my recipe for bubble and squeak, then? Why not? Who doesn't like mashed potato and finely chopped cabbage mixed together and fried? You may not know this, but once upon a time, beef was the key ingredient. It was rationing in the second world war that—'

'Enough! I don't need a cooking lesson from you. That dish is the sort of slop Richard would call peasant food. Isn't that right?'

Dickie said nothing.

'No scathing remark, your lordship? Not like you to hold back where commoners are concerned.'

'Sounds beastly.'

King's phone pinged. 'You remember Gareth, everyone? He'll be here soon. Now, where was I? Yes. Phones. You gave the wrong passcode, Mr Windup. When my man gets here, you can try again. Make no mistake, I *will* check that phone.'

'Three Michelin stars, Monty? The pinnacle for any chef. Exceptional. Remarkable. Exquisite. You've reached the top, but like I said in London, the only way is down.' Wendy's needling prompted a terse reply.

'Or staying put if you're smart. *Where is that blasted Gareth?* He should be here by now.'

'Maybe he got detained.'

'Hardly, Richard. If your dubious behaviour hadn't convinced me a rat was in my midst, I'd tell you to find out what's taking him so long. You may not have spoken to the police yet, but you will. You're itching to do it. I suspect you noted the wrong passcode. I know too much for you to turn traitor. No one likes a Judas. No one trusts a grass.'

'And no one should fear an unloaded gun,' Wendy gambled.

'You have some gumption, but way too reckless. I've a good mind to prove—'

'I wouldn't goad him,' Dickie warned.

'That's the most sensible thing you've said so far, Richard. Should we try out your theory, Wendy?' King chuckled.

'Come, come, Monty. I wager your area of expertise is chess, not shooters. You know I told you chess wasn't my game? I lied. Played for years. Learned when I was knee high to a gnat. Not master level, but good enough to hold my own. In the day, your sweet student girlfriend was your queen, but she craved the knight Tom to take her. She owned her domain. Could go wherever she chose. But didn't.'

Wendy rode her chance. Gritted her teeth and stabbed at her chest. 'Not this queen. She's nobody's fool. Until I hit an obstruction or capture an opposing piece, I can and will move forwards or backwards. Side to side. Diagonally. And I have. *With guile*. Closer, closer, I now stand one move away from the King. I've waited for this moment and I'm ready to take you. Check.'

Jon gawked at Wendy. Had she gone mad? Winding up this sociopath?

But Wendy hadn't finished. 'You're one angry man, Monty. Whoever stood in your way had to go. In came the baddies to help you out, and whatever happened, you had one man marked. The centuries-old family feud. You know your local history. Pengelly didn't. No surprise there. I know my local history too. But just because the archives cracked it means nothing. The police always want proof. Proof. Proof!

'You aren't gentry, but like your ancestor, who changed his name, you are deluded. Same trash. Different name. Why King? To sound regal? Grand? Of course, but I say, yellow. Like Nasty Ned. You're a coward, Monty. And no likes a coward.'

A loud thud in the corridor followed shouts and the turbulent drum of running feet. The door flew open and four armed police burst into the room. At the doorway,

DCI Slate watched DS Uttley cuff and caution, then uniform led Dickie away. He shuffled out with his head down and didn't look back.

As a defeated King headed out, Wendy hijacked Jon's do-or-die quirk. This time, she would have the last word. 'Looks like patience paid off, Monty. My wait for the King's over. Checkmate.'

92

Keep it Under Your Hat

'Never thought I'd be thrilled to see you.' Despite her ordeal, Wendy's fervent candour returned. What joy to see her big fuzzy friends break dancing. Eyebrow popping at its finest.

'My feelings exactly. You pair have cost me time, energy, and a serious bellyache.' Though sarcasm tickled his tonsils, Slate's tone sang of relief. He dismissed armed response and sat down opposite Jon and Wendy. 'Notes, Uttley. And take a seat.'

'Thought you were convinced King was innocent and Tom Trebilcock was the one?' Wendy fired.

'Turns out Trebilcock and his lady love had a dossier of evidence proving Lord Biggin-Smythe and Chief Constable Bowden had a cosy arrangement. Money would flow one way. The mandatory blind eye would flow the other. Not in an obvious way. Staff paid with the business account, then the chief drew the money and claimed a mountain of expenses and bonuses. Deception of that magnitude isn't easy to investigate without attracting suspicion. Ever tried going over your boss's head? Especially when he's head of one of the biggest rural police forces? Even trickier with tied hands.'

'What swung the pendulum?'

'Mr Treblicock told us he had irrefutable proof of events when his lordship died. Said he'd copy in the local and national press. Imagine what damage that could do to a force's reputation? The public will demand blood. At the very least, heads will roll. Most officers have their reputation to think about. I will never be complicit in someone else's corruption. Boss or not.'

'Glad to hear it.'

'The other helpful tip was the message you left after researching the archives. Funny how some people hold grudges, even centuries later. King was as bothered about his family's repute as Biggin-Smythe. Wasn't Ned a nasty creature? And King. Had Ross Pengelly marked from the get-go. The postman's demands mattered not.'

'I thought as much. King's one of those types with a permanent grievance. Will never find peace. I'm glad my findings got through and had a teeny influence on your decision.' Wendy pulled off her cap and showed Slate the pocket voice recorder. 'If needed, this little beauty might've picked up further proof. It's small, but mighty. Had to hide it from prying eyes. Under my hat was the best place. Let me have it back as soon as. Comes in handy for my interviews.'

'Or your sleuthing, Miss May. You'll never lose that leaning for justice, will you? A dog with a bone.' The bags under Slate's eyes wobbled.

'What about Tom?' Jon spoke for the first time since police arrived.

'He's a free man. And happy for it. We haven't spoken to your friend, but will when she's ready. The thug responsible for her being in hospital is on his way to the station. We collared him outside, making his escape from a window. Murder and manslaughter are just two of a long list of offences. It will be done. Familiar territory for you, Miss May?'

'Yes. I remember it well. And King?'

'Went quietly, along with the man in the van. King's crimes add up. He'll be doing a long stretch. You can bank on it.'

'Dickie tried to help us,' Jon said. 'Only because he thought armed police were on their way and he'd been exposed. Anything to make himself look good in the eyes of the law.'

'Don't know all the ins and outs until I review, but he's up to his neck. He's a silly man.'

'The gentry don't relish scandal,' Wendy said. 'Seymour must be turning on his slab. Risking life, limb, and title to be kingpin. But the deal wasn't big enough for two. No doubt the family'll take Dickie to the cleaners, after the law scrub him down. Doubt you'll get him clean. You can't polish rot.'

'Agreed. I wouldn't want to be in his shoes.'

'Fancy conspiring to kill your own father,' said Jon.

'Some folk'd sell their granny if there's money in it,' Slate sniffed at the air.

'Wonder if we could take out a contract on Atom Annie,' Jon mumbled.

'What's that?' Slate asked.

'Nothing.'

'I'll need statements, of course, and we'll have to hold your car for a while, Mr Windup. I'm happy to give you both a lift to the station, then home. Do you recognise anything in these evidence bags?'

'Everything,' Wendy said. 'Gareth told us to empty our pockets. We didn't argue.'

'Wise move. Thought the little bottle looked familiar. Remnants of pink liquid. I'm curious to see what's in the plastic pouch. Looks like an interesting muddle of mischief.'

'Will the crime scene investigators want to examine what's there?' Jon asked.

'Afraid so. Don't worry, if all's legit, we'll get it back to you soon. Now, anything else? If you don't mind, we have vital work to do here.'

'Could murder some gloop, chief inspector. Any flavour'll do.'

93

The Quizards of Tor

Jon pulled into the Noose & Gibbet's busy car park. He and Wendy had a guaranteed space. It was the least Honest Tor could do for celebrated heroes, Windy & Darling, TA. The caretaker at St Mark's had agreed to keep the cemetery gates open for the expected overspill. Eddie suspected quizzers and supporters would pack The Noose to the rafters. The intervillage quiz final was only an hour away.

'Ready for this, Windy?'

'Ready as I'll ever be, Darling.'

'Now, don't get stage fright. We've done a ton of research and our combined knowledge is ace. Tonight, we are Windy and Darling, Team Awesome quizzers. This is our moment. Savour it!'

'I'm all set for a different type of interrogation.'

'Should be a breeze for one serious geek. Fancy changing the jumble in your drat pack every day. That's inspired.'

'Not just the contents, the pouch too.'

'Genius. Limits any DNA. Don't want forensics linking your molecules to any found at crime scenes. Apart from those you can easily fudge your way through. We have all our belongings back now and a clean slate.'

'Until the next time. Got a feeling Windy and Darling's adventures have just begun.'

'I have that feeling, too. Shame. We'll have to grow up. Ready for showtime?'

The warm August evening cloaked the couple in a fuzzy, feel-good aura. Powder puff cotton clouds dotted an enchanting blue sky and leafy trees whispered thanks for a sleuthing job well done. Birds twittered, bees hummed. Life as they knew it was back in gear.

Through the front door into the crowded lounge and there behind the bar, his radiant smile warming, stood Eddie. Weeks earlier, the Noose was a scene of carnage and chaos, and, for a time, Tor had the smell and feel of a deserted ghost town. Now, it was back to its charming, garrulous old self. And, with its steady vibe, the Noose was back in full swing. A motley mix of happy customers, some here for drinks, some for culinary delights, and all looking forward to crowning the quiz champion of champions.

'He's there, Wendy. Let's go say hello. While I've been on holiday, I've decided. I'm getting a cat.'

'About time.'

Jon and Wendy edged to the red-cushioned stool, where pernickety Mr Quince groomed his beautiful long hair. Unruffled by the pub's buzz and beat, he was only fussed about working his barbed pink tongue over the tangled white bib. Quick, slow, slow, quick, the fastidious feline picked off grime, grit, and a heap of stray fur until the glorious apron looked pristine.

Jon tickled Mr Quince under his chin and behind his ears. 'How I've missed this big bundle of ginger fluff.'

'What a character. Couldn't care less about the din.'

With coat, face, tail, and limbs washed and brushed, Quincy was ready to doze. Sleepy green eyes swept the room, then he sprawled across the cushion, one eye open, one ear up, and slipped into his mid-evening nap.

'He'll close both eyes soon,' Jon said, 'but we'll never know if he's out. That cat makes my heart sing. Hope he doesn't cough up any hairballs. Not nice.'

'I'm glad Slate didn't corner him for DNA. Tried a few times, but failed, much to Eddie's and Quincy's amusement. He's a card.'

'Who? Slate or Mr Quince?'

'Both.'

'Our snooping stars are here, folks,' Eddie boomed to a resounding, welcoming committee. Applause and cheers went on and on. 'All set, you two?' Eddie asked when the ruckus died down.

'Yes, indeedy. Ready for battle. Bring it on!' Jon's excitement oozed from every pore.

'When do you take up your new job, Eddie?'

'In a month, Wendy. Tomorrow's my last night in the Noose. I'll have a nice, long break—some serious me and Gina time—then, Brock and Sett, here I come.' He pointed to a corner table. 'Your seats, honourable guests. Buffet's served during the interval. Usual drinks, or is it champagne?'

'Give over,' Wendy laughed. 'This peasant wants a glass of red. Any grape'll do.'

'And this pleb wants a fresh orange juice. And water. Filtered,' Jon grinned.

'At least let Anna bring them over.'

'You're on,' Wendy said.

Absolved as chief suspect for killing his boss, Tom had finally returned to work after an unauthorised leave of absence. Normally a sackable offence, but the Noose's new owner showed compassion. George Biggin-Smythe had assumed the title of lord and taken the reins of Honest Tor's popular watering hole. He was thrilled Tom Trebilcock had played an important role in bringing down his father's killer. Delighted that he'd rid the family of his tiresome older brother, who'd brought dishonour and shame. Two choice reasons why George showed kindness. The new lord of the manor was still getting used to the title he never expected to own. Undoing the ravages of his father's grabbing hands.

No need for head chef Tom to get used to the kitchen. Donning his chef's whites, he'd put on his own show and devised a gourmet buffet. Aided by Will and two agency chefs, quirky cuisine was back. Prepped, cooked, arranged, and covered on four trestle tables, Tom covered the goodies, then disappeared. A prior engagement, he said. He couldn't be late.

Jon and Wendy joined Will Dalton, enjoying a night off after his six-hour buffet stint, and Antonia Biggin-Smythe, who'd returned from Norfolk following her brother's arrest and detention. Wendy detected a closeness between the canoodling pair. She hoped Antonia's new beau wasn't a rebound romance. Will deserved more than that. The lad knocked spots off Pengelly. Wendy crossed her fingers and wished the couple well. Jon did likewise.

Anna brought drinks, congratulated Team Awesome on their detective work, and wished them luck in the quiz. Eddie headed to the opposite corner of the lounge, where the PA system and microphone awaited.

'Ladies and gentlemen. Your attention, please.'

The ambient noise faded to silence.

'Welcome to the tenth annual intervillage pub quiz. You should know the format by now. Six rounds covering different topics, as well as the picture round, anagrams, and this year's bonus round. Flags.'

'Your area of expertise, Jon,' Wendy said.

'And you're a dab hand at anagrams.'

Eddie boomed again. 'In case anyone needs reminding, I'll ask a question and you *write* it down. Don't shout out the answer. Unless you want the whole pub to know. Questions are worth one, two, or three points. You'll see what's what on your sheet. Hand your answers to the next table for marking. One more thing. If

I catch anyone searching their phones or any other suspicious activity, it's instant disqualification.'

'Seriously?' Antonia giggled.

'Always,' Wendy confirmed. 'I kid you not. Some take this competition beyond the limit. Jon's one of those some. Right, my windy friend?'

'What can I say? I'm a nerd. Come on, Ed. Let's go.'

And so the quiz began. Pairs of eyes contemplated flags and anagrams and images. Although Jon and Wendy didn't live in Honest Tor, they were treated as villagers for the time they spent there. Their latest escapade had awarded them celebrity status. A couple of grumbling locals always got iffy about non-residents being team members, but most weren't sticklers for niggling.

The first round passed with a breeze. The Stan Clan made a double appearance, prompting Jon to wear a "told-you-so" grin. 'Knew all those hours of stan research'd pay off,' he gloated. 'And those fishy facts of mine weren't so smelly after all.'

'Gets harder from here,' Wendy warned, savouring the dark fruits and full body of a fine Cabernet.

'I hear Lucinda's moved into the dower house, even though she has her own place,' said Jon, gulping another glass of iced water to keep himself hydrated.

'It's a mansion. Much bigger than her cottage. She gets to be queen of her own castle. Some people,' Wendy said.

Antonia pricked her ears. 'Yes. queen of hearts. Now probate's almost complete the move was inevitable. Dickie would've stuck his oar in, but George is kinder. Both him and Royce are good souls. You wouldn't think they had the same parents.'

'And you, Antonia. Surely you didn't spring from the same pool as Dickie Boy. He's a definite apostrophe. You're an enigmatic ellipsis. And, while she may be an interrobang, I admit to secretly thanking milady for her exclamations and questions. Her blabbing gave me a sweep of info. Plenty there to help our cause. Windy's an interrobang, too. Has more in common with Lu Brush than he thinks. Right, Windy?'

'Over my dead body.'

'Any chance you can pop off when the quiz's finished? Need your supreme research, and I'm not quite ready for more sleuthing, though I'll never tire of Slate's gyrating eyebrows,' Wendy snickered. 'Not to worry, Windy. You also have qualities of the ellipsis.'

'Ellipsical, you mean?'

'Wacky word and all. Tell me, Antonia. Is Lu still calling herself milady?'

'Yes, but not for long. George marries in nine months. His wife will become the new Lady Biggin-Smythe. Anyway, Wendy, you know my thoughts on all that pomp, but when you're born into it, what can you do?'

Everyone laughed. It was refreshing to see a member of the gentry despair at the nuances of her class. Antonia was a reluctant member and often said she'd love to opt out. Destined for a career in PR, she'd have no problems taking care of herself. No need to rely on her wealthy family. Her disgraced brother, Richard, along with Montgomery King, was on remand awaiting trial.

'Richard's lawyer fancies his chances,' Antonia said. 'No doubt he'll pay off the judge and jury.'

'With any luck, George'll pay them more to find him guilty,' Wendy quipped, bringing belly laughs.

'No one's in a hurry to have him back. Even some of his puffed-up shooting friends.' Antonia's expression wasn't complimentary.

George had established a beautiful calm to the Biggin-Smythe family and business proceedings. Unlike his late father and older brother, he didn't have grabbing hands, nor did he consider hiking rent a priority. Scant consolation for Ross Pengelly. George had even told Eddie he'd reconsider his position at the Noose and

Gibbet. Though grateful, Eddie said he'd stick by his decision. He and Gina were looking forward to a change in direction, and Bogus Hole offered that chance.

'The Rutters' origami's coming along a treat,' Wendy said. 'Have you seen their works of art? I'm well impressed.'

'They deserve a lot of happiness,' Jon said. 'Long live love.'

After round one of the quiz, there was a four-way tie for the lead. Round two, and Jon stormed through geography. Wendy did the same in the music round before the interval. More drinks. More chat and chuckles. And a stack of hungry hands heaping Tom's decadent delights onto large square plates. Hungrier mouths chomped and relished a feast of pure indulgence. No one could say there was little choice. Sandwiches galore. Chorizo slices. Satay skewers. Pizza, with six different toppings. A selection of world cheeses and Tom's assorted baked biscuits. Caramelised onion mini scotch eggs.

'This food's scrumptious, Will,' Jon mumbled through a mouthful of sun-dried tomato and capers. 'You've done yourselves proud.'

'Thanks. We followed Tom's menu. He knows how to satisfy.'

'In more ways than one,' Wendy said. 'Shame the kitchen's closed and there's nothing hot, although some pastries are still warm and taste divine. The whole spread's finger-food paradise. Windy can't wait for the sweet treats, can you, my friend? He was eyeing up the chocolate cherry pavlova. And that peanut butter and meadowsweet ice cream won't last long. Those mini freezers have come in handy.'

'Another plate of savoury first.' Jon was up and off to the food fest, but took his time to return.

'Jon must be eating all the profits,' Wendy giggled. 'While we wait, tell me about Norfolk, An … What the hell?' Wendy shrieked, reeling back in her seat, hypnotised by the huge baguette waving back and forth in her face.

Jon put his loaded plate onto the table and sat down. His silly grin had Wendy in fits, then she demanded to know what in the name of dough he was playing at.

'You said it, Darling. Dough. Went on a snoop and found this. Look at the logo.'

'Crikey. That's it! The deadly one. Dough by Artie San. And there was me thinking it was *artisan*. A brilliant play on words from a clearly creative company. Delicious bread too.'

'I'll say,' Jon agreed, stuffing a hunk of blue Stilton and two pickled onions into his mouth.

'You can tell me about your jollies later, Antonia. Looks like Eddie's ready to roll out the second half.'

Hush fell over the Noose as Eddie posed more questions in each round. Eventually, he had the unenviable job of checking answer and bonus sheets before announcing the winner. While waiting, Jon was on pins. He'd polished off his second plate of food, guzzled chocolate cherry pavlova and a bowl of heavenly ice cream, and downed the lot with two glasses of filtered water and one of orange juice.

'Hollow legs Windup,' Wendy said. 'Where do you put it, Jon? I've had half a plate and couldn't eat another mouthful.'

'Lightweight. Wish Eddie would tell us who's won. I'm bricking it here.'

'It's a quiz, Jon. Not the end of the world. Don't milk the drama.'

'Why not? I have a reputation to keep. Don't want to ruin it.'

Wendy sipped Cabernet and regarded Will and Antonia. Giggling at something silly, you bet, and gazing at each other all doe-eyed and dopey. Wendy lowered her voice to talk to Jon. 'Had a message from Ems. She won't be back for a couple of months. Still fragile, poor thing. Pengelly really did a number on her. Hope she recovers from it all.'

'Ladies and gentlemen, your attention, please. I have the final scores,' Eddie's voice rumbled.

There was a round of applause, then hush.

'First, a big hand to everyone who took part. You've all been fantastic. Right. Here we go. There are eight teams, and I'll read the order from last to first, but not the exact score. Don't want to embarrass anyone. In eighth place, High Flatt.' Light applause followed a chorus of groans from team members. 'Seventh, Little Swell, sixth, Old Fallow.' Eddie stopped, then took a swig of lemonade. 'In fifth spot, we have Low Steep and fourth goes to Ewes Crook.'

Building up the tension, Eddie swigged again. Jon's right leg pumped up and down, up and down.

'Would you believe it? Three teams have the same number of points. Bogus Hole. Boggy Bluff. And our very own Honest Tor. That can only mean one thing. Tiebreaker time.'

The Noose erupted with whoops and cheers.

'Okay, it's simple. One question. First team to shout out the answer wins. If no one gives the right answer, I'll ask another until somebody does. Are you ready, teams? Allowing five years either way, when did the baguette officially get its name?'

The pub fell silent. Faces dropped.

'Do you know?' Wendy whispered.

Jon shook his head. 'Nope. Hours of research and dough's proving deadly. What's Ed playing at? What about New York? Or the stans?'

'Not them again. Maybe Eddie's question about the baguette's a tribute to Windy and Darling. Not as quizzers. As sleuths. Makes no odds. I don't know the answer. 'Tis a mystery to me. Can't even ask Will and Antonia. They've sloped off somewhere. Sorry, Windy. Looks like we're doomed.'

'Seems no one knows,' Eddie said. 'I'll repeat, give you five minutes, then ask another. Here goes. Allowing five years either way, when did the baguette officially get its name?'

'Nineteen twenty!'

94

Sticky End

Team Awesome would know that beautiful, chirpy lilt anywhere. Dear friend and darling Prue Penn was back. Unaided and beaming, standing next to Tom, mike in hand, educating the fascinated room about one of the most iconic of French foods.

'That's all very well, but you've ruined the quiz,' incensed Bogus Hole captain, Brian Longbottom, bellowed. 'You're not even on a team. Just come waltzing in here and shout out the answer.'

The still in the room deepened. Wendy was out of her seat and by Prue's side lightning fast. She took the mike.

'Shut your trap, Brian. Prue's lucky to be here at all. Don't think I need to remind anyone of the tough time this woman's had. Or the tittle-tattle she's suffered about her brother. The less said, the better. Team Honest Tor's privileged to have her as a member. But what we're dying to know, quizmaster, is did she give the correct answer to the tiebreaker?'

'She did.'

'Yes! Yes! Yes!' Jon hollered, punching the air and stamping his feet in typical hammy style.

'Don't let him stand up,' Wendy warned. 'He might conk out and get carted off in the cadavan.'

Jon's celebrations went on and on.

'Honest Tor, here we go.' Another familiar voice rang out. Adam Brown, who'd snuck in minutes earlier to catch the quiz finale. He welcomed Prue and Tom, bought a celebratory round of drinks, and pulled up three chairs at Jon and Wendy's table.

'It's a fix,' Longbottom bawled, ready to leave with his disgruntled team in tow.

'Go comb your whiskers,' Wendy retorted. 'Go on. Get lost. No room in here for sore losers.'

Will and Antonia swiped the empty seats and sat down at Honest Tor's table. Adam dished out drinks.

'Can you drown a blonde in that?' Tom said, looking ruefully at the pint of craft ale.

'Right down to Davy Jones's locker,' Wendy said. 'Lucinda would still be on the chase down there. All those sailors? Ecstasy! You're best off without, Tom. Should be grateful Prue's alive and here with us, and you're no longer chief suspect for a crime you didn't commit. That makes all the difference, yes?'

'Of course. Thanks for the reminder.'

'Anyway, when my article's published next week, no one'll get near Lucinda Biggin-Smythe. Her ego will see to that. In a few months, she'll be milady no more, but that won't stop her. Now hubby's crept into the family crypt, and she's binned Tom off, the bling babe'll be hunting down her next pair of trousers. Run for the hills, fellas. And get this. She invited me to milord's funeral. As if I'd show my face there. Sorry, Antonia.'

'Understood,' Antonia smiled.

'Prue was right,' Tom muttered, 'shouldn't have got involved, but that's history. From now on, I'll stick to my own sort. No offence, Antonia.'

'None taken.'

The buzz in the Noose had returned. Team Honest Tor's laughter rang out, happy tears flowed, sides and bellies ached. Wendy and Prue played catch-up, starting with a pact to attend cookery classes again. Tom was looking for a new venue for the big marquee and Wendy said she'd see what she could do. Mr Quince stirred, shuffled around on his cushion, then floated off for his late evening nap.

'You know, Wendy, don't think you ever revealed your mark.' Prue's eyes shone through misted tears.

'Could only be one. Right, Windy?'

'Right.'

'The full stop. And there's nothing more to say, so let that be an end to it. Period.'

Prue giggled. 'Won't argue with that.'

'Just like her punctuality. *On the dot*. Looks like our cue, people. We're off,' Jon cheered.

Still light-headed with the win, Jon shook hands with Eddie and accepted the champion of champions intervillage quiz trophy. Wendy stood next to him, feeling a triumphant rush. An energising push and pull, not just for the quiz, but justice for Prue and Tom.

Back at the table, Wendy held up the prize. 'Twill take pride of place on Jon's bookcase. Next to his atlases and maps and crazy collection of pylons. You deserve it, my windy friend.'

'We both do. Thanks for letting me keep it. Means a lot, Darling.'

'Room for a little one?' a voice squawked.

Wendy couldn't believe the gall of the woman. Standing at the entrance, clutching Jemima, brazen Annie Clegg and her overzealous overbite.

'In you come, Annie, but that heap of scrap stays out. And no trouble, or you're barred,' Eddie warned.

'Trouble? The very idea.' Annie sat in a corner, mean eyes scouring the room.

Wendy kept one eye on her friends, the other on the village scold. Annie was up to something. Agitated twiddling thumbs weren't a good sign. 'What's brewing, Adam? Any new concoctions on the horizon?'

'None, but you know me, Wendy. Can't keep creativity at bay. Forever brewing up something. Kate's the same.'

'You're not the only one. She's consistent. I'll give her that. Slap on your waders, people. Drool's come to town.'

Annie Clegg and silence were sworn enemies. She'd wasted no time. Standing inches from Tom, doing what she did best. Once a shrew, always a shrew. 'So, you're back, are you? Not the kilted killer now, but you can't blame me for doubting. That's what happens when you mess around. Let that be a warning.'

'She's off again. Raking it in,' Jon hissed.

'Time for a moratorium,' Wendy decided. 'Give me that baguette, Jon. The night ain't over till the she-devil dies. Hey, Annie. What's this?' Wendy wielded the loaf in mid-air.

'It's a French stick.'

'Wrong. It's deadly dough. And it kills!'

Revellers cheered as Annie's scrawny legs hurtled from the Noose. Eddie saluted. Even Mr Quince raised his weary head and hissed to send her on her way.

Prue raised her glass to toast. 'Breaded. Windy and Darling win again.'

'Indeedy,' Jon chimed.

Wendy didn't hesitate. 'Always!'

ABOUT THE AUTHORS

Wenark Green, a collaboration of writers and earth friends, Mark Hallworth and Wendy Wilson. Polar opposites. Zen connected.

Scottish-raised, environmental science grad Mark writes cosy crime and sci-fi and co-manages a self-publishing house. He's also an avid reader and loves music. A fondness for maps, hugging trees, or pondering pylons takes whimsical to a new level. Laughs and cheer are high on Mark's priorities. He's a nature lover, vegetarian, and loves animals. Ask Tahlula, his fussy old tuxedo cat.

Born in the original Washington, NE England, Wendy's a crazy word nerd. Helps keep her studious mind company. Amid a diverse range of vocations, and now as co-owner of a self-publishing house, Wendy's lust for language never wanes.

She adores writing and editing. Other hobbies are music, yoga, museums, and comedy. She loves cooking, wine, and hats, is animal qwackers, and salutes the great outdoors. A sworn bookworm of anything and everything, Wendy devours dictionaries daily.

Deadly Dough is the couple's feature-length debut.

www.wenarkgreen.com

SUPPORTING OTHER READERS

Readers have a world of choice, and thank you for choosing *Deadly Dough*. We hope you enjoyed reading the book as much as we loved writing it. Feedback is vital. To help readers decide their next escape, please give a quick review on Amazon. Many thanks in advance for your valued support. We appreciate you.

ALSO BY WENARK GREEN

FATAL FUNGUS
When pies meets lies, there's not mushroom for error

One great bake-off
Twelve golden pies
Windy & Darling, back in stride

On a crisp autumn evening, in rustic Bogus Hole, the village committee proposes a charity pie auction to celebrate Sycamore Medical Centre's first anniversary. To attract doctors' bids, secret bakers contend for a place on the prized gingham table, setting the scene for a spiteful showdown.

The following week, when a ruthless doctor collapses at the Christmas fair and later dies, the gossip train rumbles. Whose evil hands baked a deadly golden pie and killed the not-so-fun-guy?

Geeky mapman, Jon Windup, and odd-eyed hat freak, Wendy May, hit the fatal fungus trail. Can our offbeat, sparring amateur sleuths sniff out the villain before murder strikes again?

Read on for an extract …

1

In the Brock

Wendy May and Wednesday. A fragile affair. Marooned midweek was how Wendy saw the day. Try a little tenderness, she told herself. Look for common ground. Your name's tucked up in the day and appeals to your love of wordplay. Yes? No! Whenever life came crashing down, you bet it crashed midweek. Wendy blamed the wasp and an odious onion who both invaded many Wednesdays ago. Since that deviant day, no matter how hard she tried, she'd never quite hugged the hump.

In the warm glow of the Brock & Sett pub, in the cosy village of Bogus Hole, Wendy sipped a robust, smoky Malbec reliving when her standoff with Wednesday began. A long time ago. In a different world. Another life. Her waggish gaze and rhythmic closing of her blue eye prompted dear friend and colleague Prue Penn to nudge a tale from Wendy's bulging, comical archives.

'You're dying to tell me. Go on, do it,' Prue's velvet brown eyes coaxed. Sipping chilled house white, she strapped herself in, expecting the unexpected when Wendy went off on one of her outrageous, nostalgic capers.

Basking in the roar of the blazing fire, Wendy painted vivid memories. 'Picture this. A cold, dreary Wednesday moons ago, and my first proper job as office junior in a small legal firm. Two weeks in, and clueless. The day didn't start well when a pesky wasp tailed me into the office and evaded capture for an eternity. Not that catching it was my intention and I was glad when it buzzed off.

'My colleague, Dotty Doris—because her name was Doris, and she was dotty—had work to do in the back office and left me alone out front. One pest had gone, when in waltzed another. All airs and graces, she was. So far up her own rump, she'd lost her way. What my wacky word partner Jon'd call a proper pompositor.

'She wanted to sell her *enormous* house and move into something grander. Could I quote for the legals? Sure, I could, and asked her name. "Sylvia O-ni-on," came the affected reply. I had to hold it together and asked her to repeat. "O-ni-on," she snapped, huffing and puffing. Asked her to spell it. And she did. And I hooted. Not a gentle hooted. A parliament of owls hooted. "That's onion," I shrieked. Couldn't keep a straight face, Prue. It split in half, but the onion's withering glower never cracked. At sixteen going on seventeen, essential legal etiquette was alien to me. My professional poker face would come, but not that day.

'Mrs O was a can't-get-much-further-up-my-rear sort. The desperate-to-reach-the-top-of-the-social-ladder-type. But why she was trying to impress me, I do not know. I was a working girl, without a care in the world. Not a rich, successful debutante gadding around the globe quaffing fine champagne and dining on Beluga caviar in St Moritz or Monte Carlo. Half a cider and a chippy tea was more my bag. How I hate snobbery, but I passed on telling the overbearing onion she was wasting her hoity-toity time. Anyhow, didn't matter how fast she tried to climb the social ladder. The rungs had collapsed, along with her aspirations. Damn people's egos and quirks. Can't work them out.'

'Takes all sorts. What punctuation mark did you give her?'

'Wasn't into such cuckoo stuff back then, but now you've put me on the spot. She's a definite apostrophe. One serious niggle. And fractious, like dotty Doris, who wasted no time in thundering from the back office in a right old hoo-hah, giving me severe earache for losing a potential new client. The rest of the day was disastrous. *The* classic Wednesday from hell, and the reason I have a funny old funk with the middle of the week, my dear Prue. Since I tore a strip off the onion, any niggle seems to land on Wednesday and gives me the right hump. The name's derived from old English after the Germanic god, Woden. But in my book it's *Woe*den. I'll never forgive that bleeding wasp. It's got a lot to answer for.'

Prue almost choked on her wine. 'Don't worry, it's long gone. Pollinating in yellow jacket heaven. Or hell. And what about the onion?'

'Yes. The odious onion. Didn't make me cry, just stormed out in one almighty huff, taking the door with her. Anyone who crossed her path was in for it. But enough scurrilous pantomime. Halloween and Bonfire Night are done and now we're on a Christmas go-go-go. I can sense snowflakes falling and see Rudolph's red nose. 'Tis the season to be jolly, which gives Jon the perfect excuse to fill his face with advent choccies while counting down the days. From our recent banter, I know he can't wait for Santa to bring the new hearing trumpet I've earmarked. Thought I'd go all bespoke and have one made for him. Might have it engraved, too. Jon "Windy" Windup. Full of gas, indeedy. What do you think?'

'You're a scream, that's what I think. Where is he tonight?'

'Out with the MAC. The Map Appreciation Club. It's monthly meeting and curry night. Mapman loves a curry.'

'MAC?' Prue twisted her face. 'What *do* they find to talk about?'

'Could be wrong, but I think it's maps.'

'Trust you,' Prue chuckled, admiring the huge pine tree standing in one corner of the inn. 'Don't the Christmas decorations look stunning? Especially the tree.'

'When the pine's dressed up, it always looks fabulous. Bogie's dressed in its best, too. Most locals want that festive twinkle in November.'

'It's the same in Tor. The village looks beautiful.'

Wendy checked the big wall clock, dulling her groan with a slurp of Merlot. 'Why *is* our chair always the cow's tail? Come on, Longbottom, get this meeting started.'

2

The Chair

'Is this delay normal?' Prue whispered to Wendy, beginning to wish she'd stayed home to bake a Persian lemon cake or a batch of ginger and orange muffins.

'Should've warned you. Duty chairman Brian Longbottom's always behind. If he ever starts on time, I'll show my butt in Spragg's farm shop window.'

This was Prue's first meeting since becoming a member of Linkville, the village community council Wendy joined last year. Its slogan, *Where Village Matters Matter*, saw a random number of members meeting to discuss rural affairs. Not just issues concerning Bogus Hole, but all eight villages on the fringe of county town, Treeton, which had now crept into the mix. As the biggest village, Bogus Hole was the preferred meeting place, the Brock & Sett or village hall, the chosen venues.

Because of her new role as daring Darling, amateur sleuth, Wendy hadn't been active of late, but word had it meetings and members missed her, and would she mind coming back sharpish to pepper debates with her wit, wisdom and wiles? Of course, she wouldn't mind. Prue wanted in too, so here they sat around a rectangular table with ten other members waiting for Longbottom to get on with it.

Without Kitty Clegg, treasurer and number cruncher, who had other plans and couldn't make this evening's gathering, Wendy likened the count to the last supper. There was no supper, but wine still flowed. Next to Brian, his long-suffering wife and committee secretary, Nellie. To dodge writer's cramp while taking notes, Wendy offered Nellie her pocket mini recorder, but she declined. 'Thanks, but I'm old school. Happy with pen and paper. Not into all that technology stuff. Robots confuse me. Ask Brian.'

'You're all right, Nellie,' Wendy said, mystified by Brian's methodical preening of his discernible trio of shaggy muttonchops, over-curled handlebar moustache, and coiffed hair. All three eccentric gingers had his unswerving attention, but the silly man was oblivious to the waiting audience. 'That robot definitely confuses me,' she muttered to Prue. 'He's one big apostrophe. Or should that be robotstrophe? Now there's a wacky word for Windy's lexicon of life.'

'A gem of a word, and I agree. Brian is a robotic, strange man.'

'I fear he's still in a grump because he didn't get to switch on the Christmas lights this year. The honour went to Dr Kenneth Cotte—him, there—Sycamore Medical Centre senior partner and recently appointed cricket captain of Bogus Hole Badgers. Cotte usurped Longbottom there, too, causing ructions. They've never got on. Like two big kids squabbling in the playground and so many face-offs. I'm surprised Cotte hasn't scored a hat-trick and seized the chair's chair. He upsets everyone. As does Longbottom. On that note, I'm off for more drinks. Same again?'

'Fresh orange juice, please.'

Leaning on the polished bar, Wendy eyed the pleasing pictures of beautiful black-and-white-striped faces, stocky grey bodies, and short furry tails. Badgers had always been a big part of Bogie's history, and the muse for the Brock & Sett's name when opening its doors centuries ago. With six well-equipped guest rooms, the Brock kept one half of its popular coaching inn status, offering bed-and-breakfast for two legs, but not nosebag for four.

She wallowed in the warmth of Eddie Rutter's sweeping smile. 'Hey, you. Must say you're doing a sterling job as new manager, and Gina's the housekeeping queen. Got it all stitched up, boss.'

'It's busier than the Noose, but we love it here. Our new home's only a stone's throw away, meaning we can roll out of bed and be here in a blink.'

'And the origami?'

'Coming along a treat. Doing some new bird shapes and hoping to perfect the lotus fold soon.' Eddie flashed a beam of super white teeth.

'My dear friend, I won't ever tire of that grin, but go easy. The last time 'twas that wide, someone got hanged.'

'You're a legend, Wendy. Never lose that dark sense of humour.'

'I won't, though it won't ever be as grim as Jon's. He sends his best, by the way.'

'Thought he'd be here.'

'He loves debating a pothole fiasco, but when the Gerardus Mercator crew begs his good ear he'll pass. Our would-be cartographer won't miss a chance to mull over maps before dabbling with dal or whatever curry takes his fancy.'

'What's all that? Apart from the curry bit, haven't a clue what you're on about.'

'Is Mercator's reputation as the best known mapmaker of all time only true for mapmen like Jon Windup? Didn't he tell you he'd joined the Map Appreciation Club? As for Mercator, he was a Flemish geographer, cosmographer and cartographer, who in fifteen sixty-nine, created a world map based on a new projection. His greatest innovative renown's still used in nautical charts today. Can't tell you how many times Jon's told me that. It's embedded in my brain. He loves a slice of theatre.'

431

'Oh, yes. Don't remind me,' Eddie chortled. 'Where does curry come in?'

'The mapsters always have a meal after their deliberations, and tonight's curry night. Jon's a slave to curry. Indian. Thai. Malaysian. He'd eat it every day. But not flaming hot. If he was here, he'd tell you they don't call it curry in India. The British invented that term during the Raj. You know what he's like for trawling the web to net random, fishy facts.'

'I should know. Tells me often enough when he's pulling pints.'

'Bless his gammy ear. He asked me to thank you again for the shifts you're dishing out.'

'No bother. Not sure of his next one, but shouldn't be long. We're getting busy for Christmas.'

'And only one more community meet, then we're done until January. Serving solo this eve?'

'Lol's on his break and Amy's in at eight. Once you lot push off, the locals'll come and I'll need the extra hands.'

'Wish I could push off now. Longbottom's playing dawdler—he's worse than Jon—and Cotte's so puffed up over his recent wins, he'll likely explode, but that wouldn't be a bad thing.'

'Still happy to be back home?'

'Always. Back in Bogie three weeks and feels like I've never been away. Didn't take me long to get back with the beat. Charm. Cobbles. Incredible wildlife. And that irresistible perfume. Oh, how I've missed that country smell.' Wendy's laughter rang out. 'Same old village doctrine. Same old gossip. Same old gripes. One magnificent vibe.'

'That's village life.'

Wendy gazed down at the great ginger feline sprawled on his cushioned barstool throne. Mr Quince, resident pub cat and superstar mouser, had adopted the Rutters months ago when Eddie was manager of the Noose & Gibbet in Honest Tor. With more attitude than Brian Longbottom, Quincy's disarming charm and character ensured he was a puss you couldn't ignore. 'Mr Q looks settled. Wherever he lays his paws.'

'He's the don again, right enough. Your drinks, madam. Give my best to Prue.'

'Will do, thanks. Better dash.'

It was no surprise to see Brian still preening his whiskers. As vain as Mr Quince, though not as handsome. Suddenly, he banged his fist down, declared the meeting open, and off he railed. Toneless. Monosyllabic. Wearisome. Everyone looked bored at his tirade. He looked the opposite.

'He keeps giving me funny looks,' Prue said, nudging Wendy and taking a sip of juice.

'Reckon he still hasn't forgiven you for the baguette debacle at the quiz championship, nor me for making him eat humble pie after his bellyaching. Or was it the humble pie that gave him bellyache? No matter. Bring back the wasp. I'd even vote for the onion instead of bumptious Brian. By the way, Eddie sends his best.'

Prue smiled at Eddie's sentiment. Pretentious know-it-all Brian rambled on.

Finally, Wendy's tolerance could take no more and waved a white flag, but scathing remarks never surrendered. 'Scintillating stuff, Mr Chairman, but is it possible to talk about potholes without reciting War and Peace, part two? Forget the magical mystery tour with no stop-offs. Get us there with time to spare, so we can all enjoy the experience.'

A roar of laughter and animated murmurs thronged the air. It wasn't village issues that made community meetings worthwhile, but the raucous drama when Wendy swapped barbs with Brian. Wit versus belligerence, and may the best talent win. Bottoms shuffled in seats, but not

Longbottom's. Irritated at being cut off mid-sentence, he sat ramrod straight, po-faced and peeved.

'Mr Quince got your tongue, Brian? We were talking ruts, remember?'

Brian gave one of his infamous prickly stares. 'Well, Miss Wendy May, you might not drive, but many villagers do, and the state of the roads are unacceptable. Something must be done.'

'Is unacceptable, Brian. "State" is the singular, not the plural. Look, I appreciate the point, but your grousing's nothing new. We know the roads are bad. We know the local authority must do more. And I do drive. Remember when the Mell burst its banks and the floods that followed? Course, you do. Almost washed Bogie away. Water, water everywhere and all *my* boards *did* shrink. Shrank enough to cause extensive damage to my cottage, warranting a complete renovation. The car had to go, but I'll be back on the road soon. Now, can we please get on? We don't have time to listen to you cite the shipping forecast for the North Atlantic, or grumble about how many potholes you saw or drove through yesterday. Next item on the agenda, please.'

'Why don't you run for chair, Wendy?' Co-owner of Beans & Leaves tea queen Kate Brown suggested with a blatant chuckle.

'Can we get back to the meeting?' Brian was purple in the face, whiskers twitching, channelling Quincy. He downed a mouthful of ale, wiped the froth from his handlebars with a big brown handkerchief and brought his fist down again.

Sensing a tantrum, Wendy flashed a crooked smile. 'Sorry. Must say it's refreshing to see the new name and logo for Linkville. The chain design's inspired, and the slogan. Of course, we can get back to the meeting, Brian. Didn't I ask for the next item on the agenda?'

'The main reason for tonight's meeting is Sycamore Medical Centre.' Brian choked.

Prue glanced at Wendy with a look that said, "At last."

'My Nellie has a proposal she'd like to share with us. Get on with it, Nell.'

'Yes, Brian dear, and thank you. Next week, the practice is a year old. As you know, the main surgery opened in Treeton, but also covers eight villages on the outskirts. Since opening, residents have experienced exceptional service.'

'Yes, it's a shocking disgrace why they keep building houses, but no new doctors' surgeries, schools, and the like,' said Kate.

'The infrastructure's all skew whiff. Like most things in this cockeyed country,' Wendy said.

'At least there's a village practice here in Bogus Hole, even if it's only open a few hours a week,' Nellie said, 'and as a way of saying a big thanks to the partners, I propose a charity pie auction.'

'*A what?*' Baffled looks joined a chorus of strangled voices. Had Brian Longbottom finally sent his poor wife around the bend?

A WORD FROM WENARK

A megantic, super-duper thank you for choosing *Fatal Fungus*. If you enjoyed the story, and want to keep up to date with new releases in the Windy & Darling Cosy Mystery series, please visit our website and socials using the links below. We'd love to hear from you.

wenarkgreen.com/contact

linktr.ee/wenarkgreen

@wenarkgreenauthor

@wenarkgreenauthor

ALSO BY WHISPER PRESS

FINDING BILLY
Coming soon

One girl
One boy
One cruel summer

Rejection and loneliness are all Jane knows, until she meets Billy, and a bond that will last for eternity. With Billy, Jane feels alive again, but a dark secret threatens to destroy everything.

Will Jane never have a happy ever after, or will fate bind the two lost souls together?

Available soon from Amazon in paperback or Kindle.

ALSO BY WHISPER PRESS

WHAT THE KNOCKER-UPPER WOKE UP

Old London

Sideways. A stinking, ghostly hell, where time stalls and torment is endless. Among the blackened bones of a burned Victorian asylum, something stirs. Clutching her pea-shooter, the fate of Alice, the Knocker-Upper, is sealed. Now, she's Sideways, and fading to grey.

London, today

In her grandfather's old clock shop in a forgotten corner of London, Tess smells something wrong. Feels it in the ticking of her heart. When she stumbles Sideways and meets Alice, Tess knows life may not work out the way she planned.

While fighting her own demons, is Tess of the Clock Shop the one to destroy evil? What sacrifices will she have to make along the way?

Available from Amazon in paperback or Kindle.

Printed in Great Britain
by Amazon